BURIED SECRETS: THE THREE-STORY COLLECTION OF DOMINIC RIVERS AND BERT TOMLIN MYSTERIES

a detective thriller

DEEPIKA VISWANATH

Kindle Direct Publishing

Copyright © 2021 Deepika Viswanath

This is a work of fiction. Names, characters, places, and incidents either are the product of the author's imagination or are used fictitiously. Any resemblance to actual persons, living or dead, events, or locales is entirely coincidental.

All rights reserved. No part of this book may be reproduced or used in any manner without written permission of the copyright owner except for the use of quotations in a book review.

Front and back cover created by Deepika Viswanath (via Canva.com)

Cover image credit: Canva.com

Chapter header picture credit: Canva.com

ISBN: 9798712491063 (paperback)

For my family

TABLE OF CONTENTS

Story 1: Know Your Neighbors

Story 2: He Saw it Coming

Story 3: In Her Eyes

Author's Note

Acknowledgements

Story 1: Know Your Neighbors

CHAPTER 1

November

Dectective Dominic Rivers, a tall, attractive, and tanned man of thirty-five years, was sitting in his small, but cozy office, located in the Homicide/Missing Persons division of the Boston Police Station headquarters. It had a single desk, a chair in front and piles of case files on his desk. Dominic, one of the department's top men, had brown curly hair that adorned the top of his face, making him look like a young Hugh Jackman.

The BPS headquarters was a unique place to work at— after all, the top officers of the state, like Dominic, worked there. A senior member to the force, he had been named the Detective of the Year for the past couple of years. He had decided to become a detective because his father was also one, and he had worked in the very same building. Sadly, his father had passed away recently. Detective Clarence Rivers instilled in his son that it was important to take whatever path he wanted in life. Since Dominic was so used to visiting his father at the police station, at a young age, he decided that he would become a law officer too.

Fast forward to nine years ago, when he arrived to the Boston Police Department for his first day on the job within the Homicide/Missing Persons unit. Being a new detective meant that Dominic wasn't well-versed in different procedures or tactics, which caused him to not to question suspects properly, and instead come across as a 'nice cop'.

On one occurrence, a few months into his career, when he finally had all the proof that a suspect was guilty of a murder rap, it was too late. The suspect, in trying to flee the country, had died when a car hit him. On top of that, a lot of the senior officers and detectives at the time thought they knew what they were doing better, and made sure Dominic knew it too. Over the years of working alongside experienced detectives, his knowledge of what it meant to serve in the police force, grew.

Now, Dominic was no longer the amateur he once was. He didn't take nonsense from anyone. He had even become like those detectives—tough, no nonsense and to the point. He had become known for his hard work and dedication in all his cases.

At the moment, though, Dominic was feeling different. He had a disdained expression painted on his face as he pondered over something. He had gotten assigned to the case of a missing couple in the town of Newbury. They had been missing for a week. This seemed strange to him, because as a native Bostonian, he knew that there was never a lot of missing persons cases in Newbury. That town was safe as could be. He checked his phone for the time. His home screen read: *7 am, November 6th*.

Dominic's boss, Police Chief Oscar Tonew entered Dominic's office, after a quick knock on his door. Police Chief Tonew was a stout man of sixty years, with slightly balding hair, and sharp brown eyes. He had been on the force even before Dominic was born. His age was catching up to him, which showed in the wrinkles on his face and his lack of energy. In his hands he had a file.

"Hey Dominic, are you going to get started on looking into the missing couple in Newbury?" he asked.

Dominic knew exactly what he was talking about and was up for it. Having a new case meant more rapport and more experience for him. He nodded affirmably.

"Yes, I'm going to do that. Seems strange that a missing persons case would occur there. It's a pretty safe town. I wonder what happened to them."

"Good. The Police Chief there told me that they wanted your help on this, as well."

"They're probably interviewing possible suspects, am I right? And have search parties been able to find anything? After all, the couple have been missing for a week."

Chief Tonew nodded. "Yes, the Chief told me his men are doing so. A few community members have organized search parties to scour though forests and areas far away from the town. They haven't found anything yet. Which is why they need our help as well. That's why you're assigned to the case. Talking about which, why don't *you* go over to the neighborhood where the couple live, to get started? After all, everyone, including their Police Chief knows you are our best man."

Dominic couldn't help but feel his ego rise. "You know I'm the best man for *any* job. What've you got?"

His boss handed him the file. It was quite heavy, and looked to be filled with lot of information. "Get on it before the media arrives," he said. "I have a file on the couple here. Read it over."

Dominic perused the file. Then he looked up. "I'm going to need to ask questions afterwards."

Chief Tonew smiled. "Yes. Afterwards. *After* you've read the file." His tone was fatherly-like, as if he were lecturing his own son. After all, the two had a strong bond over the years, with Dominic gaining a lot of insight from the experienced Chief.

"Go over to the neighborhood and ask some questions," he continued. "We got some of our people already on the scene. You know what to do." He waved his hands away as if to indicate 'Go on now! Hurry!'

"On it, boss." Dominic took the file and got up. As he left the station, he looked through the file again, this time looking at it in more detail. The couple's names were Alvero and Catalina Trent. He'd get more information by asking questions to the officers, hopefully already on the scene. He was surprised that no new leads had come about so far.

When Dominic arrived to the neighborhood, he parked on the opposite end of the street from the house. Unfortunately, a media crew truck was hanging out by the Trent house. He shivered as he got out of the car. Surprisingly, there hadn't been as many snow days yet, but the winter chill was still starting to engulf the city.

As he neared the front of Alvero and Catalina Trent's house, he was dismayed to see a female reporter already standing outside, holding a mic in her hand as she talked in front of a camera.

"The Trent couple who lived in *this* house are still missing," she said, as she pointed in front of her. "According to witnesses, they were last seen pulling into their house on Halloween night after a dinner party..."

Dominic shook his head, dismally. He disliked the fact that the press had made their way to the neighborhood, and somehow figured out what had happened before he had a chance to. Once he was at the front door, he noticed there were neighbors about, clad in their PJ's, standing outside their houses, gawking at the scene of the crime. He could hear their murmurs and see them pointing at the Trent house.

The house, which was blue in color, looked like an average two-story house. Stairs led to the front door. The garage was tucked in to the left of the house. The adjacent houses in the area also looked identical to the Trents' house. In all, it was a decent neighborhood to be living in. It shocked Dominic that two people had gone missing in such a peaceful place.

Multiple officers walked in and out of the house and around the premises. Dominic walked over to one of the officers standing nearby, who was a young man with a mustache. He recognized the man as a fellow officer in his department.

"What exactly happened?" Dominic asked.

"Couple who lives here has not been seen since returning from a dinner party around 11:05 pm last week. Neighbors reported them missing, after not seeing any signs of them after a few days. Call was made this morning by one of the neighbors. The names of the missing couple are Mr. Alvero and Mrs. Catalina Trent. They are both thirty-one years old."

"Any signs of foul play? Or perhaps they've just gone for a little vacation?"

"Not yet. We looked around their house. There are no signs of robbery. Wallets and jewelry were found in their bedrooms, indicating they hadn't gone out for a "vacation," as you say. Everything looked orderly and neat."

Dominic patted his shoulder. "Well, keep looking around the house for more clues. The Chief asked me to go around to the other houses and ask questions. I want to know if anyone saw their car pull into their driveway."

With that, he walked away. He needed to get more information as to what could have happened. He decided to make his rounds to people living in the adjacent houses first, one of which made the call to police reporting the couple missing. He wanted to get a general sense of who lived in this neighborhood. They all said that they either didn't see or hear anything, or were fast asleep by then. They made sure to add that either they didn't know the couple well, or that they were busy that night trick-or-treating, just to draw suspicion off of them.

An elderly woman with close-cropped hair and a pearl necklace, who lived a few houses away from the Trents' house, had reported the couple missing. She said she usually saw the glare of headlights reflecting from her windows from cars passing by. This was common in this street, as cars came and went, even late at night.

With no new information to guide him towards a suspect, Dominic then decided to direct his question to the people in the houses to the left and right of the Trents' house, aka, their direct next-door neighbors. These two sets of neighbors probably knew the Trents better and could account for where they might have gone.

He first made his way to the house that was to the left of the Trent house. As figured, it looked exactly like the Trent house —blue exterior, stairs leading to the front door, etc. There was only one car on the driveway—a Hyundai.

He knocked on the door.

At first there was no answer. All of a sudden, the door opened slightly. There stood a small boy around seven years old. He had freckles on his face, and tousled brown hair, and wore a red sweater and blue pants. He had a Spider Man toy clutched in his hands.

"Yes?" he asked, quite confidently.

"Hello there. My name is Detective Dominic Rivers." He flashed his badge to the boy. "Is your mother or father home?"

The boy looked it over as if he understood what his badge stood for. He paused, then said, "No, they both have gone out."

"When will they be back?"

"In an hour."

"So, you're all alone?"

"Not if you include Jeffy."

"Who?"

"My dog. He's sleeping."

"Oh...I see." Dominic then told the boy he'd be back, and asked him to make sure he had his doors locked.

When he arrived to the house to the right of the Trent house, he knocked on the door. No one answered at first. Then, a young woman opened the door, just a crack. She looked around her late twenties and wore thick nonprescription fashion glasses, jeans, and a cropped green sweater. She had black hair pulled back in a ponytail. She looked like she had been painting due to the paint stains on her jeans.

"Yes?" she asked, a confused look plastered all over her face.

"Hi, I'm Detective Dominic Rivers." He flashed his badge to her. "I was wondering if I could ask you a few questions, if you don't mind. It's about Alvero and Catalina Trent's disappearance. They live next door to you. I'm sure you heard about them being missing?"

The young woman eyes widened. As if she just got caught doing something wrong. Then she composed herself.

"Oh. Right. I heard about it from the news. To add to that, there's all these press people and police cars around, which I can see from my window."

"I know it must be a disturbance but I'm afraid we are only doing our job," Dominic said, with a sigh. "By the way, what's your name?"

"Jessica."

"Jessica what?"

"Jessica Douglass."

Dominic noted this; his astute memory allowed him to remember names well.

"Alright, Jessica. Could tell me if you saw the couple any time in the last week or so?

She hesitated. "Well, I don't know. I didn't really pay attention to them usually, but I did see a car pull into their driveway around a week ago."

"Are you sure you saw *their* car pull in their driveway a week ago?"

"Yes. They drive a Ford Sedan. Well, it's actually Catalina's. I know because I always see it in their driveway. Every time I leave the house, that is, to get groceries and stuff."

"Okay, and from where in your house did you see them pull into the driveway last week?"

"From my living room window."

"Can I look inside?"

"Don't you need a warrant? To enter my house?" She gave him a sharp look.

"I'm not searching your house. That's what you need a warrant for. I just want to look through your living room window."

"Oh." She looked down, feeling relieved.

Dominic couldn't help but be suspicious of her demeanor. *Did she have something to hide?*

Jessica then allowed him to enter. He made his way from the foyer to the living room, which was to the left of the foyer. There were shades made out of cloth that were drawn back. He peered through the window that she was referring to.

He could see a clear view of the entrance of the Trents'

driveway.

"When did you see them pull in? Last week? What day and what time?" he asked.

"I remember clearly, around 11 pm on, um... October 31st. Halloween. I was just going to sleep, but I forgot to turn off all the downstairs lights. As I went to turn them off, I heard yelling coming from outside. When I looked out the window, I saw some kids in costumes, yelling and throwing candy at each other. That's when I saw a glare of headlights reflecting from the side. I looked closer and saw it was them, inside the car. Then I closed the blinds before I could see them get out of the car."

"And do you always go to bed around 11? Or just that day?"

"Always at 11." She was firm in her answer. Dominic couldn't help but wonder how she was able to remember exactly what she did before going to sleep on that particular night, other than the fact it was Halloween night.

"Okay. What you say does check, as other witnesses report seeing the glare of headlights from their windows."

Jessica seemed taken aback by his comment. "What do you mean 'does check'? Am I a suspect?"

Dominic could see the creases of her brows go wider.

"No. Not yet. I'm just keeping my tracks all covered."

Jessica gave him a blank look, a look that was trying hard to hide her fear. It was as if she was thinking, *Not yet? Am I a suspect or not? There should be a straightforward answer to that.*

As he kept looking out the window, he then asked, "Do you live alone here?"

"Yes, I do." Her blunt answer made it apparent she was more than eager for him to leave. She pulled something out of her pocket and looked down at it, clearly indicating she didn't want to continue talking with him.

"That the latest iPhone?" Dominic asked, looking at the object in her hands.

"No. It's an old phone. Smartphones aren't really my thing."

Jessica then walked up to her front door, leaving it wide open, while staring at him. In a conclusive voice, she said: "Have a good day, Detective."

"Have a good day, ma'am," he said, tipping his head down and walking out the door.

CHAPTER 2

Twenty-seven-year-old Jessica Douglass watched as Detective Dominic Rivers departed her house. Surely, she would not be considered guilty, or as a suspect in the case of the couples' disappearance? She was not about to be a one.

Not this time.

Nothing could tear her away from her house, or this neighborhood that she loved so much. She might not always have had the money to afford it, but through her sly ways, she was able to pay the home owners dues and her taxes.

Importantly, she had lived next door to the Trents for almost a year now. Whenever she was invited over to their place for dinner parties and such, she gathered that Catalina and Alvero seemed like sweet people, even if she wasn't very close with them.

She remembered one time a few months ago, she got invited to their house, as Catalina was hosting a dinner gathering with all her friends and neighbors. Whether they were close with her or not, it didn't matter, as Catalina was the friendly type and loved having people over at her house.

There was one close friend of Catalina's, in particular, that Jessica remembered not liking. This friend, a woman named Greta Owens, kept staring at Alvero throughout the night. Jessica thought this was not proper behavior, considering that Greta was married, with a son.

"Don't you think it's rude what that woman is doing?" she whispered to one of Catalina's friends, Erica, that night.

Erica was Catalina's college best friend. She was a flushed-faced individual with soft brown eyes and dyed pink hair, who reveled in gossip and drama, turned her head towards the woman Jessica was referring to, with interest.

"I know, right? I thought I was the only one who noticed that," she whispered back.

"It's obscene. To me, that is. I'm surprised Catalina hasn't noticed yet."

"That woman is in her own world, busy with her job and all. Not every woman is a Senior VP, you know," Erica pointed out.

Jessica gave a little shrug. "True, true. I might bring it up to Catalina, but don't really know her that well, so I don't think it's my place to say anything..."

Erica let out an irritated 'hmm', as she secretly hoped there would be a confrontation. She gave Jessica a slight nod as she walked over to her husband, who was standing by the kitchen counter. Jessica watched as Erica chatted with her husband; gazing at him lovingly.

In a crowd of married couples, Jessica hoped to find someone for herself. She was happily single for now, but she wondered when that day would be, when she would find someone permanently...

Her thoughts returned to the present, as she went over to her living room window, and watched as Detective Dominic Rivers stood outside the Owens' house.

CHAPTER 3

Meanwhile, Dominic took note of his interaction with Jessica. He would come back to her later, if the need arose.

He then decided to go back to the house where the young boy lived. Maybe his parents were back by now. As he did so, he turned back and saw a face from the window of Jessica's house. She was watching him. It gave him the creeps. He walked over to the young boy's house. He noticed a Nissan was now parked in their driveway. He knocked on the door of the house.

An old thin-looking man opened it. *He's probably the boy's grandfather,* Dominic thought. After all, he looked to be in his late sixties. He wore a grey sweater that didn't compliment his pasty, wrinkled face and was almost balding on top of that.

"Yes?" the man asked, as he pursed his brows.

"Hello. I'm Detective Rivers. I came by earlier. Your grandson opened the door and said his parents were out. I'd like to speak with them?"

The old man gave him a hard look. "What's this about?"

"Can I get your name first?" Dominic asked.

"I'm Michael Owen. And the boy you are referring to is my son." Dominic's eyes widened. *Doesn't he look a little too old to be having a young son?* he thought incredulously, but didn't say anything.

Michael continued, "My wife and I were out getting some groceries earlier.

"I see. Well, I'm here investigating the disappearance of Alvero and Catalina Trent. They live next door to you. Did you happen to see a car pull into the Trents' driveway around 11:05 pm, last week?"

Michael's face looked like stone, and he didn't appear to have a reaction.

"It was Halloween," Dominic probed. "They were just returning back from a dinner party at that time."

"I didn't see anything…I was out like a log."

"When did you go to bed that night?"

"Heck if I know. I don't even remember what I did yesterday. I usually go to bed around 10 pm. I'm not getting any younger, am I?"

"I see…" This man's nonchalant tone irked him. "So, it's likely you went to bed at 10 pm that day? And did anyone else in your house see anything? Your wife or son maybe?"

"My wife was asleep too. And so was my son."

"Are they in now? Can I talk to them?"

"Sure. Honey! Grant!" he called out.

A few seconds later, a *much* younger, prettier woman in her thirties, and the young boy he saw earlier emerged. Dominic raised his brows, even more taken aback by the fact that *this* woman was supposedly the old man's wife.

"Hello," she said with a calm voice. She had wavy blonde hair that reached her shoulders and wore a knit sweater. Her seagreen eyes brightened up her still baby-face. She resembled the actress Reese Witherspoon. Grant stood next to his mother, looked up at the detective, and shuffled his feet back and forth. The kid had no idea what was going on.

"Hi, what's your name?" he asked the wife.

"Greta. Greta Owen." She shook his hands firmly.

"And this is our son Grant." Michael pointed to the boy. Dominic smiled at the boy, acknowledging his presence.

He then directed his attention to Mrs. Owen, repeating what he said to her husband earlier, "I'm here investigating the disappearance of Alvero and Catalina Trent. They have not been seen since the night of October 31st. They were just returning back from a dinner party at around 11:05 pm…" He noticed a blank expression on her face. "…Mrs. Owen, did you or your son see a car pull into the Trents' driveway, around that time that same day? It's important to know as the Trent couple were reported to be missing the day after. I'm sure you've heard."

"We have. It's all over the news and we can see the reporter from outside talking about it…it's so sad." She shook her head.

"I didn't see anything," Grant blurted.

"Really?"

"Yeah. I was too sleepy."

"At that time, we were at home," Greta clarified. "I had just gotten back from a party. I arrived home around 8."

Dominic raised his brows. "A party? What type of party?"

"A small, uh, gathering with my friends. I was not in the neighborhood that night as I was out with them."

"How long did it go until?"

"Well, it started at 7 pm, but I left early, around 8 pm. It went until midnight, I think."

"Who all were there? I need to know so I can verify whereabouts. You know, Catalina and Alvero were *also* at a party that night—"

Michael interrupted this time. "I think she's said enough."

Dominic drew back, surprised by his sudden burst. Greta turned to her husband, looking eternally grateful.

"I'm just trying to figure out—"

"I just said I was at a party." Greta looked at Dominic, distastefully. "You should probably be out there focusing your attention on other neighbors— like Jessica from next door."

"Already talked with her."

"Oh."

"What did you do next?"

"Well, I told you I was at a party, and then got home, put Grant to sleep around 9:30 pm, as I always do. He had gone trick-or-treating with his friends. As you know, Halloween is a big deal in this town, but... people go to bed very early, even on a festive holiday like Halloween."

"What happened after you put Grant to sleep?"

Greta sighed. "Michael went to bed at 10 and I was awake for a little while longer till around 10:30, and then I went to sleep."

"What were you doing until 10:30?"

"I was cleaning up the kitchen. It was a mess. I had to clean the dishes and the countertops."

So far, nothing seemed suspicious yet.

"Is that all, Officer?" she asked, a glint of fatigue reflected in her eyes.

"Yeah. That's all. Sure, you didn't see anything from your windows or hear anything?"

"Nope, we heard nothing. Thanks for stopping by Officer, but I really think you should focus your attention on other neighbors," Michael insisted, mimicking his wife's words from earlier.

"Okay. Well, if that's all, then I'll leave then. Thank you for your time." He then shook the couple's hands again and walked away.

That was an interesting interaction. But there was no one concrete to suspect, yet.

Dominic decided to go back to the Trent house to investigate. As confirmed by the officer he first spoke with, nothing seemed out of the ordinary on the scene. Everything was in place. Catalina's purse and her wallet were inside the house. There was a strong, tangy smell of perfume and cleaning supplies that filled the air. The inside of the house looked just like the inside of Jessica Douglass's house. Two-story, spacious, and clean for the most part.

When he explored the upstairs, he saw that the Trents' bedroom was squalid. The pillows and sheets were messed up, and clothes were strewn on the ground. This made Dominic have a hunch that foul play might have occurred. If not, it might have been that they had gone to bed, and something must have happened afterwards. Seeing nothing to look into further, and with no potential lead in mind (other than Jessica and Greta, who came across as suspicious to him), he decided to return back to the station. Other than that, he had no leads.

He relayed these facts Chief Tonew by phone. Although he was a senior officer, Dominic still felt the need to report his findings to him. Saying things aloud helped him get his thoughts out in the open and helped provide new leads.

Chief Tonew acknowledged what Dominic told him, as he sat in his office. "Okay, so you have potentially two suspects, right? But there needs to be proof. To start, I will see if Jessica, has a file on her or not."

After he hung up, Dominic couldn't help but think how grateful he was for Chief Tonew's assistance.

CHAPTER 4

If anyone asked what type of person Greta Owen was, this is what she would want them to know:

She was not an ordinary woman. At least not in her own eyes. She had a great job at the local gym as a trainer. And she knew she as soon to be promoted as Head Pilates Trainer of the whole gym. But this was not what made her extraordinary.

It was the fact that she was married to a man who was two times her age. And on top of that, she had a son with him. *Grant Owen.* He was such a sweet child, according to her. When he was younger, she used to care for him a lot, but as the years went on, work had taken over, among other things. So, she didn't spend as much time with him as she would have wanted. If things didn't work out with Michael, she definitely wanted to keep Grant with her forever, that was a given. As for her marriage to Michael, people gossiped that she must have married him for his money, which was true.

But over the last eight years of marriage, she thought that she could really love him. After all, Michael Owen, her husband, was a charmer at first. He was kind-hearted and dotted on her. But this was not the case now. Michael was now distant towards her, whined all the time, and made her feel guilty for marrying him. She realized that the older he got, the more he began to have a complex that Greta might fall out of love with him. He reminded her that she must still be with him for his money. After all, he was now retired, and was reaping all the benefits of a retired veteran. He used to be a soldier in the military, during his younger days, in the 1980's. With all the money he had saved, he was able to provide nicely for his family.

But money doesn't buy everything, Greta realized.

Greta craved love, affection. Things she would not get from Michael. So, when she met Catalina Trent's husband, Alvero, about a year ago and found out he worked out at the same gym she was a trainer at, she figured this was a great reason to get to know him better. He was exactly her type, physically. He had the muscles, the height, piercing eyes, impeccable dress sense—in all, everything she desired in a man.

On one occasion, when she was at the Trents' house a few months ago for a gathering, she couldn't hide how she felt about him. Alvero was aware of her stares and warned her to keep her body language on the down low—using his eyes, of course, as Catalina didn't have a clue about their affair. This was the same day Greta met Jessica Douglass for the first time. She thought of Jessica as quiet, demure and boring. She noticed as Jessica whispered something to another friend, Erica. Whatever they were talking about had to be dull. After all, what could a single woman have to say at a gathering filled with people who were married?

Drawn back to the present, she knew that with the Trents' now missing, suspicion was on anyone who knew the couple personally. She only hoped that the police wouldn't be on her back about it.

She also hoped they wouldn't find out that she and the Trents were at the same dinner party the night before Catalina and Alvero disappeared...

CHAPTER 5

After sitting in his car for bit, Dominic waited for a call from Chief Tonew to see if he had any information on Jessica.

A few minutes later, he finally called back and told him she was a clean slate. There were no outstanding reports on Jessica's file. No priors, arrests, etc. All that was listed on her file was her occupation and where she lived. Because of this, there was no reason to pursue any lead on her, just yet.

Dominic decided to now look into the Trents' personal life a little deeper. How they were at work, what they were like as people, etc. Alvero and Catalina had been married for 15 years. No kids. Dominic also knew from his file that Alvero worked at a non-profit organization, called Sacred Wish Center, helping impoverished families, and that Catalina worked as a VP at a company called Sumpter Productions.

A few minutes later, Dominic had arrived at the Sacred Wish Center. It was a one-story building with beige walls and a glass door. There was a bright red sign on top displaying the name of the center. When he entered inside the building, there was a stout woman at the front desk.

"Hello, how may I help you?" she asked, smiling. He smiled back at her, as he showed her his badge.

"Hi, my name is Detective Dominic Rivers. I have some questions to ask about Alvero Trent. I understand that he worked here. He's been missing since October 31st. His wife, Catalina, is also missing. If you could answer a few questions about how Alvero Trent was as person, I'd appreciate it."

The smile immediately vanished from her face.

"Yeah. I heard about his disappearance. It's all over Twitter." She then narrowed her gaze at him. "I only work front desk here; I usually see Alvero in passing as he comes and goes. I think you might want to talk to his supervisor, Kathy Barnes, as she knows more about him. She's just as upset about his disappearance. She's in her office right now. Take a left and it's the first door to the right."

Dominic thanked her. "What's your name by the way?"

"I'm Jocelyn Ortiz."

"Okay, thank you."

He walked up to the office of Alvero's supervisor, Kathy Barnes. He knocked on the door, which was cracked open.

Kathy Barnes, a tall lanky woman who looked younger than Dominic thought a supervisor would be, turned around. She looked to be in her mid-twenties. She wore a turtle neck sweater and jeans. Her blonde hair was put up into a ponytail. She had just filtered her coffee from the coffee machine, and was stirring her mug, having added cream to it.

"Yes?" she asked, turning around.

"Hi, I'm Detective Dominic Rivers. I have some questions to ask you regarding Alvero Trent's disappearance. I take it you are his supervisor?"

"Come on in first," she said, in a soothing voice, as she walked to her desk and sat down. "Want something to drink?"

Dominic told her no thanks, and entered the immaculate office. Barnes' desk stood in the center of the room, facing the door. Two painted white chairs stood in front of her desk. He sat down in one of the chairs, and faced her, expectantly. She sat down a few moments later, sipping on her coffee.

"To answer your question, yes, I am his supervisor, Kathy Barnes. What about Alvero do you want to know?" she asked.

"What was his job here exactly?"

"He was a coordinator for the families who asked for assistance. He gave them resource packets and ran trainings at times."

"And these families are—"

"They are families whose kids qualify for reduced lunches at school. They are families whose kids attend Tier 1 schools. Families who are living below minimum wage. They come here for free clothes, school supplies. We even supply health care packages, especially for women—"

Dominic stopped her. "I get it. So, did Alvero like his job here?"

"Yeah. He was a pleasing face to work with. I enjoyed coaching him. Everyone has nothing but good to say about him."

"And when did he start working here?"

"Practically his whole career. For about 10 years now."

"Wow. And he never thought of going up the ladder, switching jobs, or maybe becoming someone like you for instance? Someone in a higher position?"

"He was a very simple man. He appreciated what he had. He didn't ask for more or have that drive to "go up the ladder", as you say. He always valued relationships, especially the one with his wife. He told us how much he appreciated her contribution to their marriage. This goes back to his disposition as a simpleton. Plus, if we lost him as a coordinator, who would we hire in his place? We are banking on a budget as it is."

Seeing Dominic take note of this in his notepad, the silence that followed was deafening. "Is that all?" she then asked.

"Yes, that's all," he said, getting up. "Thanks for your time." He shook her hands.

◊◊◊◊◊◊◊◊◊◊◊◊◊◊◊◊◊

Dominic now had a better picture of Alvero as a person and as a worker— a simple man who appreciated his wife.

Now he had to investigate Alvero's wife, Catalina Trent. According to her file, she worked at a prestigious job as a Senior VP, at a technology company similar to the likes of Apple, called Sumpter Productions. Their company handled the production of products like cameras, phones, etc. Her job paid her about six figures a year. Between her and her husband, she was the bread winner.

Dominic took a nice drive into the city where her job was. Her job was at least a 20-minute drive from their house, whereas Alvero's job was just a 10-minute walk from their house.

He arrived at the fancy, glass building of *Sumpter Productions* that had multiple stories. He went inside and walked around the first floor. There were glass walls, wooden roofs, and well-lit rooms. People were at their cubicles working at their computers. Overall, it seemed like a comfy work environment.

"Can I help you?" asked a man's voice.

Dominic turned around. Standing behind him was a young man, only around twenty-five years old. He had the looks of a college kid—brown hair that reached his shoulders, and blue eyes that reflected the sparkle of youth.

"Hi, I'm Detective Dominic Rivers," he extended out his hands and introduced himself and the case. "What's your name?"

"I'm Collin Afshin," the young man replied. His hands were shaky. He seemed nervous.

"And what do you do here?"

"I'm merely an employee. I work at one of these cubicles. I type the inventory of products and train interns who want to work here in the future."

"I see." Dominic nodded. Then he changed the topic. "I'm here to ask some questions about Catalina."

"I heard about her. It's so hard to believe. It's so terrible." Collin shook his head. "She's such a good worker too."

"I take it she was the Senior VP here?"

"Yes, she was. Or is. Hopefully when she turns up, that is. We have our VP taking over both positions for now."

"So, what did Catalina do here?"

"She managed the production of our products. We sell multiple technology devices. Cell phones, recording devices, camera, etc."

"And how was she as a worker? Hardworking or—"

"She was very hardworking. She would work all the time. She has great relations with everyone. Our boss, Don, loves her. She's his favorite he's had in this company. You know, she doesn't even have time to go home and rest? Once, she stayed here the whole night and went home only at 12 am."

Dominic whistled. "Wow. That's dedication right there."

"She's good on tight deadlines and budget proposals. She's the best."

"And did she tell anyone about wanting to go somewhere, on a trip or something, with her husband, maybe?"

"Nope. Not recently."

"Had she given the impression that she was not happy?"

"No, why would she be? She has the life— a loving husband and a good job. Heck, I'm jealous of her life."

Collin then shuffled his feet, like he wanted to say something more. He finally mustered the courage to do so. "But... there was one thing about Catalina..." He looked at Dominic right in the eyes. "You know what I was saying earlier about her staying here until 12 am? The thing is, she'd do so only when deadlines for product releases came up. She insisted that she be the only one here, and would even urge everyone else to leave before her."

"Did she usually do this, or only during deadlines?" Dominic wanted to make certain.

"No, just as I said, during deadlines only. Once a month maybe?"

"So, she was a workaholic, you'd say." Dominic wondered if she really was a workaholic, wanting to stay long hours, or maybe she was hiding something. He couldn't be too sure.

"For sure. I don't know anyone who's more of a workaholic than her."

"And will the others in the company attest to what you say?"

"For sure."

Dominic nodded. "Thank you for what you've just told me. One last question, though. Did Catalina bring her husband here ever? To show him where she worked?"

"No, not since I've worked here. But I'm pretty new here. I just got hired last year."

"And how long has Catalina been working here?"

"She told us at least 8 years. She would always bring it up during our work trainings and meetings. I wouldn't forget.

She sort of bragged about how much she loved this job."

Dominic shook his hand again. "Okay, thank you, Collin. You can go now."

"Anytime." Collin walked back to his cubicle. His coworker from the opposite cubicle peered over and asked him something, looking at Dominic at the same time.

Once Dominic walked away from sight, he knew he had to talk with the CEO of Sumpter Productions to get an even better picture of Catalina, as a worker. Collin said that Catalina was well liked by everyone, including the CEO. Perhaps he could find more from him.

He asked around and found out the office was on the top story. His name was written on a plaque on his door, in dark black lettering and all capital letters:

DON SUMMERS, CEO

Dominic knocked on the door.

"Come in," called a voice from inside.

Dominic entered, standing awkwardly at the doorway. He saw a man sitting at a desk that faced the door. Don Summers was a good-looking man in his forties—he wore a coat and suit, and had a crew cut hairstyle.

The CEO noticed Dominic's badge sticking out from his holster belt, and immediately straightened in his seat. He gave the detective a questioning look. He tried to hide his confusion by appearing confident.

"What can I do for you?"

Without answering, Dominic entered the room and stood close to Don's desk, like a tough detective. He focused his attention to his surroundings. The CEO's desk was made out of glass. On top, there was a coffee cup, stacks of papers, and a computer. There were also two chairs seated in front. The giant glass windows surrounding the office gave a beautiful view of the city.

After observing the surroundings of the office, he turned to Catalina's CEO. "Don Summers, I assume?"

"Yes, that's right. Says so on the plaque outside my door. Call me Don, though. And come in and have a seat."

Dominic obliged.

"I'm Detective Rivers," he motioned at his badge. "I'm here to ask you some questions regarding Catalina Trent. She worked here as Senior VP?"

"She did," Don nodded affirmably. "Is this about her disappearance?"

"It is. I want to know more about Catalina's disposition. I just talked with Collin Afshin, one of your employees, downstairs, and he told me about Catalina's workaholic tendencies. Did she always appear to be focused on her work?"

"She sure was. She's the best senior VP we've had. She would work even later than me. I told her one evening around 5, to go home but she insisted she stayed here."

"Was that a deadline week?"

"Yep, it was. But she wanted to take care of it. We had some products being released for the first time and she wanted to go over the inventory."

"Isn't that the job of the employees? To go over inventories? Collin told me that was *his* main job."

"It is. But Catalina wanted to go up and beyond in her work."

"Did she ever mention to you that she wanted to hopefully become a CEO in the future?"

"She did, as a matter of fact. Recently, like a month ago. She was telling everyone about some bucket list she wrote for herself. And "running a company" was on her list."

Dominic took in everything that was being said. "She seems like a very intelligent person. Since she is a prominent person in this company, we are doing our best to make sure she is found."

"As you should. I hope she's found. It's so terrible." Don seemed sincere in his words, as he shook his head sadly.

"I know... I have another question for you. Did she mention her husband to you or anyone else, at all? Maybe about what he did for work, how loving he was, etc."

"Not really. She'd only talk work related stuff when she was here."

"Really?" Dominic was not convinced.

"Yes. Even if she did talk about her husband to employees, I wouldn't know and I wouldn't care. I'm not privy to my employees' personal lives."

Don looked around the room, restless. "Is that all, Detective? I have a lot to do now."

"That all for now."

Dominic got up and headed out the door.

"Have a good one. Keep me updated on the case," Don called out.

CHAPTER 6

As of now, Michael Owen was the kind of man that no one wanted to be around. He was irritable, impatient and cranky. It got people to wonder what his wife Greta saw in him. When people asked how he and Greta met, this is what he'd tell them:

They met more than eight years ago, at a restaurant. Greta was with another date at the time, and Michael was dining with some of his ex-marine friends. When he saw Greta for the first time, he was interested in her. She was, after all, a beautiful woman. But the man she was with, seemed a bit off. He didn't seem to care about her, as he kept glancing around the room at other women.

Michael wanted to know Greta a bit more, as she seemed very jovial and energetic. But he knew she would never be interested in him. He was too old for her. His wife had died a few years prior, and the fact that they had no children made him lonelier and yearning for affection.

Little did Michael know that his life would change for the worse, by one first interaction with Greta. He walked over to her table and asked if she would like to join him and his friends. After she found out he was rich, and a retired marine, she was interested.

After dating for a few months, they decided to marry. He genuinely thought she loved him, as she acted as a caring wife to him. But he was wrong.

Almost a year ago, Greta started acting strange. She became more preoccupied. Distant. Aloof.

She would be looking at her phone all the time, as well as be awfully giggly when she returned back from the gym, where she worked. She'd been working at the gym for a few years and never did she act so childish like she was acting at the time.

With their son Grant in the picture now, Michael wanted his wife to be there for him, and fulfil her role as a mother, even if she didn't like him anymore. Michael, after all, was home the whole day, and had all the time in the world to care for Grant. So, a little bit more effort on her part would make their marriage more balanced, in his eyes.

Little did he know that what Greta had on her mind would change the course of their lives.

CHAPTER 7

Dominic now had a good picture of the people related to this case:

There was a workaholic wife, who had no time for anything other than work. Then, there was her husband who claimed to appreciate her, but also worked at a job that paid less than his wife. Sounded like the opposite of a loving couple.

Then there were the couple's next-door neighbors, one of whom were a couple with a significant age gap. Dominic doubted how they could be happily married.

Additionally, there was the other neighbor, a mysterious young woman who lived alone. He didn't know where else to go. He didn't have a clear-cut idea of what happened. Maybe he would ask his boss what happened at the dinner party that the couple was at the night before. *Maybe his suspect was in one of the party attendees.*

He had a late lunch with Chief Tonew at the Pavement Coffee House. It was a popular dining spot for locals and college students, who wanted a quick bite, as well as a popular spot for police officers who wanted to unwind after work. But he was far from wanting to unwind. His mind was on the case right now. Dominic ordered a sandwich with soup and Chief Tonew ordered a bagel with cream cheese. They both talked about what to pursue next.

"I have one of our guys, Detective Bert Tomlin, talking to the people who were at the dinner party that night. After he gets back to me, I will tell you what to do next, even though I'm sure you know what to do, being a senior officer and all. But it will help speed up things if multiple people work together in getting this case solved. In the meantime, why don't you tell me what you think."

Dominic ate his sandwich as he listened on. "I think that Jessica seemed suspicious," he said. "She said she saw the Trents' car directly from her window that night. No one else reported seeing the couple return back home—meaning, seeing their car. She even knew Catalina drove a Ford Sedan. She might be hiding something. I don't know. I also know that Catalina is a workaholic wife who doesn't have time for her husband Alvero. This might hint at trouble in paradise between them, but I'm not sure yet."

"What about the Owens? The old man and his young wife?"

"They seemed alright. Nothing *very* suspicious." Dominic emphasized the word 'very', as if he couldn't help but wonder if there was more to the couple than what was seen on the outside.

Chief Tonew shook his head and sighed.

"You saw the pictures of the Trents, right? On the news. And in their files? Catalina looks worn out and tired. Whereas Alvero looks cheerful. He's retained his good looks from his youth. Did you know he used to model for Calvin Klein when he was young?"

"Really?" Dominic asked, surprised. This was news to him.

"It's all in the file," Chief Tonew said, matter-of-factly.

Dominic knew his ignorance was not faring well with his boss. "I must have missed it when I was looking it over," he said, a cheap excuse.

Chief Tonew shot him a look. "Careful, Dominic, you need to be vigilant when dealing with a missing persons case. You are our best man for this job, aren't you? Or do I have to assign that status to someone else? Now tell me. How did Greta Owen seem to you?"

"The young wife? She seemed…" Dominic put his fingers under his chin, pensively thinking what to make of her. "I couldn't help but notice that she looked like a younger version of the actress, Reese Witherspoon. Which was why I was surprised at why she married an old man and had a son with him on top of that. In terms of her manner, she seemed as she was just following what her husband was telling her. She didn't want to reveal any more than she did. Good looks aside, I think what I got from her was important. Apparently, she was at a party the night that Alvero and Catalina disappeared."

He searched Chief Tonew for a reaction, but didn't get anything from his facial expressions. It appeared that he was more focused on his food than what he said.

Dominic then watched with disgust, as the Police Chief bit into his bagel rather quickly and proceeded to shove everything in his mouth at once. *We might not be at a five-star restaurant, but at least have some table manners,* he thought.

The Police Chief, taking a break from his food, said, "You don't think she could have been at the same party as Alvero and Catalina, right?" He might have looked like he wasn't listening, at first, but he had sharp ears.

Dominic mused this over. "That's a possibility. If Bert Tomlin, or whoever, is following up with the attendees of the dinner party, I guess we'll know." He then started on his tomato soup, which was delicious.

Chief Tonew spread more cream cheese on his second bagel.

"Going back to what I was saying, regarding their files, you wouldn't suppose that Greta would think of having an affair with anyone, say a handsome former model? If she and Catalina knew each other, that is..."

Dominic looked up. This seemed possible.

"Likely. But *Alvero* having an affair is not likely. He seemed like he loved his wife. His supervisor, Kathy Barnes, told me that he mentioned how much he appreciated her."

Chief Tonew's tone tuned sharp. He had a dislike for people who assumed things without getting all the facts. "*Seemed? Would, could, most likely, etc.*, are not words that hold up in an investigation. You have to be sure. An affair *is* a possibility, according to me."

"But Barnes told me his coworkers had nice things to say about him. Nothing to suggest he's *that* type of guy."

"That doesn't mean he isn't lonely. Imagine your wife staying at work, late all night, every month. How would you feel? I'd feel horrible."

"Well, I'm not married, so I wouldn't know."

Chief Tonew rolled his eyes. "That's the problem. Try putting yourself in someone else's shoes for once. *If* you were..."

Dominic thought for a moment. He'd be pretty upset, he gathered.

"Now that we know all this information, wait for Bert Tomlin to brief you on what he has on the dinner party folks. He's right now finding out more information or else I would have invited him here with us. Once you meet him, I'm sure he'll have a lot to say. He will also be working with you on the case, by the way. Since he's relatively new to the force, I had him do the work of finding out names."

Dominic nodded in interest. He was looking forward to meeting this Bert Tomlin. He'd never heard of him before.

After the day ended, Dominic was on his way home. He stared at his watch. It read: *5:30 pm*. He entered his car and was about to start the engine when his phone rang. He picked it up, seeing it was from an unknown number.

"Hello?" he asked.

"Detective Rivers?" asked a woman's voice, sounding frantic. Or what *appeared* like a woman's voice. The pitch was way too high and the frequency of the voice hit Dominic's ear like a needle.

"Who is this?" he asked, paying close attention.

"I think I know who did it."

"Did what? Who are you?"

"I know who killed Alvero and Catalina. This is Elene."

Click. The line went dead.

CHAPTER 8

Given the current situation with the couple's disappearance, Michael Owen didn't want to reveal to the police what he knew.

He knew that Greta was not at a small gathering with friends, and in fact was at a party with Catalina and Alvero on the night of October 31st. He didn't want to tell this to police as he intended to keep his family intact no matter what. He didn't want anyone in his family to be under suspicion, even if one member of his family might have a few skeletons in her closet.

A few months ago, Michael Owen asked someone to spy on Greta, and find out what was going on with her, as she was acting out of the ordinary. She seemed more than eager to be at the gym every day, dressing up, in her expensive work-out clothes. She would always be looking at her phone at night.

Michael then told this someone to follow Greta at the gym and see who she's meeting or talking to. He had an inclination that she was having an affair. Why else would she be acting like a teenager, who's just had her first crush?

He received a text from this someone saying that they could see Greta pull up to the gym: *There's a man standing at the entrance. He's very good looking. Fit, muscular. Greta is now walking towards him.*

Michael texted back asking them to send him a video and take some pictures. When the person did so, and sent them to him, he was shocked.

In the video he could see Greta greet the man and hug him. The person zoomed in on the two of them. To Michael's utmost horror, he watched as the two of them...*kissed!*

He scrolled through the pictures that were simultaneously being sent to him. They were all of Greta and the man kissing. Michael's heart began to race as he rubbed his temples in anticipation. His heart felt weak. This is what it felt like to be humiliated. This is what it felt like to be betrayed.

The man Greta was with was no stranger, but rather he was none other than their neighbor Alvero Trent!

Thank you, Jessica, Michael texted back. Jessica, his trusted companion and someone he knew he could rely on.

The following day, Michael decided to confront Greta about what he found out about her.

"Who is this?" he asked, showing his phone screen.

"Who's who?" Greta absentmindedly asked, looking down at her phone, without bothering to look up.

The two were sitting in the living room couch, a few feet away from one another.

"You know exactly who...," He extended his hands out to give her a better look at his screen. Greta turned and saw a picture of herself kissing someone. Someone that was not Michael.

"Uh...where did you get this from?" her voice reflected slight panic.

"I don't need to tell you. What's important is that I know what you're doing. It's not right." His voice was flat.

"Wow, I expected that you'd be a little more upset about it," she said, responding to his lack of tone.

"So, you're admitting you and Alvero Trent are having an affair?"

"I'm not admitting anything."

"I shouldn't be too angry, and I'm sure you know why. What I'm more upset about is that you're trying to blow our cover!" His voice now seared with anger. "What have you told him?"

"Nothing! I haven't told him anything!" Greta was agitated now. She was surprised at his little outburst.

"I need to know. You really need to be careful about who you talk to or who you decide to have relations with." He then looked down at his phone, staring at the pictures of Greta and Alvero with disgust.

Greta rolled her eyes. "You don't tell me what to do or who to talk to. I can decide that for myself. Regardless, I know you won't leave me. Plus, there's an added bonus to my little affair. Want to know what that is?"

"What?"

"Alvero's bank account."

This time, Michael looked up. His expression changed from anger to intrigue.

CHAPTER 9

The Trents were now missing for seven days.

They were not confirmed dead yet, however. Whomever called must have known something, Dominic gathered, as he dressed up for work the next day morning. He could only wonder who made that call to him the previous evening.

When he arrived to the station, Dominic told Chief Tonew about the call. The two of them were seated inside Chief Tonew's office, with Dominic directly facing the Police Chief. When they both tried tracing the call, it came back as an unknown number.

"This person might have called from a payphone," said Dominic.

"Maybe. Who is Elene, though?"

"No clue."

"Do you think it was Jessica?" Chief Tonew asked, based on Dominic's suspicion of her from the day before.

"I'm guessing so. But the voice from the phone didn't match Jessica's."

"There are such things as voice altering devices you know."

Dominic paused, upon hearing the words "voice altering devices". He then remembered something.

"You know Catalina Trent worked on producing devices like phones, cameras, etc. Do you think her company made voice altering devices as well? If Elene is really Jessica then does this mean Catalina knew Jessica? Maybe Jessica bought a voice altering device from Catalina's company?"

It was a long stretch, but worth exploring.

Chief Tonew considered this. "You will have to check with her company to see if they made these devices, and if one was bought from them. I'm surprised people buy voice altering devices these days. These days, there are apps that do that work for you."

"I know. But at the same time, Jessica doesn't come across as someone who would know about voice altering devices. She didn't even know what a search warrant was, and she doesn't have a smart phone. I don't think high-tech fancy applications are her style."

Chief Tonew gave him a reprimanding look. "Well, even if that's the case, you never know unless you check. First, find out a complete list of products that Catalina's company made. Then, find out who bought what when. Then be *sure* that Jessica *is* the one who called you."

Dominic let out a sigh. This was getting more complicated than he thought. He looked at his boss, cocking his head to one side. "Did you hear from Bert Tomlin yet?"

"Not yet. He still has one more couple to talk to."

The detective rolled his eyes. "Really? Too slow for me. Would be helpful to have that information by now." It would save him a trip to Catalina's company, if there was a lead, stemming from anyone who attended. But it seemed like he would have to make another trip.

"He's new, okay? Give him a chance. That's why I'm having you do the harder work."

Dominic groaned. So much for nine years on the force. The leniency got less and less.

"I will get on that inventory list. In the meanwhile, brief me on what Bert Tomlin finds out. *If he finds out anything that is,*" Dominic muttered the last sentence.

Chief Tonew didn't say anything. He gave Dominic a thumbs up, instead.

⌂⌂⌂⌂⌂⌂⌂⌂⌂⌂⌂⌂⌂⌂⌂⌂⌂⌂

An hour later, Dominic went back to Sumpter Productions, the company Catalina worked at.

He saw a tall, lanky, employee wearing a name badge, standing near the entrance. Dominic asked where he could find Collin Afshin. As the employee was about to point to a direction, he spotted Collin in front of him. The young man looked startled to see him.

Dominic walked over to him, after thanking the employee and motioning him to leave.

"Hi Collin. I'm glad you're here right now. Nothing to worry about, I just have something to ask of you. You told me you do inventory of all products that Catalina was in charge of overseeing, right?"

The young employee nodded.

"Can I have a list of products you have on your inventory list? From this past week until now? I want to know if you guys manufacture voice altering devices."

Collin looked up. "Why? What's happened? Have you found anything on Catalina?"

"Not yet. We're still getting there. Now, will you get me that list?"

Collin's eyes widened in shock. "Y-yes. Follow me this way," he said, stumbling as he moved.

Dominic reached the young man's cubicle, where an Apple Computer and piles of handouts lay on his desk. The observant detective took in his surroundings before looking up. He noticed everyone was staring at him, probably wondering what a cop was doing there again. Dominic ignored it. *People were always fearful of something even if there was nothing to fear in the first place.*

Collin hurriedly clicked on the computer before pulling up the spreadsheet on the screen.

"Here you go. This is the Excel spreadsheet of all inventory accounted for that people bought, from the last week till now. The first column is the name of the product, the second column is who bought it, and their address. The third column is the amount, like how many of the product was bought. The fourth column is the exact date of purchase."

"I see. And are there any voice altering devices that you guys manufacture here?"

"Yes, there are. We manufacture them in small quantities and we deliver them fast, since they aren't very popular. We deliver all products, usually by mail to the specific addresses, or through pick-up as well—people come to the office and pick up their order in person. According to this spreadsheet, three voice altering devices were bought this past week by three people." Collin highlighted the names, as Dominic wrote them down.

"The first person on the list, Lisa Arcort, lives two hours from here based on her address. The second person, David Michaels lives a few minutes away from this office building. And the third person, Michael Owen—"

Dominic froze. "What did you say? *Michael Owen?* You mean Catalina's next-door neighbor?"

Collin didn't know who he was, but he showed him the address, nevertheless. It matched the address of the Trents', except it was one number off.

"So, Michael Owen bought a voice altering device from Catalina Trent's company," Dominic said to himself. "When did he order it?" he then asked.

"Here is the date." The young employee showed the date on the spreadsheet. It read, *November 6th*. Dominic also saw the timestamp of the order—5 am. *The morning that he met Michael Owen for the first time.*

This meant that Michael couldn't have used the device to crank call him, if he had ordered it before talking with Dominic. He could have ordered it for his personal use, perhaps? Maybe he needed it for a project he was doing? Dominic mused through all possibilities he could think of.

"And did he come here to pick it up or did he have it delivered to his house?"

"He came here in person to *'pick it up*—*"* Collin made air quotations. "—with his wife too."

"How do you know that? What time did he come here to pick it up?"

"He came around 7:30 am. I was here, early. I was covering for a coworker who usually deals with handling pickups from customers."

"So, you handled the delivery of the voice altering device to Michael Owen, I'm guessing?"

"Yep. I personally delivered it to him. I know for a fact."

"How do you know his wife was with him? Did she come with him inside?"

"No." He chuckled. "He did something funny, actually. He

parked outside our building, but he called in the office asking for someone to bring his delivery to his car. Like we were a curb side delivery service, or something. That's what I meant earlier with the air quotes. He didn't come here to "pick it up"—he expected us to bring his order to him. So, I was the one who brought it to his car. I saw a woman next to him, so I assumed it was his wife. I couldn't see her face properly, as it was covered with her blonde hair."

Dominic thought—*That would explain why both Michael and Greta were not home, when he approached their house yesterday morning and found their son at home alone.* This meant they were not getting groceries after all. Or they could have been getting groceries, but they most definitely made a stop to Sumpter Productions. This revelation changed everything.

"Thank you, Collin. Do you mind if you printed this spreadsheet out? I would like to keep it for our investigation."

"Sure thing."

After Collin handed him the printed copy, Dominic walked to his car. He called Chief Tonew and asked to meet him in person at the station to tell him about what he just learned.

"Good thing you called," Chief Tonew said on the other line, happily. "Bert Tomlin is back as well. He has something to tell you."

CHAPTER 10

When Dominic reached the station, he saw another man waiting for him at the entrance.

The man gave him a little wave. *Finally,* he thought. *I guess this must be Bert Tomlin.* This officer looked like the younger version of Antonio Sabato Jr. He was thirty years old, tall, handsome, muscular in build with a smile that most people would kill for. His brown eyes were mesmerizing and sharp, and his black hair was slicked back.

Bert Tomlin was relatively new to the Boston Police department; it was his third year. He had become an officer a few months after graduating from college. A few jobs later, he decided that being a police officer was his ultimate calling. His charming good looks and lively personality immediately made him popular with his coworkers as well as with the ladies outside work. He'd have a few dates or two every now or then.

His confident demeanor didn't prevent him from being vigilant with cases when the need arose. Talking about being vigilant, he knew he was about to meet his "partner in crime"—Dominic Rivers—for the Trent case, so he made sure to be at the station beforehand.

His boss, Chief Tonew, had told him stellar things about the experienced officer, so he was looking forward to hearing what he had to offer to this case. He was also eager to relay new information he had gathered regarding the dinner party. *Maybe this will show off my expert interrogation tactics,* he thought to himself.

"Hello, I'm Dominic Rivers," the older officer greeted Bert, with a firm handshake.

"Nice to meet you. I'm Bert Tomlin. I've been looking forward to meeting you. I've heard great things about you from our boss."

Dominic smiled at him. A bit of flattery never failed to excite him. It was, after all, a boost to his ego.

"Thank you, I appreciate it. How long have you been on the force? I haven't seen you before."

"This is my third year. But I just got switched to Homicide this year."

"I see. Well, nice to meet you. I guess it's good to have someone who will assist me with this case."

Dominic and Bert then entered an empty interrogation room. There were three chairs, and one wooden table in front of them. Two minutes later, Chief Tonew walked in, taking a seat next to Dominic.

Bert said he had all the intel regarding the dinner party that the Trents' attended. He explained that the dinner party was at an upscale ballroom at the Hyatt Regency Hotel, which was in the city. Alvero and Catalina took Catalina's car for the event. It started at 7 pm and ended around midnight. The couple got back around 11:05, as previously confirmed. It was hosted by Don Summers, Catalina's CEO, but he wanted to make it sound fancier and called it a "party" to get more people to come. Most of Catalina's coworkers and employees were there. All the attendees that Bert talked with said that the Trents' acted normal and were full of life. Bert handed a list of names of people who he talked with.

"They didn't say anything or cause a scene, if that's what you're expecting happened," Bert said, turning to Dominic.

Dominic looked down the list and paused at one name. *Greta Owen.*

"Greta Owen was at this party?" he asked, surprised. *Was this the party she was referring to, when he interrogated her for the first time?*

"Yep. She left early though. Around 8 pm."

"Did you talk to her in person at all?"

"Yes. I did. I did so right after you talked with her yesterday. She told me that you questioned her and her husband."

"That's right. Greta told me that she was at a party that night. I guess I hadn't surmised that the party would be the same party that Catalina's boss was hosting. Anyways, now that we know, what was she doing at the dinner party? Did she know Catalina well or something?"

"Not Catalina, but Alvero. She knew Alvero well."

The two detectives gave each other a look.

"Greta told me Alvero invited her."

"Why would he invite her? Were they close, if you know what I mean?" Dominic asked.

"They were on good terms, she'd said. She didn't say anything else about their relationship with one another. Greta and Alvero both went to the same gym, the Sunview Gym, the same one she worked at. Greta apparently works there as a trainer. Anyways, she claims that she is on friendly terms with Catalina, too. Greta said she planned to be at the dinner party for a little while then she had to leave, because Michael and her son Grant were at home. And she wanted to spend time with her family."

"Did witnesses see Greta and Alvero talk with one another during the dinner party?"

"No, but Greta told me herself that she had words with Alvero for a brief while and then left."

"*Words*?" Dominic perked up. This was definitely a start, somewhere.

"Words. That's all she said."

Dominic paused before letting his thoughts come out.

"Okay. So, this means that Catalina and Alvero knew Greta. There's a connection there. I have another piece of evidence that would connect Michael, Greta's husband, to this whole case."

He then explained about the phone call he received last night, to tracking down voice altering devices, to this leading him to the fact that Michael Owen bought a voice altering device from Catalina's company. Even though Michael ordered the device before talking with Dominic, one never knew. Michael could have still made the call.

As if Bert read his mind, he said, "So maybe Michael called you under the name Elene, even if he bought the device before talking with you, Dominic. He's trying to distract you from the case. For all we know, Catalina and Alvero are on a vacation and didn't tell anyone. Or it may be that he knows something."

"Atta boy, Bert!" Chief Tonew praised.

Dominic smiled. "That's good deduction on your part. It's what I figure as well. As for the words Greta and Alvero exchanged, I believe Greta was trying to tell Alvero that she wanted to be with her family and didn't want to have an affair anymore."

"Whoa, an affair?" Bert asked, shocked. Dominic nodded. This revelation came upon him, after hearing the fact that Greta was at the dinner party and had exchanged words with Alvero.

"I have reason to believe Greta and Alvero, two good-looking people, might have been having an affair with each other. Alvero is a sad husband who was a former Calvin Klein model, now has a wife who is a workaholic, and Greta has a husband twice her age and wants some love in her life, likely from someone younger. It makes sense. And the fact that they go to the same gym and that Alvero invited her for the dinner party makes this even more certain that they might have been having an affair."

"What about Michael Owen?" Bert asked. "Do you think he suspected his wife was having an affair?"

"We don't know that yet. I still need to talk with him about why he bought the voice altering device. Maybe I'll get a clue from him," Dominic stated.

"You do that..." Chief Tonew said. "...And Bert, you talk to Jessica again."

Dominic perked up. "Why are we talking to Jessica again now?"

"Bert interviewed her again after you did yesterday and found out that she might have seen something that night. Something about a shadow-y figure."

Dominic raised his brows in shock. "Wait, what? What shadow-y figure? Why did she tell this to Bert and not me, when I asked her if she saw anything? When were you going to tell me about this?" he ranted.

"Relax, maybe Bert is presenting himself as less tough than you are."

Bert looked up, surprised by this comment. His expression turned to anger, as he glared at the Police Chief.

Dominic held in a breath.

"You know what? *I* will talk to Jessica. Bert can follow along with me, but I want to question her about what shadow-y figure she might have seen. I was the one who questioned her first."

"No need to get antsy about this, Dominic. Sure, you can do that. Take Bert with you too. But first talk to Michael Owen."

"What do I do in the meantime?" Bert asked.

"You can check on any updates from the search parties who've been looking for the couple. I also have another case for you to look at. Until Michael Owen's story is all covered, you both will not talk to Jessica. I want closure on his part before one of you get all excited on who is dealing with what part of this case." Chief Tonew shot Dominic a judgmental look before getting up and leaving the room.

Dominic gave Bert a cold stare before walking out of the room as well.

Dominic went to his desk, thoughts clouded his mind. He was thinking about his conversation with Chief Tonew and Bert regarding the theory that Greta and Alvero may be having an affair and that Michael might have known about it. Even though there was no proof yet, he surmised the phone call revealing that the Trents' were dead might have been used with a voice altering device so that he wouldn't know the identity of the caller.

Maybe the caller was Michael Owen. Maybe Michael Owen had something to do with the couple's disappearance.

After all, there was motive. An angry husband kills wife's lover. And Catalina, the wife of the lover, could have been the collateral damage, getting killed because she was in the way.

Since Chief Tonew told him not to investigate Jessica Douglass just yet, he decided to look up Michael's personal history. Who was he? What type of person was he?

He did a quick google search on his laptop. There were a couple of results that popped up. Two things that stuck out were a Facebook profile page and an old article from the Daily News. Dominic clicked on the page. The article was about Michael receiving a new house, (the house he currently lived in) due to his war veteran status. It was from nine years ago.

From the article, Dominic discovered that Michael was a retired war veteran, who fought in the 1980's. And the fact that years ago, he received the house as a gift from the Veteran's Association. He soon exited out of the article. He then clicked on the Facebook profile page. It was of Michael Owen indeed. His profile picture flashed a huge smile, showing off his pearly white teeth.

As Dominic scrolled though his profile (which was public) to see more about him, he stumbled upon Michael's liked pages. He noticed that he had liked numerous bank pages—Chase, Bank of America, Wells Fargo, etc. This didn't seem too odd, but Dominic couldn't help but be struck by it. Why would Michael "like" the pages of different banks? Did he want people to know which banks he had his money in?

Dominic decided to call one of the banks, to see if Michael Owen had an account there. He'd get a better sense of how money-minded the man was. When all this time, Dominic was looking into voice altering devices and affairs, money could have been a factor in this whole case. Michael perhaps was in debt, and had to use fake identities to transfer cash into different accounts. He called the first bank—Chase. He introduced himself, the Trent case, and asked the associate on the line if he knew if a Michael Owen had an account at their bank.

"Sorry, that's personal information. I can't reveal that," the associate, Tony Seiber said.

"Look, Mr. Seiber, I really need to know. I am part of a missing persons investigation."

"I know that...the case is all over the news."

"I bet they have a lot to say. Which is why, as a detective, I'm trying to figure out the truth. Maybe what you tell me could give me a lead. Did someone named Michael Owen have a bank account here? He's one of the neighbors of the Trent couple and may or may not be a suspect," he emphasized.

There was a brief pause.

"That's confidential information I can't reveal."

Dominic let out a frustrated sigh. "Sir, I am asking politely. If you can't tell me, could you connect me with someone who can? If not, you wouldn't want us to get a warrant for your arrest, for withholding information in a missing persons case, hmm?"

Mr. Seiber gulped. "Well, I—uh...I guess I can say that I am Mr. Owen's direct associate—I wouldn't want you to bother my other associates—"

Before he could say another word, Dominic cut in.

"Good, that means that Michael had an account here. Was it under his own name or another name?"

"His own name, but—"

"So, he didn't have another alias, or other names he used by any chance?"

"Not to my knowledge." Mr. Seiber spoke with brevity.

"Really? Are you sure? Because we can double check what you say."

Silence.

Dominic was about to hang up when the bank associate cut in.

"Actually, no, wait," his voice was rushed. "He uses one other name. Walter Schuman. S-C-H-U-M-A-N. He didn't tell me if this name was an alias or his real name or not. But he asked to make an account with this name."

"Really?" This was intriguing. Why would he do that? It was illegal for the same person to make another account, under a different name. Perhaps Michael paid Mr. Seiber off? He wrote down the name **WALTER SCHUMAN** on a piece of paper that was on his desk.

He resumed his questioning. He wanted to play his cards cool. He didn't want to alert Mr. Seiber by asking too many detailed questions. "Was he in debt by any chance?"

The bank associate answered immediately. "No, not to my knowledge. He never stated so."

"Hmm, alright, thank you." Dominic hung up.

After calling the other banks on the list, all associates said the same thing.

Michael Owen apparently used the names Walter Schuman, Donny Spelling, and Chris Sheppard to transfer his money into their accounts. Which of those names was Michael's real name, he didn't know. But for now, he had to speak with Michael in person to get more information about the voice altering device, and if he still had it or not. Having it would make Michael's suspicion of guilt even stronger, in addition to the fact that he used fake names to open up different bank accounts.

He got up from his desk and went out the door. .

CHAPTER 11

The Trents' two neighbors had different problems:

Jessica Douglass, in addition to being aware of Greta's affair with Alvero, and who had worked alongside Michael to figure this out, was thinking about what she saw the night of the couple's disappearance. She also had a lot to hide. She told Detective Tomlin she might have (*might have*) seen a shadow-y figure that night.

But she lied. She knew exactly who the shadow-y figure was. How could she forget who it was, when it was someone she knew, all too well?

Michael Owen on the other hand, was irritated that the police had questioned him and Greta about the Trents' whereabouts. To be honest he didn't really care about them. He was not as close with them, as his wife was...

But one thing he did have to worry about was not getting caught by the police regarding his bank balance. He had recently purchased a voice altering device, under his own name, to use with Grant.

At the moment, he had finished buying some new clothes and household items at Target. Before he started the car, to go back home, he went on his phone to check his current balance.

That's when he saw that someone had called him a few minutes ago.

"Hello?" he asked.

"Hello, is this Michael Owen?" the voice asked.

"Yes, who is this?"

"This is Mr. Seiber."

"Oh." Michael knew exactly who he was. "What is it?" he asked.

"I got a call from a detective today asking about you. I was wondering if everything was alright on your end."

At this, Michael didn't know what to say; he was quite shocked. Michael had come to Mr. Seiber for problems regarding his bank balance and wanting to put his money in different accounts, under different names. It was not legal at all, but Michael paid him off well.

"What did you tell him? What did he say?" He knew it must be Detective Rivers.

"His name was something Rivers, and he was asking if you had several accounts under different names, at our bank, and I said yes."

Michael was enraged. "Now why would you tell him that? Isn't that supposed to be confidential information?! I paid you so that you wouldn't reveal anything. Everybody knows its illegal to do that!"

"I know, and I shouldn't have taken your money in the first place. But I didn't know it would lead to a missing persons case that would hover around you and eventually lead to me. That detective has to know the truth eventually. I didn't want to get arrested for not telling the truth. They will eventually find out everything, you know."

Michael clenched his teeth. "Why'd you call me, then? To tell me this?"

"Yes. See, I like to warn my clients when I think something is amiss."

"Nothing is amiss, and even if there is, it's none of your concern."

There was a pause on the line.

"Hello?" Michael asked, restless by the silence.

"I have to go, actually. I have to deal with a client right now."

Mr. Seiber hung up, leaving Michael perturbed. He knew from now on that he had to be careful. Careful of not having his cover blown.

To the world, he was Michael Owen and he intended to keep it that way. Not even Detective Rivers or Mr. Seiber would do anything about it.

CHAPTER 12

The sun was looking like it was setting, leaving a cold chill in the air, even though it was only 4:00 pm. Entering the winter season definitely was a curse, especially when a missing persons investigation was happening during it. Everything seemed so much duller and more frightening.

Dominic made his way to Michael Owen's house twenty minutes later; the spreadsheet of the inventory purchases made from Catalina's company, was clutched in his hands. He was very pressed at the moment. Why had Bert extracted more information from Jessica than he had? Did nine years of working as a police detective not matter? All these younger, newer officers were more likable, he surmised, angry by the thought. Time to loosen up and get on with closing Michael Owen's part of the case, even though he knew the loosening up part would be hard for him to do. Regardless, he would solve this whole thing no matter what.

As he arrived at the house, he saw that the lights were mostly off. He knocked on Michael Owen's door. There was no answer. He knocked again, yelling, "Police!" The door opened. It was not Michael Owen. It was Greta. She had on an apron over an orange sweater, looking a bit disheveled. On top of that, she didn't look too happy to see him. She asked what he wanted.

"I was wondering if your husband Michael was at home. I have a question to ask him," Dominic said.

"He's not at home now. He'll be back in an hour."

"Where is he?" He couldn't help but be curious.

"That's none of your concern."

"Alright, if that's what you say. I'll wait for him to get back. It's very important I speak with him today."

"Why do you want to speak with him? We answered all your questions."

"Not all of them, actually. Maybe you can help me out. Can I come in?"

She hesitated. "Uh— sure?" She led him to the kitchen, where the smell of something delicious met his nose. There was a big island in the center of the room. The oven door was open, revealing a tray of chicken or...turkey? It was hard to see from his angle.

"It smells good in here," he said. He sat down in one of the high chairs that faced the big island.

"I'm making pot roast. Want some? It's almost done," she offered, in a rather flat tone.

"Sure, I could use some. I'm hungry. It's been a long day."

"I'm sure it has. Now what did you want to ask me, or my husband rather?"

Dominic showed her the spreadsheet he got from Collin Afshin. "Your husband ordered a voice altering device from Catalina Trent's company. You and he went to pick it up on the 6th, which was yesterday morning, the morning that the Trent couple were reported missing. Your husband told me, you both had been out to buy only groceries, when I questioned him, later that morning. That was a lie. Now, I want to know, do you still own the voice altering device?"

Whatever good cheer Greta had, vanished from her face. She stared at him with cold menacing eyes. There was a long pause before she replied: "I don't know...I don't know if he still has it...I don't know why he'd order that in the first place."

Dominic grimaced at her words.

"But you went with Michael to pick it up just recently. Don't tell me you don't still own the device. He even asked someone from inside to deliver it to your car. I have his name. Collin Afshin," he said, trying not to sound like he was confronting her.

Her manner, in turn, made it seem like she was indeed guilty of covering something up. She hesitated, as she looked down at the ground. "I don't know. Really. He told me that morning that he had something to pick up and asked me to come with him. What he did with it afterwards, I don't know."

"I find that hard to believe. You have a young son at home who was all alone with the dog. Michael could have gone to pick it up himself. How does that look, the fact that you both went to pick it up? Sounds to me like reckless parenting. Or maybe it sounds like a plot to do something with the device... perhaps crank call someone with it."

Greta quivered her lips and shook her head, agitated. "Don't go insulting me in my own house! I have no clue what you're talking about!"

"I'm sorry. But it is what it is. Tell me the truth. Why did he order the device in the first place? Why did you both go to pick it up?"

She turned away from him and pulled the pot roast out of the oven. She sliced into it hastily and put a piece on a plate. She shoved the plate in front of him. "Here you go. Eat this! But I'm not saying anything. Not until Michael gets home."

"Why don't you just tell me the truth? I know you two are lying to me. You also didn't answer my question from before. Did he need the device for work or any project he's doing?"

He wanted to test Greta to see if she would now tell him the truth, even if he knew that Michael was now retired. She seemed to read his mind.

"Michael's retired," she said.

"Oh." Dominic tried to act like this was the first time he knew of this. "So, how do you keep money flowing in? Do you have a job too?" He wanted to make sure she stated she worked at the gym, as Bert had mentioned.

"Michael's retirement money is keeping us afloat. And I work at the local gym."

"The same gym that Alvero Trent worked out at?"

His name brought a jolt to her.

"Yes." Dominic noted the look of surprise on her face with the mention of his name.

"His name does mean something to you, huh?" he asked.

"I have no clue what you mean. I will not answer any of your questions until Michael gets home."

"Fair enough. I will wait here then. This is great by the way. You are a great cook," Dominic complimented, biting into the delicious pot roast. But she remained stone-faced, staring her wide eyes at him.

Michael returned, five minutes later. He wore a black sweater and jeans, and had his glasses perched on top of his head, holding a bag filled with items, in his right hand. He walked through the kitchen door, calling out Greta's name. He paused when he saw Dominic.

"Honey, he's back again. He has some questions to ask you." Greta shielded herself protectively behind her husband.

Michael let out a huge sigh, looked at his wife and then at Dominic. "What do you want?"

"I want to ask you a question regarding this spreadsheet. I told your wife about it." Dominic handed it to him, as the confused husband skimmed over it, appearing like he could care less.

"So?" he scoffed.

"This is an inventory of all items bought from Catalina Trents' company, this past week, as well as the names of people who bought them. Your name is on this list. You apparently ordered a voice altering device and picked it up in the morning, right before the news of the Trents' disappearance broke. I was telling Mrs. Owen that you lied to me when you said you were out getting groceries when you really were out picking up this device. That same evening, I got a call from someone with a strange high-pitched voice named Elene, saying they know who killed Alvero and Catalina. Now I want to know, do you still own the voice-altering device that you ordered?"

Michael shuffled his feet, uncomfortably. He was not expecting such a long speech from the detective. He looked at the ground, as he didn't want to give Dominic any form of eye contact. He knew that Dominic thought he was guilty, but he knew he wasn't.

"Sure, I still have it. It's in my study room. But for my personal use, only. I bought it so I could use it with Grant. To mess around with the voice controls and make it sound like I had a high squeaky voice. I knew he'd be amused by it. And he has been. I've used it with him a couple times since I got it."

Dominic looked at him closely, trying to take in Michael's defensive manner at the moment. He didn't believe a word of what he said. "Really? So, you perhaps didn't, I don't know, crank call me, using the voice altering device? Cause the voice was high-pitched, like I said—"

"Honest. I didn't make any call to you using the device, if that's what you're insinuating. And who's Elene?" He looked at his wife. Greta shrugged, then looked down, not even saying a word.

"I didn't call you," he continued. "I don't even know your number. Honest to God. Fine, I lied about getting groceries. I couldn't tell you I was picking up a voice altering device. Not at that moment—it would have been too hard to explain at the time. I had just found that police were swarming the Trent house and I was pretty disturbed and upset about it, right honey?"

Greta looked at him with sad eyes. "Yeah. I was upset about seeing all the commotion too. Especially in a quaint street like ours. It made me worried for Grant, especially. But as Michael said, he didn't make any call."

Dominic gave her a sharp look.

"Then did you make the call, Mrs. Owen? Is there something you know that you aren't telling me?"

She glared at him. She had nothing coherent to say. "I—uh, well—"

Michael put up his hands and edged closer towards Dominic "I think that's enough, *Detective* or *Officer,* or whatever you are. I've had it with your questions. Leave us alone or else I will file charges against you on the basis of harassment. We told you we didn't make any calls to you, and I told you why I bought the device."

The detective put up his hands in defense. "I'm sorry I'm upsetting you two. I'm just trying to get the truth. Why would someone named Elene call me, convinced that the couple is dead, when they are still considered missing?"

"I think you have to figure that out for yourself," Michael said with a sarcastic little tsk as he walked the confused detective out his front door.

CHAPTER 13

Michael Owen was belligerent at this point. As he watched Detective Rivers drive off, he let out a groan. He marched over to the kitchen, where Greta stared at him.

"That insolent cop! If I see him again, I'll kill him!" he exclaimed, slamming his fists against the big island counter.

"Michael! Not so loud! Grant is taking a nap," his wife reprimanded.

"I don't give a damn! I want this guy to stop asking us questions! If I see him again, standing even an inch from our mailbox, that's the end of him!"

"Michael, calm down. He's just doing his job. Besides he's got nothing on us."

"Nothing on us? Really? He's accusing us of lying and crank calling him. Even if I did lie to him once, who cares?"

He then gave Greta an accusatory look. "Did *you* call him by any chance?"

Her voice went up a few decibels. "What, me?! No! Why would I do that?"

"Answer me now. Did you call him pretending to be Elene or whatever?"

"No, I didn't!" she insisted.

He stared at her until he finally cooled down. His expression changed from that of anger, to that of tenderness. "Fine, I believe you, honey," he said as he hugged her.

Greta, half-heartedly obliged his hug. She then took a bite of her pot roast and calmly thought about everything so far.

She couldn't help but think about how to use this situation to her advantage. After all, she had always been about herself. Her wants, her desires—they all came first. She thought about how Detective Rivers suspected Michael of crank calling him, admitting that the Trents were dead. And that because he bought the voice altering device, this immediately put him under suspicion. Maybe he made that call to throw the officer off, to divert the detective from the truth.

Let Detective Rivers keep thinking this, she thought. Anything to get him off *her* back, specifically. What he or the police in general don't know is the truth.

The truth she was not willing to reveal.

And no, she was not referring to the truth regarding her affair with Alvero. She was talking about a different truth. Something more sinister...

CHAPTER 14

The next morning, the two men were sitting in the same interrogation room, as the one they were in when they first met. Dominic relayed to Bert what had happened at the Owens' house and the fact that he was disconcerted by the fact they didn't reveal anything to him. Bert, in turn, revealed that he had checked in with the search parties, but nothing had been found yet.

There was a long pause afterwards.

Bert knew that Dominic was feeling down because of his lack of information from the Owens. "That's interesting that they weren't able to say anything. I guess that's their form of being defensive."

"What do you know?" Dominic's tone of voice was hostile. "They will have to let out the truth one of these days."

Bert scoffed. "I know about people like you who try to act like they're always entitled to getting information."

"Watch your mouth. As far as I'm concerned, I'm the one who should be allowed to give the lectures to people like you."

"Wow..." Bert whistled. "You really are the hardest person I've had to work with. No offense." Bert put his hands up in defense.

Dominic banged his hands on the table, in frustration, not paying heed to Bert's words. He was more frustrated because of the case. The sound resonated loud enough that it was heard from a few feet away.

Chief Tonew happened to be walking by when he heard a loud bang coming from inside the room he was next to. When he peered through the doorway, he saw it was only Dominic and Bert.

"Hey, what's going on? What did you find out, Dominic?" he asked, as he stood there with his arms crossed.

The disgruntled detective repeated what he told Bert. He finished with: "I basically got nothing. I know he was not telling the truth regarding why he bought the voice altering device. His wife didn't know anything either. And they both claimed they didn't call me."

"So, what do you know now?" the Police Chief asked.

"What I do know is that Michael lied to me. He even admitted to it. He lied about getting groceries when really, he was picking up the voice altering device with his wife, the same morning. And most importantly, I know Michael Owen is not who we all thought he was."

"What do you mean?" Bert asked, curiously. He placed his hands against his chin, listening with interest.

"I called up one of Michael's bank. Chase. He apparently uses more banks than any person would." Dominic proceeded to explain what he found out from the article he read, as well as seeing the pages of different banks on Michael's liked pages on Facebook.

"From there, I called Chase bank first and spoke with his bank associate, Mr. Seiber. Then I called the other banks. Apparently, our man here has more names than we thought."

He produced his list of names he wrote:

Walter Schuman

Donny Spelling

Chris Sheppard

"So, you're telling me that one of these names must be Michael's real name?" Chief Tonew asked, intrigued.

"Maybe. Mr. Seiber told me that Michael used another name, which is on the list—Walter Schuman. I wonder if that is his real name. Because I doubt Michael Owen is his real name. It sounds so…generic. But you never know these days. It proves that Michael may be doing something shady with money, like using different names for different accounts, to keep his balances flowing with cash. Where is he getting all his money from anyways? He's retired, isn't he?"

Dominic paused, waiting for a reaction from the other two. There was none, just pure silence.

"And on top of that, he lied about why he bought the voice altering device. He's obviously hiding something, so I'm not crossing him off my list of suspects. Maybe he knows something about the Trent couple's whereabouts."

"What about Greta?" Chief Tonew asked.

"I can't pin point it but she looks like she has a lot to hide. She wouldn't tell me straight up why she thought her husband bought the device or not."

"Maybe she didn't know," Chief Tonew said.

"She knew enough to go pick it up with him. So that doesn't fly." His voice seared with anger and frustration. It appeared as if he was worn out.

"Geez, Dominic. Take a break, will ya? You seem to be acting up," Chief Tonew said, not amused by Dominic's attitude. "While you mule over your theories, now that you got more on Michael, why don't you and Bert talk to Jessica now?" He walked out of the room, shaking his head.

The detectives looked at each other.

"Fine," Dominic muttered.

Dominic Rivers and Bert Tomlin went in the same car to Jessica's house. When they arrived, they parked outside, opposite her driveway. Her house looked identical to the Trents'.

It was a two-story residence that was blue in color. There were also stairs leading to the entrance of her property.

Bert approached Jessica's house first, and knocked on it. Dominic followed him, standing a few feet behind. The door opened slightly. It was Jessica. She was wearing a red sweater and blue jeans, and had her hair in a bun. She wore no makeup which only made her look more fatigued.

"Yes?" she asked.

"Do you always wake up this early?" Bert joked.

"I do." She cracked a playful smile and continued to look at him as if Dominic not there.

Annoyed at their gazes towards one another, Dominic took charge. He stood in a commandeering manner and asked if they could ask her some questions.

"Can we come in?" Bert added, flashing the kind of smile that women would not be able to resist.

Jessica blushed. "Sure, come on in." She led them into her living room. The living room was quite spacious with white couches, arranged neatly in an L-formation. A plasma TV stood perched against the wall.

It was obvious she fancied Bert and therefore would reveal

more information to him, as she'd clearly done before. This infuriated Dominic. He was not about to have competition from a newbie.

The officers sat down in one of the couches, while Jessica brought them a tray of breakfast, from the kitchen.

"I always over-make everything. Have some eggs and bacon."

Dominic's mood changed upon hearing she was offering food. Maybe it was hunger that was making him cranky. He took a bite of the eggs and smiled.

"Mmmm, so good!" he said, heartily enjoying it.

She laughed. "I'm glad you like it." She looked at the younger detective, who signed the "a-okay" sign. She took this as a cue to sit down, awaiting their questions.

"So, you said that you saw a "shadow-y figure" by the Trents' house the night they returned from the party, right?" Bert asked, after mouthing a spoonful of eggs.

"Yes, I did."

Dominic gave her a look. She avoided his gaze, looking down at her feet.

"What time did you see it?"

"It was after I had gone to sleep. Around midnight. I first went to bed at 11 pm, but couldn't sleep. So, I came down and got some water. That's when I saw that the moonlight was seeping light in through the living room window, shining brighter than usual. I decided to look out the window." She pointed to the window behind her. "I saw a shadow-y figure walk up to their house. It was dark, so I couldn't see how it looked, but it was wearing all black."

Dominic shook his head. "Wait, you just said you couldn't

see much because it was dark outside, but yet the moonlight had been shining bright enough for you go to the window and look out, in the first place? You seem to be contradicting yourself. It either was too dark to see anything or just bright enough to see something."

This seemed to scare the young woman a little because she sat straighter in her seat and shook her legs nervously. Bert gave Dominic a reprimanding look. Dominic was obviously aware of his rude way of questioning, but he had no time to be a softie, not when it revolved around a missing persons investigation.

"I, uh—might have seen what looked like a man."

The detectives straightened in their seats.

"A what now?" Dominic asked again.

"A man. Who wore all black and walked in the front door of their house—"

"Wait, wait, wait. So, you saw a man walk through the front door of the Trents' house. From which way did he enter, the right or the left?"

"How do you mean?" Jessica asked, confused.

Dominic sighed. "I mean— from which direction did the man you saw seem to enter the house? Did he look to be coming from the next-door house or from a house across the road?"

"I don't know. I just saw enough to see him walk from about their mailbox to their front door."

"So, you really wouldn't know which direction he came from, even just as a guess?"

"She said she doesn't know. Let's drop it," Bert said, in a stern voice.

"Fine." Dominic decided to move on. "I have another question. Did you happen to make a call to me saying you know who killed the couple? The evening of the same day I met you for the first time?"

Jessica looked taken aback. "What? A call? I don't know what you're talking about."

"Did you make a call to me or not?" Dominic repeated.

"No, I didn't. I don't even have your number."

"Didn't go to a payphone recently?"

"No, I didn't. What are you talking about?"

Bert interjected. "Hold on, Dominic, let me handle this."

He turned to Jessica. In a gentler tone, he asked, "Do you use your phone a lot? To text or call people?"

"Not really," Jessica said. "I don't really use social media either. It's too distracting."

"Really? In this day and age, that would sound unbelievable for someone to say." Bert's tone was not insulting, but instead one of genuine surprise. His softer questioning tactic was working, as Jessica was warming up to his questions, and took no offense to previous comment.

"I'm an introvert, sort of an anti-social character, so I am just happy with my own company."

"I see. And do you work at all?" Bert probed.

Dominic listened on, as he was also intent knowing more about Jessica's personality. Maybe there would be some connection to it and the missing couple.

"I do. As a graphic design artist. A year ago, I had been drawing on my iPad, and afterwards, I decided to pursue that as a part-time living."

"Artists in general don't get paid a lot. How do you upkeep a home like this one?" Dominic asked. looking around at her well-built two-story suburban home. He didn't want to sound rude but it was a reasonable question.

"I have personal connections," she said, tersely, shifting her gaze around the room.

"Like what?"

"I get money from a different "business". Her tone of voice faltered down, as she enunciated the word "business".

"Doing what?"

She sighed. "I'm too embarrassed, I—I don't know if I can say."

"No no, it's alright, you can tell us. We are on your side, Jessica. Maybe what you say can help us with the case," Dominic said, suddenly lowering his voice.

She paused. "Well, I get paid by someone each month."

"By whom?"

"For doing what?"

Dominic and Bert exchanged glances, realizing they both talked at the same time.

"I can't say explicitly," Jessica said, after a few moments of silence. "But it's what's giving me dough for the month."

To this, Dominic creased his brows. "Who is paying you, Jessica? And what line of "businesses" are you involved in? Drugs? Illegal stuff?"

He was now returning back to his blunt way of questioning as he had now raised the tone of his voice.

Bert turned his head towards Dominic, slightly taken aback by this. He was hoping that Jessica would eventually reveal more about herself, rather than get riled up from experience detective's hard-hitting line of questioning. This was one of the things he didn't like about Dominic.

"You're going to have to tell us," Bert started. "I know you don't want to. Based on what you've told us previously, makes us more curious about you. You are a witness of interest; I hope you know that. And now when we want to know more about yourself, you're backing down and refusing to tell us more? We won't allow that. Now...will you answer Detective Rivers' questions?"

Jessica's eye widened, as she nodded vigorously. Then she said, "It's like something from a Lifetime movie, you know? It's "that" kind of business that college-aged girls use, in order to pay for tuition, when they don't have enough money. You know what I mean?"

Dominic didn't know what she meant, but decided to act sly. "What *do* you mean? Enlighten us like we don't know a thing." He gave her a stern look.

Jessica didn't know how to respond. It was already embarrassing enough to admit the truth.

"Like a sugar-daddy business?" Bert suddenly asked. Dominic raised his brows.

"Yes." Embarrassment was evident all over her face, as she turned bright red,

"Who's paying you?" Dominic asked.

"I don't think I should say," she said almost immediately.

"I think you do have to tell us. Or else have fun telling us more downtown. I mean, you already started telling us, so you might as well let us in on who it is."

This got Jessica's attention.

"D-downtown?"

"Yes. If you don't tell us, we will have to keep you there until —"

"Okay, fine! It's Michael. Michael Owen."

Wow. His name was somehow getting involved in every aspect of this case.

"And how long have you been involved in this "business" with Michael?" Bert asked, calm as a cucumber.

"For about four months. I moved to this neighborhood last November. Oh, I forgot to say. Before I had my job as a graphic artist, I was a barista at Starbucks. But they fired me in late December, as they had over-hired for the year. I took the boot as they thought I was not doing a good job, which honestly, I didn't care, because I hated that job."

She was silent for a few seconds, looking at the two detectives' monotone reactions.

"I then applied for the graphic artist job and got it. But it was still not enough, I realized. This new job would not pay me much. I had to find another way to earn money. I wouldn't have time to apply for a second job. I was already getting tax notices that I would not be able to meet by the end of January, of this year…"

Jessica realized she was rambling, as she tended to do when she was nervous.

"Go on," Bert urged, gently.

Dominic didn't know where she was going with her little spiel. "What does this have to do with Michael Owen? How did you get involved with him?"

Jessica snapped back. "I'm getting to that, since I assume you two have all the time in the world to listen to what I'm saying!

I thought this was what you both wanted to hear. If you don't want me to say anything, I won't."

Someone's got an attitude, he thought.

She continued anyways. "In early January, I was sitting on a bench at the local park, when Michael sat down next to me. He engaged in small talk with me at first. I found out he lived next door to me and all. Then I got all personal and started talking about how I wouldn't be able to keep up with rent for the month. I told him I had no time to apply for another job in time for the payments due that month. That's when he suggested this deal with me. He would pay me every month if I, you know, *keep him happy*."

"And how much is he paying you? Is he still paying you?"

"Fifty an hour. And yes, he's still paying me."

"With cash?"

"Yes."

"I see. So, when do you go to his house for 'business'?" Bert asked.

"We made an agreement, two times a week in the afternoons on weekdays, for two hours, since that's when his wife works at the gym."

"So, his wife doesn't know about this whole arrangement between you two?" Dominic asked.

"Of course not." She gave him a "duh" look.

"I see. What you told me about yourself has been very helpful. But it still doesn't answer my questions about the call from the payphone or the shadow-y figure," Dominic said.

"I don't know what to do about that," Jessica said.

"You could help by telling us the truth," he insisted. "I don't think you know what the word introvert or antisocial means. You say you are an introvert, yet you decide to do something like this with your very "older" neighbor. What were you doing in the park in the first place, chatting with a stranger, that too?"

Jessica hesitated. She didn't answer him at first. Finally, she gave in.

"Okay fine, I was lying. I'm not an introvert. I was scared to tell you the truth, that's all. I'm just a bit lazy. That why I agreed to this whole deal with Michael. Plus, this way, I won't need another job."

As the detectives took in her words, Bert suddenly asked, "Do you know about Greta's affair with Alvero?"

Jessica turned white. "Affair?"

"Michael didn't tell you about suspecting his wife or anything?"

"No...." Jessica's voice faltered.

"Really?" Now even Bert was having his doubts.

"I don't know anything about his wife's life other than that she works at the gym. I just go to his house and do my business with him, get my money, and leave."

"Fine. We believe you," Dominic said. "Going back to what we came to talk to you about—you said you don't know where you saw the shadow-y figure coming from. Did he carry anything in his hands?"

"I didn't see anything, just his figure walking in."

"What exactly was he wearing?"

"Black pants, black shirt."

"How do you know it was a man?"

"The figure looked tall to me, so I assumed a man."

"How tall would you say Michael Owen is?"

She thought for a bit. "Hmm six feet maybe?"

"Would you say he fit the description of the shadow-y figure you saw?"

"I couldn't tell you for sure. I really don't know."

Dominic and Bert looked at each other dejectedly. They had asked her enough questions for now.

"Alright. I guess this is it. Thank you for telling us all that you know. And as for your embarrassing secret, it will stay with the both of us for now, okay?" Dominic reassured her. Obviously, this was a lie, but he wanted her to trust him so that he could get more information from her later on.

She thanked the two men. Then she smiled at them both of them as they walked out.

In the car, Dominic expressed what he gathered from their meeting with Jessica.

"So, now we know she's connected to Michael based on what she revealed about having an affair with him. Now we have Michael connected to everyone's name at this point, but we can't fully determine that the shadow-y figure is in fact him. And we still don't know who made the call to me."

Bert nodded. "I say you call the number again. The number you received a call from."

"That's a good idea, let me try now."

He got his phone and called back the unknown number. The phone kept ringing on the other end. A dead line.

"Sounds like they are busy. Let's wait for her call once more. Now that this person knows I'm getting close to the truth, they will call again. I have a feeling this person is someone I've already talked to."

"How do you know?"

"Just a gut feeling," said Dominic, with a twisted frown.

CHAPTER 15

After the detectives left her house, Jessica went back to her graphic art work on her iPad. She thought about what was happening so far in her life.

She knew she was now a suspect in the disappearance of Alvero and Catalina. It was so obvious! After all, she did a great job of appearing guilty in front of two detectives—how stupid could she be? But she couldn't help herself. She was horrible under pressure. Detective Rivers and Detective Tomlin definitely must be thinking she had something to do with it. But one thing was for certain—she really had no clue what Detective Rivers was talking about, regarding someone calling him from a payphone.

Her thoughts then went back to what she told the detectives regarding her arrangement with Michael. She shouldn't have said anything to them. Now what if Michael found this out?

As if on cue, her phone rang, making her jump.

When she saw who was calling, she was shocked to see it was Michael.

"Yes?" she asked, trying to hide the dismay in her voice.

"Did that detective come to see you anytime, recently? Detective Rover?"

"You mean Detective Rivers? Yeah. He also brought his friend, Detective Tomlin, with him. They just came to my house to ask me some questions."

"What? Now? Two of them?"

"Yeah, they just left from my house. Why?"

"Whatever you do, don't talk to them again. Got it. Or else I won't pay you anymore."

Jessica was startled. "Wha—what do you mean? Do you know something? If so, tell me. I promise I won't tell anyone."

"Bull. I know you well. You like to tell everyone's secrets, don't you? If you don't stop talking to those cops, I will not pay you anymore, got it?"

Jessica heard him hang up immediately on the other end. She was speechless.

⌂⌂⌂⌂⌂⌂⌂⌂⌂⌂⌂⌂⌂⌂⌂⌂⌂

Meanwhile, Greta thought about how she told Detective Tomlin that she spoke with Alvero the night of the party. She didn't tell him what they spoke about. Surely, they might suspect that she and Alvero had an affair together, but that was not all.

Her mind flashed back to what happened after the party…

It was a little after midnight. Greta made her way inside the Trents' house. The house was dark for the most part, except for the streak of moonlight that gave way from the paneled window next to the front door.

She was now near the stairwell, careful not to make any loud footsteps. Alvero Trent was most likely sleeping, along with his wife, Catalina, upstairs.

Creak.

Too late. She had accidently made her next step sonorous enough to cause a sound from within the floorboards. Greta stopped. They must have heard her!

She looked around, just in case, making sure no one was

coming down the stairs just yet. As she looked down for a split second, she suddenly felt that someone was staring at her. She looked up.

It was Alvero Trent.

He stood at the top of the stairwell in his robe, as he stared down at her.

"What are you doing here?" he asked.

Greta gave him a stern look.

"I wanted to see you. I was hoping we could continue what we were talking about at the party," she said, in a put-on voice.

"There's nothing to continue. I thought I made it clear to you. I said I don't want to see you anymore. I love my wife, and I intend to stay with her."

"Really? That's not what you said to me at the gym all those times we worked out together. Didn't you call her a bore? A workaholic? And then later on, in the locker room, when we were the only ones there—"

"Okay, alright. What do you want? You know what time it is?" His tone of voice was filled with annoyance.

Greta crossed her arms.

"I want you to be with me. Leave Catalina. I'll leave Michael too."

Alvero shook his head. He could not believe what he heard. "You must be out of your mind."

"I'm not. I'm honestly telling you the truth. Leave your wife and I'll leave my husband."

"I don't know what's gotten into your stupid little head, but all I know is that I love my wife." His voice turned harsh.

Greta stared at him with cold-blooded eyes.

"What? What do you mean?" she asked. "You are *not* breaking up with me!"

"I am. And *shh*! My wife is upstairs!"

"Who cares? Let her hear! After all, I have something against you that I think your wife will find very interesting."

Alvero scoffed as he leaned one side of his body against the stair post. "Oh yeah? And what is that?"

"I can't tell you now. Let's just say it has to do with our affair."

"You better not tell her…"

"Well, say that you'll be with me. Or else…," Greta had a kitchen knife in her hands and twirled it around in a menacing way.

"Threatening me won't work. I'm going to tell my wife about you, right now. And I will call the police. So, I ask that you leave my house, before I do that."

Greta stood like a statue, in an at-ease stance.

"What if I don't want to? I won't leave until you promise to stay with me," she insisted.

"Really? Well, that's not going to happen. If you want to play games, like an immature fool, go ahead and do it. But you don't have me fooled. I know all about you."

Greta stiffened. "What do you know about me, huh?"

Alvero walked over to her. He came close enough to her face, that their noses nearly touched.

"I know who you are, *Eliza Schuman*."

Greta Owen, or what people used to think of her as, took a step backwards. She clutched the knife in her hands, as hard as she could. She knew having the knife was the best thing for her to have, the way the conversation was headed.

"Eliza Schuman. Who's that?" she asked.

"Don't play dumb with me. I know about you. And Michael as well. He does a great job in playing the devoted husband, am I right? When really, he's just as conniving as you."

He came down the stairs and started walking closer to her.

Greta didn't respond to this. Instead, she continued to twirl her knife in her hands and stared at him, without blinking.

Alvero spat, "I know that both of you are con artists. You steal people's money. Like you did, mine."

"Oh yeah? How do you know? And how do you know that is my real name?" Greta challenged.

"I know everything. I have connections—"

"Yeah right."

"It's true. I do. That's how I figured out that you aren't Greta Owen and that your husband isn't Michael Owen, but instead Walter Schuman, who I know isn't really your husband."

"If you don't shut up already, I'll kill you. I swear."

But Alvero continued, "I know that you two are Swiss nationals who moved here pretending to be a married couple. And that son of yours, I don't even know if he is really your son. But I know that you two are cons. You steal money."

He pointed directly into her face, much to her annoyance. "You faked Michael being a veteran so that you both could be given a house, and benefits. I didn't say anything about this before, because I liked you, I really did. But now that I know the truth about you, I don't want to have anything to do with you."

"One more word and you're dead meat...," Greta warned.

She couldn't believe that he knew everything and was going to rat her out. It was one thing to be dumped by one's lover, but it was another thing to risk going to jail. There was only one thing left for her to do.

"I'm going to expose you...," he went on. "I'm going to call the police and tell them who you are! And have you both arrested after I get my $50,000 that you stole from my credit card!"

"SHUT UP!" she yelled.

Alvero reached for his phone in his robe pocket. By the time he could look at his screen, Greta made her way towards him, and plunged the metal into his flesh. There was a loud thud, as Alvero fell at the edge of the steps. His groans filled the air for a few seconds. Then there was silence.

Satisfied with what she had done, Greta then turned around, when she saw Catalina standing at the top of the stairwell.

The glow of the moonlight shone right in Catalina's face, showing her horrified expression. Greta knew she had been caught and had to do something about it.

She darted towards Catalina up the stairs. Catalina's eyes widened. She tripped on her feet, turned back and crawled wildly, trying to avoid Greta, who held her knife high above her head.

"No! Don't!" the timid wife screamed.

That's when Greta plunged the knife into Catalina's chest.

"Goodbye now...," Greta said with an eerie smile.

Those were the last words Catalina ever heard.

CHAPTER 16

That evening, Dominic couldn't stop thinking about the case, especially the call he had received. He also didn't know who the shadow-y figure could be, other than it must have been a man. Nothing substantial yet.

He then decided to have a drink with his brother, Mario Rivers at the City Bar Back Bay. Maybe that would help calm his nerves. It had been a while since the two caught up. Mario Rivers—tall, dashing, and just as handsome as his brother—was a lawyer who lived in Boston as well. He was a few years younger than Dominic but he looked like he could be his twin, with his equally curly brown hair and bright eyes. Tonight, he wore a suit and beige pants.

The two brothers were sitting and discussing their lives, when Dominic interjected some quips about the Trent case.

"I know for a fact someone with a voice altering device called me. I don't take friendly to crank calls. And the fact that I don't have anything yet frustrates me."

Mario took a sip of his drink and gave his brother a serious look. "I know I don't have a say on how to solve your cases, and I hope that the couple is found, but you got to take your mind off the case for once. You're not on duty now."

Dominic shook his head. His expression gave it all that he was not willing to listen to his brother. His mind would always be on any case he was assigned to. He then looked up and smiled halfheartedly. "So, tell me, how are Grace and the kids?"

Mario was married to a wonderful woman named Grace and

had two kids. He was what everyone would call the perfect family man. Something Dominic wouldn't be, for a while, that is.

"They're good. At home at the moment. I told Grace I was going out with you. She doesn't know I'm at a bar." He said the last sentence, drooping his mouth sideways.

"Well, where else does she expect you to be at, this time of night?" Dominic laughed.

"I don't know... but she's very trusting though. That's what I love about her."

Dominic couldn't help but smile at this. He was happy for his brother, for settling down and for living a life that everyone dreamed about. He thought about his own life and how he wanted to settle down eventually. His parents had been on his back about it the past five years. But work was work, after all.

"I think I should go back home," he then announced.

His brother looked up. "Why?"

"Because its late."

"And this is why you won't settle down, right? You're always busy with your work, you won't let it rest for one night." Mario reprimanded.

"That's the way I am, I can't do anything about it. Sorry." He then got up and waved to the woman, sitting two seats away from him, wearing a black buttoned jacket and bright makeup. She had been giving him "the eye" when he and his brother arrived to the bar. She saw him and waved back.

As he walked out, he knew what Mario was thinking about him: When will he learn to balance things because life isn't all about solving cases and playing the macho "bad cop" ? But he couldn't help it. It was his nature after all.

CHAPTER 17

The next afternoon when Dominic arrived at the Homicide/Missing Persons floor, Bert was already there talking to Chief Tonew enthusiastically. They were standing near a wooden table alongside other officers, who were chatting. Dominic cut in the conversation to tell the Police Chief what he and Bert had learned about Jessica.

"Yes, Bert was just telling me about it," Chief Tonew said, right after Dominic finished his whole spiel.

"I have so many questions still..." Dominic said, shaking his head.

"Who are you going to question now?" Chief Tonew asked.

"Well, I thought of asking more questions to the Owens', but they said they will file for harassment against me if I come to their house again."

"Ouch," Bert said, feigning hurt. "So, do you suspect them?"

"Yeah, they know something they aren't telling me."

Chief Tonew suggested, "How about Bert question them again? Maybe he could get more information on what they know about the call and about their real intent of having the voice altering device."

Bert put up a hand. "I can get more information on the couple, too. Do some digging myself?"

Dominic gave Bert a nod as he turned to his boss. "There's Michael Owen who never admitted to lying about their grocery trip- I had to expose him. Then there's Greta, who I don't know if she's telling the truth or not. She failed to mention to me that she knew Alvero well. And then there's the deal with the voice altering device. She didn't want to tell me that she had gone to pick it up with her husband. She refused to talk about it until Michael returned home. All this sounded weird. Basically, everyone's been lying to me, except Jessica for the most part. She's told the truth the whole time to Bert and myself. For now, that is."

"We have to get it out of them somehow. How about if we crank call them? Say something along the lines of 'we know what you did'?" Bert suggested, as a joke.

Chief Tonew laughed. "I didn't know we were amateur police detectives. That's not our style. We shouldn't resort to cheap tactics like that. Bert should go to the Owens' again, and bring up Michael's business with Jessica. In front of Greta. Then we'll see where we'll go from there."

⌂⌂⌂⌂⌂⌂⌂⌂⌂⌂⌂⌂⌂⌂⌂⌂⌂⌂

Bert Tomlin decided to do some digging on the Owen couple, before heading to their house to reveal Michael's affair with Jessica.

As he walked to his car, Bert thought about them. Since Michael Owen obviously had some tricks up his sleeves with his numerous bank accounts and lying about going to the grocery store, it made it all the more certain that he was involved in something deeper than what met the surface. His wife Greta was not off the grid, either. She'd been secretive about her relationship with Alvero, as Dominic said, and didn't want to admit she went with Michael to pick up the voice altering device.

Come to think of it, what did she see in Michael? The two of them looked so mismatched for each other. And their son on top of that looked way too young to be their kid. Everything about them appeared suspicious. Most importantly, if Dominic Rivers suspected something was wrong about them, given that he was one of the best men on the force, it probably meant something was wrong.

Since Bert was relatively new to being a detective, he sought outside help, to assist with digging dirt on the couple. Once he was inside the car, he got out his phone and called a good friend of his— Larry Enger.

Larry was an ex-FBI informant who, when he was active, specialized in digging dirt on people.

When Bert rang him, Larry picked up, after a few rings.

"Hello?"

"Hi, Larry? How's it going? This is Bert. Listen, I have something to ask of you."

"Sure, man. What's up?"

Bert explained the case and what he needed. "Could you find something on the couple, especially Michael Owen? For example, why does Michael have so many bank accounts under different names? Is Michael Owen not his real name or—? I gave you the list of names, right? Maybe one of them is his real name. Just anything that proves that he and his wife are people we should look into. I need proof."

After finishing, he was impressed at how well he was able to convey his message.

"I see," Larry said, after listening intently. "I could do that...I would assume this is on the down low, because I don't want to get in trouble doing something that can be traced later on."

"Oh, come on Larry. This is your specialty. Nothing will

happen to you. I really would like to know. Plus getting this information would prove my skill as an experienced detective, which I'm trying to be."

Larry could be heard laughing on the other end. "Well, you're good regardless. I'll do it because you're my friend. I'll see what I can find."

"Thanks, you're the best." Bert smiled and hung up.

CHAPTER 18

Michael was livid. He was starting to become paranoid. The police were on his trail about the Trents' disappearance because of a phone call made to them. He had to do something. He could run away with Greta. Take an overnight trip to an upscale cabin in the woods for a few days?

No. That sounded suspicious.

How about they go to New York? Take a day trip or something?

That way it wouldn't look too fishy and the police would think he's just vacationing for a while.

He mentioned this to Greta, when she came back from the gym that afternoon. Jessica was not allowed at his place that afternoon, and he even refused to call her. His anger for her had increased, because she talked to the police.

So he was alone at home when he brought up his idea:

"Want to go to New York?" he asked.

"Why?" she asked, suspiciously.

"Because…I'm scared of those two police officers questioning us all the time. I need a break. Let's go there for a day or so. Leave today and be back tomorrow morning?"

"Won't that look suspicious? Us leaving all of a sudden?"

Michael said he thought about that. But all he wanted to do was leave here. *For now, that is.*

"Talking about being suspicious, why did you buy that voice altering recorder?" she asked him. "Tell me the truth."

He shrugged. "It looked cool. I'd been looking at Sumpter Production's website for a while and saw their voice altering device. Since I am old school, I prefer a device rather than an app. I thought it would be cool for Grant to use. And Grant loves it."

"Really? Was it just for Grant, or did you use it to call Detective Rivers?"

"Why would I do that? I have no reason to."

"Just wondering… I don't know why he'd think we made the call to him."

"Who cares what he thinks. Let's talk about us now? How about that day trip? To get our mind off this case. Grant could use a distraction from all this mess."

Greta finally relented. "A day trip doesn't sound bad at all. As long as we are back in a timely manner."

Michael looked down. He held his wife's hands. "And this is exactly why I "married" you," he said, smiling. Greta gave him a half-smile and pulled away quickly.

He went to Grant's playroom to tell him about their plans.

Right before Bert Tomlin arrived to the Owen house, he got a call from Larry.

"I got some information for you," he said, clearly. Bert's eyes widened. *Already?* It had been less than twenty minutes. He parked on the side of the road.

"Well, that was fast. What is it?"

Larry inhaled as if he was about to give a lengthy speech. "Michael Owen's real name is Walter Schuman. And turns out he's not even a war veteran, like you said he was."

The detective couldn't believe his ears. "Really? This is something. And Walter Schuman—that name sounds familiar..." He then remembered it was one of the names on Dominic's list from earlier.

"Yeah. Turns out he's not even really born and bred American, like he claims in this one article. He's really from Switzerland."

"And what about Greta?"

"Her real name is Eliza Schuman—"

"Wait, so they're *really* married?" Bert asked incredulously.

"No, but get this. Both of them are total strangers. They met on a train, and they happened to have the same last name. Coincidence, huh?"

"So, if Michael is not a war veteran, what is his occupation?"

"That I don't know. But he seems to be some sort of con man, if you ask me."

A con man that wants more money perhaps? A con man that uses a fake name and fake identity to trick people into getting their money? Bert wondered if Greta Owen perhaps had some ulterior motive with Alvero, that had to do with getting rich. After all, his wife, Catalina, made a six-figure income. And Michael had to use different bank accounts to store his money in. This seemed to make sense now.

"And what is Greta's real occupation?"

"Doesn't say."

"And the kid? Their son?"

Larry shrugged, which Bert obviously couldn't see. He then wanted to make sure of something. "I would like to know, where are you getting all this information from?"

Bert had to get his sources cited.

"I have access to a data base that has information about everyone in a neighborhood. Specifically, I have access to information on anyone's location history, where they've lived, marriage records, and if anyone has any priors or arrests, and more. I narrowed my search to the Newbury neighborhood that the Owen couple live in, and came up with this," Larry explained.

"Can I have access to the information that you just gave me about the Owens?"

"Uhh...," Larry hesitated. "It's confidential information that only I can have access to."

"Really, because as an *ex*-FBI informant, I would assume all access such as personal data information would be taken away, since you've left the job."

Larry paused. He knew Bert had a point.

"You're right. It is. But I do have some connections that allow me to hack into certain databases, even if I'm retired. I may not be an FBI informant anymore, but that doesn't stop me from knowing the loops. But you can't tell anyone. Just tell your cohort that you got this information from an FBI informant who's a good friend."

Bert didn't know what to say to this. He figured he had to agree to Larry's request. Obtaining personal information is sensitive and if he mis-communicated anything to Dominic or Chief Tonew, then Larry would get in trouble.

"Thanks so much Larry. I guess I owe you a drink or something."

Larry chuckled. "For sure. Let's meet up one of these days."

Bert hung up. He felt satisfied. He now had more information on Michael Owen. But he then realized Larry didn't provide much information on Greta Owen's persona. Her real occupation, her history, etc. He thought of asking Larry again, but he decided to do some research of his own, to prove that he was learning to become an experience detective, just like Dominic.

So, he looked into Greta's bank accounts. What he found surprised him.

⌂⌂⌂⌂⌂⌂⌂⌂⌂⌂⌂⌂⌂⌂⌂⌂⌂

A few minutes later, Bert made his way to the Owens' house. He wasn't going to say anything to them, regarding Michael's bank account and the fact that his real name was Walter Schuman.

Right now, his focus was to tell Michael and Greta about Jessica and how he knew that Michael was paying her money. He was confident he would get a confirmation from them now.

He knocked on their door.

Grant opened it. He smiled at the detective. "I know you. You're that same police guy."

Bert chuckled. "It is I, indeed. Are your parents' home?"

"Yeah, they're inside. Packing."

Bert frowned. *Packing?* "Are you all going somewhere?" he asked.

By the time, Grant could answer, Michael made his way to the door.

"You?!" he boomed.

"Yeah, it's me, this time. Don't worry, my friend won't be joining me today. I am here because I have something to tell you. Something of importance to the Trent case."

"What is it?" he asked sharply. He motioned for Grant to go inside the house.

"Are you guys going somewhere? Grant mentioned you guys were packing."

"No, he's just saying that. He doesn't know what he's talking about," Michael said, as if he was trying to brush it under the rug. *Lying, yet again.*

"Okay. It would be a good idea if you didn't leave town, as our investigation is still underway."

"Why, am I under suspicion?" Michael asked in a condescending manner.

"Not exactly," Bert lied. "But we still have questions unanswered. Can I come in? It's important I do so. Please." He put his hands on his hips, highlighting his holster belt that held his gun.

Michael was unfazed by the gun. He did his best not to punch the detective. He'd had it with these cops bugging him. He led him in, forming his hands into fists.

"Is your wife here?" Bert asked casually, oblivious to Michael's sentiments. "She would like to hear my important news, too."

"She's upstairs."

"Packing?" Bert asked slyly.

"No..." he paused. "I'll be right back." Michael went upstairs.

A few seconds later, Greta came down, with a look of worry on her face. Michael stood next to her, crossing his arms.

"What is it now?" she asked.

"I have something to tell you. Something related to your husband."

"Okay...?"

"Did you know that Michael was paying your neighbor Jessica Douglass, who lives two houses away, for a solicited business arrangement, between the two of them?"

Michael's eyes widened. Jessica Douglass.... That little.... she just had to reveal the truth. Open her big fat mouth and ruin everything. Didn't he tell her not to talk to the police?

Greta turned to Michael. "What's he talking about?"

Michael tried with all his might to hold in the anger he held in. He stuttered his words, "HE'S LYING!" He lunged at Bert

"Whoa, hey!" Bert drew his gun out.

Greta screamed. "Everyone, calm down! What arrangement?!"

Michael drew back, put his hands up defensively and stared at Bert.

"Michael, why don't you tell her?" Bert asked, panting.

"I have no clue what you're talking about,"

"Really? Jessica begs to differ."

"She's a lying SOB. She doesn't know what she's talking about."

"Wait, Jessica Douglass, the art geek?" Greta asked, as if she suddenly remembered who she was.

Bert nodded. "Her indeed, if that's what you call her. Why don't I enlighten Mrs. Owen? Mrs. Owen, for four months, your husband has been paying Jessica in exchange for the sort of thing broke college girls' resort to, to earn money. Jessica had no money. She had to find another way to earn it. Who better than from a rich older man, with a lot of retirement benefits?"

Greta stared at her husband. "How dare you? You pig!"

Slap. The sound was deafening. The manner of the slap left a red mark on his cheek.

Michael gasped, as he clutched his cheek in agony. He stared at Greta and then at Bert. He had no words.

"Is it true or not?" Bert asked, softly. He didn't want to aggravate them even more.

Michael looked down. He sobbed. "Yes. Yes, it's true. I didn't know how to tell you this, Greta, but I—"

Greta turned away from him, tears streaming down her face.

She faced the detective. "I might as well tell you something now. Now that I know my husband is a lying pig, I might as well admit the truth."

"Which is?"

"I made the call to your friend, Detective Rivers. I called him. I said all that about the Trents being dead to scare him a little." Michael was shocked at his wife's actions. He didn't know she would actually resort to this sort of thing.

"So, are they dead, the couple?" Bert asked.

"I don't know. I just made it up to distract him and get him to stop asking us questions."

"Why? Are you hiding something?"

"No. I'm not." She looked down and avoided her husband's gaze.

"Why'd you lie about it to Detective Rivers then?"

"I don't know. I was scared. I didn't like him, or how in-our-face he was, in his way of questioning."

"And you used the device to alter your voice?"

"Correct."

"Well, that settles it then. I got my question answered," Bert said, walking to the front door.

"So, you what you said about Jessica, is it really true?" she asked, following him.

"Yep, that's true. Your husband really has been involved with her for four months. We have Jessica's testimony on it. All I needed to know was who made the call to Dominic. Now I know. Thank you for your honesty."

Bert walked out the door, leaving Greta in tears.

CHAPTER 19

After Detective Tomlin had left, the Owens' plan for going on a day trip was out of the books.

Yes, Greta Owen had made the call with Michael's device.

She did it to throw the police off their trail. She was getting a promotion in her job. She would become the Head Pilates trainer of the whole gym. More money would be coming her way. She couldn't dare have a missing person's case linger on her back. Already people at the gym were asking questions about the case.

But after finding out about Jessica's arrangement with her husband, in a fit of anger, she had to tell Detective Tomlin the truth. She was furious that his affair with Jessica had been exposed, further making him a person of interest in this case. Why was he doing this? Affair aside, he was wasting money, paying Jessica. Already they didn't have enough and were barely scraping through. The last time Michael obtained a lump sum of money was a year ago when he was part of a successful bank heist at Wells Fargo, where no one figured out who the perpetrators were. But that money had been spent since then.

"What you're doing is not right. Our cover is going to be blown if you continue to see Jessica," Greta said, calming down.

"I'm sorry, alright," Michael seemed apologetic. "Let's move on and try to figure out how to not get caught now."

"You know I don't care who you have an affair with. The fact that you're wasting money out the window is what's making me angry. We need the money." She wasn't buying his apology.

"Yeah, like you're not blowing our cover by having an affair with Alvero. Who knows what *he's* figured out." Michael sneered.

Greta drew back. Michael didn't have to know that Alvero already did know about them. She tried to hide her fear by turning harsh.

"Shut up, okay. At least I got something useful out of it."

"Like what?"

"I haven't told you this but I have fifty-grand in my possession. I'm waiting to cash it in slowly."

Michael whipped his head around, like he just heard the world was ending.

"*Excuse me*? What? You have fifty-grand with you and you didn't tell me? Where'd you get it from?"

"Who else? I got a hold of *his* credit card and withdrew fifty-grand."

"Where's the money now?" Michael was expecting the worse; perhaps Greta had spent it all.

"It's with me. In our closet. In a duffle bag."

Michael gave her a quizzical look and went into their bedroom. He emerged, carrying a blue bag with a white logo. "Is this it?" he asked.

"Yes," she said flatly.

"Wow." He tsked. "And what were you planning to do with this? Wait to cash it out or just keep it for yourself?"

"Well, I was planning to cash it in, but now I can't cash it all at once. Those detectives will be suspicious. I'm waiting for the right time."

"I say the right time is right now," Michael said, as he ushered her out the door. "Go to the bank. Cash all the money in, or else."

"Is that a threat?"

"It is. Go, before I do something I'll regret." Greta was frightened by his tone so she went out the door.

She grudgingly cashed the money in to her account. On her way back to home, thoughts flooded through her mind. She didn't know why Michael was so insistent on cashing in the money all at once. *Oh right.* Maybe he intended to use the money to keep paying Jessica. He'd ask Greta to give him money any time he needed it. If this kept going on, they'd get bankrupt eventually, get caught, and put into the slammer for good. She didn't want that. So how was she going to fix this problem? After a few moments, she had nothing. Minutes later, as if a light bulb went on in her head, she got it!

What if she could put the blame on Michael for everything? For the calls, the disappearance of the couple, everything. After all, Michael making her cash the money was only the start. She knew that things would not be getting better from here. Also, now that the police knew about his affair with Jessica, they could find out more. So, after all, it wasn't a bad thing that it had been revealed. So why not make Michael a suspect again?

Fifteen minutes later, Greta came back with the empty duffle bag. $50,000 had been added to her account.

In order for Michael's guilt to be believable for police, she first had to do something about Jessica Douglass, that money-hungry leech. Her involvement in Michael's life had to end, for the time being. Just until the police stopped questioning Greta for good. In other words, if something happened to Jessica, Michael would immediately be blamed for it.

This thought permeated through her mind as she put the duffle bag away.

CHAPTER 20

That night, Dominic Rivers, Chief Tonew and Bert Tomlin were sitting in a booth at IHOP, eating a late-night dinner, consisting of pancakes and eggs. The mood was quiet and somber. It was just them and a young woman, a college student, sitting in the adjacent booth with her laptop in front of her. She seemed to be in her own world.

Bert sat across from Dominic and Chief Tonew. He had just revealed what he found out from his friend Larry, about Michael's true identity as well as the fact that he was having an affair with Jessica.

"I found out that Michael Owen is in fact not his real name. And Greta Owen is not her real name either," Bert started. "You were right, Dominic. Michael Owen's real name is Walter Schuman—one of the names on your list, and Greta's real name is Eliza Schuman. They're from Switzerland, and came here nine years ago. They both are most likely con artists. That's what Larry thinks. That's what I think too."

Dominic looked at him in shock. This was getting more bizarre.

"In addition, I looked into Alvero Trent's bank account after I came back from the Owens' house. He had $50,000 withdrawn from his account a few days before he died. I then checked with Greta's bank account—she has her money in Wells Fargo. Apparently, she has only one account. And that one account magically got $50,000 richer, as of tonight.

"Now that we know this information, we can target Greta.

Get her supposed affair with Alvero out of the bag. The money transfer proves that she might have had access to his account and stole the money somehow."

Dominic perked up. "And this shows that Michael may have done something to the couple, due to the fact that Alvero may have found out about Greta's true identity. What we need to do is find a way to trap them."

CHAPTER 21

It was 11:00 am the next morning. Dominic was at inside his office, sitting at his desk.

The top of the desk looked like a mess, with papers scattered all over the place—papers that were case files from previous cases. Given that he had no time to sit still, he never bothered to be tidy about his workspace. He still had a Skittles wrapper from a week ago that he forgot to throw away, as well as gum wrappers on the ground, near his chair.

Right now, all Dominic could think about was how he going to get Greta to confess to having an affair (if she was having one in the first place) without directly confronting her about it? And what about the search parties that were helping find the couple? Was there an update on them?

He was about to ask Chief Tonew about his questions, when he got a call from his phone. It was from an unknown number. He picked it up.

"Hello?" he asked.

"I know something," said a woman's voice. Her voice was muffled, as if she was partially covering her mouth, speaking close to the phone. Was it Greta?

"Greta? Is this you?"

"I have something to tell you, Detective Rivers."

"Who are you? How did you get my number?" he asked, straightening up in his seat. He was going to have to change his phone number soon, with the amount of spam calls he was getting.

"Doesn't matter. I have something to tell you about Michael."

"Michael Owen?"

"Yes. Michael Owen. He knows more than you think."

"Knows more about what?"

"He knew that his wife was having an affair."

Dominic stood up. "Really? How do you know? What's your name?"

"I won't tell you. All I know is that he knows."

"Who is his wife having an affair with?"

"Alvero. That's all I can tell you." The woman on the other line hung up.

Dominic looked at his screen in confusion. He ushered for Bert Tomlin to come over, from the other side of the room.

"I got another weird call again, from a woman. Trace this call. I don't know who it was. It didn't sound like Greta or anyone we know."

Bert raised his brows. "What did she say?"

"She said that Michael Owen knew that Greta was having an affair with Alvero."

"And how does this help us?"

"This proves motive, like I said. Maybe Michael fell in love with Greta for real, and couldn't bear the thought of her with another man. He had to have her all to himself. Alvero must have figured them out, so Michael decided to get rid of him. All I have to do is confront Greta about having the affair."

"Wait, you're saying *this* proves motive for Alvero's death?"

"We don't know he's dead yet. But this proves that Michael

had a reason to dislike Alvero because of it, maybe even want to harm him. I still think the shadow-y figure Jessica saw was Michael."

"So, what we do now?" Bert asked.

"Let's think on it. By the way, have you heard from the search parties yet? Have they found anything?"

"Not yet. They're still looking. Everyone's extremely worried, though."

Dominic didn't seem too happy. "What about Alvero and Catalina's family? Parents or relatives? Do they know about their disappearance?"

"I tried to get in contact with Catalina's parents, but they aren't on speaking terms with their daughter. Something about how she married beneath herself. As for Alvero, his parents are no more. No relatives that live close by."

"How convenient," Dominic said, rolling his eyes. Then he remembered, when did Bert get all this information? And how? Bert didn't bother to consult him on how to go about finding out about all this. *I guess he doesn't need my advice, when he knows what he's doing,* Dominic thought.

"...but Catalina does have a sister who lives in Miami,"

"Get in contact with her then."

"I did. I reached out to her yesterday and she seemed to not really care. She's not very close with Catalina, she told me."

"And when were you going to tell me you talked with their family members?"

"I, uh—well the Chief asked me to get on it yesterday, after dinner, so I did. I figured since you were pursuing the lead on getting Greta to admit her affair, I thought I would get more insight on the Trent family."

Dominic brushed it off. He didn't really care at this point. He just wanted this case to be solved.

"Alright. That's good. You're just learning, so it's good that you are taking charge of this. Try talking to Catalina's sister again. What's her name by the way?"

"Ana."

"Ana what?"

"Ana Castillo. Catalina's family are from Spain, by the way."

"Hmm. Well, thank you for enlightening me on all this. Now, could you help me trace the call on my phone?"

After a few minutes, Bert found out that the call was made from a restaurant. When Dominic called back the number, it connected him to IHOP.

The same one that he, Bert, and Chief Tonew had been at the night before!

Was the caller following them? Who made this call? This was all getting more and more bizarre as time went on.

"The next step is for you get in touch with Ana Castillo," Dominic said, as he walked out of the station.

He was going to grab something to eat. He knew it was going to be a long day.

CHAPTER 22

Greta, in the meantime, stood outside Jessica's front door, looking around anxiously. She didn't want anyone to see her there. Her main purpose for meeting Jessica, was that she wanted to make her leave, so that she didn't find out about hers or Michael's true identity. Although, she couldn't help but wonder if Jessica already knew or not. Perhaps Michael told her, during one of their rendezvous? She also wondered if the police would find out soon enough. About her, Michael, and even Grant?

As for Grant, she hoped that she would be able to have him with her forever, but she knew that since the detectives were on her trail, her chances of getting away scot free would be slim. Grant wasn't even her real child. Greta and Michael adopted him under their fake names after Greta established herself as a successful trainer at the local gym, nine years ago. Who Grant really was or what his real name was, didn't matter now. What mattered was how to slow get rid of hindrances that could expose her. It was better to be safe than sorry, if she wanted her covers tracked.

She knocked two times. The door finally opened.

"Yes? Oh, hi Greta!" Jessica greeted with a smile.

"Yeah, hi. Can I come inside?" Greta asked in a rather rude manner.

Jessica pursed her brows. "Uh, sure..." She let Greta inside her house. "Want some tea, cookies—"

"Cut the bull, Jessica, I know what you and my husband have been doing behind my back. Well, I am not stupid any longer. I first ask that you stop your little "arrangement" with him. Secondly, whatever you told the police will only get them on our backs, especially mine, even more. So, I ask that you do something for me."

Jessica stared at Greta. She was not expecting a full-on confrontation.

"What should I do?" she asked.

After she was told everything, Jessica then nodded. "I see…" She then asked Greta, "Do you still want some cookies?"

CHAPTER 23

Bert Tomlin made another phone call to Ana Castillo. Ana, turned out, didn't want to get involved in the investigation so she refused to comment about any more than she knew. "I wasn't even there. I was and still am in Miami. I don't understand—"

"We aren't suspecting you or anything. We know you were nowhere near here when they disappeared. All I ask is that you tell me how Catalina was as a person."

"Catalina? She was a self-entitled prick. Now don't get me wrong, I don't wish harm upon her, but she could be a little self-absorbed."

"Like a workaholic?"

"Yes."

"Did she love her husband?"

"Alvero? No. I don't think she did. When she would come to family gatherings once a year, she and Alvero wouldn't even talk to each other in front of us."

"Did she directly tell you that she didn't love him?"

"Well, I think she loved him, for real, during the early years of their marriage. Then her work got the best of her, and she had no time for him. That's what she told us several months ago, when we had our family gathering."

"Was the gathering here or out of state?"

"Out of state. She came down to Miami with him."

"Would she be the type of person to leave her husband?"

"No, *pshhh*. Never. She wouldn't dare."

"She wasn't having an affair?"

"No! That's not her style. Alvero, on the other hand...he was a friendly, good-looking guy. He'd glance around at other women during the gathering and chat with them."

"Did Catalina know that her husband tended to stray a bit, at times?"

"No...I wouldn't know. I'm not her. How'd I know? Maybe he did have affairs, but that's not my business."

"Well in this case, an affair seems to be the motive of their disappearance."

"How do you mean?"

Bert said he couldn't explain more, as it was all speculative at this point.

Ana seemed upset to hear this. "Really? That's too bad. I was hoping to know more."

"I know. But once we figure out everything, we'll let you know. The real reason why I called you was to get some insight on Catalina."

"Well poor her! Ugh! Alvero is such an idiot to be cheating on my sister. I never really liked him in the first place..."

"I mean, I don't have proof that he did have an affair with Greta, but it's a high possibility. Greta and Alvero went to the same gym together and were at the dinner party the night before."

"Well if that's the case, let me know if that turns out to be true. Keep me updated." Her voice was now tearful.

"Will do. Thanks for talking to me, Ana."

Once he hung up, he thought for a minute.

Catalina's sister was mostly clueless about her sister's life. But based on what she said about Alvero chatting with other women, it could be that he's capable of cheating on his wife.

He waited for Dominic Rivers to return, to tell him about this conversation.

CHAPTER 24

Jessica Douglass was not seen entering her house, or even leaving it, the following day. Her car was gone too. Her not being seen around was not unusual. She was mostly indoors (she had a studio inside her house that she did all her art work in), with the exception of going out to dry her artwork.

But today, there was really no sign of her.

Michael tried calling and texting her in the afternoon but she wouldn't pick up her phone. He hadn't talked to her, since Bert showed up to his house revealing their arrangement to Greta. He realized that what he said to her about not paying her because she talked to the police, was in a fit of anger. He was apprehensive at this point. What had happened to her?

He walked over to the dining room, where he sat down at the table, across from Greta, with a tense look on his face. He proceeded to text Jessica again. Greta looked over at him, as she ate her lunch.

"Texting your girlfriend?"

"No..."

"Talking about her, haven't seen her around. I was just out and I didn't see her about. She's usually outside doing her art nonsense—"

"Why don't you shut up, okay?"

"Just saying..."

Michael looked down at his phone again. He was worried.

And Greta was not making things better.

It was now about 1 pm. Dominic Rivers had returned from getting food from a close by cafe. He had bumped into an old female friend and ended up chatting with her for longer than necessary.

Bert Tomlin was waiting right outside the building, leaned against the front door. His eyes expressed confusion, as he had been wondering where Dominic had been.

"Got something?" Dominic asked, ignoring his partner's look.

Bert nodded. "Yep. Talked with Catalina's sister, Ana. Confirmed from her that Alvero was the straying type." He explained their whole conversation to Dominic. "So, your caller was correct. Alvero could have been capable of having an affair. Especially with someone young and pretty like Greta. Thus, making Michael's motive to want to harm Alvero, stronger."

"I feel like I need something more substantial to confirm that he was having an affair. An anonymous call and testimony from a sister who lives out of state, is not very convincing. We got to get something to convince us that Michael is our man. Who knows something, and is hiding it all?"

The two men went inside. The Police Chief, seeing them at the entrance, motioned for Dominic to approach his desk.

"Just got a call reporting a missing person. Guess who it is?" he asked, tensely.

"Who?" Dominic asked.

"Jessica Douglass."

CHAPTER 25

Dominic and Bert got in their squad car on their way to Jessica's house.

The person who had made the missing persons call was Michael Owen. Both detectives were even more convinced that Michael had something to do with the Trents', and now Jessica's disappearance.

There were officers at Jessica's house already. They were searching the premises. After they got news that she had not been seen that whole morning, they decided to talk with the Owen couple to get more intel on what happened. They knocked on the front door of the Owen house.

"Police!" they yelled.

Michael opened the door as fast as he could. When he saw Dominic, the anger on his face increased, but when he saw Bert, it subsided.

"Come in," he said, forgetting that he had threatened Dominic in his last visit.

When they entered, they saw Greta inside sitting down in the high chair, with her head in her hands. Michael was seated next to her.

"I understand you made the call to us reporting Jessica missing?" Dominic asked, turning to Michael.

"I did. She's not picking up her phone and Greta said that she hadn't been out of her house. Her car is gone too."

"When did you realize that she may be missing.?"

"An hour ago."

"Well maybe she will turn up. It's only been a few hours. The day hasn't passed yet," Bert said.

"Maybe she won't." Greta burst. "What if the person who did something to the Trents did something to Jessica?"

Dominic nodded. "Perhaps that is a possibility. Maybe it's the case that she just left for a few days. But my strongest bet is that she's left because she might be involved somehow and is trying to escape. I'm pretty sure foul play isn't the case just yet."

Michael asked, "But it has to be related, right? Her trying to escape and something happening to her?"

"Well why don't you tell us what you know? You seem to be benefiting from everyone's disappearance lately, haven't you?" Dominic eyed Michael sharply.

"What do you mean?"

"I mean pretending to care by calling in that she's missing. Why don't you first tell what you really know? Starting with your reason for hating Alvero. We know about your true identity, Mr. Walter Schuman, so don't try to act smart here. You're fooling nobody. I know that you are a con artist from Switzerland, who takes on new names in order to get more money. You're also Donny Spelling and Chris Sheppard. I have more information as for the illegal stuff you did. Pretending to be a war veteran, obtaining a house, and annual income. It's the biggest scam I've seen in a while."

Michael and Greta's face widened in shock.

"How did you—how—why?" he stuttered.

"Never mind that. I also know that Alvero must have figured

out your scam, and you got rid of him. Am I right? Am I right?!" Dominic raised his voice loudly, that it made Bert jump.

"What about Jessica?"

"We'll get to her later. Why don't you tell me your real motive for causing the disappearance of Alvero?" he repeated.

Michael looked confused. "I don't know what you mean."

"Really? Why don't you tell us all that you knew about Greta's affair with Alvero? I'll tell you why. Because that's not what's bugging you. You were angry that Alvero figured out your true identities and was going to expose you. Am I right?"

Michael looked at the two detectives. All the color drained from his face. It was now white.

"Greta's affair?" he asked, deflecting from the rest of Dominic's words.

"Yes. Affair. Don't tell me you don't know about it." He was glad Michael had pointed out about the affair.

By the look on Bert's face, Dominic knew that the younger detective was smart enough to figure out where this line of questioning was going.

Michael stared at Greta who had a look of horror on her face. When Michael didn't respond, Bert asked, "What did you do to Alvero?"

"I didn't do anything!" Michael burst. "Sure, I knew about Greta's affair with that gym junkie. I saw her texts to him." He stared at his wife.

"This is all a lie. Someone set us up!" Greta yelled.

"No one set you up. It's not a lie. I got an anonymous phone call from someone saying that Michael knows about your affair with Alvero."

Greta didn't know what to say. "It's all lies! Just because you are cops doesn't give you the right to—"

"We are just doing our job. If this were any other case, we could care less who is having an affair with whom. But this correlates with our investigation. Now out with it. The truth. Or else we can have this conversation downtown."

She looked down. "Fine. I was having an affair, but we ended it. The night of the dinner party. That's what Alvero and I were talking about then."

Bert then asked, "So those were the "words" that you exchanged with him then? Wanting to end it with him?"

"Yes."

"And how long did this affair with Alvero last?"

"8 months." At this, Michael glared at Greta.

"I see. Now, let's talk about Jessica. Dominic?" Bert motioned at his partner to begin his questioning.

Dominic cleared his throat and began: "So now Jessica has mysteriously disappeared. Did she know about anything she was not supposed to? Did you, Michael, tell her anything about knowing about Greta's affair?

"I didn't tell her anything. Even if I did know about anything why would I tell her. Maybe she saw the two of them together, who knows."

"You don't seem to care that your wife was having an affair?" Bert asked. Michael's calm reaction didn't fare well with him.

"Well, I am not exactly perfect either. Look what I was doing with Jessica? Anyways—"

"I find it strange that Jessica wouldn't know anything about your married life, Michael. It's strange after all those meetings with her, you don't tell anything your life? You better be speaking the truth. Did you tell her anything or not?" Dominic's patience was being tested now and he didn't like that.

Michael looked down. "Fine. I told her that I had my doubts that my wife was having an affair. She'd be at the gym longer than usual, and would be grinning at her phone at night. I told this to Jessica, a week before Alvero and Catalina disappeared."

"And?"

"Jessica told me she would do some investigating for me. She said she would go to the gym to see if she could spot the two of them or not."

"Really? And what did she do?"

"She went to the gym. She told me that she saw the two of them walking hand in hand outside the gym's entrance. That they hugged and kissed each other too. Jessica took a few pictures of them, and sent them to me, which I deleted since."

Greta looked down in shame.

Bert cut in. "Okay... now that you knew for certain, she was having an affair, how'd that make you feel? Furious?"

"Yeah. I was mad about it. But then, I decided not to confront Greta about it. I had Jessica, so I didn't really care. Greta's not really my wife, after all."

"So..." Bert pointed at Greta. "Did you love her at any point?"

"What love? I'm old enough, as it is. I was in love with her at the very beginning, I'll admit. But you know all pretty women are frauds. As for her affair, I don't really care, to be honest...."

Greta was incensed by his words. *How dare he insult her like that in front of the detectives?*

"How dare you—"

Dominic stopped her, by putting his hands in front of him.

Michael continued. "…As for Jessica…she doesn't know anything else; I swear."

"Okay, so when did you both last see Jessica?" Dominic asked, moving on. He then turned to Greta. "Could I have some water?"

This was a way of getting her to leave the room for a bit, so that he could resume his questioning with Michael, without interruptions.

Greta let out a *hmph* and marched away.

"I last saw her yesterday. She was walking to her car and then went back into the house," Michael said, turning his attention to Dominic.

"And when was this?"

"In the morning."

"Didn't see her after that?"

"Nope."

Greta returned with a glass of water and handed it to Dominic. He thanked her.

"When did you see her last, Mrs. Owen?" he asked sipping from the glass.

"I saw her, uh, yesterday morning."

"And what was she doing?" asked Bert.

"I just saw her from the window, she walked out to check the mail."

"What time did you see her?"

"9 am."

Dominic sighed. He still had reason to believe Michael was responsible for Jessica's disappearance, even if he didn't have definitive proof.

"So, you both really have no clue where she could have gone?" Bert squinted his eyes at them.

"Nope, we don't know," both of them said at the same time.

"Fine. I see how it is. Mr. Owen, we still suspect you of foul play, so I wouldn't advise you to leave our sights any time soon," Dominic warned, lowering his voice.

Michael was incredulous. "Foul play? I had nothing to do with Jessica's being missing. I don't know where she is!"

"Don't know what to tell you, but until she's found, then you are a suspect. In her case, and in the Trent couple's disappearance. So, don't plan on going on a vacation anytime soon."

Dominic took a last chug of the water glass. Thoughts ran through his mind. Before Jessica disappeared, he wondered if she was the one to call him the second time. She had all the reason to—she wanted to make Michael look guilty, as he knew about Greta's affair with Alvero, turning this into a scenario of an 'outraged husband who kills wife's lover'.

Seconds later, he and Bert got up, thanking the couple for their time, and headed over to Jessica's house.

As they walked over, they briefly stopped for a moment, talking about how they laid the trap for Michael, revealing that they knew about his true identity as well as Greta's affair with Alvero.

They reached Jessica's house. The officers there said they couldn't find anything substantial to indicate she was "missing". Her wallet and ID were gone. Her car was also gone. Maybe she had gone away for a few hours or days and would be back.

The only explanation for her sudden disappearance was the fact that her affair with Michael had been discovered.

A few hours later, Greta told Michael she had to go out to get some food from Safeway. She just had to get out of the house.

When she reached Safeway, she sat in the parking lot and called Jessica.

"Hey, where are you at?" Greta asked.

She nodded her head as she listened to Jessica on the other end. "I see. Stay there for now. The same detectives came to our house asking about you today. So, stay there until I tell you to."

She hung up the phone and went inside to buy some random food items that she was never planning on getting in the first place. She was now restless, thinking about someone else who was on everyone's minds now.

Alvero.

Now that her affair with him was brought to light, she realized she missed him. She didn't just miss his physical physique (his chiseled face, marked with sharp features), but she missed him as a person. He was great company and gave her a bigger incentive for working at the gym. She felt like she was on cloud nine when she was in his presence. She wondered if he felt the same about her. She knew he considered her beautiful, he'd admit this to her several times, but that was about it. She always wondered if whatever it was between them, was solely physical or something more. She sadly knew she would never get these answers ever again.

Presently, though, she had two bigger things to worry about — one being the fact that the detectives knew about her and Michael's true identities. And the second one being Michael's guilt. The detectives were on to Michael now, but they hadn't arrested him yet. What if they got onto *her*, next? It wouldn't be long before they nailed *her* for the murders of the Trent couple. She had to do something to incriminate Michael for real. Something that would make him officially guilty. Her eyes widened.

Unknown to everyone, she had something in her possession that would make sure her "husband" went in the slammer for good. Something she hadn't known would prove useful...until now.

CHAPTER 26

A few hours later, after Bert Tomlin had returned back to the station, Dominic Rivers decided to go back to the Owens' house to loiter around. He wanted to see if there was any concrete proof he might have missed to show that Michael was responsible for Jessica's and the Trents' disappearance. As he walked around their front yard and along the sides of the house, he didn't see anything. Just plants, flowers, and mud. Then he reached their driveway. He saw that one of their cars was not there. However, Michael's car was still there.

Dominic knew it was his car because he had done a background check on everyone involved so far. He knew that Greta owned a Nissan and Michael owned a Hyundai. The Hyundai was still parked on the driveway. The Nissan was gone. He peered through the windows of the Hyundai. There was nothing too suspicious. There was a milkshake cup in the cupholder next the driver's seat. Some clothes were tossed in the back seats. Dominic shifted his gaze to the front of the car. Something caught his eyes.

There was a wallet on the passenger seat.

Whose was it? Greta's or his? He assumed since Greta's Nissan was not in the driveway, the family must have taken that car to go out. With Greta presumably driving, she must have her license with her. As for Michael, he probably took his own wallet with him. Then it hit him.

A wallet!

Catalina and Alvero's wallets were the only things left behind in their house. Dominic checked his notes from his notepad. According to them, he had written down the description of both wallets. Catalina's was purple and Alvero's was black. The wallet in the passenger seat was indeed black. Maybe Michael had a black wallet too. He couldn't be too sure. He knew he couldn't bust open someone's car door without a warrant. He took a picture of the passenger seat with his phone. Then he thought: *Why would Michael be having Alvero's wallet?*

He decided he had to call in Bert. He waited for the dial tone. Dominic's partner finally picked up.

"Bert, I have a situation here. Alvero Trent's wallet could be inside Michael Owen's car. I need to have it checked out. I need someone to come over here and see if we can get this door to open. And to take proper pictures. Before the Owens arrive, I need this to be checked out. And bring the pictures of Alvero's wallet that were taken from his house."

"Are you snooping around their house?" Bert asked incredulously.

"I am. Now will you come over here or what?"

A few minutes later, Bert Tomlin and a team of police arrived to Michael Owen's driveway.

"Bert, do you have the pictures of Alvero's wallet found inside his house? We need them to compare to *this* wallet," Dominic asked once he saw his partner walk over to him.

Bert pulled them out from a file folder. Upon seeing them, Bert realized that Alvero's wallet and the wallet found in Michael's car looked to be the exact same1 Both were black and had the same intricate border pattern on the front.

"Do you think that this is, in fact, Alvero's wallet, which

Michael had all along, and was trying to get rid of?"

Dominic scoffed. "Well, that would make him look stupid, because why would he leave Alvero's wallet out in the open for everyone to see? And how did he get Alvero's wallet from our possession in the first place? Perhaps this was someone trying to pin this on Michael?"

"Wait, I thought you considered Michael a suspect."

"I did, but I'm now confused by Alvero's wallet showing up in Michael's car. It feels like a set up to me. Maybe someone planted this here. Unless…this wallet really belongs to Michael.

CHAPTER 27

A few minutes later, Greta's Nissan pulled into the driveway, just to see police officers all over the perimeter of her house.

Greta got out of the car and yelled, "What's going on?" as she looked around frantically. Michael followed his wife out; Grant held on to his father's hands, scared. Greta hurried her son to go inside the house. When he did, she then turned her attention to the two detectives.

"Mr. Owen, can we see your wallet?" asked Dominic, approaching them.

"My wallet? Why?"

"Do you have it with you?"

"I do."

"Can we see it?" Bert asked. Michael reached into his pant pocket, and showed his wallet to him. It was *brown* in color. Bert examined it for a bit, then gave a Michael a look.

"Can you come over to the right side of your car for a minute?" Dominic asked. Then seeing Greta start to follow, he added, "Michael only." Michael obliged, following Dominic.

"Look at the passenger seat, will you?" Dominic instructed. "Could you tell me what that is?"

"That's a wallet. But whose is it?"

"I don't know, why don't you tell me?"

"I don't know."

"Can you open the passenger door for us?"

"I have to get my car keys from inside the house."

"Okay. We are waiting. "

Michael went inside and came back a few moments later. He unlocked the car.

"*Don't. Touch*," Dominic cautioned, as he saw Michael about to reach for the wallet.

"Whose is that? What's going on?" Michael asked.

Bert took the wallet with his gloved hands and opened the wallet. *Alvero's license was there, tucked under the clear plastic pocket.*

Michael was shocked. "What? How did that get there? I don't know—Greta! What is this?"

His wife looked just as bewildered. "What is that doing in his car?" she asked.

"I don't know, maybe it's time that Michael be taken downtown and explain himself more." Dominic dragged Michael by the arm.

Greta then screamed. "No! He didn't do anything!"

"Greta, go inside the house or else you will be arrested too," Bert said sternly.

Michael was handcuffed and put into the police car. In the car, Dominic asked him how he got Alvero's wallet. "Did you kill him and then steal it from their house? We had it in our possession the first day we looked at the Trent house. How did you get a hold of it?

Michael cried. "I didn't do anything! I swear! I don't know how Alvero's wallet got in my car!"

"Tell that to a lawyer. In the meanwhile, you better tell us the truth."

Greta went inside the house, crying. Grant was asking a lot of questions about where his dad was. She comforted him and told him he was going to the police station to answer some questions. He walked to his room, head down, clearly upset.

Once Greta found herself out of sight of Grant, she straightened up, wiped her tears, and called Jessica.

"They've arrested Michael! They think he had something to do with Alvero's disappearance. It's time you came back."

CHAPTER 28

Jessica was on her way back from where Greta had instructed her to stay for a few days in exchange for a thousand dollars. Greta had seemed upset on the phone to her about her husband's arrest. Jessica couldn't help but wonder why after she was paid to disappear, Michael was now arrested. Perhaps Greta wanted to pin the disappearance on Michael? Or perhaps the police had some other evidence against Michael?

As confused as Jessica was, as long as she got her money, she was happy. She didn't bother to ask any questions. Jessica knew that Greta was doing all she could to clear her own name. But what she didn't want Greta to know is that *she* was the one who had made that second phone call to Detective Rivers revealing Michael's knowledge of Greta's affair.

And what Dominic and Bert were unaware of was that she was connected with this case more than they knew.

◊ ◊ ◊ ◊ ◊ ◊ ◊ ◊ ◊ ◊ ◊ ◊ ◊ ◊ ◊ ◊ ◊ ◊

Inside one of the interrogation rooms of the Homicide/Missing Persons unit were Dominic, Bert, and Michael Owen.

They sat at a small table, with Michael facing the two men. He sat handcuffed, in a wooden chair.

The two detectives started interrogating Michael about the wallet found in his car. Dominic told Michael that there were no recognizable finger prints found on the wallet, other than

Alvero's, but he couldn't help but be suspicious that Michael was responsible for placing it inside his car.

That was, until he said something that made Dominic change his mind.

"There's no reason for me to keep Alvero's wallet, and in my car, that too. Or even know the difference between his wallet color and mine. That's because I'm color-blind. Been so since my early twenties. The only colors that I can properly see are any shade of blue, like your coats for instance, and yellow. All the other colors, like black and brown, look greyish to me."

Dominic and Bert looked at each other, their mouths hung open.

They never bothered to check up on this fact, when looking at Michael's file! This meant that Michael couldn't have put or had Alvero's wallet in his own car, because both wallets would look the same color to him! Whomever put the wallet there knew the difference between the two colors. So, whoever put the wallet in his car wanted to frame Michael for Alvero's disappearance by having his wallet.

Given this fact, this individual had to be someone who wasn't color blind.

As for Catalina and Alvero's wallets themselves, they had been in police possession all this time, with no report of a break-in or evidence tampering, so this same person could have somehow taken Alvero's wallet to place in Michael's car. How could someone steal an item under police custody without getting caught? Unless they stole it on the first day when police arrived at the Trents' house...

"Is your wife color-blind too?" Dominic asked.

"No, she's not. It's not a common thing, you know. I do know the difference between black and brown in my head, but my brain tells my eyes something different and I can't tell."

"Can we do a quick test just to see if what you're saying is correct?"

"Are you challenging me?"

"No, I just want to confirm the facts. Don't think that by passing the test, you are in the clear. We will need a search warrant for your house—"

Just then, the door opened. Chief Tonew walked in.

"Guys, sorry to interrupt but I have news for you. Jessica Douglass has returned back to her house."

"Bert, go over there right now. I will handle Michael."

Chief Tonew motioned Bert to leave while he watched what Dominic was doing. Dominic grabbed his own wallet (which was black) and placed it on the table, to the left. Then he placed Alvero's wallet—which an officer at the Owen house had given back after dusting it for prints—to the right of his own wallet.

"Tell me now. What color is the wallet on the left?" Dominic asked Michael. Michael squinted. "Black?" he asked.

Correct.

Then he asked about Alvero's wallet. "What color is this wallet?"

Michael squinted again. "I don't know, black?"

Dominic raised his brows and gave Chief Tonew a look.

Michael really was color blind.

Or maybe he was lying.

"I would like you to get a doctor's note confirming you are color blind. This simple test doesn't really hold up in court. Will you do that?" Dominic asked.

"I surely will," he scoffed. "Anything to prove my innocence. I thought I wouldn't have to see your smug face again, but here we go again. I guess I'll be seeing you even in my dreams."

Dominic rolled his eyes. People hated him; he knew it. But he wasn't here to make friends. He was here to solve a case and do his job.

"Can you call your doctor right now and ask for your color blindness results. Please?" he asked politely.

Michael groaned. He called his hospital. When they picked up, a nurse was on the line, as his doctor was busy. Michael explained the situation. The nurse told him his results would be sent by mail.

Michael was relived. "There. See? You will get the results in a few days."

"I kind of need those results sooner. I can get them picked up later today. In the meantime, let's go back to your house. I have to talk with Jessica."

"That's good she's finally back. I bet she ran away or something. After trying to blame things on me."

"No one's blaming anyone. Stay here until further notice."

When Dominic reached Jessica's house, he saw Bert and her talking seriously outside her front door. Bert was leaned against the ceiling post, while Jessica had her arms crossed. She seemed unfazed as if nothing had happened. She was unusually dressed up today, clad in a gold t-shirt and leather pants. Maybe it was the sunny weather that seemed to uplift her spirits. She didn't seem to care that people believed her missing. She appeared elusive and shady.

After walking up to the two of them, Dominic said to Jessica, "You're back, finally," She nodded. "Where were you all these days?"

Bert interjected hastily. "About that...Jessica has something to tell us."

Dominic fixed his gaze on her. "Really? What do you have to tell me?"

Jessica paused. Then she spoke: "You must be wondering what happened to me, right?"

Right, he thought impatiently.

"Well, I heard that Michael got arrested. I was just telling your partner that I don't think Michael did anything."

"What makes you so sure of that? And where were you all this time?"

Bert was about to cut in to reveal what Jessica told him, when she said, "I was staying at a motel, alone. I was sent to "disappear" for a few days."

"Sent? By whom?" Dominic asked, surprised by this revelation.

Jessica didn't answer his question. "I was paid to disappear then I got called to return."

"Wait, you got paid to disappear and now came back? Why?"

"Once the news broke that Michael got arrested, I got called to return," she repeated, as if he should have understood the first time. "But I don't think he is responsible for this whole thing. His wife, on the other hand..."

"His wife? What about Greta?"

"Uh..." She looked at Bert who urged her to repeat what she told him earlier.

Dominic asked, "Did Greta ask you do to something?"

"She is the one who asked me to disappear."

His eyes shot wide open. "What?"

"Yeah. She's the one who paid me to leave for a few days. Then she told me Michael got arrested. Is he going to be in jail forever?"

"We don't know. He's still in custody though."

If Greta paid her to leave, then…

"Do you think Greta is responsible for the Trents' disappearance?"

Jessica shrugged. "I just got her money, so I don't really care. I think she could have done it."

An idea popped into Dominic's head. *If Jessica was sent to get out of the way, the only remaining suspects they had were Michael and Greta.* With the detectives suspecting Michael already, was sending Jessica to disappear a way to confirm their suspicion of him? By making it seem like he was responsible for Jessica's disappearance?

"Do you think the Trent couple are simply missing or do you think something happened to them?" he then asked.

"I really don't know. At this point, they're probably dead. Or doing a really good job of hiding in an isolated cabin in the woods. But why would they do that?"

"Unfortunately, you're probably right. It seems that Greta may know something. She seems to be hiding a lot of secrets, doesn't she?"

Jessica nodded her head. "For sure."

With that, the two men walked away.

Dominic couldn't help but suspect Jessica. She might have been truthful in her words right now, but he never knew if there was something more she was hiding. The fact that Jessica seemed more than eager to say Michael was not guilty and say that Greta might have secrets to hide, made him to think that Jessica could be hiding *her* own guilt. Guilty people always did this. They put the blame on someone else, trying to distract the police from the truth of their own faults.

Now he had to get Greta to confess what she knew. He was now certain she might have put Alvero's wallet in Michael's car. And might be one of the people responsible for the Trents' disappearance.

CHAPTER 29

Later that day, Dominic went to Michael's hospital, specifically the optometric department, to get the color blindness test results from the doctor. Although he had perfect vision and didn't wear glasses yet, as he walked inside the corridors that led him to the optometric department, he couldn't help but think that the hospital was such a dreary place for anyone to be at. It reminded him of his experiences of being there as a patient, from the many times he injured himself playing sports.

He opened a door to a waiting room. As he made his way to the front desk, he noticed there were many people sitting, some young and some older, either on their phones or reading a magazine.

He cleared his throat and introduced himself to the nurse sitting at the front. He explained what he was looking for, and how he needed the results as soon as possible. The nurse sitting there was young and had a well-rounded face to reflect it. At the same time, by her candor and listening skills, it was evident she possessed a lot of knowledge. He found out her name was Marcie.

Not soon afterwards, Marie handed him the results (a large manila file folder filled with papers). Dominic looked through the folder of papers. He then asked Marcie to explain the results to him.

"Numbers and everything aside, it says that Michael *is* color blind. See, he took the Waggoner PIPHRR color vision test a month ago. It's a test we use to see if our patients are color blind or not," she explained. "It's approved and used by the

Navy even. To pass, he must get 26 out of the 29 questions correct. But he missed a lot of them—as you can see here. His score was a 16 out of 29. However, he was correctly able to identify yellow and blue, when it was displayed within its plates$_2$."

"*Its plates?*"

"Basically, this test was given on a computer. He had to identify the color of a bubble-shaped number that is within a plate made out of dots of the same color. The color of the number is a different color than the color of the dots. He did do a multitude of vision tests too…" She showed him some examples from his results.

"Okay, I see. So, he is colorblind," Dominic confirmed.

"For the most part, yes."

"Thank you very much."

"I had administered the test for him myself, which is why I know his results personally." She smiled at him.

"Thanks a lot. Can you make a copy of this report and give it to me?" he asked.

She said she'd do so and left in a jiffy. After a few minutes she brought the copied results to him.

"I appreciate it," he said, as he shot her a little wink and walked out of the hospital.

CHAPTER 30

The next day, Dominic and Bert decided that they would talk to Greta, as she was their number one suspect. After all, she was the only one who could have put Alvero's wallet in Michael's car. Who else would have had access to Michael's car if not her? Jessica had just arrived back home around the same time they were investigating Michael's car and Alvero's wallet.

Dominic decided to follow Greta around town to see what she was up to. And hopefully arrest her.

⌂⌂⌂⌂⌂⌂⌂⌂⌂⌂⌂⌂⌂⌂⌂⌂⌂⌂⌂

Greta was currently shopping for some medications and some magazines for herself at CVS.

Anything to get out of the house, she thought. She wanted to escape all the pandemonium surrounding the police and this case. If anything, she wanted them all to go away.

She paid for her items quickly and exited the store.

Unknown to her, Dominic and Bert were parked outside in a regular "undercover" car, and saw Greta walk out with a bag in her hands. She seemed cool and collected. She dumped the bag in the back seat.

Just as they saw her about to start the car, Dominic said he was going to do something. He then moved his car and stopped just behind hers. Bert looked at him in confusion. What was he going to do?

Greta started to back out. Not seeing his car, she rammed her rear into his front bumper.

"Christ! What the actual f—" she cursed. She hit the brakes and got out of her car. She marched over to Dominic's car angrily. She rapped on his driver's side window.

When he rolled it down, her face turned to sheer shock when she saw who was the driver.

"You?!" she blasted. "Are you trying to kill me? What are you doing, coming right behind me when I'm trying to back out?!"

Dominic gave her a satisfied nod, as if he were proud for what he did.

"You ruined my rear end!" she continued, motioning to the back of her car, which was banged up badly.

"Why don't we take a look at it then?" he asked calmly. He was still sitting inside his car, along with Bert, which infuriated her even more.

"No, I will call my insurance agent and make sure *you* pay for this!"

"It doesn't look *that* bad," he said, nonchalantly.

"How do you know? Are you a mechanic? It looks pretty bad to me. I'm calling someone to fix this."

"You do that…Wait, is that—I see smoke coming out from the back."

Greta whipped her head around and saw that small traces of smoke appeared from the back pipes. She was now at the peak of her melting point. She groaned loudly as she got out her phone and called a mechanic.

When he saw that Greta was far from their earshot, Bert asked, "Why'd you do that? You ruined this car."

Dominic didn't seem to care. "It's not my car. It's the BPD's. Even if there is some damage, consider it part of the cost of this whole investigation. All I want to do is make sure she doesn't run away. Maybe what I did will get her to confess."

A few minutes later, Greta came over to the driver's window. "I called him. He will be here in a bit," she said. She then pointed to Dominic in a menacing way. "In the meantime, *you* will be paying him after he fixes my car, so get your money ready."

"Sure sure, no problem. I'll do that. I was wondering, now that we are reunited again for what seems to be the umpteenth time this week, why don't you tell me if there is something about this case, I should know." He showed a poker face, which she saw through.

"Uh, no. I don't think so."

"Alright, fine. I won't pay for the damage then."

"You wouldn't dare. You can't do that. I will get a lawyer, file a lawsuit...you know. I'm not scared of you."

"Oh yeah? Why don't you tell us the truth then? Before you 'file anything against us.'" Dominic couldn't help but be sarcastic.

"You suspect me, don't you? That's what this is about right?" Her eyes widened, as she smacked her hands to her forehead. "You followed me here. Oh my god!"

"I think you did something to the Trent couple and I think you're trying to frame your husband." Dominic's words came out as smooth as butter.

She glared at him. She crossed her arms and looked away.

At this point, the mechanic arrived. He fixed the back of her car as well as the slight damage on the squad car Dominic was driving. Dominic ended up paying for it all. He looked at Greta with a type of look that screamed "I'm not letting you off the hook, even though I paid for the damages."

He was playing the bad cop, he knew. But he wanted her to confess.

After the mechanic left, Greta sat in her car about to start her engine when she saw someone tap on her window.

She rolled it down. "What do you want, *Detective Rivers?*" she asked with a sigh.

"Just the truth."

"You won't get it from me."

"How'd you get Alvero's wallet and put it in your husband's car? That was very sly of you to do."

She looked down. "I didn't."

She was lying, Dominic knew.

"I know you can be a good person; you were after all adept in your job at the gym. If only you'd tell me what you know, we will all be happy at the end."

Dominic wanted her to be affected by his words. He half-heartedly meant what he said. He knew she was really a conniving person who was capable of using more people, in order to clear her own name.

Greta sighed in defeat. Then she started to cry. She put her head down on the steering wheel

"I'm done. I'm done. I'm finished. I can't do this anymore!".

"No, you're not. Please, tell me." Dominic's voice was soft. A few seconds passed; the silence was unnerving.

Then as if some force overtook her, she rammed her feet on the accelerator and drove away from Dominic, almost running him over.

"We have to follow her!" he shouted. He ran to the driver's seat and trailed after her. She was speeding like the dickens! He flashed his overhead lights and sounded the siren.

The two cars were now engaged in a high-speed chase. They dodged different cars in an attempt to get Greta to stop. Bert got out a loud speaker and announced, "Stop the car now!"

Greta didn't listen. She kept driving. She then made a sharp right, into an exit. The road following led to a motel. She stopped her car at the entrance. Dominic stopped right behind her.

He and Bert got out of their squad car and pointed their guns at her car.

Greta rushed out of her car, and started to run the opposite direction. She looked like she was trying to figure out where to go.

"Greta, stop or else I will shoot!" Dominic demanded.

She wouldn't relent. She kept running. Dominic let out a warning shot that hit her car window. Hearing the gunshot, Greta screamed and quickly turned around, shielding herself with her arms.

"You better 'fess up. It's better to do so here than downtown in a dingey room." Dominic taunted as he approached her.

She gave them both a hard, menacing look. Then she scoffed. "Get away from me! Is that all you got, Detectives? I bet I could do a better job in catching criminals."

"So, you're admitting you're one? A criminal?" Bert asked.

"I'm not admitting anything."

"Well, you're going to have to." Dominic still had his gun pointed at her.

"What are you going to do, shoot me? Well, I don't care."

He ignored her. He wasn't going to shoot. He wanted her to speak. "Did you have something to do with Alvero and Catalina's disappearance? Or worse, did you kill them? Are they dead?"

Dominic motioned for Bert to start recording whatever she was about to say next. Anything was better than nothing.

"Dead? Well, if you consider the life Alvero lived, yeah, I'd consider him dead. He should have been with me."

Bert walked closer to her. "So, you didn't want to end things with Alvero?"

She shook her head.

"So, is he really dead or…?"

"Why should I tell you?" she sneered.

Dominic lowered his hands. "You should because it's the right thing to do."

"I don't care."

"Well, you should. If Alvero were beside us right now, he'd want you to do so. He'd even take you back."

This reverse psychology type of tactic was an excellent way of playing into the emotions of a guilty person. Dominic had dealt with people like Greta before, where he had to resort to using this tactic to get under the skin and get a confession from them.

Greta let out a gasp. This hit a nerve. Her guilt pricked her as she thought about how much she loved Alvero.

"I don't want to incriminate myself though," she said.

"You know all this will be over, I promise," Bert said. "All signs point to your guilt anyways, so spilling the truth is the only way to go. I know who you are. Detective Rivers knows who you are. You're Eliza Schuman, a Swiss national, who's also a fraud.

"You came here to Massachusetts under the pretence of working at a gym and even having a son, who I doubt is really your son. I also know about the money that you stole from Alvero—$50,000 that magically turns up in your account, after that same amount is missing from Alvero. He probably knew who you were and you got rid of him before he exposed you."

The look in Greta's face was that of shock, horror and disbelief. It was as if she'd seen a ghost.

"It can't be! How did you find out?" she exclaimed.

"We have our ways. Just like you have yours. You and Michael are both very sharp and know how to get things done your way."

Greta looked irritated. The wrinkles under her eyes were more prominent than ever.

Bert continued, "Now I can tell you straight, you will never be able to see the light of day. Or go back home. You will remain here until you confess what you know. Running off and engaging us in a useless chase is not helpful for you or me."

After speaking, he waited for a few seconds. Greta was now crying. She sniffled as she rubbed her nose.

"What about my son, though? I will never see him again!"

"Given he's not your real son, neither was he adopted legally by you both, it will be hard. But we'll see what we can do to have him visit you in custody."

This was a lie, but he wanted to get her hopes up so he could get the confession out of her.

Greta put her head down and plopped on the ground in defeat.

"Greta? It's alright. Know that you will have a clean conscience by telling the truth. And your son will be just fine." Bert's voice was soothing. Greta quieted down.

Once Dominic saw that she had cooled down for a moment, he interjected: "Did you have anything to do with Alvero and Catalina's disappearance? And did you pay off Jessica so that we'd focus our attention on Michael? Blame him for everything?"

He waited for a few moments, until she finally looked up at both of them. It was too late now for her to do anything. She was caught, and not only she knew it, Detective Rivers and Detective Tomlin knew it too.

In a monotone voice, she said, "*I did it.*"

CHAPTER 31

Dominic wanted to make sure he heard right.

Often times with confessions, people just say something under pressure, or in the spur of the moment. But here, Greta Owen or Eliza Schuman, or whoever she really was, had confessed to a brutal crime as if she cared less.

"You killed them?" he asked again.

"I did. I killed them both."

"Why is that?"

"I did it because Alvero wanted to break up with me and wanted to tell his wife about us, that same night—"

"The night of the party."

"Yes. I lied. *I* didn't break things off with him, *he* did. He told me he wanted our relationship to end and that he'd tell Catalina about it, regardless. But I didn't want him to tell Catalina. He also was going to tell police about my true identity. I couldn't have it.

"So, I snuck up to their house later that night and confronted Alvero at the entrance of his house. Catalina was not there when we conversed. That time, she was upstairs. A few seconds later, I'm guessing she heard us arguing..." Greta let out a cry, as she struggled to finish.

"Then what?"

She sniffled. She then revealed everything, from their fight, to seeing Catalina, to stabbing them in the chest.

"Where did you put the bodies?"

"I buried them. In my backyard."

"How did you get the bodies to your house?"

"I dragged them. They live next door, so it was easy to dispose of them."

"*You* carried both their bodies *on your own*?" Bert asked.

"Yes."

Dominic placed his hands in between his brows, creasing the lines. He had a hard time believing this.

"Really? Both Alvero and Catalina? Alvero works out, doesn't he? He's a big guy, tall too. I find it hard to believe that you carried him, disposed of his body, and got rid of all evidence, all on your own."

"Unless you had help…," Bert interjected.

Greta's eyes shot wide open. "I did it on my own." She seemed insistent. Was she scared that this other person would be out to get her if she revealed their name?

"We don't challenge your strength—we know you work at a gym and you seem very fit, physically. But I find it unlikely you dragged two bodies on your own in the dead of night," Dominic pointed out.

"Who is your accomplice?" Bert asked.

She didn't answer. It was futile for her to keep insisting she did all on her own, when she could just rat out her helper. Nothing mattered anymore, she was done for anyways.

"Fine. I had help," she said, in a confident voice. "Jessica Douglass helped me."

Dominic and Bert looked at her with shock.

"She did?" Dominic asked.

"Yes. She told me she saw a shadow-y figure from her window enter the Trents' house and waited for a while, until she decided to come over to investigate."

Jessica had never mentioned this to the detectives. This was the first time they were hearing anything about Jessica and Greta interacting with each other the night of.

"Then what happened?" Bert asked. "You never told us about any of this before."

She sighed. "I don't know if I should go on."

"No, please, continue."

"What did Jessica do then?" Dominic interjected, this time in a louder voice. "It's your word against hers, you know. That is if she was involved in their death."

"So, she will go to jail too, right?"

"Well, she hasn't done anything yet. How can she go to jail? Or am I wrong?"

Greta stiffened. She was not going to take the bait for something they both did. Jessica was going down too. "No, no wait. She's just as involved. And she knows that too."

"What did she do? Please tell us."

Greta clasped her hands together and looked down. "Jessica then saw me with two bodies. I told her to help me dispose of them. I had the bodies covered up; that's why she didn't know who they were at first. Only when she asked and I told her, did she become hysterical. She told me she would call the police. I grabbed her phone from her hands stopping her. I told her she would be doing this for Michael's sake. That she would still be able to see him, and not go to jail if she listened to what I said. I also said that if she called the police, I would make sure she would go down. That she would never see the light of day. After my threats, she said nothing. That's when I knew she must really care for my "husband" if she was willing to help me out. She helped me bury the bodies in my backyard."

Dominic cracked a half-smile. "You seem to know a lot of about covering up your tracks and making sure people dance to your tunes, huh?"

Greta didn't say anything to this. As humiliating as it was to be confessing to her own crime, she seemed more than contented that she had exposed Jessica as well.

She continued: "Then she went back to her house. I made sure that she was not talking to the police too much. That's why I sent her away. I thought I could focus your attention on my husband, and blame him for the disappearance of the Trents."

"That's why you used Michael's voice altering device to call me, in order to introduce his name into the picture, am I right?"

"Yes. I just didn't tell you both the truth, because I was just promoted as a Senior Pilates trainer at work. If this whole thing broke, then everything would be gone. My job, my life, everything."

"I'm afraid it's a little too late for that now," Dominic tsked. "I don't feel sorry for people like you who plot and connive to get their way. After doing all this, you have the audacity to pin the blame on your husband, who's innocent? I find that extremely shocking, but not surprised as I've come across many cases like you. I do have one last thing to address—did you take Catalina's wallet as well?"

"No, I didn't. Just Alvero's."

This meant that Catalina's wallet was still in police possession, he figured.

"How did you get Alvero's wallet in Michael's car?"

"I took it from his house, while the police were investigating, the first day. When no one was looking."

The expression on her face and the lack of fear in her eyes showed something—she had nothing more to say.

It was time to arrest her.

Bert put her in handcuffs, and held onto her, until backup was called.

Jessica was also questioned later that day, and she confessed to the cover-up, given the fact that Greta had dragged her name through the mud, earlier. She was arrested soon afterwards. She asked if she would be given a lighter sentence. Dominic told her that was between her and her lawyer and the court to settle.

He then called a forensic team to dig up the backyard of Greta and Michael's house. The two bodies were indeed right under the mud, next to the grass.

CHAPTER 32

A day later, the forensic team came up with an official autopsy report on the bodies. According to them, the two victims died by multiple stab wounds in the chest from a kitchen knife.

This confirmed what Greta had confessed.

The same knife was purchased under her name and was found hidden under Michael and Greta's bed. Dominic finally obtained a search warrant due to Greta's confession, and went through the Owen house in its entirety and found the knife.

The following day, Michael, Greta, and Jessica were arrested. Michael was found guilty of tax fraud, theft, and robbery—he was finally caught for that bank robbery he pulled off at Wells Fargo. Greta was arrested for two counts of first-degree homicide. And Jessica was arrested for conspiracy and cover up.

Reports of this caused a scandal and rocked the headlines in Newbury. But it was the news of Greta's arrest that garnered the most interest. Newbury's local newspaper wrote about it in a recent article:

SWISS NATIONAL—TURNED—LOVING WIFE SHOCKS COMMUNITY WITH DOUBLE HOMICIDE SCHEME

The arrest of Greta Owen has shocked the Newbury community. She was arrested yesterday afternoon for the deaths of Alvero and Catalina Trent, after she stabbed them in a brutal manner, according to the medical examiners.

Her arrest brought shock to those who knew her. She was well-respected as a trainer at the local gym. She was known as a devoted wife, married to retired war veteran, Michael Owen. They share a seven-year-old son together.

But there was more to Greta and her husband, than what people knew. It turns out that Michael Owen is not even a retired war veteran— there is no report of a Michael Owen having served in the 1980's. Records searched by the FBI have proven this fact. And Greta Owen is a self-proclaimed thief, who cons men and takes their money. According to sources, she allegedly stole $50,000 from one of the victims, Alvero Trent.

In a bigger twist, Greta and Michael Owen are not their real names. Their real names are, in fact, Eliza Schuman and Walter Schuman, and they are Swiss professional con artists. They came to the US nine years ago.

Prior to coming to the US, they first met on a train in Switzerland, and concocted a plan to make money. They found out they had the same last name and used this to their advantage to move to Boston and create their fake identities and make it seem like they were married.

Posing as local community members, the couple cheated their way into earning a few perks. A free house, veteran benefits, and a yearly check of $500, all while making fake bank accounts, and stealing money.

As for their "son", Grant Owen, the boy is currently in custody of the state. Whether he is their real son or not, the Child Protective Services are currently looking into the matter...

When news of the arrests broke on the TV inside the Boston Police Station, everyone was watching with interest. Dominic and Bert had their eyed glued to the screen, as they leaned their hands on their chins.

Bert turned to Dominic. "For what it's worth, thanks for the support during this case. We finally solved it. I know you may not like me much, but it means a lot to have a senior officer by my side during such a heavy-duty case like this."

Dominic was taken by his comment. He didn't know Bert appreciated working alongside him. "Why, thanks. I guess I have been too hard on everyone lately. It's part of my nature. Sorry about that. But I appreciate your words."

Chief Tonew stood aside, observing the two men proudly. He noticed how their partnership was starting to grow as the case went on.

"Good work you two. I think for the next case, you two should work together," he said.

Dominic and Bert looked at each other. Dominic then shook his partner's hand. "I think I could get used to that, *newbie*," he said, with a smile.

THE END

Story 2: He Saw It Coming

CHAPTER 1

Two months later, *January*

DAY 2 *of* ERIC BODEN'S DISAPPEARANCE

Dominic Rivers sat in the patio of his new house on a Monday morning, wearing his comfortable clothes—a grey t-shirt with sweatpants. It was 8 am. Due to his work from his last case, regarding the Trent couple, he earned a promotion, as well as a two-week break. In addition, he could now afford a house in the heart of Boston's suburbs. He'd had his eyes on the house for the longest time, but back then, it was previously out of his budget.

His new house was two stories and cast away from the other houses. It was beige in color, with a concrete roof top. Old vines slithered around the sides giving the place a rustic look. One advantage of having a house like this, was that he could now host gatherings and parties with a large crowd. It was such a stark difference to the cramped apartment he used to live in.

He lived alone then and planned to do so even now. He had no plans of settling down soon, as his work took over the majority of his time.

At the moment, he was admiring the view from outside—the blue skies, and the trees that swayed in the wind. The misty cool air swept in his face, making him feel like he was in another world. Little did he know that his vacation would come to an abrupt end, by a phone call.

Dominic went inside to get some juice from the fridge, when he heard his phone ringing. He always had his ringer on, just in case. He rushed to his bedroom and picked it up.

"Hello?" he asked, without properly looking at his home screen.

"Dominic?" asked the all so familiar voice of Bert Tomlin, his partner in Homicide/Missing Persons.

"Bert? What's up?"

"Hey! How's it going? Hope you're enjoying your new house."

"I am. Very much so. You calling just to check up on me, or is it something else?"

"You know me too well. Of course, I care about your well-being. Actually, there's a case that Chief Tonew is on my back about. It's a serious one. I thought I could use your help—"

"But I'm on vacation. I need my two weeks."

"I know. But it's urgent."

Dominic felt tense at Bert's pleading tone. If Bert Tomlin said something was urgent, it very well had to be the case. That man always spoke the truth.

"What's this case about?" he asked.

"It's a school-related case."

"What is it, unruly kids up to no good?" Dominic's voice was flat and monotone.

"No...a high school student has gone missing." The unwavering tone in Bert's voice made Dominic perk up.

He had been used to solving many cases, from murders to disappearances. But school-related disappearances hit a note.

He valued education to a high level and would one day give

his kids the same advice: to do your best, and value your education as if it were a god-send. Not that he was religious or anything, but the fact that a student goes missing, puts an enormous strain onto the entire school community. That sense of continuity is disrupted. The motivation to study and do well is overshadowed by a missing persons case. And this bothered him.

A few minutes later, Dominic was back at the Boston Police Station, specifically in Chief Tonew's office. He had changed into his coat and tie attire, looking dapper as ever.

"Hey, Dominic, thanks for stopping in," the Chief said casually, as he sat at his pristine and clutter-free desk. "Sorry to cut your two-week break short. You don't have to be here if you don't want to."

As if he even had a choice to be here, Dominic thought. *He could be relaxing in his new house. But no, that's not the life of an official of the law. He had to help out at any time given.*

"No worries. I couldn't stay still after Bert told me all about a student that's supposedly missing. I had to come here."

"Well, I appreciate your hard work and dedication. You aren't this department's most valued cop for nothing. Here's a run-down of the case: Name of the student missing is Eric Boden. He's a senior at Everest High School, a private school near the city. Hasn't been seen since yesterday *afternoon*, when he was supposed to be back from school."

"And when does school get out at Everest?" Dominic asked.

"At 2:15. But Eric had basketball practice until 3:30, as he does so every Monday. He didn't show up at home afterwards."

This got Dominic to think. Could it be that Eric was at a friend's house for the night? It was too soon to declare him as "missing" yet, but given that the kid was only in high school, he could understand the concern over him not showing up.

"Who was he with when he had practice?"

Just then, as if on cue, Bert Tomlin appeared. He had gotten a haircut and had put on a few pounds (in a strong, muscular way) since the last case.

"A few of his friends who are on the school basketball team with him. I made a list," he said, smiling as he handed a list to Dominic.

"You make my job so much easier, much faster too. I like that," Dominic said appreciatively.

He used to be irritated at Bert for doing his work for him, but now he was relieved of this fact. It took a load off him for a change. Grunt work like getting people's names wasn't always enjoyable; it was tedious.

He looked at the list. It read (in Bert's messy handwriting):

Eric Boden

Charlie Davis

Tom Lee

Kirk Codd

Carter Everest

Derek Marbury

"And were all these boys accounted for at the practice yesterday afternoon?"

"Yes, they all were. I checked in with the gym teacher, Matt Nendler."

Dominic scoffed, but in an impressed way. "Good on you! You did 90% of the work I would have started with doing. Now that that's out of the way, have you talked with Eric's family?"

"Briefly. I thought maybe you could do more digging on him. He lives with his mother, father, and younger sister. Oh, and by the way, Eric is an honors student. Has a 4.1 GPA."

Chief Tonew whistled. He never had that sort of GPA growing up. "Wow…that's impressive. I sure wish I had that GPA when I was in high school." Shifting his focus to the case, he then said, "I guess you better start talking with them then."

Dominic gave a thumbs up. "I'm on it. In the meantime, Bert, why don't you talk with his homeroom teacher, or advisor, or whatever they call it these days— anyone who's like a mentor to Eric, to see what he's like outside of academics. Talk to the school counselor as well. He's a senior, right? Find out what colleges he's applied to or thinking of going to. Everything is important, no matter how irrelevant it may seem now."

Bert nodded in affirmation.

"Good. I'm going to Eric's house. Get Eric's address for me, will you?"

Bert handed Dominic a file before leaving for Everest High School. It had an address, date of birth, social security number, and family information.

This time Dominic read through it carefully before going to Eric's house.

CHAPTER 2

The Bodens lived in an upscale suburb in Boston. Their house was quite big—with two stories and a patio in the front. Every other house next to or across from the Bodens looked just like theirs.

A woman sat on a swinging bench next to the front door. She was around forty-five or so. She wore a white tank top, blue jeans and her brown hair was put into a messy bun. She had her eyes closed, inhaling the air.

Dominic greeted the woman as he approached her. "Morning, ma'am," he said, cheerily.

Her eyes shot open. She eyed him suspiciously, trailing her gaze up and down.

"Police?" Her tone was that of surprise and also of calmness.

"Yep. I'm Detective Dominic Rivers." He flashed his badge. "Are you related to Eric Boden?"

"I'm his mother," she said, her voice unwavering.

"Oh." Her attitude struck him as strange. He expected her to be a bit more worried for her son. Shouldn't she be asking questions inquiring his whereabouts or any progress made?

"What's your name?" he asked, making sure her name matched the one on file.

"Taylor, Taylor Boden."

Good, so it was the same name as the one on the file.

"Mrs. Boden, nice to meet you. I wish we were meeting under more pleasant circumstances, but I believe you or someone in your family reported your son missing?"

"We sure did. My husband, Steve, reported him missing two hours after Eric didn't come home yesterday. The police told us to wait till the next day to see if he'd show up. And he hasn't."

"Could he have run away from home?"

"No way!" she huffed. "Eric running away from home, when he got accepted into Dartmouth? No way!"

"He was going to Dartmouth, you say? What does he want to study there?"

"Chemistry. He likes all them plants and stuff about ions and bases, and what not. I'm happy for him. I'm proud of him, that he likes things like that."

"So, did he usually have basketball practice every Monday afternoon?"

"Yep, sure did."

Dominic swore he heard footsteps from inside the house.

"Is your husband inside? Maybe I could talk to him as well," he suggested.

"He's sleeping; so is my daughter. She's eight, by the way. Anyways, Steve barely got any sleep last night let me tell you that."

"I mean, I wouldn't too, if my son was missing."

Mrs. Boden brows raised at his snarky comment.

"So...Eric is eighteen now?" Dominic moved on before she could say anything.

"Yep. Eighteen. Legal now. He can do whatever he wants in his life."

"But since he's still in high school and living with you guys, he is still very much financially obligated to you and your husband. So, it's essential we find him. We want to know how Eric was yesterday. Was he acting off, like he was hiding something? Or did something happen at school, perhaps?"

"Whoa there, Detective, way too many questions. Ask them one at a time."

Dominic sighed in frustration. "Okay, my first question is, was Eric acting normally yesterday?"

"Sure was."

"Walk me through what he did yesterday up until the time he didn't come home."

"So, he woke up around 6:30. Got ready, ate breakfast till 7:30. Bus came at 7:45. School started at 8:10. He texted me that he would be at basketball practice till 3:30. He always texts when he has basketball practice...so that wasn't a big deal. He walks home too, as our house is five minutes from his school. Anyways, it became 3:50. Then 4:50. No sign of him showing up home."

"I see. And I assume this was his schedule every Monday. Did he have other extracurriculars?"

"Nope. Just basketball. Kid is a nerd, by other means."

Dominic didn't like Mrs. Boden's choice of words when describing her son. She should be grateful to have a son who is a jack-of-all-traits. "You must be proud to have an intelligent son, you mean."

"Well, yeah. But a lot of the other parents are jealous."

"For Eric being smart?"

"Yeah. But Eric is not very social. He has a few friends from basketball and that's it."

"Who are his friends? His close ones?"

"Kirk Codd and Derek Marbury."

Those names sounded familiar. Dominic pulled out the list of students on the basketball team that Bert gave him. Those two names *were* on it, he confirmed to himself.

"They are good kids. Their families are good people. They also want what's best for their sons," Mrs. Boden confirmed.

He didn't want to agree with her just yet, as he still had to talk with everyone's families. His legs were getting tired, so he leaned against the ceiling post in front of the patio.

"Does he have a girlfriend?" he suddenly asked.

Mrs. Boden looked at him in alarm. "No…no he doesn't." Her voice hinted that something was amiss, but he couldn't put his finger on it yet.

"Alright, well this leads me to my third question. Did something happen at school to Eric? Maybe he was bullied or something?"

Dominic put out these options, based on a hunch. He wanted her to open up more about her son. Because so far, all that he heard was that Eric was a "nerd, honors kid" who played basketball and loved chemistry. Nothing suspicious.

She shook her head. "Nope, he was not bullied, as far as I know."

"Eric didn't use social media or anything?"

"He used Twitter and Instagram."

"How do you know?"

"I check his phone every now and then. He barely has anything on it. Just gaming apps and word puzzles that were popular from, like, 2012."

"So, he was a good kid overall."

"Very."

Dominic didn't have any more questions for her. It was too early to tell if she was telling the truth about her son or not. He asked if she could wake up her husband, Steve so he could ask him questions.

While he waited, Dominic looked around, thinking about his interaction with her. What he thought was strange was the fact that she, as Eric's mother, didn't seem concerned about her son's disappearance.

Perhaps it was due to the fact she didn't make the call to police reporting her son missing.

Or maybe it was she still thought he was at a friend's house. Or maybe it was something else...

Steve Boden stood at the front door, a few moments later, looking dazed. He was around forty-nine, stout, and short with a mustache and balding hair. The blue night robe he had wrapped around his body added to his sleepy look. He had overheard his wife's conversation with the detective.

"You are here about my son, right? Any updates? Have you found him yet?" he asked in a groggy but worried tone.

Dominic was relieved. At least one of the parents was concerned for their missing son.

"Not yet. We're just in the beginning stages. I take it you called the police reporting your son missing, am I right?"

"Yep, I did...what do you have so far?"

"As I said, not much. We have search parties all around the school and in the surrounding areas. I wanted to come here to get an idea of what Eric was like. Besides being academically studious."

"He's a nice kid. Always friendly to everyone. Making us proud too. He's going to Dartmouth!"

"So, I've heard. Congratulations!"

To Dominic's surprise, Mr. Boden kept a solemn face. He didn't say anything for a few seconds. Then he spoke: "Nothing is wrong with him. He doesn't get in trouble in school. If there's one thing about him, it's that he likes to back answer you at times. He won't listen to directions when we tell him to make up his bed, for example. He does it afterwards, anyways. But you know, I thought this would be useful for you police to know, for your high-end investigation."

Dominic pursed his brows in confusion. This was not that kind of "high-end" investigation, where he was uncovering a government conspiracy or something.

It was a missing persons case.

Simple as that.

Mr. Boden definitely got the wrong idea when it came to *this* particular case.

"This is a missing persons case, sir. Don't get carried away with the fact I'm questioning you. Don't worry, all that high-end stuff is FBI territory, which this is not."

"Oh." Mr. Boden's face fell.

Dominic thought that maybe Mr. Boden wished it was. *Perhaps he was hoping a high end case would draw more attention towards his family?*

"Well, now I have a better picture of your son as a person. I'll come by if I have more questions. Thanks for your time," he said diplomatically, on his way out.

CHAPTER 3

Eric Boden had everything going for him. Bright-faced, brown haired, with sea-green eyes, he had it all. He was an eighteen-year-old high school senior on the basketball team, affable and well-liked among his group of friends.

Most importantly, he had a girlfriend, Samantha Beaumont. They were a power couple for as long as they were a couple, which wasn't for a long time. Eric became interested in other things and having a lasting relationship was not one of them. He instead wanted to become something that no one would expect him be. He was tired of being labeled the "honors kid". He would rather be labeled as "basketball star" instead. Which he also was, but his parents didn't want to see that side of him. Grades were the number one priority for them even if other parents constantly compared Eric to their kid, annoying the hell out of them. It was their effort of making him be something he didn't want to be.

Which is why he, in an effort to defy them, went on to have a girlfriend behind their backs, when he was forbidden to date.

He met seventeen-year-old Samantha Beaumont, a junior, at a football game two months ago. She was with her group of friends when he saw her. She seemed spunky, funny and a bundle of nerves with her brown hair that complimented her youthful face, and her impeccable fashion sense. He loved her laugh, her smile, everything about her. When they started dating, everyone in school knew about their relationship, including faculty and staff. When he told his friends from the basketball team about Samantha, they were curious to see what was so great about her.

As Eric introduced her to them, he noticed the looks on his friend's face. They didn't seem overjoyed that he had finally found someone. He sensed they were a bit jealous of him. Especially one person in particular. They also seemed more than excited to chat with Samantha as if she were their long-lost buddy, which made no sense. At the time, he thought he was imagining his friends' odd reaction to their relationship and maybe it was they didn't care.

Little did he know, he would be dead wrong.

CHAPTER 4

Everest High School was located on a big open field, near a residential area in the Boston suburbs. It was founded in 1945, originally as an all-boys private school, then later turned into a co-ed private high school.

The buildings within reflected its elite status as a private school. All of the buildings looked rustic in nature as they were made of brick. The main office was located on the bottom floor of a two-story building, with the top floor dedicated for the English classrooms. There were two other buildings, adjacent to the main building—one was the Math/Robotics building and the other was the History building.

On the inside of each classroom, however, it was like attending a school straight out of a sci-fi movie. Each classroom had glass windows that reflected light to the inside, plastic desks with attached chairs, and Smart Boards (instead of traditional whiteboards). And of course, there was a track and field and football stadium.

Bert Tomlin was in awe as he strode through the corridors of the school. He wished he could have attended a high school like this one. The buildings at *his* high school looked like prison cells, no joke.

Mr. Victor Garcia, Eric Boden's homeroom teacher, led him to his office inside the Math/Robotics building. Mr. Garcia was a man of average height—five feet six inches. He wore a Red Sox hat, a plaid t-shirt, and beige pants. He was around forty and appeared lethargic. Who could blame him though? With all the turmoil surrounding Eric's disappearance, it seemed normal for him as a faculty member, to feel the brunt of everyone's emotions.

There was a student outside Mr. Garcia's office holding a binder, most likely there to ask a homework-related question. When he saw Bert, he put his head down, trying not to make eye contact. Mr. Garcia turned to the student. "Sorry, Greg. I have an appointment that's very urgent. I will see you after school. I'll set my office hours then, if that works for you."

The student, who appeared to be an antsy freshman, with his mopped hair and perplexed look, nodded and walked away.

The two men entered inside Mr. Garcia's office. Bert sat down in the comfy leather chair in front of Mr. Garcia's desk while Mr. Garcia sat across from him in a wooden chair.

"Alright, so you said that you wanted a better picture of Eric Boden, right? Being his homeroom teacher, of course I'd have all the intel. He's a good kid," he said, matter-of-factly. "He didn't have a lot of friends. But he was studious."

"Yeah. I gathered that. He is an honors student, I take it?"

"Sure is. He is in my Calculus Honors class too. I also teach math here."

Bert wrote this down in his notepad.

"So, did you notice who all Eric is friends with? Going back to your previous comment about him not having lot of friends."

"He had two friends from the basketball team. They are also in my homeroom. Derek Marbury and Kirk Codd. That's all I know."

"And was Eric bullied at all?"

"Bullied? No way. People wanted to be like Eric. Smart, studious, and popular with the ladies."

The detective looked up. "You mean, he had girlfriends?"

"Sure did. I mean I don't bother to know about my students' personal lives, but other teachers were talking about it. You know how teachers all talk about their students outside of class? One of the teachers was saying how they were surprised that he was the type to have a girlfriend because he's so serious in class."

"And who was the teacher that said that?"

"Mrs. Amber Allen. She teaches Chemistry Honors. Was his teacher last year."

"I see. And who's a specific girl that Eric liked recently?"

"Her name is Samantha Beaumont. She's an exchange student from France. She's a junior."

"And how do they know each other?"

"From word of mouth I heard that she often hung out with him at his basketball practices."

Bert took his time to take everything in. "So, what I have is that Eric is studious, and has a girlfriend. Do his parents know about her?"

Mr. Garcia shrugged as he crossed his one foot over the other. "I don't know." He then shook his head. "It's so terrible. He's a nice kid."

"I'm sure he is. Thanks for the talk."

Bert left the office and went to talk to Eric's guidance counselor.

He found out from the front office that Eric's counselor was Mrs. Anita Hong. All the counselor's classrooms were in a separate but smaller building next to the History building. The three counselors' classrooms were right next to each other. He was surprised to see that each the rooms looked very high tech with its sliding glass doors. He could see her inside, on her laptop.

He knocked on the door.

Seconds later, she opened the sliding door. It made a slight screeching sound. Upon seeing her, he saw that she had short black hair that was styled into a bob. She donned a pink shirt and a black dress skirt.

"Oh, hello," she said, cheerily. "You are that detective who's talking to everyone right? About Eric Boden?"

"Sure am. I'm Detective Bert Tomlin." He shook her hand.

"What do you want to know?" she asked with a smile. She stepped outside.

"I want to know more about Eric. I heard he was set to go to Dartmouth, right?"

"Yes, he was. He didn't seem too happy about it. He wanted to go to NYU."

Bert raised his brows. "Really? But Dartmouth is a better college."

"I know. That's what I told him. But he said that NYU had what he wanted."

"Which was?"

"A life, sir. The party scene is big in New York and he thought that would be a good change for him."

"But isn't he the studious kind and an honors student on top of that? Wouldn't that be a misfit for him? He wanted to study chemistry, right?"

"He did. Up until this year. He changed his mind. He told me not to tell his parents anything that he confided in me about. I did email his parents to tell them that he didn't want to go to Dartmouth. And valuing his confidentiality, I didn't tell his parents the other half of the truth."

"Which is?"

"That Eric not only had no intention of going to Dartmouth, he wanted to accept NYU and then drop out."

CHAPTER 5

Two weeks ago

"What?! You're kidding!" Samantha Beaumont said to Eric Boden, one day at lunch.

The two of them were sitting underneath the brick stairs of the Math/Robotics building, which was the largest building of the campus. Everest High School was famous for their math and robotics program, so the trustees decided that a bigger building dedicated to those two departments was much needed.

Samantha, one of Everest High's smartest students, had heard the news of a lifetime from her boyfriend. "You want to drop out? Why?"

Eric, with his phone clutched in his hands, a sign of nervousness, looked at her with earnest eyes. "I just don't want to be labeled as an honors kid anymore. I have aspirations too!"

"Which are what? Why would you apply in the first place, if you were just going to drop out? That's a huge waste of everything, money, effort, you know."

"The thing is, I won't remain a drop out," he insisted. "I will do something with my life, but at the moment I don't want to go to Dartmouth." His firm tone made Samantha believe he was truly serious in his words. She crossed one arm over the other and looked away. She gazed at the other students walking by who looked so carefree, laughing. She returned back to reality. She was still in shock over Eric's words. He had so much potential in life to become college drop-out. What would her family think if they found out she was associated with someone like him? Someone with no real purpose in life. They wouldn't bear it!

"I see that you're mad about it. But it's my life, I can choose what I want to do," he said, amidst the silence between them.

Samantha huffed. "You're right. It's your life, your choice. I think we should also break up while we're at it."

Eric gave her a double look. "Excuse me?!"

"Yeah. We should see other people. After all, it's what you're probably going to do in college next year, right? Or— I'm sorry —it's what you're gonna be doing while you're partaking in other activities that include *not going to college*!"

"Samantha, I thought you would understand that I have my own dreams too. I want to do something creative with my life."

"Like what?"

"I want to start my own business."

"Okay?" Samantha was surprised that he actually had something in mind and that what he wanted to do was not out of the ordinary. She had assumed he had his own bizarre reason for wanting to drop out of college. If he wanted to start a business, why drop out of college for that? She didn't want to question him anymore, as he had made up his mind.

She had also made up her mind too. She wanted out of the relationship.

In a clear voice, she said, "If that's what you want, let me tell you this. I'm not comfortable, nor will I ever be comfortable, with the fact that I am dating someone who won't go to college. For this reason, I think we should take a break."

In response, Eric stormed away, without another word.

CHAPTER 6

"Excuse me?" Bert Tomlin asked, shocked, upon hearing the news that Eric planned to drop out of college.

He couldn't fathom that someone who got into Dartmouth wanted to go somewhere else...and then drop out? It seemed unbelievable to him but he guessed that given the change in times, people were more enterprising in their lifestyle choices.

Not anymore did people have the "go to school, find a prestigious job, marry, and live happy" mentality. Bert definitely took these life choices into consideration, given that he was also young himself. Understanding why people made certain decisions that he didn't necessarily agree with was also in his line of work as a detective.

"Yep. He was tired of being labeled as a "nerd", as he said, or as an "honors student." Mrs. Hong spoke in an exasperated sigh, as if she was also disappointed at Eric's mindset.

"I would think the opposite."

"Yeah, so did his girlfriend."

"Samantha Beaumont?"

"Yes. She's a junior. I gathered that she wanted him to have dreams as well that extended beyond just studies. As for his decision to drop out, I don't know if she agreed with it.

"Don't tell me she is also considering going to NYU to be with him?" Bert asked, rolling his eyes. This was a recipe for disaster among high school couples that tried to maintain long distance relationships after graduating. He knew it all too well.

He was once that kid who tried to make things work with his high school sweetheart, but ended up breaking it off before his college freshman orientation. Not something he recommended anyone else doing.

"No, she's probably still deciding. I don't know. I'm not her counselor. And she's a junior still, remember? So she has time to decide. Anyways, he had the support of Samantha and his two friends from the basketball team—Kirk and Derek—on anything he chose to do, I'm guessing."

"So, did he have enemies? People who'd want him out of the way?" Bert had to ask.

"No, not really." She hesitated.

"What do you mean, *not really*?"

"Well, there was a teacher who didn't like him at all. Eric mentioned this to me once, last year."

"What's their name?" The young detective was now curious.

"Mrs. Allen. She teaches Chemistry."

That name sounded familiar. Wait...was she referring to Amber Allen?

"His homeroom teacher mentioned her name—Amber Allen. I'm guessing she's one of the teachers who was talking about him in passing to other teachers. Something about how he didn't seem like the type to have a girlfriend," Bert explained.

"Yes. That's her, alright. She still teaches here, by the way, so I wouldn't push on her too much. She's a good teacher. The other thing I wanted to say is that Eric has had attitude "issues" as you can call it. He would back answer his teachers, especially her. No wonder she thought like that."

"So, amongst students, his attitude was fine."

"Yeah, for the most part. I guess he likes to defy authority as a way of making a point to them."

"Making a point that he's not a 'nerd' but a cool kid who can talk back. Maybe that's also making a point to the students as well."

"Seems about it."

"Do his parents know about his so-called attitude problems?"

"Yeah, they do. They had a talk with myself and Mrs. Allen about it, last year. They told her that Eric behaves like that at home too."

"So, he's a bit of a spoiled brat but only to his elders."

"Correct."

"Thank you very much, Mrs. Hong, I appreciate this conversation. I wish I were talking about Eric in a livelier note, but it is what it is," Bert said, in a diplomatic manner.

"I'm hoping for the best." She shook his hand again and walked him out.

◊◊◊◊◊◊◊◊◊◊◊◊◊◊◊◊◊

Bert waited for Dominic at the Boston Police Station. In the meantime, he jotted down notes and outlined what new information he gathered:

Eric Boden, 18

Senior at Everest High School

Has girlfriend is Samantha Beaumont

Friends are Derek Marbury and Kirk Codd

Teacher that doesn't like him is Mrs. Amber Allen, who was his Chemistry honors teacher last year, had attitude in her class

Counselor is Mrs. Anita Hong; told me that Eric wanted to go to NYU and then drop out, likes to defy authority to look cool in front of peers

HR teacher is Mr. Victor Garcia, who is also his Calculus Honors teacher, Eric was studious in his eyes, noticed the fact he had girlfriend

CHAPTER 7

Dominic Rivers walked into Homicide/Missing Persons, as Bert sat writing down notes. Dominic's head ached from not having time to eat properly and his throat was parched. He had even bought a bottled water at one of the vending machines in the hallway.

He then peered over Bert's shoulder. "So, got any news for me?" he asked. Bert handed him his notes.

"Hmm…" Dominic perused through it. "This is good. You'll have to explain this to me at lunch. I also have to tell you what Eric's parents told me. Now let's get something to eat. I'm starving."

The two had lunch at a Mediterranean place called The Pita House. The restaurant was a quaint joint—crystal decorations hung from the ceiling made of wood. The place was dimly lit, with black booths and wooden tables. Classical music played in the background, adding to the homely surroundings. Lot of people were present inside, chatting in a lively manner. Waiters were carrying trays of food and drinks; the strong aroma of flavors filled the air. Dominic's stomach growled in anticipation.

Both of them ordered a falafel wrap filled with falafel balls and lettuce, and a side of pita bread and ranch. When the food came, Dominic proceeded to stuff everything in his mouth, pita bread and falafel balls and all.

Bert looked on in disgust as he sipped on his coke, with more class. He decided to start a conversation.

"So, Dominic, when are you finally going to settle down? It's a question we've all been wondering. The Chief included. Cause I'm sure your wife or girlfriend or whatever wouldn't be too pleased seeing you gorge your food like that in front of them."

Dominic gave him a look. "What you said makes me want to get a drink."

"Well, we are on duty—"

"I know. That's the point."

"Oh," Bert said, trying not to laugh.

"Who even cares in the first place?" Dominic continued. "What does this have to do with the case?"

"It doesn't. I thought I'd just ask—"

"Well stuff it. It's my life and I'll "settle down" when I want. I don't need you to keep asking me abot it."

Bert threw his hands up defensively. "Alright, fair enough." He then diverted the conversation to the case—which he knew his partner was dying to hear more about. He explained how he met Eric's homeroom teacher and counselor, mostly covering what he had written down in his notes.

After he finished, he looked at Dominic with serious eyes. "So, what did *you* find out?"

Dominic took a break from his food. He hadn't realized how starved his was, and the food they were eating at the moment was the ultimate comfort food. He went on to explain what he discussed with Eric Boden's parents.

"So, his parents seemed a bit strange to me. His mother didn't act concerned at all. She seemed cool as a cucumber as she explained about Eric's daily schedule. His father on the other hand, played the more convincing parent as he seemed genuinely concerned for their son. But they both said that Eric was a good kid, as he would text them every time he had basketball practice."

"Okay...?" Bert started. He knew Dominic had something more to add.

"...but his mother said that she checks his phone all the time and he had nothing on it, except some word games and puzzles. Nothing that would give us information on where he could have gone."

To this, Bert kept a puzzled face. "That doesn't sound like your average high school kid. I would assume he'd have text messages, social media accounts, you know, the works."

"Well, it doesn't sound like your average high school kid, I agree. But it does sound like this is the phone of a studious kid. The ones that don't use social media that much 'cause they're too busy with their studies. But then again, I may be wrong. Everyone this day and age uses social media or their phones. I know I do," he said, with a wink. "I'll ask one of our men to check into Eric's social media profiles to see if he disclosed his last location. It would also give us information on how Eric was as a person."

Dominic proceeded to make a quick call, phoning a fellow detective to look into Eric's social media profiles and give him updates.

When Bert saw his partner had finished the call, he added, "I found out that Eric had another side of him that not everyone knows. If you read my notes, you'll see that he had a girlfriend. And he also liked to talk back to teachers."

"Not your average goody-two shoes, right?" Sarcasm hit Dominic's voice.

"Do you think that Eric had a secret phone where he kept his real text messages, social media, and conversations to Samantha and his friends?" Bert proposed. "I don't know why but it seems likely. If Eric's mother told you that he only has word games on his phone, it's likely that he must have another phone that he doesn't want anyone to know about. I also talked with his counselor and she said that it's possible that Eric was acting out or rebelling, just to look cool to his friends. This proves that he might have been having another phone."

Dominic considered this. "I can see that. Peer pressure is real nowadays."

"Do you think Eric was forced into doing something he didn't want to and disappeared that way?"

"Maybe, we don't know."

"Well, we do know something too. Maybe this relates to his tendency to "look cool"—the fact that Eric didn't want to go to Dartmouth, but NYU."

Dominic was stunned. He didn't think anyone would be dumb to make a choice like that. Unless he didn't like Dartmouth. But then again, why apply there, in the first place?

"But I asked his parents if he was the type to run away from home and they told me he wouldn't be that type, because he got into Dartmouth. And they seemed proud of it."

"They're probably lying," Bert said, with confidence.

"Yeah. So, what now? We got nothing so far except an honors kid with a secret dark side that his parents don't know."

"I'm onto the parents." Bert seemed so sure in his answer, Dominic had to give it to him.

"Will you talk to them, then?"

Bert thought for a moment. "Why don't *you* do that, since you talked with them before? I will go talk to Eric's girlfriend,

Samantha Beaumont's family."

Dominic stopped eating his last bite of his wrap. He was not just getting orders from an "amateur". He didn't want all the credit to fall on Bert once this case was solved. Dominic didn't see that he had a bloated ego. It was a matter of both of them doing the work. After all, who was the older and more experienced one?

"How about this, why don't we both go to his parent's house again and both go to Samantha's house? That way we won't need to be briefing each other on what we learned," Dominic asserted.

"Why, do you suspect me of withholding information?"

"I don't. I just want us to work as a team. Tonew will be impressed…"

"Dom, you have a promotion already. I don't think you need to be reporting to him all the time. He's probably already impressed with your work. At least for me, I'm still new, trying to work my way up. But you…don't mess it up by letting your bloated ego get in the way."

The proud detective sat up straight. "It's not my ego," he lied. "It's just that I want to be in the loop about every aspect of the case."

"It doesn't work that way. It's not just you. I'm also there. And I am briefing you on everything I've learned so far, too."

"I see what you're saying. And I thank you for that. But I still insist that we inform each other on everything."

He was not relenting.

Bert sighed. "Fine. We can both go together," he grumbled. "Not because I agree with you, but because I know you won't have it any other way."

Dominic smiled. "Good."

Bert took a last bite of his falafel wrap, reluctantly.

As they walked to their car, Bert could not help but think about the kind of person Dominic Rivers was and how different he was from himself. Bert Tomlin was the type of detective to not take things lightly. Especially when it had to with deciding what part of an investigation to dive into next. Each step was crucial and to be successful in getting answers, he and Dominic had to work together. Dominic's way of handling things was not effective. Being an experienced detective didn't mean he could bark orders and demand things to go his way. Now that the two of them were handling a school- related case, it took his back to his younger days, when he was a scrawny, unpopular kid in school. Bert used his words to get back at the bullies.

But that wasn't a major turning point of his life, that made him the way he is today. It was when he was in college that he decided to become a police officer…

It was Bert's senior year of studying political science at Boston College. One day, as he was walking on campus, he saw a police officer reprimand a young teenager for pushing his friend off a skateboard in a menacing way. The friend who got pushed off didn't say a word and just sat there on the ground. The words Bert overheard the officer say stuck with him: *"Be the person your friend or anyone else would want to respect. Your friend here may not have it in him to call you out on your actions, but I am. So, change your act, kid. Start by being nicer. It all begins at a young age…."*

That officer was right. Helping others, defending others when they don't have the ability to, was something Bert wanted to do.

After college, he dabbled in a few jobs here and there, but found no real interest in them. He finally decided to officially become an officer for the Boston Police Department. He passed his training with flying colors. It was after two years of being a police officer that he decided to broaden his horizons and delve into case solving. Which is why he decided to become a detective in the Homicide/Missing Persons unit.

On his first day, he vividly remembered meeting Police Chief Oscar Tonew for the first time. He found the experienced officer to be kind, compassionate and a strong leader. That man introduced him to a life that he would no longer back down from. One that he would never forget for the rest of his life…

⌂⌂⌂⌂⌂⌂⌂⌂⌂⌂⌂⌂⌂⌂⌂⌂⌂

While Bert and Dominic were having lunch, Chief Tonew received a phone call.

The body of a fourteen-year boy, who had been missing for a week, had just been found in downtown Boston, near the intersection of State Street and John F. Fitzgerald Surface Road. It was declared a shut and close hit and run case, as no perps had been identified for being responsible. But he decided to let Dominic and Bert know about it due to one fact.

The boy happened to attend Everest High School.

CHAPTER 8

Since Dominic had already spoken with Eric's parents and Bert had spoken with Eric's teachers and counselors earlier, they had to speak with the Beaumonts in order to figure out what Samantha's family was like.

They drove to her house, which was a few minutes away from Eric's house. Samantha's house was a smaller version of a Tudor house, nicely decorated with holiday lights around the front door and roof. It seemed like they still had yet to take down their Christmas decorations, given they were in the month of January. Based on the appearance of the house, Samantha's family Her family seemed to be reasonably well-off.

Dominic knocked on the door, as Bert stood next to him. No one answered. Then, a middle-aged woman emerged. She had an apron and wore a flowy blue dress. Her blonde hair was let loose.

"Yes?" she asked, clearly surprised to see them.

"Hello, Mrs. Heidi Beaumont? My name is Detective Dominic Rivers and this is Detective Bert Tomlin. We are here regarding the disappearance of Eric Boden and would like to ask you some questions."

Her face lifted in alarm. "Disappearance?"

"Yes. I don't know if your daughter, Samantha, told you?"

Mrs. Beaumont shook her head. "She doesn't know anything."

Of course, she wouldn't, he thought. *Cause no one seemed to know anything around here.*

She didn't invite them inside. Instead, she left them standing there, awkwardly, in front of her. All of her hospitality seemed to have vanished.

Dominic continued, "Eric Boden, your daughter's boyfriend, has been reported missing. Didn't show up at home after his basketball practice yesterday afternoon around 3:30. What I'd like to know is how your daughter's relationship with Eric was like."

Mrs. Beaumont looked surprised. "I'm not aware of my daughter having a boyfriend," she said, with a hint of a French accent

Dominic grimaced. *What was up with parents not knowing anything that was happening in the lives of their children?*

"Well, according to the school—" (Bert made sure not to mention names) "—he was seeing your daughter. Maybe we can return when she's back from school to verify this fact."

"Why, is she a suspect or something?"

"No. No. We just wanted to know more about Eric as a person. But given you weren't aware of Eric being Samantha's boyfriend..." Bert noticed she wasn't paying attention to him. She was looking left and right, appearing as if she didn't want be there.

"Do you live here alone?" he suddenly asked.

"Yes. Alone. My husband is in Paris. I came to the US with my daughter a few years ago."

Dominic whispered something into his partner's ears. Mrs. Beaumont looked on, impatiently.

"Did your daughter like to play basketball by any chance?" Bert asked. He had been asked by Dominic to take over the questioning and bring up basketball, due to the fact that Eric was on the team.

"Yes. She did. She told me she'd also watch some of her friends play basketball after school, sometimes."

Bert nodded. "Was she watching her friends yesterday by any chance? After school? Or did she come home immediately?"

"I picked her up at 2:30 as usual."

"So, she didn't stay back?"

"No. What's this about? I don't understand."

"It's not anything for you to be too worried about. We would like to speak with your daughter today."

Mrs. Beaumont nodded her head. "Uh, okay…You can talk to her. I'm sure she's got nothing to hide."

The detectives gave her a little nod as they left her house.

"How come she doesn't know anything?" Bert asked regarding Mrs. Beaumont. They were sitting in their car, across the street from Samantha's house.

"I don't know. Maybe Samantha is not telling her mother anything like our buddy Eric isn't telling his parents anything."

"That's weird. The teachers know more about the students than their actual parents.

"I think that's the point," Dominic said. "These students might have something to hide and aren't willing to disclose anything to anyone, especially their parents. My bet is that there's something fishy going on with Eric and Samantha."

Bert sighed in frustration. "I guess this means we won't get anything else by talking to Eric's parents again."

There was a brief pause.

Suddenly, the sound of a phone's ringtone blared from Dominic's pockets, making them both jump.

The older detective swiftly picked up. "Yes?" He listened for a few seconds. Then he hung up.

He told Bert that the detective he had called earlier had intel on Eric's social media—which was pretty fast by Bert's standard.

"What did he find out?" he asked.

"Apparently, Eric's social media are all private. There's nothing there. We don't have his phone, his *real* phone, that is, to dig up more. I thought we would have something by now."

Disappointment crossed Bert's face. "So, what do we do now?"

"Why don't we go back to Everest High? To where the kids have basketball practice. Maybe there's something there. Did you ask where they hold basketball practices, when you were there, by the way?"

"I didn't." Bert looked down, not feeling proud of himself. He was so wrapped up about finding out about Eric, that he hadn't bothered to find where the school held basketball practices.

"That's okay, actually. I can help with that. If I know better, they probably hold them in the gym." Dominic said slyly. Seeing Bert miss out on one detail made him feel more powerful. In a horribly good way.

On the way to the school, Dominic got another call, this time from Chief Tonew. He held his phone to his ears in stunned interest, as his boss went into detail about something.

"A body? How old's the kid?"

Bert looked over at Dominic in a questioning manner.

Dominic heard Chief Tonew's response on the other end. "Alright, I'll let him know," he finally said before hanging up.

"Who was that?" Bert asked.

"The Chief. He wanted to let us know about a hit and run case that was deemed accidental that occurred downtown. Kid's fourteen years old. Name's Anthony Rugen."

"Damn, that's terrible. But why did he call to tell us about this?"

Dominic gave him a glum look. *"Because Anthony Rugen was a student at Everest High School."*

⌂⌂⌂⌂⌂⌂⌂⌂⌂⌂⌂⌂⌂⌂⌂⌂⌂⌂

Everest High School was a lively scene, especially when school was in session. And especially so when it was break or lunch time. Kids chatted or ran around. Teachers often yelled, "No running in the hallways!" Others sat in circles in the hallways, staring at their phones. The school went by a block schedule that consisted of rotating class schedules. On some days, school would end early or later, lunch would be early or late, or free periods would be at the end of the day, meaning the students in that free period could leave early.

Today, the students had a different schedule so lunch was pushed forward. By the time the detectives made it to the school, it was lunch time. The sight of detectives with badges in the pristine and clean-cut school created jolts in everyone who walked by them.

Once at the front office, Dominic asked the representative at the front desk where basketball practices were usually held. She told them that it was held in the gymnasium.

"Go straight ahead and exit to the right. The gym is the big white building to the side."

"Got it, thanks."

When they reached the gym, they observed students laughing and running around. Some of them stared at the two detectives, whispering and gossiping.

Bert focused his mind on the surroundings of the gym. Cafeteria tables with students, the yellow painted walls, the mascot on the center of the gym floor. With all the students about, any DNA evidence would be erased.

A few minutes passed. Among everything in the gym, there seemed to be no real evidence that something must have transpired during Eric's practice.

He whispered to Bert to search the boy's locker room for any evidence or clues. Maybe Eric's locker was a good starting point. Even if he didn't know his locker number yet.

Once Bert left, a girl then walked up to Dominic and tapped his shoulder. She looked around seventeen, with short brown hair. She wore a striped t-shirt and jeans with the edges of the legs folded neatly.

"Are you guys here about Eric's disappearance? People are talking, wondering what detectives are doing on campus," she said, in a slight accent.

Dominic turned around, looking at her in alarm. "Yes, we're here regarding his disappearance. Who are you?"

"I'm Samantha."

He froze. "Samantha Beaumont?"

She gave him a startled look. "How do you know?"

"We talked with your mother today. Maybe you could tell us more about Eric. Now, perhaps?"

Samantha looked shocked at the fact that they had spoken with her mother. Her manner was as if she just got caught doing something bad.

"S—Sure," she hesitated. Dominic led the way as they walked outside of the gym. "So, tell me about Eric. Did you watch his basketball practice or see him after school yesterday afternoon?"

Samantha thought for a bit. "No. I went home. My mum picked me up."

"I see. And did you always watch Eric play during his basketball practices?"

"Not always. Just on some occasions."

"Yesterday, did you talk with him in between classes or at lunch?"

"Yeah. Just in the morning. He also told me he was going to talk with his friend about something important after school…."

"Something important? Like what? And what friend?"

"Derek. He was going to ask Eric something."

"Derek Marbury?"

She nodded her head. Then she pointed at him. "Don't tell anyone I told you this."

"You haven't told me anything." Dominic was getting impatient. "What did Derek want to ask Eric?"

By the time she could respond, Bert came out and announced that he spotted something in the boy's locker room.

"I'll be right back, Samantha. Here is my contact card. Keep it and tell your mother about it too. We'll talk later."

She looked down at the card, then back up at the detectives as they left the classroom.

Samantha's heart pounded as she walked towards her locker. Even the clamor of students was not enough to distract her thoughts. As she stuffed books in her backpack, many thoughts came to her mind. The first thought that came to mind was why Eric hadn't been found yet. The second thought was that if the police found out that she was not really happy about Eric's decision to drop out of college, they would suspect her for being involved in his disappearance. This would be a strong motive for her—the fact that she wanted to be with him forever and not get him into the wrong crowd. That she would go to all lengths, even harm him, to make sure he stayed with her forever.

But the reality was, she was the one who wanted to break up with him. She and Eric even broke up not too long after that conversation they had about him dropping out, and expressed their desire to see other people.

But would the police believe her if she told them that? Would they also believe the fact that Eric Boden had a bet with one of his friends regarding another girl they liked, thus proving that her and Eric's relationship was never a committed one?

She had to reveal this information to the detectives before suspicion fell on her. She had to wait for the right time, though. If the police don't question her again, she wouldn't say anything. If they did, then she would have to say everything.

Everything, including the fact that she knew more about

Eric's disappearance than what she let on.

In other words, Samantha knew where Eric was.

CHAPTER 9

In the meantime, Dominic followed Bert to the boys' locker room, which was a separate room next to the gym. It was empty for the most part. Students bolted upon seeing the detectives, with their badges and intimidating demeanor.

When they entered, they saw the room was relatively small. Grey lockers stood next to the door and curved all the way inside. They were lined in rows of two, with numbers on them (odd numbers on top, and even numbers on the bottom). There were locks on all of them.

All except…

Eric's locker. His locker number was 134. It was on the bottom row, and stood further away from the door.

Bert asked Dominic to look at what he found inside Eric's locker. He had gotten Eric's locker information the previous day, after questioning teachers and counselors.

Inside the locker was a hoodie with a Stranger Things logo and a pack of gum. But most importantly, there was a cell phone. A black iPhone X.

"Whose phone is this?" Dominic asked.

"Don't know. Thought you should see it."

"Is this Eric's phone?"

"We don't know that. We can charge the phone, since it's out of battery."

They immediately called for for an officer to bring an iPhone charger. Minutes later, an officer, Fred Duer, came in with the charger. He also worked in the Homicide/Missing Persons department, and had the looks of a rookie.

Dominic plugged the phone into the charger.

A few seconds after scrolling through the phone, he realized that this was the phone with no text messages, as it had just apps and word puzzle games.

Dominic thanked Officer Duer and told him he could leave.

He then turned to the phone in his hands, and looked at his partner questioningly. "Wherever he is, he must have taken another phone with him. I wonder— did he have PE at the end of the day? That would explain how he had the opportunity to go to his locker and leave this phone inside."

Bert said he would find out. Minutes later, he came back from the main office. He told Dominic that Eric's specific schedule that day was a regular day. Eric's first class was English, and his last class was a free block. He had no PE at the end of the day.

This convinced them that Eric must have made a stop to the lockers only *after* basketball practice to drop off his phone. *Why would he leave his phone there? Unless he knew he wasn't going home...*

When the two of them got back to the gym, they saw that lunch had ended. Samantha was nowhere to be seen. That figured. She was in class, most likely.

Dominic decided to talk with her after school to finish their conversation about Derek asking Eric something important, the day before. Maybe this had to do with the phone in the locker. To Bert, he explained about his interaction with Samantha and how her testimony might bring new insight into the case. After all, this confirmed their suspicions that the students might have something to do with Eric's disappearance.

They both went to the front desk and asked for Samantha Beaumont's schedule for today. The lady at the front, a frail-looking elderly woman, was hesitant to give it out. The two had to remind her that she had to disclose this because given that Samantha was a person of interest, it was essential they know everything about her.

"Her last class is US History. Room 234 in the History building. You can take the elevator," she said in a frightened tone.

The two thanked her.

Since they had some time until school ended, they stood near the sitting area, next to the front desk. Dominic read a copy of the current school handbook that was placed on top one of the chairs. He was strangely engrossed in it. He read that Everest High School didn't have uniforms, but they had a free-dress code enforced. No ripped jeans, low cuts, midriffs, the works. Bert turned to see what Dominic was reading so intently. Out of sheer curiosity, he took a look through the handbook once Dominic was finished with it.

After a while, they went upstairs and stood in the hallway, where room 234 was located. Her class would end any minute now. After all, this was the last class of the day after lunch. Dominic couldn't help but scoff at the lockers that stood next to the row of classrooms. Some of them were plastered with celebrities and group photos. He remembered his days in high school. It was definitely a time he wouldn't want to go back to. If people from his class knew he had become a detective, they wouldn't believe it. And now coming back to a high school to solve a case, made him feel empowered.

The bell rang soon after, drawing him away from his thoughts. Students flooded out of the multiple classrooms on the floor. Dominic found himself bumping into students left and right. Bert was a few feet away, equally cornered. It was going to be hard to find Samantha amongst the plethora of students. He had to do something.

"SAMANTHA BEAUMONT!" he yelled at the top of his lungs.

Everyone kept walking by, not one heeded to his call. Some students even darted faster away after seeing and hearing him.

"SAMANTHA BEAU-MONT! WE NEED TO SPEAK TO YOU!" he repeated.

Suddenly, a girl rushed over to them. She had heard someone calling her name. Once she realized it was one of the detectives, she hastily made her way towards them.

"Yes?" she asked.

"Samantha, thank god," Dominic said in relief. "My voice was going to become hoarse. Can we talk more? I need to speak to you regarding Derek."

Her eyes widened. "Derek?"

"Yes. You said that he wanted to tell Eric something important afterschool," Bert said. He waited for her answer.

"I didn't say anything." She crossed her arms.

"Oh really? Then why'd you bring it up?"

"I have to go—"

Dominic blocked her way. "Not so fast. We want to know what he wanted to tell Eric. You won't be considered a suspect if you tell us what you know."

"*Suspect*?! I didn't do anything!"

"I'm sure you didn't. But we need some answers. Why don't we go inside the classroom you were just in? It's too loud out here."

To this, Samantha gulped. But she relented. She led the two inside.

The classroom was spacious with rows of painted desks. A Smart Board was at the front. Posters of famous historical figures as well as art projects hung on the walls. The large windows gave view to the tall trees and blue skies, outside.

Her teacher was still in the classroom. He sat at his desk, which was located in the right corner of the room. Bert explained that they were interviewing Samantha for "the case" and that they needed to talk with her alone.

Her teacher nodded. After gathering his papers and laptop, he walked out.

Once he left, the three of them sat in the student desks. Samantha sat in the first row, and Dominic and Bert sat in the row behind her.

Dominic cut to the chase. "So now, tell me about Derek."

She took a deep breath as she said, "Derek's a good guy for the most part. Except he could be kind of egotistic at times."

"Meaning?"

Samantha sighed. "Don't tell anyone what I'm telling you, not even Derek. I don't want any blame to fall on me. Anyways, Derek has this ego, that he needs to match up to someone else. He doesn't like to be the person who loses; he likes to be victorious at all times. So, what happened was this: Derek was asking Eric for money. They had a bet on who could ask out one of the popular girls in school—Jamie Mitchell. She's a senior, like Eric. By the way, if everyone's saying Eric and I are a thing, that's partially true. We were a couple for a year, exclusively, but now we are kind of seeing other people on the side, not that either of us mind. So, I don't really care that they made this bet. Anyways, Eric bet that Derek wouldn't ask Jamie to go out with him. But Derek asked her out in the end and she accepted. So, he wanted money from Eric. Eric wouldn't give it to him."

She paused, trying to catch her breath. "Now that I told you all this, I'm not a suspect anymore, right?"

Bert ignored her question. "Can't make you any promises at this point. How much was bet?"

To this, she shuffled in her seat, and turned her head from the detectives to the door. She looked like she wanted to be anywhere but there. She also kept a face, as if thinking 'When are they going to stop questioning me? Am I done yet?'

Finally she said: "$100."

Could she be hiding something? Bert thought, seeing her expression of uneasiness.

"Wow. That much? Did Eric have the money with him and he forgot to give it to Derek, or did he just refuse to give it to him?" Dominic asked.

"I don't know. I just know about the bet and the money I assumed that's what Derek wanted to confront Eric about, after school."

"And after that, where did Eric go, do you know?"

"No. As I said, I was picked up after school." After a brief pause, she said, "Is that all? Am I done?"

They nodded, reminding her to tell her mother about their conversation. Samantha gave a curt nod and left the room, practically bolting out the door. Dominic looked at Bert, wondering what to make of their conversation. They got the intel on the bet Derek and Eric had made. But it didn't explain the phone being in his locker.

With that, they walked to the parking lot. Bert wrote down what Samantha told him in his notepad.

"So, the two boys had a bet about asking a girl out and Eric wouldn't give Derek his money," Dominic said flatly. .

"Sounds like your average high school guy drama," Bert said, shrugging.

"We need to find out more about Derek, now that Samantha told us a bit about his ego problem."

"I can talk to his family," Bert said enthusiastically.

Dominic smiled. "You do that. I will go to the station and do some more digging on Eric to pick up from where you left off."

CHAPTER 10

"So, Samantha, how was school?" Mrs. Beaumont cheerily asked her daughter as Samantha slumped into the front seat.

Mrs. Beaumont still had to drop and pick up Samantha, as her daughter didn't have her driver's license yet (she was going to work on getting it this summer). She knew the written test was a breeze, as that's what some parents had said. As for the road test…that was the part she knew Samantha was going to be worried about.

But for now, she couldn't be more than happy of the fact that she could still drop and pick up Samantha to and from school. This would enable her to find out more about Eric Boden and his relation with her daughter.

Samantha replied, "Good, I guess," as she put her backpack under her seat, in an absentminded manner. She was still thinking about her conversation with the two detectives today.

"Did you know that two detectives questioned me today?" Mrs. Beaumont didn't hesitate to get to the point.

Samantha turned to her mother, looking her dead in the eye. "I know. They told me. I was just going to tell you—"

"What's going on? What's this about a boyfriend and that he's missing?"

Samantha could not stop her mother. She had every right to be concerned. After all, she was in the dark about mostly everything. Samantha was not very close with her mother. Coming to the U.S a few years ago had put a big strain on the relationship between her and her mother. Her father was in France, meaning they had to manage alone in the States. Samantha didn't have time to tell her mother everything that happened in school, as her mother was busy on her own trying to adjust and make new friends. Because of this, Samantha wanted her high school life to be separate from her home life. She thought everything would go smoothly and she would leave high school on a happy note.

But that's not things turned out. At the moment, Samantha knew she was faced with a lot of troubles. Which was why when Eric was announced as missing, Samantha had to tell the truth (most of it, that is) so that suspicion would not be drawn to herself anymore.

So she told her mother *everything*. Everything, from her relationship with Eric, to the bet about Jamie Mitchell, to Derek demanding money from Eric.

The only thing she didn't disclose is that she knew where Eric was.

As Samantha spoke, the look on her mother's face turned from confusion to anger.

"I knew we shouldn't have come here. I knew you'd get corrupted."

"I didn't do anything, though!" Samantha screamed.

"I don't care if you didn't do anything! You hid the truth from me! If those detectives didn't show up. I wouldn't have known anything! You are grounded. You will not go out with friends, or use your phone before finishing your homework! You hear me!"

Samantha crossed her arms around her chest as tears streamed down her face. This was getting to be too much! She hated everything right now. Eric, her mother, life, those detectives. Everyone.

Eric, you stupid idiot, she thought. *Look what you're putting me through, and you're not even here.*

CHAPTER 11

Derek Marbury's house was smaller in comparison to Eric's or Samantha's. His house was a single-story house, with a driveway and a three-car garage. Lights adorned the single framed door made out of plywood.

From looking through the names in the handbook from the front office, Bert Tomlin knew the names of Derek's parents were Sid and Maggie Marbury.

He was about to make his way to the front door, when he saw a man exit. He was tall, had black hair and piercing eyes. The man looked stunned to see someone he didn't recognize, standing in his driveway.

Especially if that someone looked to be a cop.

"Yes?" he asked, narrowing his brows.

"Hi, are you Mr. Marbury? Derek's father?" Bert asked.

"Yes. Who are you?" he said, in a British accent.

"I'm Detective Bert Tomlin."

"I'm Sid Marbury. What's this about?" Mr. Marbury, without shaking hands, crossing his arms instead. His cold demeanor was obvious.

"I'm investigating the disappearance of Derek's friend, Eric Boden, who didn't come home yesterday after school. And I've come to know that Derek and Eric talked right before he was not seen again. Do you mind if I ask you some questions about your son?"

Mr. Marbury sighed. "Fine. But I'm heading out somewhere."

"Where?"

"To the library. Got to pick out a few books."

"Mind if I ride with you? I'll leave my car here and we can come back together.

Mr. Marbury didn't like the fact that Bert was forcing his way into his space. He showed this by his irritated expression. Bert, in turn, got the sense that everyone involved in this case seemed to not care one bit. They didn't want to get into trouble, it seemed like.

Finally, he responded. "Fine. Come along."

The two of them rode together to the Boston Public Library. It was a ten-minute drive.

Mr. Marbury started: "What is this that you're saying about my son and Eric?"

"You do know of Eric Boden…he's your son's friend, right? They both play basketball together and are in the same homeroom? Ami right."

"Yes, I know of Eric. Good kid."

Good kid. Where had he heard that from? Bert thought. Everyone seemed to be saying the same thing about Eric.

"As I said earlier, Eric has been missing since yesterday afternoon. Mind if you tell me how well Derek knew Eric? I understand they had a bet with each other over a girl in school."

Mr. Marbury looked shocked. He turned to Bert. "A bet? You must have the wrong student. Derek wouldn't do that."

"Well, he did. And apparently, Eric owed Derek some money because he lost the bet."

"What bet? What are you talking about?"

Bert explained what Samantha had told them earlier about the bet the two boys made about a girl named Jamie Mitchell.

"Oh. So, my son is under suspicion because he had a bet?"

"Well, he had a bet with someone who is now missing. There's a difference. And we don't know if Derek got his money or not."

Mr. Marbury shook his head. "Derek has nothing to do with this."

"Look, I'm trying to get all the facts, alright? So, let's back track here. What exactly did Derek do after school yesterday?"

"He had basketball practice until 3:30."

"And then?"

"He came home."

"Did he walk home or drive home or did you pick him up?"

"He drove home. He has a license now. He's a senior like Eric."

"Okay and what did he do after basketball practice? Did he text you and let you know?"

"No. He just came home at around 3:50. It doesn't take long to get here from his school."

"I see. So you really don't know anything about the bet that Derek had?"

"I don't."

"Alright…" Bert let out a loud sigh of frustration. He was getting no answers so far from anyone!

They had reached the Boston Public Library by then. The library was an architectural wonder. The name of the building was brightly displayed at the front entrance. Underneath were doors and windows made of glass, giving a full view of the brightly lit interior which was filled with books, toys, and educational resources.

Mr. Marbury parked in the street opposite the building. He told Bert to wait in the car and said that he'd be back in ten minutes.

Bert agreed to wait. As he did, he couldn't help but look around the car. This was illegal, he knew that, but he wanted to get a better sense of what Derek's family was like. Maybe snooping around would give him answers. He opened the glove compartment. There were documents of purchase for the car, which was a Toyota. Other that that, there was nothing else that stood out.

◊ ◊ ◊ ◊ ◊ ◊ ◊ ◊ ◊ ◊ ◊ ◊ ◊ ◊ ◊ ◊ ◊

Meanwhile, Mr. Marbury was in the library picking up the books that he reserved. Once he was away from sight, he called Derek, who was on his way home from school.

"There's a detective who showed up at our house, asking about you. Something about a bet you made? I want to know what this whole thing is about! Get home now!" he blasted.

When Mr. Marbury finally exited the library, he was composed in front of Bert. He drove them both back to his house.

◊ ◊ ◊ ◊ ◊ ◊ ◊ ◊ ◊ ◊ ◊ ◊ ◊ ◊ ◊ ◊ ◊

When they arrived, Derek had just pulled his car into the driveway. He got out, his backpack slung around his shoulders, and stared at his father in shock. Bert got out of the car and asked, "Derek?"

"Yeah?" Derek had brown hair, wore a plaid shirt and jeans,

and his hazel eyes that usually shone bright were filled with fear.

"Now that you're here, I'd like to ask you some questions regarding Eric Boden. I understand that you spoke to him last yesterday afternoon," he started.

Derek's eyes widened.

"Let's go inside and talk," Mr. Marbury said, motioning his son to go inside.

They went into the living room, which was lit by tube lights, and contained three couches arranged in a horse shoe formation.

A woman in her early forties with bright red hair, appeared. She wore an orange shirt and loose-fitting brown pants. "Who are you?" she asked, upon seeing another man standing next to her husband. Bert gathered she was his wife.

"This is Detective Bert Tomlin. He has some questions for Derek," Mr. Marbury explained.

"I see. I'm Maggie Marbury. Derek's mother."

"Nice to meet you, ma'am. As I was saying, I wanted to talk to your son about the disappearance of his friend, Eric Boden. I got information from Eric's ex-girlfriend, Samantha Beaumont, that the two boys talked before Eric disappeared. I want to know from Derek what it was that he talked with Eric about. Something about a bet?"

Mrs. Marbury looked confused. "I don't know what you're talking about. Derek didn't have any bet with Eric."

"Well, I'd like to have Derek speak, please," Bert insisted. Mrs. Marbury nodded, then rushed to the kitchen to get some water for the detective. Mr. Marbury, Derek, and Bert sat down on the couches.

"Now, Derek, please." He motioned for the boy to speak.

Derek sighed in frustration. "I guess since she opened her mouth, yes, Eric and I had a bet about a girl we both liked. Eric said I couldn't or wouldn't be able to rather, ask her out. I said I could. He bet $100 on me. I asked Jamie out—that's her name—last week. Eric lost the bet. I let it slide for a week. Then yesterday, I reminded him that since he had lost the bet, he had to pay me the $100. He said that he didn't have the money with him."

"And was this after basketball practice or before?"

"Before. It was right after school that I talked with him. He told me to leave him alone. He seemed troubled."

"Troubled how?"

"Like he was running away from something..."

"Like what?"

"Dunno."

Bert let out a deep breath. He seemed to be getting nowhere, other than knowing about a bet the two boys had. He then remembered about the Chief's words about the hit and run case of Anthony Rugen. He decided to ask if Derek knew the kid. Maybe this could help him get more information.

"This is random, but do you know an Anthony Rugen? Freshman at Everest? He was involved in a hit and run accident."

Derek's eyes widened at this. He looked like he was going to be sick.

Mrs. Marbury came back with a glass of water and handed it to Bert. "Here you go,"

"Oh, thank you," he said, as he lifted his head up and took the glass. She sat down next to her husband. Bert turned to Derek, waiting for a response.

"I know *of* Anthony. He's in my guitar elective, and that's it."

"Are you talking about Anthony Rugen? He was in an accident, you know. So terrible." Mrs. Marbury said while shaking her head. "The principal emailed us about it. It makes me question the safety of the school now."

"Well apparently he was killed outside of school grounds. He was found near downtown." Bert explained.

"*Killed*?!" Derek shot up in alarm. Somehow the word caused some sort of stir in him, other than genuine horror. Was he possibly hiding something?

"Well, yeah. It's an open and shut hit and run case, though. I was wondering if this had any correlation to Eric Boden. Did Anthony know Eric?"

"No." Derek's reply was curt and tense.

"Okay…" Bert didn't want to push the matter further. After all, he had other questions to ask.

"So, going back to Eric, did you see him leave after basketball practice?"

The Marbury boy seemed relieved to be switching topics, which Bert noted, by his sigh of relief.

"No, I didn't. I got changed into my regular clothes and drove home. Got here around 3:50." This was the same time his father brought up earlier, so Derek was speaking the truth.

Derek then hesitated. "I don't think I should say this too, but Eric told me that his parents had found out something about him."

Bert stopped his sip of water. "What did they find out?

"*They knew he didn't want to go to college and planned to drop out."*

CHAPTER 12

As Detective Tomlin sat in front of him, Derek Marbury couldn't help but feel queasy. His heart palpitated like never before.

The police now knew about the bet.

What were they going to do about it? They didn't know anything else. Would this prove that Derek did something to Eric because he didn't get his money? There was no evidence of this, so the police couldn't pin him to anything. But he still was at fault: he didn't tell his parents anything about the bet. After all, what teenager tells their parents about something like that? A bet is a bet, no big deal.

Derek was also used to being in the company of Eric Boden, a self-proclaimed rebel. All the terrible advice and ill-suited actions that Eric asked him to follow was not his own fault. But the police didn't have to know about all that. What Detective Tomlin should know is that the bet was the *only* thing that happened right before Eric disappeared.

No questions asked.

Nothing else happened.

He certainly was not going to share the fact that he and Eric were present when Anthony Rugen took his last breath.

CHAPTER 13

The Bodens were your typical family—the typical Bostonian, suburban family who were just like everyone else.

But there was one thing that made them stand out. They were the most hardworking family anyone had ever seen, always cheerful with smiles on their faces in front of friends and acquaintances. Steve Boden worked at a bank, and his wife Taylor was an architect. They managed to balance work and raising a family, effortlessly. Both of them had grown up in poor conditions, sometimes struggling to have food on the table. They never took their work for granted, whether it was school or extracurriculars. Which is why they ensured that their children—their younger daughter and their older son Eric would turn out to be like them, to be successful in life. They didn't want him to take attending a private school for granted. They went through certain measures to make sure he did well in school—they gave him a phone with only word games, and other learning apps, didn't allow him to date, etc. Less distractions, the better, was their logic.

But this year, they noticed Eric had struggled to maintain his image as an honors student, as well as his motivation to do well in school. They found him to be edgy, distracted, and absent minded at times. Especially when they found out his college results. He had applied to Brown, Dartmouth, Cambridge, NYU, and three UC's. He hadn't received his results from the remaining colleges, except one—Dartmouth. He had gotten accepted into their chemistry program.

It was a month ago, when the Bodens had broken the news

to their son, and showed him the college acceptance letter. They then noticed he had no reaction on his face. He looked like a statue. They found this odd. Shouldn't he be happy? they thought.

Eric had taken the acceptance letter and had read through it quietly, in front of them.

"Oh cool," he had said afterwards.

Oh cool...

Those words lingered in Mrs. Boden's mind that afternoon, as she remembered about the argument that ensued afterwards.

Eric had looked up from the letter and let out a defeated sigh. "Actually, I want to drop out. I don't want to go to Dartmouth," he had said, as if he were refusing to have a certain flavor of ice-cream.

One could only imagine the look of horror on both the parents' faces when they had heard these words.

"What do you mean?" Mr. Boden had asked, wide eyed.

"I want to go to NYU instead. I might drop out during second semester, something like that. You know, I want to get a taste of college life, then start my own business. Yes, that's what I'm going to do."

"What the heck do you mean by that? Do you even know what you're saying? You must be nuts!" Mrs. Boden had cried out. She had snatched the acceptance letter from his hands.

Defiling the family name like this was unacceptable.

She couldn't have helped feeling hatred towards her son at that moment, as she continued to yell, "With talk like that, you don't deserve to hold this in your hands. Do you know how much we had to struggle to get where we are today? Huh? We had to put up with not being able to eat a proper meal, at times. And you're telling us that you want to *drop out*?"

"Yes. I want to drop out."

The anger in Mrs. Boden's voice and Eric's refusal to listen had riled Mr. Boden up even more. He had come close to Eric's face and pointed his finger at him.

"You don't know what you want," he had sneered. "You're still young. That's why you should listen to us. We know what's best for you. You better commit to Dartmouth. Now, if you think of disagreeing or arguing again, you will be kicked out of the house. Understand me, son?"

Eric didn't say anything. He just stood there silently. No emotions had crossed his face. Mrs. Boden had let out loud sobs as she put her face in her hands. Mr. Boden had comforted his wife by embracing her. He then looked up at his son. "Well, what are you standing there for? Get out of my face…or else!"

With that, Eric had gone to his room.

Mrs. Boden's thoughts went back to the present. Where was he now? Was he alright? She felt worse when she remembered that this was the last argument she had with him, regarding his college decision.

CHAPTER 14

Education, which is supposed to be a privileged thing, was no longer taken seriously by the current generation. Eric Boden was a prime example. He had it all—a good school, solid group of friends, teachers who supported him. But no, he just had to use his worst judgement and squander everything away by deciding to drop out. *What more did he want in life? Why did he have to resort to secrets and lying to get what he wanted? And what more was he hiding from everyone?* Bert Tomlin wondered this as he sat inside the Marburys' residence.

"Wait, so you're saying Eric's parents knew about his decision?" he asked, not hiding the look of surprise on his face.

"Eric said he told his parents himself," Derek said.

"What was his parent's reaction? Did Eric tell you?"

"Yeah, he said they were furious at him, and that he better change his mind and accept Dartmouth."

If this were the case, why did Eric's parents lie to Dominic saying that they were proud of their son and that he's a good kid? When in reality, they were hiding their feelings of shame towards him.

"How did Eric react to this?" Bert leaned in forwards, waiting for an answer.

"He was upset, of course. He said his freedom was now gone."

"So that explains why he left his phone in his locker," Bert said.

Derek had a questioning look on his face. "He did?"

"He did. He left his phone that his parents know about. Did he have another phone that he used?"

"No, I never saw it. He always had an iPhone with him."

At this, no one said a word as Bert wrote all this down in his notepad. The tangible silence resonated in the air as Mr. and Mrs. Marbury looked at one another, then at Derek.

All of a sudden, Bert's phone rang loudly, interrupting the temporary stillness.

"Sorry, I have to take this", he said apologetically. He walked over to the front door. "What is it, Dominic?" he asked.

On the other end, he heard Dominic say with excitement, "We got a confession of sorts, from a teacher at Everest! She says she knows what happened to Eric!"

Bert's face lit up. Finally!

He ran to the living room and announced, "We just got news that someone may know where Eric is! I will be right back!" Then he ran out the front door.

Dominic was faced by a woman with short black hair inside the floor of Homicide/Missing Persons. She was leaned next to a desk, looking distraught as ever. People walked in and out, the clamour of voice overlapped over one another. The wait for Bert Tomlin rattled their nerves.

When Bert finally arrived, Dominic told him this was Mrs. Anita Hong, Eric's counselor. Bert acknowledged this fact. "Yes. We just met today."

Mrs. Hong cut to the chase. "I know what happened to Eric. I was too scared to say anything on school grounds. So I came here after school."

"Before you say anything, lets go into a quiet room," Dominic said. "There's too much chatter here."

They three of them entered an interrogation room, similar to the one where they interviewed Michael Owen months ago.

She sat down on the wooden chair and faced the two officers. She rested her hands on the table, clasping them together.

"I know what may have happened to Eric. Eric told me that he wanted to go to NYU. He had no intention of going to Dartmouth. He also said that his parents knew about this decision. I failed to mention this to Mr. Tomlin because I was scared before, like I said. Eric told me that his parents were very disappointed at him."

"When did he tell you that they knew about his decision?" Dominic asked.

"Less than a month ago. During one of his appointments. He was terrified, the poor boy."

"Did you have a follow up appointment with the parents to discuss this with them?"

"I didn't. He requested that I don't talk to them, since they already knew and would probably try to further convince him to go to Dartmouth. He didn't want to push this matter further. He seemed terrified to talk about his parents. I think they —"

She paused, reluctant to say anything further.

"You think his parents might have done something to him? Because they couldn't bear the fact that their son had humiliated them by wanting to drop out of college?" Bert asked.

"I do think so. That's why I called. That's what I think." She seemed relieved to get this out of her mouth, as she got up. She had nothing more to say.

Once Mrs. Hong left, both detectives mused over her words. What she had told them validated what Derek had said to Bert minutes ago.

"Derek Marbury's family seemed clueless but Derek told me about the bet he had with Eric and how Eric never paid him. He also told me that Eric told him that his parents were aware of his decision to go to NYU. He felt like, quote, 'his freedom was gone.' This matches what Mrs. Hong told us, doesn't it? This does prove as strong motive, right?"

Dominic nodded. "This could indeed be a tell-tale sign that his parents might be somehow involved."

"I also asked him about Anthony Rugen, you know, the kid who died, and Derek didn't seem to know if Eric knew him. But Derek is in the same elective as Anthony, so I feel like he might be lying. But it's just a hunch. What about you? What did you find out about Eric? Anything more?"

"Not much. I looked in his file, but he has nothing else that stands out."

To this, Bert made a face. "And that's all you've done until this point?" He couldn't believe that Dominic had been doing nothing, while *he* had been doing most of the work the whole day.

Seeing his face, Dominic scoffed. "Now you know what its like to do the hard work. Welcome to the force, baby!

CHAPTER 15

It was a vibrant scene inside the Pavement Coffee House later that day. The quaint coffee joint was a brick building with glass windows, located about a minute away from Fenway Park. There were an unusual number of people ordering food, or eating and chatting in the various booths and wooden chairs.

As Dominic looked at the menu board that stood above the barista's desk, Bert looked to his right and observed two women drinking tea in plain white cups. Next to them was a man wearing a giant green parka jacket, reading a newspaper. Both looked like they were engrossed in their own worlds.

Bert turned back to the menu. "I guess I will have to go with the veggie sandwich."

"I'll get an apple turnover pie and a milkshake," Dominic said.

"Feeling like eating healthy, huh?" Bert joked.

"Sure do. Jokes aside, this is my cheat meal for the week. After all, it's cold outside. Boston in the winter is a big no for me, but it has its perks—being able to enjoy seasonal treats that are only suitable for cold weather."

Bert couldn't help but agree. After ordering their items, they made their way to a table behind the barista's desk, next to the man with the parka jacket. He cleared his throat as he sat down. "So, I don't know if you heard, but the Chief is out for today."

"Why, what happened?" Dominic asked casually, as he

turned to his apple turnover, and put a huge scoop in his mouth.

"His wife apparently broke her arm, so he's going to visit her in the hospital. He left just moments ago right before we arrived at the station. That's what I heard from a fellow officer."

Dominic's face lifted in concern. "That's terrible. Hope she's alright. I can't help but feel sorry for the Chief. He does so much for the Boston Police department. Never once have I seen him take a break, like how we're doing."

"Makes us seem like we're not taking our jobs as seriously..." Bert said, guilt pricking him.

Dominic nodded sadly. He then looked around the café feeling nostalgic.

"This place brings back so many memories. I used to come here all the time as a kid, and enjoy Oreo shakes. Sadly, they don't have that anymore."

Bert looked up from his sandwich as he surveyed his surroundings. "Certain things in life that used to be can never come back, can they? We are grown men now, so things that happened in our life, we are bound to forget as we get older."

He immediately remembered about his parents and how he wished they were here today, seeing him as a detective. He never would have imagined he'd become the person he was today. He was always very shy as a kid...

"You alright there?" Dominic asked, looking at Bert's morose face.

"I guess I struck a nerve with my thoughts. I was just thinking about my parents and how they would have loved to see me today the way I am."

Dominic smiled. "I'm sure they're proud of you. They're watching from up there, I'm sure."

Bert hadn't realized that he would feel sentimental from being inside a café. Having Dominic Rivers as a partner was not too bad after all. He might be tough, but under that tough exterior, he really did have emotions, like himself.

The two men continued to chat about other things, unrelated to the case. After eating, they set out to Eric Boden's house to talk to his parents about their newfound revelation regarding their son's college decision.

When they arrived at Eric Boden's house, Mr. Boden opened the front door.

"You again?" he asked, not so much irritated, but surprised at their appearance to his house once again.

Dominic pursed his brows in confusion. Shouldn't he be happy to see that the police were back? Maybe they have updates on his son? Maybe he's found? *This is one strange family*, he thought.

"Yes, it's us again. We wanted to ask you about Eric's college decision. We have reason to believe you have been lying to us —"

"Who's there?" asked a voice from inside. It was Mrs. Boden. She stood next to her husband, defensively. She glared at the two men.

"Hello, Mrs. Boden, we were just saying to your husband that we have reason to believe you both have been lying to us," the tough detective repeated.

"What do you mean?" Her voice was sharp like knifes.

"Did you both know that Eric wanted to go to NYU and then drop out, instead of going to Dartmouth?"

He had finally got the question out and could only anticipate their answer.

"What? What do you mean?" they both asked, acting completely clueless.

What liars, Bert thought.

Dominic shook his head. "Don't give us that. You both very well know he never wanted to go to Dartmouth. He even had a girlfriend. Or are you not aware of that, as well?"

Mrs. Boden looked horrified. *If looks could kill*, was written all over her face.

"*Girlfriend*? I'm sorry, but we forbade him from having one."

"Yeah, which is why he went out of his way to have one. Her name is Samantha Beaumont. She knows all about Eric's decision. And so do his friends and counselor. It seems like you both know about his decision too and are pretending not to know anything," Dominic said flatly.

"So? What are you saying? That *we* had something to do with him being gone?"

"Well, we're not saying that outright..." Dominic barely had time to look up before Mrs. Boden lunged at him.

"How dare you?" she screeched.

Bert blocked the way, putting his hands up.

"Careful, Mrs. Boden, you don't want to get arrested," he warned.

Her actions indicated some form of guilt. What that was, he didn't know. Her face now softened. She looked like she was about to cry. Mr. Boden stood close to the detectives with a scowl on his face.

"The fact that you are insinuating that we had something to

do with our son's disappearance, is despicable. I can't imagine why you'd think so," he said.

Mrs. Boden put her hands on her husband's shoulder, in an attempt to prevent him from saying more.

She turned to Dominic.

"We did know, okay? If we had known he'd make such a terrible choice, we never would have encouraged him to be an honors student."

"*Encouraged*? You mean you *pressured* him to study well? He wasn't academically inclined by free will?" Bert asked, incredulously, turning his head back to his partner.

"Well, he definitely had potential. But he wanted to take regular classes and we told him not to. We told him it would look better for colleges."

"And if he didn't want to go to Dartmouth, why'd he put up with what you told him?" Rivers asked.

Mr. Boden was quick to jump in. "Because, the boy is a listener like I said before. He doesn't do things on his own. He always copies everyone else, and is influenced by them. Which is why we had to set him straight. Be studious or become a gone-case. He listened to us before, but now that he's a senior almost done with high school, I guess he started getting what they call *senioritis*."

Mrs. Boden added, "I really want my son found, detectives. I regret all the things we put him through." She seemed shaken up by the questioning, as she put her face in her hands and let out a loud sob. Her husband glared at the detectives.

"Thank you for ruining an already horrible day. I hope you won't be offended if I don't wish you a good day."

After they left, Dominic and Bert both believed that his parents had nothing to do with his disappearance and that someone else was behind it. Dominic could tell when someone was lying, and these people didn't look like they were, based on their emotional responses. Every parent of a missing child is bound to react harshly to an accusation such as the one he insinuated. Maybe it was part of their personality to look like they didn't care, when they really did. In this case, he believed the dislike and the disappointment they had for their son made them react in such a defensive manner.

CHAPTER 16

DAY 3 of ERIC BODEN'S DISAPPEARANCE

That morning at school, she couldn't concentrate on anything.

She had been thinking about Eric. How his disappearance was after all not a real one.

When Eric told her what he planned to do: hide away from everyone and run away somewhere, she thought it was foolish. An angry snarl crossed her face as she thought about the threat, he made to her, afterwards.

Don't tell anyone where I am, or else.

She hadn't planned on doing so—that was until Detective Rivers and Detective Tomlin questioned her and her mother. She was frightened at the prospect of being a suspect in his fake disappearance. She wasn't going to tell them she knew where he was, but given that she had been questioned twice, she might continue to be hounded and maybe arrested. She had to do something about it.

She texted Eric:

I'm going to tell the police where you are

⌂⌂⌂⌂⌂⌂⌂⌂⌂⌂⌂⌂⌂⌂

A few hours later, during her free block, she walked over to the gym. The time was 1:45 pm. She entered the cream-colored building from the side entrance.

She was about to continue walking further inside, when she paused. She swore she heard footsteps behind her. But there was nobody inside the gym. When she slowly turned around, she almost screamed.

Moments later, she slumped to the ground. Whomever she saw ran away in a hurry, leaving her lifeless body lying on the gym floor.

CHAPTER 17

That afternoon, around 2:15 pm, Chief Tonew received a frantic call.

He had just come back to work, after taking a day off. His wife had broken her arm the day before and had to spend the whole day in the hospital. Now, she had a cast and was resting. Chief Tonew told his wife he had to be at work today, as he felt like he wasn't as involved in the case of the missing Boden boy as he should be.

As he made his way to the station, his phone rang.

⌂⌂⌂⌂⌂⌂⌂⌂⌂⌂⌂⌂⌂⌂⌂⌂⌂

Dominic Rivers and Bert Tomlin were in the lobby of the Boston Police Station, discussing what to pursue next, when they saw the Chief running towards them.

"Guys! It's urgent! I got a call from Everest High School. They said they found a body on the gym floor of a female student!"

Both detectives shot their heads up in alarm. *Another student?*

"What?! Who is it?" Bert asked.

"They said her name is Samantha Beaumont."

⌂⌂⌂⌂⌂⌂⌂⌂⌂⌂⌂⌂⌂⌂⌂⌂⌂

Police cars and paramedics swarmed the perimeter of the school. Student were crying and screaming and were told to stand away, by officers.

Dominic and Bert went to the gym, first thing. The paramedics team were placing the body of Samantha onto a wheeled cart. Before they could cover her, Dominic asked one of the EMT specialists to show her body to them and explain what happened.

"She was strangled. See the marks on her neck?"

Both of them saw slanted, block-like indentation marks on the front of her neck, on both sides. Her entire body looked normal though. Her clothes were neat and there looked to be no sign of an assault. "So, she was strangled from the front. When was the body found?" Dominic asked.

"Just a few moments ago. Ask Mr. Garcia. He was the one who found it."

Mr. Garcia, Eric's homeroom teacher, was standing right in front of them, his faced drained of all color.

"Mr. Garcia, I'm so sorry that you had to find this," Dominic said, as sincerely as he could.

"Mind telling us when you found her?" Bert asked.

"I found her about twenty minutes ago. I don't teach at this time, so I was in this area, walking around."

Dominic looked at his watch. It was now 2:35 pm. If Mr. Garcia found the body around twenty minutes ago, around 2:10, she must have died before or at 2:00.

"Why were you just "walking around"?" he asked.

"I just finished talking with the gym teacher, Matt Nendler outside the gym. He's a good friend of mine, so we were chatting for a bit about our families and what not. Then Mr. Nendler left. Then I got a sip of water from the gym water fountain. That's when I saw her body lying there. I thought she was just lying down, but as I got closer, I saw that she looked pale. Her eyes were wide open. I called the police soon afterwards."

"Why was she here in the gym?" Dominic asked.

"I don't know." He shrugged.

"Bert, get Samantha's school schedule for today. Find out why she was at the gym before 2:00, when she should be in class."

The younger detective was on it. Meanwhile Dominic continued questioning Mr. Garcia. *Maybe her death had something to do with Eric's disappearance.* He had to get some answers.

Mr. Garcia explained how he knew of Samantha and that she was Eric's girlfriend.

"Yes, you told Detective Tomlin that, yesterday," Dominic nodded.

"Do you think her death is related to Eric's disappearance?" Mr. Garcia asked.

Dominic seemed pensive. "That's what I've been thinking. There might be a correlation."

As he was about to ask another question, a woman came running into the gym, in such a manner as if she were partaking in the 100 meters race for the Olympics.

"Whoa whoa whoa!" he yelled, restraining the woman back, as she tried to see Samantha's body.

The woman was Samantha's mother—Mrs. Beaumont.

"My baby!" she yelled out.

The paramedics quickly covered the body. But Mrs. Beaumont saw her daughter's face already. She let out a huge sob.

"Who did this?! Who? Who?!" she continued screaming. Students and faculty, including Mr. Garcia kept horrified faces at her outburst.

"Mrs. Beaumont, I understand you are upset, but you need to calm down," Dominic said reassuringly.

His words had no effect on her, as she started to yell even louder. "NO, I WON'T! WHO DID THIS TO HER? WHO?"

"We don't know yet."

"Was it Eric? Was it him?!"

What made her think Eric had something to do with her daughter's death? Unless Samantha had known something...

"We don't know anything yet. Once the autopsy report is released—"

"I DON'T WANT AN AUTOPSY REPORT UNTILL I FIND OUT WHO DID THIS!" She was hysterical at this point, not making much sense. She continued ranting and screaming. Dominic had enough of it. He put his hands up at her.

"Mrs. Beaumont, we are doing the best we can, okay? We will find everything out. You have to remain calm, and step away until you are in a better frame of mind."

She finally calmed down, still hyperventilating, as she stepped away.

A female police officer led her away, as she did her best to console the poor woman.

Dominic having been momentarily distracted by Mrs. Beaumont's outburst, turned to Mr. Garcia. "Sorry about that. So, let me hear you again. You said you saw Samantha after you got water from the water fountain. Then what did you do?"

"I already said, I turned around and saw her body lying there."

"Was there anyone else in the gym?"

"Not that I saw. I saw her lying down, face up. I walked over to her and saw that she looked passed out. I saw the marks on her neck. I knew something had happened and I called the police." His voice was shaky. Dominic believed he was telling the truth. He thanked the teacher and told him to stay aside, for the time being.

Bert then came walking in with Samantha's school schedule.

"On Wednesdays, this is her schedule," He handed Dominic a paper copy. It read:

8:10-9:10 Algebra II

9:10-10:10 U.S History

10:10-10:30 Break (Recess)

10:30-11:30 English III

11:30-12:30 Lunch

12:30-1:30 Collaboration (*HR meeting,* Bert had said)

<u>**1:30-2:15   Free Block**</u>

Bert had underlined the 1:30-2:15 slot—*Free Block*—meaning she didn't have a class that time. It was the perfect opportunity for someone to do this to her. This enraged Dominic. How could someone do this to a high school girl? Who would want her dead? He turned to Bert.

"I want you to check in with the schedules of everyone on Eric's basketball team. Account for their whereabouts from 1:30 to 2:00 today. Especially Derek Marbury. I think I'm onto something."

CHAPTER 18

Since news of the murder broke out, all students were required to stay on campus that afternoon, as it was announced the police were going to interview students.

Dominic and Bert each interviewed students who were on the basketball team with Eric. With Samantha being Eric's ex-girlfriend, they presumed there was a correlation between her death and Eric's disappearance. Bert took on Derek Marbury, Kirk Codd, and Carter Everest, while Dominic interviewed Charlie Davis and Tom Lee.

◊◊◊◊◊◊◊◊◊◊◊◊◊◊◊◊◊

Bert sat in a quiet study room at Everest High's Library. He stared at the morose faces of each of the three students before him. For the most part, he got what he considered to be normal responses from them:

Bert: "Where were you from 1:30-2:15?"

Derek: "I was my Algebra II honors class. We had a test today."

Bert: "Where were you from 1:30-2:15?"

Kirk: "I was in Biology class." (*Kirk was a sophomore*).

Bert: Where were you from 1:30-2:15?"

Carter: "I was in the front office, helping print flyers for our Spring Dance coming up in a month."

⌂⌂⌂⌂⌂⌂⌂⌂⌂⌂⌂⌂⌂⌂⌂⌂⌂

On the other hand, Dominic interviewed Charlie and Tom outside on a bench that faced the gym. Being outside didn't ease the nerves of the two boys who sat next to the intimidating detective, nervously shaking their legs and looking around.

Dominic: "So where were you from 1:30 till about when school ended, at 2:15?"

Charlie: "I was meeting with my counselor, Mrs. Hong. We were talking about college decisions. Ask her, you'll know. Meeting ended right at 2:15."

Dominic excused Charlie, and finished by interviewing Tom Lee, a junior. What he said changed everything:

Dominic: "Where were you from 1:30-2:15?"

Tom: "I don't remember."

Dominic: "What do you mean 'you don't remember'?"

Tom: "I think I was washing my hands in the restroom."

Dominic: "What class did you have then?"

Tom: "I had a free period—"

The detective looked at him with alarm.

Tom: "—but I had nothing to do with her death!"

Dominic: "Where were you exactly, during your free period? In the library? Or outside?"

Tom: "I was walking around outside, on my phone, not doing anything. I did see Samantha go into the gym and that was it."

Dominic: "You *saw* her? Now you're telling me."

Tom: "I saw her go into the gym and then I went to wash my hands."

Dominic didn't believe this kid. "Why would you wash your hands?" he asked.

Tom: "Be—because I saw Samantha and I was afraid she'd see me. I had to dash out of sight. The bathroom was the only place I could think of. I kind of like her, you know." He had a smug look after saying the last sentence.

Dominic: "Did she see you?"

Tom: "No, thank god."

Dominic: "What time would you say, you were "walking around", and then saw her?"

Tom: "1:32 exactly. See, I sent a text to my friend, George. He's a sophomore, by the way. I sent the last text to him at 1:32." He showed his phone screen. "Right after that, I saw Samantha enter the gym. Then I went to wash my hands."

Dominic put the pieces of Tom's testimony together: Samantha entered the gym at 1:32 and died soon after. Her body was found at 2:00, maybe a little before.

This means someone must have confronted her in-between.

CHAPTER 19

Many of the students had left after the interviews with the basketball team were given. Teachers and staff were still on campus, worried out of their wits and trying to keep composure for the students still on campus.

The two detectives lounged out by a squad car that was parked outside the school parking lot, talking about their respective interviews. Dominic suggested that since Tom Lee was the only one who saw Samantha before the time of her death, it would be good to get more information from him.

"How does this explain Eric's disappearance, though?" Bert questioned. "This could be a mass killer or something."

Dominic shook his head. "I don't think so. It has to be someone within the school grounds. Someone who knew her well."

He knew that based on the close time frame of Tom seeing Samantha enter the gym, to the time of her death, someone—a student, who would most likely be lounging about in the gym, someone she knew—might have already been inside and killed Samantha.

"We will find out from the autopsy, right? Maybe that will tell us if she knew the suspect well," Bert said with a light hint of confidence.

Hours later, the autopsy report was revealed.

Usually, the examiners took days to figure out the cause

of death. But due to Mrs. Beaumont's pressuring, or more so threatening the medical examiners and the entire police force to figure out what happened, she would make sure to use her high economic status to get justice for her daughter's death.

The ME, Dr. Aaron Howard, a younger man in his thirties, told the detectives that Samantha Beaumont died from strangulation as her windpipe had been crushed. The circulation of blood that ran from her brain down her arms, was cut off immediately due to the strangulation.

Dominic immediately surmised that it must have been someone Samantha knew well. Someone younger, with strength.

Bert shook his head as they left the ME's building. "What a way to go. She was the one that started us looking into the kids from Eric's basketball team," he said.

"Maybe she knew something and one of those kids bumped her off. Tom Lee, maybe? I should talk with his parents to get more insight on him. And the sooner I do that, the better."

"Mind if I tag along?" Bert asked, with enthusiasm.

"You're asking me?" Dominic raised his brows at his ever willing and persistent partner.

"Sure am," Bert said, with a grim look. "I want to get to the bottom of this as soon as possible."

CHAPTER 20

It was around 5:00 pm. The weather had started to chill and dark clouds hovered over the skies. When Dominic and Bert reached Tom Lee's house, they found that his parents were very much at home. They were short, had brown hair, and wore a huge frown when the two detectives introduced themselves. They let the men inside and sat them down in their family room.

"Our son had nothing to do with that girl's death, okay?" Mrs. Lee said, indignant. She was a petite middle-aged brunette who wore blue jeans, and a red tank top. Mr. Lee, her husband, who looked a little older, wore his work clothes—a black suit and tie.

"Well, I want to know what type of kid Tom is, so that we can determine if he had anything to do with it or not," Dominic said, testily.

"You can talk to him now. He's in his room. Tom! Please come down! The police are here!" she yelled at the top of her lungs.

Tom Lee soon emerged from upstairs. He had a worried look on his face. He looked just like his mother, except for his mop top hair that covered half his forehead. He sat down next to his parents on the couch.

"Tom, I want to inform you that you were one of the last people to see Samantha before she entered the gym and died. I want to know if Samantha had any enemies," Dominic said in a serious tone.

The couple glared at their son, probably wishing that he hadn't see Samantha last.

Tom finally responded. "No, she didn't. I mean, I didn't know her that well. She was Eric's girlfriend, so she was off limits. She was a pleasing person to be around. I only said hi and bye to her during basketball practices. And that's it."

"So, no mention about Eric from her to you?"

"Not really."

"What do you mean "not really"?" Bert asked, testily.

"She might have told everyone this morning that she knew where Eric could have gone."

"Who is *everyone*?"

"Me, Derek, Carter, Kirk."

"So, the people on your basketball team."

"Yeah. She told us before school started, so like around 8:00."

"What exactly did she tell you guys?"

"That she knew Eric didn't want to go home and that he wanted to run away from home."

His parents had a shocked look on their faces.

"Are these the kind of people that go to this school? Kids who want to run away?" asked Mr. Lee, infuriated.

Dominic held one hand up. "Please, Mr. Lee. Your son is saying something."

Tom continued, "She said he was thinking of running away after basketball practice the day he disappeared. He tried to make it sound like a joke, but it wasn't. And he had no way of doing it alone. After all, where would he go? He didn't have a place to stay off the top of *his* head."

As the detectives listened, they realized that Tom had said something striking. "You mean he didn't plan his runaway, alone?" Bert asked.

"No, he didn't. This morning, Samantha said that she was helping Eric plan for it."

"What?" Mr. Lee exclaimed as he stood up. "That's it! Enough questioning my son! Tom, you will not say another word! I think you both should leave."

"No, no, Mr. Lee, I'm afraid that's not possible. I'm going to need to ask you to lower your voice or else we can take this conversation downtown," Dominic said, as if he were a teacher telling his student to stop yelling in class.

Mr. Lee scoffed. "Why are you still questioning my son? I told you to leave."

Dominic and Bert sat in their seats without a word. This angered Mr. Lee further. "You know, I can file a complaint about you refusing to leave my property when asked to. Besides, Tom hasn't done anything."

Dominic rolled his eyes. "File a complaint all you want. When your son goes to jail for withholding information, then let's see where your complaint takes you."

This was a total bogus statement. Tom was not going to go to jail. He just said those words to get Mr. Lee to be quiet.

It worked.

Dominic turned to Tom. "So, Samantha was helping plan his escape?" Dominic asked.

"Sure was," said Tom, who appeared hesitant to say more, as noted by his shaky voice. But he was willing to talk and not create a scene, unlike his father. "She told us not to tell anyone anything. Now she's dead…"

"Where was he running away to?" Bert asked.

"He said he would hitch a ride with his uncle, who's headed up to Maine. Don't know if that's completely true or not."

Dominic raised his brows. "That far? Where do you think he's at now?"

"Probably on the road still."

"Was he going to have Samantha join him?"

"Maybe, I don't know."

"That doesn't explain why she's dead."

"I think Carter might be the person to help you," Tom said bluntly.

"Carter Everest?" Bert asked, looking back at the list of names from his notes.

"But how would he know anything?" Dominic pointed out. "He was in the front office helping print flyers for the spring dance during the time of her death."

"That's not entirely true," Tom said, confidently.

Everyone stiffened in their seats. No one said a word. Tom took this as a cue to continue.

"He might have been helping with the flyers during that time, but he was also texting me, saying that he thought Samantha had something to do with Eric's disappearance."

"And when was this text?" Dominic asked, intrigued.

Tom showed his latest texts, which showed the two had texted at 1:45 pm:

Carter: I know she [Samantha] knows something about Eric that she's not telling us.

Tom: What do you mean?

Carter: I know she's helping him with his "missing boy" plan. He hasn't gone missing. He's very much in town. He's just too lazy to come to school.

Tom: Dude, what? That's crazy! What the heck? That's not true! Tell me more afterschool!

Carter: Can't. Sorry. Don't want to get in trouble.

That was the end of the texts.

The two thanked Mr. and Mrs. Lee and especially Tom for giving them essential information. They were now going to track down Carter Everest to find out why he didn't tell police that he knew Samantha and Eric conspired together to have Eric disappear.

"So Carter knew that Samantha was helping Eric escape and put on a "disappearing" act for everyone? Why would Eric run away in the first place?" Dominic asked, turning to his partner, as they got in their car.

"Maybe for the attention?" Bert suggested.

"If that's the case, then who killed Samantha?"

"Carter, perhaps? Maybe Samantha was blackmailing him not to tell anyone since he knew about Eric's plan?"

"Blackmail? Is that what it comes down to these days?" Dominic put his hand under his chin, as if pensively thinking. "On the other hand, I don't think it's good enough a reason, though. It seems like too weak a motive."

"He's the only lead we have so far," Bert said, with a pout. "We'll have to talk with him and his family in depth to find out if he's guilty or not."

CHAPTER 21

Dominic and Bert approached Carter Everest's house. It was located a little further away from Everest High. Dominic hadn't noticed it before, but he now realized that Carter's last name was the same as the name of his school.

Bert had briefed him on the history of the school and how Carter having the same last name was no coincidence.

"Carter's great-grandfather, a wealthy business man, specializing in the development of educational buildings, built the school in the 1945, and named it after himself. It was his hope that his family would carry his legacy, given the advanced educational merit that students gained upon attending Everest High."

"And now his great-grandson is smearing the man's legacy, by being involved in this scandal." Dominic shook his head.

When they knocked on the door, no one was at home. They called neighbors, asking where the Everest family had gone. Luckily for them, one neighbor said that Carter and his family had gone ice-skating at the local ice rink with friends.

This was strange. Why would they be going out ice-skating when a student at Carter's school was missing and another was dead?

When they arrived at the skating rink, they couldn't find Carter's family, at first. It was hard to locate Carter amongst the crowd of kids and adults. Finally, they spotted him after asking around. Carter wore a parka jacket, and was putting on his skates. A middle-aged blonde-haired woman, wearing a purple sweater and brown pants, was kneeled on the ground, helping with tying his laces. The detectives walked over to them.

"Excuse me, ma'am. Detective Rivers here. This is my partner Detective Tomlin. I have to speak with Carter Everest."

She looked up. "I'm his mother. Who are you?"

"Police, ma'am." Dominic flashed his badge.

"What is this about?" she asked.

⌂⌂⌂⌂⌂⌂⌂⌂⌂⌂⌂⌂⌂⌂⌂⌂⌂⌂

Carter, his mother, and his father, Greg were sitting outside the rink. Dominic couldn't help but feel bad for disrupting the peace. But then again, a student was missing and another was murdered

"I apologize for interrupting your ice-skating time, but this is important. It's the third day that Eric is missing. We now believe that Eric and Samantha Beaumont, Eric's former girlfriend, plotted together to have Eric run away. The thing is, Samantha is now dead."

Mr. and Mrs. Everest seemed to be aware of this. They had heard about the death from Carter, as well as other concerned parents. It was so horrible and tragic. Never would they think that this would happen at their son's school. Their biggest concern was if this was the doing of some crazed maniac.

Dominic reassured them that it most certainly was not. "We actually have a lead that's a little closer to home, rather than it being someone from outside. And that lead is *your son*. What we want to know is how Carter knew about Eric Boden's plan to run away. He texted Tom Lee about it, the time of Samantha's death, this afternoon."

Mr. and Mrs. Everest looked stunned upon hearing this. Carter raised his brows while anxiously fidgeting with his fingers.

"I texted Tom that I knew about their plan. That was it. I didn't do anything to Sam."

"*Sam*? That your nickname for her?"

"Yeah. I liked—"

"You liked her? Like practically every other boy on the basketball team?" Dominic couldn't help but interject.

"Well, yeah, sort of..." He gave his parents an embarrassed look. "But Eric had a better shot at her."

Dominic nodded. "Okay, so what was Eric's plan? How did you find out about it?"

"He told me his plan was to run away. To get away so that people would talk about him. He was bored and tired of his life so far. His parents were pressuring him to go to Dartmouth. On Monday, he even told me to wait for him outside the locker room right after basketball practice so that he could tell me his plan. He told me not to tell anyone about it, or else I would be hurt. Anyways, he said that he was not going home afterwards, as the first step. He was going to walk until he figured out where he wanted to go. I think he originally wanted to reach New York as soon as he could. He told me that Sam knew about this too and that she told him to leave his "fake" phone in the locker before "disappearing"".

"What else was Samantha's role in Eric's disappearing "act"? That seems too small a part to be killed for. Did she blackmail you at all not to tell anyone?"

"Blackmail? No...She was way too nice to resort to blackmail. Why would you suggest that?"

"We have to consider our options, considering she and Eric

both planned his getaway," Bert pointed out. He was still thinking that Carter could be guilty of something.

"I see. She didn't blackmail me or anything. That I can vouch for." He turned to look at his parents for their reaction, but they just kept a dead pan face at him.

"So, what else was her role in Eric's plan, other than just knowing about it?" Dominic asked. "Did she provide a place for him to run away to, or…?"

Carter let out a deep breath. "Sam has a house by the beach. She told Eric to go there."

This was news to the detectives. Bert immediately got out his notepad and started writing what Carter was saying.

"Where is this house?" Dominic asked.

"Salisbury. Near the coast."

"So, he's at her beach house right now."

"Yes," Carter said.

"Why didn't you tell us this before? It would have saved us a lot of trips." Dominic kept a grouchy face but inside he felt relieved to be getting closer to the truth.

Mrs. Everest turned to her son. "Yes, Carter— why didn't you tell us all this before? If not the police, then you could have told *us* where Eric was, if you knew all along."

"I was scared, Carter said, in a small voice. "Eric said he'd threaten to harm me if I told anyone. Nothing will happen to me now that I told you, right?"

Bert reassured him. "No need to be scared of any threats. We will make sure nothing else happens to anyone. Now that we know where Eric is, maybe we can find out who killed Samantha."

Carter gave him a blank stare, not completely sure with his answer. But he let Bert's words linger, as he had other priorities in mind. "Can I skate now?" he asked.

"Sure, go ahead."

As Bert and Dominic left, they overheard Mr. and Mrs. Everest scold Carter loudly.

CHAPTER 22

DAY 4 of ERIC BODEN'S DISAPPEARANCE

Eric was hiding. He knew that people were looking for him. That they were concerned about his wellbeing. That they wanted to know where he was. Regardless of everyone's concern, Eric wasn't going to let anyone know where he was. He had no intention of going back. *Screw them all*, he thought, as he sat in the comfy chair of the house that he was given free access to.

They will never find me here, not anymore. Samantha, especially.

He looked outside the window. He could see a full view of the beach from where he sat.

No one was there.

The only thing he could see were the waves rolling. The sounds of the calm waters soothed his nerves. He looked down at his phone, the one he didn't leave in his locker. There were hundreds of texts and social media posts about him, which he happily read over and over again.

He was blissful. Content.

He took out something from his backpack that lay near the wooden dining table—the admissions letter from Dartmouth. He went to the fire place. He took a match from his pockets and lit a fire. Once the flames became more yellow and bright, he tossed his Dartmouth admissions letter in the glowing flames.

He grinned menacingly.

Now, the last thing he needed to do is take revenge on Derek. It's what he said he'd do.

How could he forget what had happened that day, in his car? And later on, when Derek demanded he give him $100? No one, besides him and Derek knew about what happened with Anthony. They made a promise, after all, to keep things mum. But now he had to do something. He pulled out his phone, about to make a phone call that he knew would change everything.

That's when he heard a knock on the front door.

CHAPTER 23

Dominic Rivers and Bert Tomlin were on their way to Salisbury to Samantha's beach house.

They got the address from Mrs. Beaumont. It would usually take them about an hour to get to Salisbury but given that they made a food stop, it took them a little over that time to reach. During their stop, Bert called for backup from the local Salisbury police.

Salisbury was a pleasant town with lots of beachfront restaurants. The sea smell was intoxicating and added to the fresh, coastal vibe. Bert had come here when he was ten years old. He remembered the memories of the freezing water in the beach every time he'd try to dip his feet in.

As they munched on their lunch, they talked about how draining this case seemed to be compared to previous ones.

"Well, at least for the last case, everyone was in the same neighborhood. This one feels like you're going on a road trip around the whole of Massachusetts." Dominic joked. "Not that I mind, of course, as this town is quite something."

Bert smiled. "True. And at least we're close to getting this case solved. Once we find Eric, everything will be alright."

◊ ◊ ◊ ◊ ◊ ◊ ◊ ◊ ◊ ◊ ◊ ◊ ◊ ◊ ◊ ◊ ◊ ◊ ◊ ◊

Meanwhile, Eric cautiously made his way to the front door. *Who is it?* he wondered. *Is it the police? Have they discovered where I am? Were they here to take me back? No, that shouldn't happen.* He would not go back. Fear pinged his chest as he peered through the small peephole on the door.

To Eric's horror, there was someone standing there with their head bent down. When he observed the person for a few seconds, he then sighed in relief. *It isn't the police.*

It only looked like a young man, but he couldn't be too sure. The person standing outside wore a hooded jacket with the hood up, covering their face. Eric waited for a few seconds before looking into the peephole again. The person was still there.

As Eric was about to draw away from the door, he heard the knocking sound again, making him jump.

Oh my god, why can't they go away?

Maybe he should open the door and tell this person to leave, or else. Yeah, that's what he'd do. He could care less who it was, unless it was someone he knew...

Eric slowly opened the door, just a crack. "Who are you? Go away," he said rudely.

The figure looked up and removed their hood.

Eric gasped.

"How did you—how—wha—?"

By the time he could continue his words, he felt himself land hard on the ground, his face numb from a single sucker punch to his face.

"That's what you get! How about you tell the truth now!" the figure shouted; the vibration of the voice hurt Eric's eardrums like nails on a chalkboard. By the time he could process anything, another punch struck his face.

Everything went black.

CHAPTER 24

By then, the detectives had arrived at Samantha's house. It was a single-story white building with glass windows. Fresh plants surrounded the exterior. There was a stoned pathway that led to the house's entrance, as well as a pathway at the back of the house, which led to the beach. The first thing they did was look around the premises. Dominic knocked on the door. There was no answer.

"Police! Open the door!" he yelled, as he drew forth his gun.

He asked Bert to circle the house.

Dominic kicked open the door with all his might. "Police! Eric, if you are here, come forward!"

There was no answer.

He cautiously looked around the foyer, which had marble floors and a high ceiling. As he walked into the living room, he noticed that the interior looked like something out of an architecture magazine, as there were potted plants, comfy couches, and a rustic fire place. Oil paintings hung on the off-white-colored walls. Everything in general looked expensive and most importantly well maintained, as if no one lived here.

Dominic then made his way through the other rooms. There was a master bedroom, a small study room, and a guest room. There was no one in each of the rooms. When he entered the guest room, he saw a bed and a closet with a sliding door. He was about to open the closet door when he heard a clattering sound and footsteps from a corner of the house. Dominic immediately ran out of the room, and frantically searched for the source of the sound. That's when he saw a dim outline of someone trying to escape. The person was climbing out the window of the living room, headed towards the beach.

Meanwhile, Bert had looked around the sides of the house. There was no sign of Eric. He was about to make his way to the back, towards the beach, when all of a sudden he heard Dominic call out, "He's getting away! He's headed for the beach!"

"On it!" he yelled. He cocked his head forwards, as he saw someone zoom past him. As he chased after them, he noticed them struggling to keep their hood on their head, momentarily pausing, as if trying to find an escape.

Bert finally managed to catch up with the individual. He grabbed onto their hood, causing them to fall backwards. Sand flew in Bert's eyes and mouth. Dominic had caught up to the both of them by then. He pushed his partner aside and removed the hood from the figure.

He saw that it was...

CHAPTER 25

The Eric Boden case had so many parts—missing students, dead students, rebellious students, academic students, the star athletes...the list goes on.

Whatever had happened so far seemed like something out of a movie or TV show or book. Instances of missing or dead students didn't happen in real life, did they? One would think students go to school to study and take their life seriously, but it wasn't the case for these teens at Everest High. Now that the detectives were reaching the end piece of the puzzle, it was a surprise that a student who was close to Eric was part of this case more than they could have imagined. That this wasn't some crazed killer or stranger, but instead someone close to home.

The figure that Bert and Dominic believed to be Eric was not Eric after all.

It was Derek Marbury!

What was he doing here?

"Derek? You?" Dominic asked, as he let go of his grasp.

Bert held on to Derek to prevent him from escaping. Derek tried to wriggle free from Bert's grip but was too weak to match his strength.

"What are you doing here?" Dominic asked again.

"Let me go!"

"No! Not until you tell me what you're doing here. Where's

Eric?"

"I don't— I don't know! I came here to find him!"

"Liar! Tell the truth!" Dominic demanded.

"I don't know where he is! Let me go!"

Bert didn't relent as Dominic continued:

"What did you do to Eric? Tell us! Did you also kill Samantha?"

"No! No, I didn't! I didn't do anything!"

At this point, Eric's parents arrived along with their young daughter. They had been informed by Bert, on the way, that they had a lead and that Eric might be found.

They were instead in shock seeing Derek instead of their son.

"Where is our son?" they demanded, staring at Derek with cold, desperate eyes. Then, turning to the open air, they shouted, "Eric? Eric, where are you? We are here!"

There was no response to their calls.

"I— I don't know where he is!" Derek kept saying.

"Would you rather do this in a dingy room downtown or answer our questions here, with a nice beach view? 'Cause I can do either. I got all the time in the world," Dominic said, putting his hands up.

"No! No! I can explain!"

"Where is Eric, then?"

Derek fidgeted with his sweater, tugging on his. He avoided all eye contact with Dominic or anyone standing in front of him.

"Derek, if you don't answer in the next five seconds, we will have no choice but to arrest you right now and take you downtown. I'm being very nice to you, young man."

Derek's unwillingness to respond was cause for him to be handcuffed. Dominic motioned for Bert to react. As Bert was about to place the handcuffs around his arms, Derek retreated and started resisting.

"Eric is gone!" he cried out, as if in shear desperation.

Bert stopped. "Gone? What do you mean?"

"Eric killed Samantha."

The air that was already tense to begin with, turned stone cold as everyone looked at one another in disbelief. Not soon after, a clamour of voices started over lapping over one another.

"That's a lie! My son didn't do anything!" Mrs. Boden shouted. "You must have done it and are now putting the blame on our son! Eric would never kill anyone!"

Derek turned to her. "I didn't do anything! I swear! I saw Eric myself! He did it!"

"But you were in class at the time, weren't you?" Mr. Boden asked, pursing his brows.

Mrs. Boden had her hands pressed to her temples, hysterically, panting in distress, waiting for Derek's response.

"I partially lied," he began. He let out a deep breath as if he were about to perform a long monologue.

"I was in class around the time she died. To start, I knew Samantha was in trouble. She seemed distressed. So, she told me to meet her at the gym to talk about it. I told my teacher I had to go to the restroom, as a lie. As I was about to make my way to the gym, I saw her go inside. I decided not to talk with her after all, as I didn't want my teacher to be suspicious why

I was gone for so long. I then saw, from the corner of my eyes, a person who was wearing a hoodie. I swear it was Eric. He entered the gym from the back door. I kept watching until he disappeared. I even took a recording of him entering the gym, from my phone. I knew it was him because he was wearing a Stranger Things hoodie..."

This was the sweater that Dominic and Bert found in Eric's locker the first time they were at the school. They never bothered to check the locker again the day after. What seemed strange was, how did Eric enter the gym again without anyone else besides Derek seeing him?

"...Then I didn't see him come out of the gym after a few seconds. I left to go to class. I figured I would talk with Samantha after school."

"Let me see that recording of yours. We will need to enter your phone under evidence," Dominic said, extending his arms out.

Bert loosened his grip on Derek, as he handed it over, reluctantly. They watched the hazy recording of a figure entering the gym from a different angle, different than the angle that Tom Lee saw Samantha entering.

"This leads us to the last question, Derek. What happened to Eric now? Where is he?"

Derek crossed his arms around his chest, pouting.

"Derek, you have to say something," Bert pleaded. "You seem to know a lot regarding Eric's last whereabouts. So tell us the truth. Your lies won't get you anywhere; it won't take you far in life. And you have a long life ahead of you."

"No, I don't! How could I have, or even want a long life ahead of me? Samantha is dead! And it's all because of Eric!"

"If you care so much about her death, I'm sure she would be

at peace knowing that you told the truth."

The boy looked over at Eric's parents, who were silently waiting for his answer. Mr. Boden mouthed to him "Don't you dare say anything else about my son." Derek then shifted his gaze nervously at Dominic and Bert

That slow dreadful feeling of despair started to take over him. "I can't...I won't tell," he insisted. His face suddenly felt warm. His head started spinning. Everyone no longer looked like people, but hazy figures.

"You better tell the truth!" Mr. Boden insisted, not caring about Derek's current state. "My son is innocent!" He started yelling at the air as if his son would appear any minute. "Eric! Come out here and tell the police you didn't do anything!"

Dominic had finally given up. Was Derek going to say something or not? In a commandeering voice, he said, "Did you have anything to do with his disappearance? Answer us, or else. Don't think we are having it easy on you because you're young."

Bert interjected, "You better spit it out. Or else we will have to arrest you." He kept an equally irritated face. Their time and energy more and more wasted waiting for Derek to answer.

"I guess the only thing to do now is arrest you. Bert, get the handcuffs."

Bert obeyed and this time put the handcuffs around Derek's arms.

"Ow! They hurt! I feel dizzy! I think I'm going to faint!" the boy cried out, tugging on his hands trying to pry the metal circles off.

"Resisting won't help. And neither is your act convincing us. You have to tell us—where is Eric and did you have something to do with his disappearance? I'm only asking you this one last time. If you don't give us an answer, we are taking you downtown."

Three seconds later, Dominic grabbed Derek's arms and started pulling him away from the beach. He stopped upon hearing Derek's loud howl.

⌂⌂⌂⌂⌂⌂⌂⌂⌂⌂⌂⌂⌂⌂⌂⌂⌂⌂

Derek Marbury had finally reached his breaking point. He couldn't take it anymore. Yes, he did want to avenge Samantha's death. Samantha, the girl that he secretly liked still cared about Eric Boden. The honors kid, the person that everyone wanted to be like.

Yeah, right. That traitor.

If only people knew who he truly was, no one would like him. And the fact that Eric's parents insisted their son was innocent, proved how messed up people could be. His head pounded, as something ached to burst out of his chest. A horrible thought came to him: The police would arrest him and intimidate him until they wrangled a confession out of him.

He couldn't live like that. Living life in fear.

He had to tell them the truth. The *truth*.

After all, Eric was not worth fearing life over. Especially after what he made him do. All the cover ups, all the lies, had to end. There was something that happened with Eric that no one knew about. Something that he and Eric promised never to tell. But Eric was dead, so he'd never know that the promise was about to be broken.

It was finally time. Anything to stop that pressure, that feeling of doom from overtaking him.

In a powerful voice, he cried out, "Fine! *I did it!*"

CHAPTER 26

Derek Marbury, a basketball standout, was the last person one would think would confess to being involved in a missing persons case. Let alone murder. He had his whole future ahead of him. Now everything was gone in one instant.

"Did what?" Dominic asked, in an attempt to pry more out of him. At this point, he was not surprised at his words, as he knew it would be a matter of time before the pressure got to him.

"I'm responsible for Eric's disappearance."

"Where is he, then?"

"He's dead."

Gasps filled the air.

Mrs. Boden let out a loud, "What?!" followed by a deafening wail as she put her head on her husband's shoulder. Mr. Boden was fighting back tears, as he looked away, in disgust.

Dominic returned back to the confession. "How did he die?"

"I punched him so hard he became unconscious."

"When?"

"A few hours ago. Carter told me that Eric was very much here. I was mad at Eric as I knew he killed Samantha. I have the video as proof, remember?"

"You *killed* him because he killed a girl that you like? That's all? He didn't threaten you or anything, like how did he did to

Carter?"

The boy did a double take. It appeared that he had no clue that Eric had threatened Carter. Carter had never told him this before.

"Yeah, that's right, Eric threatened Carter to not tell anyone that he was running away. Did Eric threaten you in the same manner?"

Derek nodded. "Yeah, Eric threatened me. I found out from Carter that he was running away here, so I had to get my revenge."

"So, he found out you knew where he was and threatened you not to tell anyone—"

"No. It wasn't about that. I only found out about Eric's whereabouts from Carter."

"Then what did he threaten you for?"

"It was right before he went missing. We were having that conversation about the money he owed me. From the bet we had about Jamie Mitchell. Remember?"

Dominic and Bert indicated they knew what he was talking about by nodding their heads. But where was he going with this? they wondered.

"We didn't just talk about the money he owed me," Derek said. "He instead told me he had secrets of mine he'd expose and that he had no intention of giving me the money he owed."

"What secrets?" Bert asked.

"It was one week before Eric's disappearance. It was after basketball practice one day, after school…"

⌂⌂⌂⌂⌂⌂⌂⌂⌂⌂⌂⌂⌂⌂⌂⌂

"Want to help me with something?" Eric had asked Derek as they were shooting a few hoops. They were in the school gym. Basketball practice had just ended.

"What?" Derek asked absently, practicing his dribbling skills before nailing a free throw shot.

"I want to do something."

"Like what?"

Eric looked around, making sure no one was listening. In a hushed voice, he asked, "Have you ever smoked before, you know, cigarettes?" He placed his two fingers near his mouth and gave two small puffs. His basketball was tucked under his left arm. He didn't seem interested in shooting baskets anymore.

"I know what that is, okay? You don't need to dumb it down for me. I've never done it before, though," Derek said, rolling his eyes.

"Well, you're about to now."

"What do you mean?"

"Let's go." Eric started to walk away.

"Where are we going?"

"To 7-Eleven. The one near downtown. Let's go in your car."

"Why are we going there?"

"To buy you know what, what else would we be going there for?"

Derek seemed apprehensive about this. He was not used to doing anything illegal.

The two boys drove for a bit until they finally reached the 7-Eleven. Derek stood outside the entrance, frantically looking around, as if someone he knew would pop out any minute. "I have to be home soon. I have homework to do," he said.

Eric patted his shoulder, reassuring him. "Relax. So do I. Do I care, though? Let's just go in."

Derek and Eric went inside with their backpacks around their backs. They scanned each isle, touching each snack or food item. Finally, Eric went to the alcohol section. He stared at a bottle of wine.

Soon Derek joined him, holding up two snacks—Teddy Grahams and Fruit Roll Ups.

"I'm getting this," he said loudly, putting them in his backpack.

"Shh… okay, fine. See that? "Eric motioned to the wine bottle. "I want it."

"You can't! You're not 21!" Derek whispered.

"So? I have my ways."

Derek froze for a second, then slowly started to walk away. He didn't even want to know what Eric meant.

"Come here!" Eric commanded. "Where are you going? I'm going to grab the bottle really quick and…" With his eyes, he motioned to his backpack. "Mind helping me?"

"You can't!" Derek mouthed. "I won't!"

"Then I guess you don't get your $100."

Derek's face turned to stone. He had been hounding Eric for the money, which he rightfully deserved but still hadn't gotten. "That's not fair," he said.

"Shh… watch me."

Eric asked him to stand away as he put the bottle into his backpack. Then, he asked Derek to grab the pack of cigarettes. Derek knew he had no other choice but to obey. He ran to the front to see if the man who worked at the cashier could them on the CCTV screen that was stationed behind the counter. The man however, was sleeping and his head was on the glass counter.

Derek took this as an opportunity to grab a cigarette packet from the shelf, behind the man. He ran back to the alcohol section where Eric was and dangled the packet in the air.

"See, I did it!" Derek bragged in a hushed whisper. "The man at the front is sleeping. Now is our chance. Let's go,"

Eric looked up in glee. His slightly red cheeks turned a bright red, almost like a tomato.

"Good. Now let me do one last thing and we can go." Eric knew how to turn off the CCTV footage from that hour. While Derek watched the man closely, Eric managed to cut off the cameras that showed the view of the liquor isle and the back counter by pressing a few buttons next to the screen. Eric was good with cameras and technology, so he knew how to work CCTVs. Being good in science really paid off.

When he finished, the two boys raced out the store and into Derek's car. This was where Eric started taking a video on his phone, showing off what they did.

"Here is Derek, who stole this pack of cigs like a boss, and here is the wine to come with it…"

Derek, having tunnel vision at that moment, proudly showed off the cigarette pack and laughed heartily…

◌◌◌◌◌◌◌◌◌◌◌◌◌◌◌◌◌◌

"After that," Derek said, "I drove us both back to Eric's house in a hurry. It was getting dark at this point, so it was hard to see our surroundings. We were driving down State Street. That day, there weren't a lot of cars on the road. That's why I might have been speeding a bit…."

He paused, not knowing if he should go on or not.

"Go on..." urged Dominic.

"All of a sudden, as I turned my wheel to take a right when we heard something scrape the bumper of our car..."

As if remembering the shock of what had happened afterwards, Derek let out a loud sob.

⌂⌂⌂⌂⌂⌂⌂⌂⌂⌂⌂⌂⌂⌂⌂⌂⌂

"What was that?" Eric asked, his eyes widened.

"I—I don't know," Derek said. He was afraid to get out and check.

"Check then."

"No, you do it."

"Fine." Eric, who was not scared of anything, even in high pressure situations, got out of the car and made his way to the front of the car. He then looked down at the ground, stunned.

Derek watched Eric liked a hawk. He was perplexed by his expression. He was curious. What had he hit? An animal, a traffic cone? He was about to open his door, when Eric ran over and blocked the way, by pressing the side of his body into the door.

"NO! DON'T!" he cried out.

Derek was confused. He rolled down his window. "Why? What is it? Did I hit something?"

Eric then got inside the car, looking morose. "Not something. Someone. And he's not moving."

Derek froze. "W—who?" he asked, his voice shaking.

"Anthony Rugen."

Derek's eyes widened, paralyzed with fear. He knew of Anthony. Both were in the same guitar elective during their third block class.

The two boys didn't know what to do.

"Is he dead?" asked Derek.

"Looks like it to me. He's not moving."

"I wanna see the body,"

"No. We should leave now," Eric said, in a monotone voice.

"Why? Shouldn't we move the body somewhere?"

"No. Just leave it here. We don't want to attract attention. Someone might see us."

With a heavy heart, Derek was forced to listen to Eric. He felt terrible.

"This never happened. No one has to know about this…Oh what have I done?!" Derek cried out. Then he started to sob loudly.

Eric shot him a look. "Shut up! Stop crying! Nothing will happen to us. Promise you won't tell anyone and I'll do the same."

"Swear on your life?" Derek asked, with utmost sincerity. He was desperate at this point. Any sort of promise, true or not, made between the both of them was satisfactory enough…

◊ ◊ ◊ ◊ ◊ ◊ ◊ ◊ ◊ ◊ ◊ ◊ ◊ ◊ ◊ ◊

Derek let out a sob as he finished explaining the first part.

"I didn't know later on that Eric would use that same video and what happened to threaten me in not paying the money he owed. The day before he disappeared, after PE, we were in the locker room. I asked Eric for the money…"

◊◊◊◊◊◊◊◊◊◊◊◊◊◊◊◊◊

"I want my 100," Derek demanded, leaning against his locker, which was two rows away from Eric's.

"Nope. That's not happening," Eric said, smugly, as he packed up.

"Why not? I won the bet! I asked her out first!"

"So? There was no written agreement. It doesn't count."

"Are you kidding me? Doesn't count? A bet is a bet. Hand me my 100 or else," Derek said, extending out his hands, as if he expected Eric to plop the money right then and there in his hands.

"Or else what?" Eric sneered. "You'll tell on me? I've got things against you too, so don't mess with me."

"Like what? Huh? Like what?" Derek walked closer to Eric, as if to intimidate him. "Why are you doing this? What did I do to you for you to act so weird now?"

"You don't have to do anything. I just realized something. I don't plan on giving you the 100 after all."

Derek's face turned to confusion. "And why not?"

"Because I was thinking about it. I don't want to land in more trouble than before."

"Then just give me the money and you won't have to be in trouble."

"I don't have the money with me right now. Even if I did, I won't give it to you."

"Why? Look, dude, I don't have time for your games." He paused. "If you don't give me the money, I'll tell everyone the truth."

"What?" This got Eric's attention.

"Yeah, I'll tell everyone about your involvement in you know what!" Derek said triumphantly.

Eric was silent for a second. Then he said: "That video on my phone."

"What?"

"7-Eleven. Ring a bell? The video in the car?"

Derek thought for a second. Then his eyes widened. He remembered. He remembered about the dumb video Eric took of him bragging about the alcohol theft.

"You wouldn't!" he cried out.

"I would! I'll show it to everyone, even the police. I already showed it to people on our basketball team, including Samantha. Wonder what she thinks of you now. She doesn't know anything else yet, regarding the other thing that happened, but for now, she's probably thinking you're the type to steal…"

"What? I'm definitely not! And it was you who talked me into it! It was your idea! You are just as guilty as me! I bet you didn't show the video to anyone. Even if you did, you wouldn't dare show it to the police. Just give me my money and we don't have to worry about all this!" After pausing to catch his breath, Derek added, "And I thought you deleted that video!"

"Nuh-uh," Eric said. "I still have it. You won't be able to get it from me, as I will go to the police beforehand, one of these days. I'll also tell them about what you did afterwards. How you did you know what with YOUR car. You know, maybe I will tell them, actually. And make sure you don't take me down as well. I've had it with your attitude. I thought I would keep quiet about it, but not anymore…"

Derek couldn't take it any longer. He lunged at Eric to swing a punch at him. But he missed. The cackles that Eric made after-

wards haunted him then and there. The humiliation Derek felt was too much to handle.

If something could be done to put an end to this, he'd be in peace. It was all a matter of figuring out how and when...

⌂⌂⌂⌂⌂⌂⌂⌂⌂⌂⌂⌂⌂⌂⌂⌂⌂

"Now you know, he was a manipulative and conniving person who didn't deserve friends," Derek finished.

"So, when you found out he had run away, specifically to this location, you decided to do away with him to hide your crimes of stealing and murder? Make sure he didn't report you to the police?" Bert asked.

Derek didn't say anything. His silence said it all.

As if on perfect timing, Derek's parents arrived to the beach house, having been notified by Eric's parents. They came running towards everyone.

Mr. Marbury turned to the detectives. "What happened? What is our son doing here?" He turned to Derek. "How did you even get here?"

"Your son just confessed to killing Eric Boden and Anthony Rugen," Bert announced.

There was a cry of shock, followed by loud screams mostly from Derek's mother.

"That's impossible. Derek could never! And stealing! That's not what I taught him!" she cried.

"Yeah, I could never!" Derek suddenly said, his voice searing with attitude. He stood with his arms crossed.

Dominic scoffed at this, wondering what caused Derek's sudden denial.

"You just confessed, kid."

"I say many things. There's no proof." Derek continued to act adamant and unrelenting.

Why he decided to deny his confession was beyond Dominic's reasoning. He got the impression Derek was acting tough to impress his parents, to make it look like he was truly innocent. A detective like himself was not going to fall for this act. And he was sure Bert also saw right through it, too.

"I know you do say many things. That's why I had recorded everything you had said to us," the younger detective said, revealing a recorder that was hidden inside his pocket.

Derek stiffened, as tears fell down his face. He was in a state of shock, unable to say anything else at the moment. Now he really looked like he was going to faint.

Mr. Marbury pleaded relentlessly. "Please is there something we can do for him to be let go? I will pay you $100k if you disregard what he said. He's a small boy, he doesn't know what he's talking about!"

Mrs. Marbury echoed her husband's words. "Yes, please let him go! He's a good kid. He didn't mean what he said! He can do community service for the stealing, but please, don't put him in jail!"

Bert glared at both of them. How could they still be defending their son was beyond him.

"He very well knows what he confessed. And I don't take bribes." He then turned to Derek. "Where is Eric's body?"

Derek, feeling the magnitude of his confession and seeing parents practically begging the detectives to excuse him, couldn't take it anymore.

"Inside the closet of the guest bedroom," he responded in-between sobs. The Bodens immediately rushed inside the beach house. Eric's poor younger sister remained outside with Mrs. Marbury, as such a grisly sight was not suitable for a girl her age.

The backup officers and the paramedics team had arrived and helped carry the body out of the house.

Mrs. Boden watched in horror as her son's body was put in a stretcher. She wailed loudly as she leaned onto her husband's shoulders. It was too much for her to bear. Mr. Boden had tears in his eyes, realizing now his life would never be the same.

Eric's body looked like it was involved in a punch-out. The right side of his face was badly bruised. His knuckles were red. Blood poured from the sides of his eyes. The only thing that seemed undisturbed was his Stranger Things jacket, which didn't have any blood on it.

All in all, it was a gruesome death.

Minutes later, Mrs. Beaumont arrived to her beach house. When she was briefed on everything, she slumped to the ground, as the overwhelming feeling of sorrow plagued her heart.

CHAPTER 27

Derek was finally arrested. After that, the detectives retrieved Eric's phone, which had the video of the alcohol theft. When they were back at the station, they stood outside the interrogation room and watched as Derek made his full statements to the interrogation officer.

"Why would Eric kill Samantha?" Bert asked suddenly.

Dominic had thought about this too. He was unsure at first, but now he had an answer.

"Here's what I think. I think Samantha texted Eric saying she was going to tell the police everything about their plan, given that we questioned her and probably frightened her out of her wits. Eric must have returned back to school and finished her off by strangling her.

"Then he went back to the beach house as an attempt to get away for good. Derek, meanwhile, knew that Eric must have killed Samantha, given that video he recorded at school. Then, he found out from Carter that Eric was hiding in Samantha's beach house. Since Eric threatened to expose Derek to the police for the theft and for the killing of Anthony Rugen, in fear of getting caught, he killed Eric."

Bert pursed his brows. "Didn't Derek's parents know that Derek was not at home, and had gone out? Why didn't they call us, reporting their son missing? Even if he had been gone for about an hour or so, him suddenly not being at home must have been a red flag for them, given everything that's happened so far. They should have been aware of where he was and what was doing."

"I think once they discovered he was not in his room, they assumed he went out to a friends house, not necessarily that he went out to kill Eric," Dominic pointed out.

"Hmm...I don't know. I still think they had something to do with Eric's death..."

Dominic said that he shouldn't assume that Derek's parents had anything to do with it. They seemed shaken up, and genuinely clueless to everything that had happened so far. When Bert added that they tried to bribe him, Dominic asked that they be questioned.

Seconds later, Bert called for Derek's parents to come to the police station. They tensed up when he told them they would be questioned further. The distraught parents entered inside another interrogation room where they were questioned for almost an hour. It turned out that they didn't know anything about their son's plan to kill Eric, as Dominic had surmised. All they knew was that their son was aware of Eric's whereabouts.

Mr. Marbury said, "He told us, he may know where Eric is and wanted to find out. I told Derek he wasn't allowed to go out late and if he knew where Eric was, he himself had no choice but to call the police."

His wife added, "Derek finally agreed to what his father said. He went upstairs to his room. So, we thought he was in his room the whole time."

"When did Derek leave the house to reach Salisbury, do you think?" Bert asked.

"I don't know, around 6:00? We watched TV for a bit, then Derek said he had to do some homework," said Mr. Marbury

Bert checked his watch. It was almost 10:00. "Derek must have left for the beach house around 6:30 and reached there in an hour, by bus. From 7:30 to around 8:30, he killed Eric after they had an altercation, etc. He then put the body in the guest closet. Then we arrived."

The two stared at the detective intently. They knew he wasn't done talking.

"So now, your son will be in juvenile prison and have to do community service, since he's not eighteen. When he turns eighteen, he will be tried as a full adult."

Given the look of the parents, Bert couldn't help but feel sorry for them. Sorry that their son had involved himself in the wrong company. At the end of the day, he truly believed their testimony.

The autopsy results for Eric's body were later released. He died from blunt force trauma to the brain, from a hard blow to the head. He died within seconds of being punched.

They did another autopsy on Samantha and they were able to find a fingerprint on the side of her neck, that they hadn't found before.

It matched Eric's right-hand thumbprint.

⌂ ⌂ ⌂ ⌂ ⌂ ⌂ ⌂ ⌂ ⌂ ⌂ ⌂ ⌂ ⌂ ⌂ ⌂ ⌂ ⌂

Mrs. Beaumont moved back to France after selling her regular house and the Salisbury beach house. The Marbury family moved out and went back to London, where Mr. Marbury was originally from. Lastly, everyone on the basketball team quit that year.

With these changes, Everest High was never the same. The sense of community was gone from the students and the parents. The elite status that the original Mr. Everest wanted his school to maintain, had gone down.

Five month later, Derek's sentence was decided. Since he was now eighteen, he was legally tried as an adult. Twenty-five years to life—one count of first-degree murder (for Eric's death) and another count for second-degree murder (for Anthony's death).

Safe to say that Dominic and Bert made sure justice was served. After working hard on this case, it was time for a well-deserved break.

◊◊◊◊◊◊◊◊◊◊◊◊◊◊◊◊◊

A few weeks later, when Dominic was looking over Eric Boden's case file again, Chief Tonew walked up to him. He put his hands on his shoulder, comfortingly.

"Take the whole month off, if needed," he said. "You deserve it."

Dominic sighed as he looked up. "I guess I do need it."

"What will you be doing?"

"I don't know, planning for retirement?"

"Already?"

"Yeah. I'm getting too old for this line of work."

"Time to marry then, huh?" Chief Tonew smirked.

Dominic shot him a look of annoyance. "You sound like Bert."

"Well he's right, you know. Take all the rest you want."

With that, Dominic Rivers walked out of the station and headed towards the travel agency store, where he would be planning his next trip to Cancun.

Bert, on the other hand, was still determined to go up the

ranks, and prove himself worthy as a senior detective, eventually. The Chief praised his work on this case, and told him he would be responsible for working on a new case. Alone.

But eventually he and Dominic would work together again…

THE END

Story 3: In Her Eyes

CHAPTER 1

One year later

The pitter patter of clear rain droplets pounded down onto the ground. It was February, which meant it was either rainy, snowy or cloudy, with occasional sunny days. Today though, the cold air from the rain left a lasting touch on everyone's faces as they hustled through the day.

All except one person.

Bert Tomlin stood on the balcony of his apartment, located in downtown Boston, watching the rain. He wasn't hustling towards any destination. He was stationary. His thoughts were elsewhere. He was debating whether or not to go to Dominic Rivers' retirement party that evening.

Why is that guy retiring? he thought.

Dominic did such a great job on the force. He even taught Bert so many useful things about interrogation, deciphering if a suspect was telling the truth, and the art of being a patient officer. People's emotions got the best of them during all types of cases. But if there was one thing Dominic did impart to him, was that one needed to be composed at all times, without showing emotions that would render them as biased.

He stared down at the text that Dominic had sent him:

You coming or not?

Should he go? He put his hands to his temples and stared

at his phone screen. He was not good at goodbyes and that's what this "party" was going to be. A giant goodbye party filled with slobbery hugs and maybe tears. Although he'd never seen Dominic emotional, let alone, let out tears, it would be interesting to see his demeanor tonight.

He made up his mind. He decided to go.

Previously clad in a white tee and jeans, he changed into a black coat and suit that fit his body perfectly. Recently, he had become more toned, due to vacationing in Miami a month ago. His tan also showed prominently. It made him quite a standout when he returned to dull, dreary Boston. He also decided to bring a small gift: a tie pin with the U.S flag on it that was enclosed in a blue box. He thought this would mean a lot for the retiring detective.

Bert finally arrived at the Boston Police Station, specifically to the Homicide/Missing Persons unit, where the party was held at. The whole floor was decorated with balloons and a bright red sign that read **10 YEARS** hung from the ceiling. Every officer of the force was present, chatting loudly. Food and drinks were stored in one of the small offices. Soft music played in the background.

The man of honor was the first to greet him. "Hey there, man! Glad you came!" He was wearing suit and tie, which that brought out his sharp features.

Bert smiled. "Congratulations on your retirement. Finally, right? I also brought something." He handed over the blue box.

Dominic looked like he was about to cry, to Bert's surprise.

"Oh. Thank you. I didn't expect any gifts, but thank you."

He gave Bert a hug.

"Are you sure you want to retire? It's so soon."

"I'm almost forty. It's soon enough," Dominic chuckled.

Even though this age was pretty young for a cop to retire, Dominic had made enough money and had worked hard to reach his elite status.

Bert pouted. "So? You've left me hanging, here to deal with all the intricacies of police work by myself."

"You got the others to help you."

"Yeah, but it's not the same."

"Even with my barks and orders?"

Bert couldn't help but scoff at this. Finally, the man was admitting to his faults.

"Yeah. I mean that's the annoying part, but at least you know what you're doing."

At that moment, Chief Tonew clapped his hands loudly.

"Everyone, gather around. I want to say something."

Everyone stopped talking and turned their heads, inquisitively listening.

"I want to thank my comrade here, Dominic Rivers and tell you all what a fantastic job he's done for the force. Ten great years. Every case he fought was fought with determination, diligence, and the utmost care for his community. Seeing as he's retiring now, I want to present him with this medal of honor. For him to remember what a force he's been to the BPD and for the city as a whole."

Chief Tonew put a shiny gold metal around Dominic's neck. The heavy metal was hung by a gold band. Dominic looked emotional as he shook hands with everyone. Everyone clapped.

"Speech! Speech!" someone called out.

Dominic made his way to the front, where he paused for a moment. Speeches were not his thing. He was not all about sentiments and tear-jerking words. He decided to make his words succinct.

"I would like to thank my fellow officers for all their work in making this department the best it is. I firstly want to thank Oscar Tonew for how much his mentorship has changed me and help make me the detective I am today. I remember coming here years ago, fresh faced, new and scared. No one had made me feel more welcome than Chief Tonew. He guided me, he told me what to do, and how to do it. He is the real reason I am standing here before you all. I also want to thank Bert Tomlin for his assistance and work on our many cases. I may not have liked him at first, but now I'm definitely going to miss him as my partner. I appreciate the gift, by the way. I also want to thank…" He went on and on thanking everyone else in the police department.

Bert couldn't help but feel a release of emotions inside him. Things were not going to be the same without his friend. He reviewed the last cases that they solved together, from the missing couple, to the missing student. Those were some interesting times. He wondered what was going to become of the Boston Police force without Dominic Rivers. They wouldn't have a tougher detective than him. Now that Dominic has now retired, Bert was eligible to go up in the ranks. Not as senior detective, but as head detective. He was now older, so he definitely knew what harder work as an officer meant.

Suddenly, the music in the background changed from calm and mellow jazz to ear-piercing party music. The Chief had made a playlist of Dominic's favorite throwback songs and made sure they got played. The song DJ Got Us Falling in Love by Usher featuring Pitbull was now on full blast, to Dominic's embarrassment. The tone of the party had changed, as people gathered in the center and started dancing.

"This song is so old!" he shouted, trying to hear himself over the song playing loudly.

"It isn't old! It's catchy," Chief Tonew said, dancing, wildly. He tried to look like John Travolta disco dancing, but he ended up looking the complete opposite. His moves were all over the place. Fellow officers stood in a circle, watching his dance, while letting out a few moves themselves.

At least he was having fun, Dominic thought, laughing. It was strange to see his boss (soon to be ex-boss), someone he valued as a father figure, dancing like he was in college. As the song played, he walked over to Bert who was munching on some Cheetos, standing behind the circle of people. Someone had now changed the song. Lose Yourself by Eminem was now playing.

"Say, Bert, this is some retirement party, eh? I appreciate it a lot. Now, let's talk about you. See that officer and his wife standing in the corner there?"

Confused by his words, Bert turned his gaze towards them. He saw a rookie officer chatting with his wife, happily. He saw as the wife put her hands on her husband's shoulder and laughed at something he was saying. "What about them?" he asked.

"Try to find someone so you can be like those two. Seeing as we're all getting old, don't you think it's time to for you look into settling down? Tonight, everyone's been on *my* back about it, which makes me wonder why they're so curious. How about I ask what *your* plans are, for once?"

Bert shook his head. "I'm not going to marry till I find the right girl. And you're wrong. This night *is* about you. You're retiring after ten years for god's sakes. So naturally everyone is bound to have questions."

"Gee thanks, but you know how much I hate sappy goodbye parties and small talk." Dominic then patted Bert's shoulder. "I also do wish you all the best in life, man."

With a smile Bert said, "Thanks, I really do want to settle down. It's just about finding the perfect match."

When the party ended, Bert offered to give Dominic a ride home. This would be their last ride together before Dominic ventured into the retirement world, where he'd probably retreat to a private coastal town, never to be seen again. That's what all the officers gossiping about him guessed he'd do.

When they arrived at Dominic's house, Bert parked outside and stepped out of the car.

"Congrats partner. I guess this is it," he said, firmly shaking Dominic's hands.

"This is it," Dominic confirmed, realizing that the moment had just hit him like a brick. He was no longer going to be called "Detective Rivers" anymore. Neither would he be working with Bert ever again.

With a wave goodbye, he went inside his house and watched as Bert drove away.

CHAPTER 2

After dropping Dominic off, Bert returned to his house.

Now in his bedroom, he turned on his widescreen TV that was attached to the wall. He flopped down on his bed without changing out of his clothes. Nothing interesting was on besides an old black and white movie and the news. He kept flipping through each channel, hoping something interesting would pop up. He stopped clicking his remote when he got to a channel that was presenting an infomercial—a QVC type of informercial. The two young women on screen were presenting highly prized diamond rings.

All of a sudden, another woman entered the frame. She looked familiar to Bert. She wore a turquoise dress that glittered brightly. She had on gold rings, pearl earrings, and a diamond necklace, as if she had slapped on random pieces of jewelry from her wardrobe. She was seventy-six years old, but her Botox and lip fillers told otherwise. Bert watched in interest as she waved to the two women and introduced herself as the owner and maker of the diamond rings. The other two women gushed (rather over the top) over how beautiful the diamond rings looked.

The woman who had just entered announced in a sultry voice, "Just for $899, these could be yours. Ladies, this would make an excellent adornment for your fingers on any occasion. And gentlemen, this would make the perfect gift for your ladies for that special day." With a little wink, she added, "I'm sure you know what I mean. Buy them now on *www.charlottebrowningjewels.co* or call ***-***-****. That's ***-***-

****. I am your host, Charlotte Browning, and I hope to see you soon on our next segment." After she finished, the commercial break started.

Bert now knew exactly who she was. She was Charlotte Browning—Massachusetts' wealthiest woman. She started a ring business at the tender age of twenty-three, back in 1967. And from there, business picked up. She grossed a net worth of $500,000 that year. Two years later, in 1969, Charlotte married William Browning. She even signed a pre-nuptial agreement with him so that in the case of a divorce, she would keep 90% of the assets. William Browning, obviously going into the marriage for the money, agreed to the prenup, which shocked many people. Now in the case that she died of an untimely death, god forbid, William Browning would get 10% of her assets. Even if they divorced (which they did in 1986), he would still get his 10%. Charlotte Browning after all was a headstrong woman and made changes to things as she seemed fit.

Now, in 2020, she was worth at least 300 million dollars. Many corporations wanted to buy her business in the years following, but she refused, as she wanted to keep the company in her name till the day she died.

Bert switched off the TV and went to sleep.

CHAPTER 3

One month later, *Costa Rica*

Dominic Rivers had found love. He had fallen for another single, American tourist who was traveling to Costa Rica with her brother. Her name was Berenice Daniels. She was a pretty beach blonde, blue-eyed thirty-four-year-old therapist from Pittsburg, Pennsylvania. Enamored by Dominic's persona and the fact he was previously a detective, made him even more desirable. There was always something attractive about handsome cops, in her eyes. The two of them spent time together going out, having drinks, and having late-night cuddles and the works.

It was now Dominic's last night here. He was currently in his hotel room, packing his clothes, with a less stylishly dressed Berenice in front of him. She was wearing only his t-shirt (which was too big for her, so it looked like a dress), as she helped him put pairs of his shorts into his suitcase. He was excited for tomorrow, as that was when he and Berenice would be headed to Pittsburg to visit Berenice's family.

As they continued packing, he got an incoming call from Bert Tomlin. He picked up his phone.

"What's up?" he asked, phone in ear, while holding a t-shirt in his hands, about to fold it.

"Hey, man. How are you doing? How's Costa Rica?" asked

Bert on the other end.

"It's good. I'm having my fair share of fun," Dominic said, smiling at Berenice.

"Well, I'm glad you're having fun there, and all. But I have to tell you something. I have another case assigned to me."

Dominic stopped folding his shirt. "Really? Congratulations!"

"Thanks. But you won't believe who it's on."

"Who?" He was interested. He turned to Berenice, who came over to him and put her arms around his shoulder, expectantly.

"Charlotte Browning. You know the richest woman in Mass state? I just saw her informercial a month ago on TV. And now she's dead! I just got assigned to investigate. It's the biggest case that the department has had to deal with, according to the Chief. So, we are taking this investigation very seriously."

The news of her death struck a chord, not in a personal way, but in a way one would react when a famous celebrity passed away. It was surprising. Dominic knew about her. She appeared in lot of ads and informercials. He also had heard of her husband, who was in the hotel business. What he didn't know was the personal details of their lives.

And did he hear Bert say, *the biggest case?* His curiosity was now piqued.

"How did she die?" he asked, to Berenice's alarm. She showed this by giving him a wide stare, her eyes widening as she did so.

"She was murdered. She was beaten to death. Her jewels, everything is gone."

"That's terrible. I've heard of her. Her husband is William Browning, right? He's made some hefty investments at the bank I go to."

"Yes, William Browning is her husband. I'll be talking with him when he gets back from Chicago."

"Why, he's not living in Massachusetts with Charlotte?"

"They divorced around thirty years ago," Bert chuckled. He had brushed up on their history but Dominic was a little hazy about it. "Anyways, William's coming back, so I will be questioning him then."

"What are you going to ask him? Do you suspect him yet?" Dominic didn't know why he was so interested in this case, but he couldn't help it. The richest woman in Massachusetts had just been murdered! How could he not be perplexed by the fact that she died such a gruesome death? He may be retired, but this didn't stop him from being nosy.

"Whoa, whoa Dominic... don't jump too far ahead here. I just got a hold of this case yesterday. Today I am piecing together all the people possibly involved. However, her husband is the first one on my list."

"Who all are on your list?"

Berenice, getting tired of the conversation, went to the kitchen to grab a glass of wine that was stored in the fridge.

Bert answered, "The husband, for starters, and then Charlotte and Williams' daughter, Felicia Browning-Mott."

"They have a daughter?"

"Yes. She's thirty-six. And a self-made woman herself. I will be meeting her soon."

"Good luck with that," Dominic said, genuinely.

"Thanks."

"See you soon." Dominic hung up. He couldn't stop thinking about the fact that Charlotte Browning was dead. He searched her name on Google. News reports of her death flashed everywhere. Obviously due to her celebrity status, it was already big news...

But someone like Bert, who wasn't so high tier as a detective, got assigned *this* high-profile case?

That was it. He wanted to help out. Maybe not officially, but maybe nose around, assist Bert when he could.

He called his friend back.

"Yeah?" Bert asked.

"Can I help work on the case with you?"

"Right now?"

"Yeah. When I get back from Costa Rica."

"Are you sure?"

"Yep."

"What about all the fun you're having? Surely you don't want to miss out on spending time with her. I thought that's what you wanted in going into retirement." Bert had been informed by Dominic that he was seeing someone in Costa Rica, during one of their catch-up calls.

"I will worry about that. But I want to help with the case."

"But unofficially, though. *You are retired,*" he reminded, even if he had no inclination of refusing Dominic's assistance. "Also, you will have to ask Chief Tonew for approval."

"I guess I will never get used to doing that," Dominic chucked.

After he hung up the phone, he walked over to the kitchen and sat down where Berenice was standing—near one of the high chairs, facing the stove. She handed him a glass then placed her hands on his shoulders. He explained to her about Bert's call regarding Charlotte Browning—and most importantly, how he wanted to help with the case. He also had to break it to her that he was not going to go to Pennsylvania with her after all.

"But why can't you leave it alone? Your friend's got it figured out," she said, a huge frown plastered all over her face. She had her arms crossed as she looked down.

"Because…it seems like an interesting case.

"But you're *retired*, right?"

"I am. But I can still assist on the side. I'm sure he'll make an exception to me helping out. I'm curious to know who committed the murder."

"But you don't have to do that!" she said, agitated.

Dominic sighed. "Can we please talk about something else? Let's enjoy the time we have now," he said, trying to divert her attention. He tried to pull her into an embrace.

"But I don't want to." She drew away. "I want to talk about *us*. Is it that you don't you want to meet my family? Is that why you're using this case as an excuse?"

Dominic had no answer. He knew in his heart that he wasn't serious about this relationship with her as she was, just yet. Going back to Pennsylvania would be rushing things. He was glad Bert called at the right time.

Berenice stared at his face, waiting for a response. His silence said it all. She understood. She took a last sip of her glass. Then she took off Dominic's t-shirt and tossed it at him, angrily.

"What are you doing?" he asked as he watched her hurry into the bedroom, and change back into her regular clothes without answering. When she was properly dressed, she stopped in front of him and shook her head.

"I guess I don't matter at all. It's all about work to you, huh? I should have known you never cared about me! You were just using me this whole time. Well, have fun with your case now! It's all you care about, isn't it?!" she blared, as she slammed the front door of his hotel room with a loud *bang.*

Dominic looked on in shock. He hadn't expected for them to have a blowout like this on the last day of his trip and for her to react the way she did. He thought she would be more understanding. That aside, he knew for a fact that his journey into retirement was going to be pushed back, for just a little bit longer.

CHAPTER 4

Boston, Massachusetts

It was a dull and cloudy day the next morning at 9 am, adding to the somber mood. A heinous crime had just taken place. Bert Tomlin was at the mansion of Charlotte Browning, taking in his surroundings. The sereneness of this Boston suburb was ruined by the swarms of police cars parked on the street and nosy pedestrians standing nearby.

The mansion was indeed something that a millionaire could afford. Firstly, it was situated in the center of the lavish neighborhood. There were a few houses adjacent to hers, that looked just as striking. Charlotte Browning lived in a two-story house, painted blue with multiple windows. A brick staircase led to the entrance. Secondly, the interior décor was just as spectacular. Everything was real. Real plywood, real cherry cabinets in her kitchen, and real limestone tiles in her bathrooms. Her mansion looked like a neatly arranged museum.

Everything was perfect about it.

Except for the fact that Charlotte Browning lay dead on her bed, brutally beaten and pale-faced with no makeup. She wore a silk pink night gown and socks. There were marks all over her face, and dried blood stained her lip. As the paramedics were checking her pulse and examining her body, the forensic experts were swiping the room for prints. Bert took this time to look around the house, specifically her bedroom, which was immaculate and orderly. The golden bedpost frames were intact. Her bedsheets and mattress were untouched, except from the indent that her body made.

After looking around, Bert knew that everything in her room and house were accounted for, except for her jewels, which she kept in a safe in her guest room. They were gone. Another officer on the scene told Bert that there was no sign of forced entry, as no windows or doors were broken. He went over to the team of paramedics who were in the process of plastic bagging Charlotte's body, and asked for more details on the manner of death.

One of the team's specialists, a bright-faced young woman, said, "She was beaten to death with a blunt object. Like a small statue or trophy or something. See the indent marks on her right side of her head. There appears to be an indent mark of an object, specifically the base of an object. Something that stood on a pedestal. It also appears that she died sometime yesterday night. Anytime from 10 pm-12 am. That explains the dry blood on her lip."

"Have we found the object that was used to kill her?"

"I don't think so. Ask one of the experts from forensics. They might have some answers."

Bert shook his head. He went over to Mr. Candance, one of the forensic experts, who was taking fingerprints and searching the room. Clad in a suit, with a badge on his right side, he wore gloves and had a focused look on his wrinkled face.

"Have you guys found any object that has blood on it? Like a small statue or something?" he asked.

"Not yet. We're still looking," Mr. Candance said. He walked away to resume his work.

Bert then went to the other parts of the house. He made his way inside the guest bedroom. There was a gun cabinet propped against the wall. Her safe (where she kept her jewels) was inside the dressing closet on the second shelf. The safe door was now opened and empty.

Bert couldn't help but be suspicious. *Why would she keep her safe in the guest room and not her bedroom? What if a guest of hers took her jewels when she had them over? And where was the object that killed her?*

Just then, he heard a man's voice loud and clear coming from a distance. Bert ran to the front of the house and watched as an elderly man, about seventy-eight years old, rushed inside and starting yelling at officers standing nearby. He wore a brown suit and khaki pants. His white hair was gelled back and slightly dyed a dark brown.

Upon seeing Bert, he reached for the detective's collar roughly and asked, "What happened to her? Huh? Tell me!"

"Whoa, whoa whoa. Cool it, man!" He pushed the man away. After a few seconds, the man relented. Bert realized he looked a bit familiar. It was William Browning, Charlotte's ex-husband!

"I'm William Browning, Charlotte's ex-husband," the man introduced, adjusting his suit. "I heard on the news that she had died. I came back as fast as I could.

"Can I speak with you regarding Charlotte? I'm Detective Bert Tomlin. I will be in charge of this case." He flashed his badge at him.

"Really? What have you found out so far? Can I see her?"

Bert shook his head. "Nothing yet so far. And you can't see her. I don't want you contaminating the crime scene. Wait until her body is brought out of the house. She's still in the bedroom, being examined. Let's step out for a bit, shall we?"

Bert led a teary-eyed William out the front door, where they stood and talked.

"So, where were you yesterday evening? We gather that she died around 10-12 pm, due to the blood on her face. Now mind telling me where you were?"

Michael's eyes widened hearing the word, "blood". "I was in Chicago, having a business meeting with some executives."

"What sort of business do you do?"

"I run a hotel business. I own a hotel called the Esquire Hotel in Chicago. I also live there now. I was meeting with some executives at the hotel until late last night, till around 11 or 12. They can confirm it, by the way. I'll give you their names." William quickly got out his check book and scribbled two or three names the back of a blank check. He handed the paper to Bert.

"Okay, and how long have you been in the hotel business?"

"For nine years."

"When did you divorce Charlotte?" Based on researching her, Bert knew that they had divorced a while ago, back in the '80's. It was all over the news that time and more so now, now that her death had sparked a lot of revisiting of her life. As for what they each got out of the divorce, Charlotte still got 90% of the assets and William was left with 10%. But he still wanted to confirm this from him, himself.

"Back in 1986. When Felicia was only two years old."

"So, you had a daughter together," Bert confirmed.

"We did."

"Where is Felicia now?"

"She lives in LA now. She's something of a YouTuber. Whatever that means."

Bert ignored his comment, but took in the information on her occupation.

"Does she know about her mother's death?"

"Yes. I called her up first thing this morning, after I heard the news. She's on her way here soon. I think her flight's delayed."

"Great. I will need to talk to her as well. I need to know where she was the time of the murder and all…"

"Sure, sure, talk to her. She won't give you anything interesting anyways. She hasn't associated with Charlotte for a while. She wanted to become a new person, have a new identity instead of being associated with her mother's name."

"And she did so by moving to LA and becoming a YouTuber?"

"Yeah. Look it up. Felicia Browning-Mott, on YouTube. She has 5 million subscribers, which means a lot to her apparently."

"That's impressive," Bert said, doing a quick search on his YouTube app.

By the time he could click on one of her videos, the paramedics team had brought Charlotte's body outside, ready to load in the ambulance. William followed them and asked to look at her body for the last time. They allowed this. He stared at her body for a good number of seconds.

"She was beaten badly," Bert suddenly said, as he stood next to William. Not a very smooth way to break the manner of death, but it had to be known in some way. "They still need to do an autopsy, but by just looking at her body, that's what they can conclude."

William bowed his head as if he was praying. He didn't say a word. It seemed like a sign of shock.

As Charlotte's body was taken away, a wave of emotion overcame him. William met Bert's eyes and said, "I want her killer to be found. I don't care how you do it; I want him found and thrown in jail where he belongs."

CHAPTER 5

Around the same time that Bert finished confirming William's alibi by obtaining the names of executives that he had met with the night of Charlotte's murder, thirty-six-year-old Felicia Browning-Mott had arrived in Boston. She was on her way to Charlotte's mansion.

Physically, Felicia was beautiful. She wore a long fur coat and high-heeled brown boots. Her long brown hair was parted in the center, giving her a glamorous look. She had competed in beauty pageants, and was formerly Ms. Massachusetts when she was twenty. She owed all her success to her mother, who had helped establish her modeling career. She moved to LA ten years ago, as she was tired of everyone being friends with her or associating with her just because she was the daughter of a millionaire ring company owner. She wanted to be her own self. Currently, she had a YouTube channel (which showcased her makeup videos, day-in-the-life videos, and fashion hauls). She even met her now boyfriend Alfred Mott at a YouTubers convention five years previously. Just recently, they had broken up. This urged her to start her own online business, to become something on her own. In other words, to prove a point to Alfred. This turned out in her favor as her business became successful, rapidly. She sold T-shirts and jackets with pictures of her channel logo.

But now, she felt anything but glamorous. She had been crying for the past few hours, upon hearing the news of her mother's murder. Her eyes, previously adorned with eyeliner and eye pencil, were now smudged. Her face looked gaunt.

She asked the cab driver to take her to her mother's mansion, hoping the police would still be there so she could ask them questions.

When she arrived, no one was there, to her surprise. After paying the cab driver, she walked around cautiously. She reached for the front door.

As she was about to turn the knob, she heard:

"I wouldn't do that if I were you,"

She jumped, startled by this other voice. She whirled around. "Who are you?" she asked.

She then froze when she got a good look at the man who had just spoken. The man was wearing a suit and tie and his tanned complexion showed off his large biceps. His eyes twinkled. *What a good-looking man,* she thought, staring at him longer than necessary.

Bert Tomlin looked back at the woman who stood in front of him. He looked stunned. She was the most beautiful person he'd ever seen in his life. Her smoky eyes left a sucker punch into his soul. Her outfit made her look more striking and glamorous.

He returned back to reality when he realized she had asked him something. He was about to answer, when she made the first move.

"I'm Felicia Browning-Mott. I'm Charlotte's daughter. You're the police, aren't you?" she asked, noticing his proper attire.

The detective stuttered his words. "Y—Yes. I'm Detective Bert Tomlin." He flashed her his badge. "I'm working on the case of your mother's death. I just talked with your father—"

"Oh, how is he? He must be a mess!" she said, raising the tone of her voice.

He was taken aback by her sudden change in tone. "He was distraught, yes—"

"Can I go inside?" she asked.

"Not yet. It's still a crime scene. I'll ask the cleanup crew to clean everything up, once the autopsy reports come and when I hear back from the forensic team on any additional information."

"Oh." She looked disappointed. "So, I can't see my mother?"

"She's not inside. Paramedics have taken her to the ME's office. They're doing an autopsy on her."

Felicia looked like she was about to cry. She covered her cheeks with her hands, in distress.

"Where's my father? I want to speak to him!"

"He's staying at a hotel, downtown. If you want to meet him, I can arrange that."

"Would you? That would be great," she sniffled.

"In the meantime, why don't I escort you out of here? You seem upset enough as it is."

He gently led her away from the house.

"What are you doing at the mansion, in the first place, if my mother is not here?" she suddenly asked, pulling away from his gentle grasp.

"I just came to investigate some last-minute loose ends."

She looked confused. "What loose ends?"

"I came here to see if there was an alternate way that the killer could have entered the house."

"Which is?"

"I'm not sure yet. I don't know if the killer entered from the front, indicating that your mother knew them and let them in, or if they entered from the back? All I know it's confirmed there was no sign of forced entry."

"You don't know anything, then why are you a cop in the first place?" Her sudden insult put him off.

"Look I don't want you to be upset—"

"Bert!" another voice called out, interrupting their conversation.

The two turned around.

It was Dominic Rivers. He wore a black coat over his unbuttoned dress shirt. The bottoms of his pants were muddied from walking outside on the damp earth.

"Who's he?" Felicia asked.

"Hello, you two. I didn't realize that you were busy, *Bert*."

"I just bumped into Charlotte's daughter," Bert said, motioning at Felicia. "She wanted to see her mother."

"Yes…and I'm sure he told you why that's not possible?" Dominic said, turning to Felicia.

"Who are you?" Felicia repeated, staring at him.

"I'm Dominic Rivers. I am a retired detective, but I've come here to help Detective Tomlin with this case."

"Oh, okay. Well, nice to meet you. I'm Felicia. I'll leave now. I don't want to interfere with your investigation here." She turned to Bert and asked, "Can you take me to my father?"

"Sure," he replied.

Bert signaled Dominic that that he would be right back and would meet him in a few minutes.

Dominic gave an a-okay sign. He didn't seem to mind the alone time.

CHAPTER 6

Bert drove Felicia to the Hyatt Regency Hotel in downtown Boston where she and her father, William were staying. Felicia sat in the front, next to him.

"It's nice to have a detective of the law so kindhearted. You must be like this to everyone I bet," she said with a big smile on her face.

Her anger from before had cooled down. She now had all the time in the world to get a good look at the handsome detective who was sitting next to her. Her inner flirt couldn't be stopped.

"Only to the good ones," he said, smiling back. He liked her already, briefly forgetting that she could be a potential suspect.

Bert had reached the Hyatt Regency Hotel by then.

As Felicia got out of the car, she turned around.

"Will you be investigating this case as the lead detective?" she asked.

"Yes. I am the lead detective of this case."

She smirked. "Well. See you around, I guess." She then went inside the hotel.

Bert let out a breath as he watched her go in. His heart raced like never before. *Whew...what a woman!* he thought.

He drove back to Charlotte's mansion where Dominic was waiting outside.

"What took you so long?" Dominic asked, slightly annoyed

but amused as Bert get out of the car.

"I dropped her off, that's it."

"Really?"

"Yeah… why?" Bert felt the inside of his cheeks turn to that of a soft blood orange.

"Your face is unusually red. What happened?" Dominic teased.

"Nothing," Bert insisted.

"Don't deny it. You like her. I don't blame you. She's beautiful. But I need you to focus."

"You're telling me? I thought you were here only to help out. Not get involved in my personal life."

"Of all the people in the world, you have to like a possible suspect."

Bert rolled his eyes. "Talking about liking someone, how did it go with the woman you had in Costa Rica?"

"She dumped me," Dominic shrugged. "Just because I wanted to come here and assist with this investigation."

"Tsk. But I do see where she is coming from. If you paid more attention to your personal life, you probably wouldn't be standing here right now. You'd instead be trying to work things out with her. But you are hard to get along with—"

"Wow. Thanks a lot. I appreciate your sound advice. At least I don't get distracted when I'm on a case."

Bert crossed his arms. "Don't get sarcastic on me now."

"You may think that, but I'm looking out for you. As for me, I don't think Berenice and I would have worked out."

After saying this, Dominic knew it was a lie. He still thought about her.

"By the way," he added. "I have something to tell you. I just got permission from Tonew to help with this case. All it took was a quick phone call, and he even asked me to stop by the station to see him before the end of the day. So even though I'm retired, I still have full jurisdiction to this case. Also, before I forget, I found something outside while you were "preoccupied.""

He saw Bert's irritated face and added, "Joking...but I really did see something. Come look at the side entrance."

Dominic led him to the side of the mansion. There was a line of flower pots standing in a row, next to the side door.

"What is it?" Bert asked.

Dominic pointed to an area. "This. A heel print."

There it was. A fresh heel print lay in the muddy earth, next to the last flowerpot of the row.

Bert bent down to give it a closer look. "Well would you look at that..."

"Looks like the heel of a high heeled shoe. Looks pretty new too," Dominic observed.

"How do you know?"

"Look at the marks. It looks brand new, like someone stepped in the mud recently. And how do I know it's a high heeled shoe? The outline is more raised and more prominent at the bottom than at the top."

"So, what are you insinuating?"

"I'm saying that this may be the print of a woman's shoe."

"A print of a woman's high heel shoe?" Bert couldn't help but feel a rush of excitement. This could be a big clue!

"Yep. It could be Charlotte's or it could be someone else's. I'd check on this. I can't believe the forensic team missed this."

The younger detective couldn't help but scoff at this. "If they were personally hired by me, I'd have made sure they wouldn't have missed out on such an important detail."

"Well regardless, get them over here now. I want this examined." Dominic had no time for silly excuses. When he had a hunch, he immediately wanted to act on it.

"Yes sir!" Bert said. He suddenly remembered Dominic was retired. "I mean, *sure*," he muttered.

When the forensic team arrived again, they examined the heel print and took a plaster cast of it. One of the members of the team said it was likely that it could be a female's shoe, but they would have to do a thorough analysis.

"Do you think Felicia is involved somehow?" Dominic asked Bert. "She looks like someone likely to wear heels." He gathered this by her outfit that she wore earlier—the fur coat and the high heeled boots

Bert thought about it. He didn't want it to be the case.

"Yeah? You think?" Dominic probed, hearing no response.

"I don't know. She wasn't even near the mansion during the time of the murder, nor was she in the same state. So it couldn't have been her."

"Well, maybe she had an accomplice?"

"We can't assume things. Let's do some digging on Felicia and find out the proper way. Remember what Chief Tonew told us? Never to assume?"

"Yeah, yeah, I remember. And I'm sure you'd like to do all the digging you can."

"Maybe I will." Bert couldn't help but be snarky.

The forensics team finished making a plaster cast of the heel print and left to take it to the lab.

For now, Bert needed the autopsy results and the analysis report of the heel print. Once he had those, he would have what it takes to find a suspect.

Dominic noticed his friend's pensive mood, and said, "Come, let's get something to eat. We haven't eaten anything in hours."

CHAPTER 7

William was having dinner with his daughter at an upscale restaurant in downtown Boston, called the Marliave. Yet, he did not participate in the chatter and banter of the crowd. Instead, he was overtly distraught.

He didn't have a clue who could have killed his ex-wife. He thought about how they had to divorce because she was extremely power hungry and didn't need anyone in her life to help sustain herself. And now he figured that Felicia had taken after her, in that department. He looked at his daughter, who sat in front of him. She was on her phone in her own world, looking like a ghost. Maybe she was doing so to keep her mind off the tension and grief.

"I can't believe mom is dead," Felicia said suddenly.

William looked up. "I know, dear. I know. It's a big shock to me too."

"How could she die? It's impossible. I hope the detectives find out who did this." She shook her head as she looked down.

"I know... If they don't find out who did this, I'll file a wrongful death lawsuit. I'll do anything to make sure your mother gets justice." Tears welled in his eyes. He wondered what was to become of he and Felicia now that they were broiled in this murder case. The fact that Charlotte was dead was too much to bear. He turned his head away from his daughter.

That's when he caught sight of two men sitting in close proximity to them, in the table opposite theirs. He recognized one of the men as the detective he spoke with at Charlotte's mansion. He watched the two men intently.

Felicia soon noticed her father's spaced-out look. She followed his line of vision and was surprised to see Detective Tomlin and Dominic Rivers seated across from them.

What were they doing here? she thought.

"Who's that other man sitting with the detective I talked with today?" William asked, staring at the two men.

"That's Dominic Rivers. He's an ex-detective. He's also helping with the case."

William sighed. "The more help, the better."

Meanwhile, as the two detectives chatted about the Browning case, Bert couldn't help but take in his surroundings at the Marliave restaurant, where they were dining. They decided to eat at an upscale place for once, given their hunger. Many people surrounded their table, chatting, drinking, and enjoying the moment.

As he looked around, his gaze stopped at one table. It was Felicia Browning-Mott and her father, William Browning. He kept glancing over at Felicia, hoping she'd catch his gaze. Finally, she looked up and met his powerful eyes. She then looked down and blushed.

After drinks were ordered, Dominic shifted his eyes to see what Bert was looking at as he perused through his menu.

"Oh, *she's* here as well? What a coincidence," he said aloud.

"Shut up," said Bert, grinning as if he were in high school and was caught secretly looking at his crush.

"Well, she may be a suspect. You never know. Talking about Felicia, that reminds me. Have you also tried contacting relatives or friends of Charlotte? Maybe they know something."

"I haven't yet," Bert said, a look of guilt crossed his face. "But I'll be on it."

Dominic pursed his brows at his friend, as if to express, 'Are you serious?' He then cleared his throat and said loudly, "You know what...enough of the staring and answer my questions. Be serious. Or else, I will take over the case for you."

This made Bert do a double take. "What? You can't do that. I actually have made a list of people to talk to. I still haven't talked with them yet. I'll be doing so soon. Don't worry about it."

"And when will that be? Before or after day dreaming?"

Bert internally controlled his anger. Dominic had no right to dictate him on what or what not to do when it came to this case.

"I have a list. Here— I made it this morning before going to the mansion." Bert tossed over a handwritten list of contacts that he had written on his notepad. Dominic read it over:

Donna Field- Charlotte's best friend

Gracie Anderson- Charlotte's cook

Look into Felicia's dating history

Upon reading the last line, he was confused. "What is this about Felicia's dating history?" he asked.

"I want to see who she's dated in the past. Maybe it's a greedy ex who wants her mother's money."

"Really?" Dominic furrowed his brows. "That's an interesting hypothesis..."

"Yeah, maybe it has relevance for the case."

Dominic thought about it for a second, then cracked a forced smile. "For the first time, you may be right," he said.

Bert didn't know if he was being sarcastic, but given it was Dominic Rivers, he must have been. In Dominic's mind, only he could come up with all the hypotheses, no one else.

"Of course I'm right. I was assigned this case. So I know what I'm talking about." Bert couldn't help but be scornful.

Their conversation was interrupted by the waiter who had their drinks in his hands—the two glasses of cranberry juice. The two of them then ordered their main course. Perhaps it was their hunger that made them more irritable than usual.

After they finished eating and paying for their food, Bert noticed that Felicia and William were still seated at their table. He told Dominic he was going to say hello to them, without waiting for Dominc's response. He walked over to their table and greeted them courteously.

At the sight of Bert, Felicia's expression changed from morose to cheery. As she looked at him, her father, William said that he hoped the killer was found. The three then continued chatting about things that were not related to the case—the Marliave restaurant, food, and places to dine, in general.

Dominic soon approached their table. He said a quick hello to William and Felicia and said he looked forward to getting justice for them.

With that, he said goodbye and walked out of the restaurant. He was now on his way to see Chief Tonew.

When Dominic met up with Chief Tonew, his ex-boss, he knew the man would be happy to see him. As his Chief Tonew gave updates about his life, he mentioned that things were not so good on his end. His wife had been diagnosed with multiple sclerosis recently. As her health was declining, so was his spirits. He was not the same jolly man that Dominic once knew. He was also thinking of retirement too. Not wanting to discuss this further, he asked Dominic about his life.

Dominic was troubled with what Chief Tonew had relayed to him. In turn, he talked about meeting Berenice in Costa Rica, to enjoying retired life. Dominic gave him updates about the Charlotte Browning case. He told him about the heel print, about meeting Felicia and William, and about the list of suspects that Bert compiled.

"That's good. I'm glad he's on top of things and taking initiative. It reminds me of the days you used to be like that," Tonew said, swiveling in his desk chair.

"I'm still like that, nothing's changed," Dominic said, as his eye sparkled with exuberance.

Chief Tonew smiled. After a few moments of silence, he said, "Regarding Bert's list of suspects, I'd keep an eye on Felicia. I've heard that she's a big sensation on YouTube."

"That's true. She's a celebrity personality. I think her behavior strikes me as fishy. She comes running all the way here after hearing of her mother's death, having not spoken to her in a long time. It comes across as suspicious and pretentious."

Chief Tonew nodded. "Have you talked this over with Bert? What does he think?"

"I did tell him that she's considered a suspect just like anyone else. But he's too enamored by her. It's quite something to see—a lovestruck Bert Tomlin who's fallen for a suspect, no less."

Chief Tonew shook his head. "Well ask him to keep his eyes open and not let his emotions get in the way of a murder investigation. He should know better."

Dominic nodded. "Will do, sir. Anyways….," he patted the desk with his hands, "…it's good to see you after so long."

"Glad to see you back, working, even if it's unofficially," the Police Chief said with a smile.

CHAPTER 8

The following morning, Bert was seated comfortably at his desk at the station. He was on his phone taking a social media break, watching some videos on Facebook and Instagram.

As he was in the middle of a video, Dominic walked in.

The first thing he told Bert was that he wanted to talk to the people that were written on Bert's list. This prompted Bert to put his phone away. He felt bad for being distracted by his phone, when all Dominic could think about was this case. He showed the list again.

"Why don't you talk with Charlotte's cook? In the meantime, I will talk with Donna Field, her best friend," he offered.

"Sure, I'll can do that. Got any suspects so far?" Dominic asked curiously.

"Not yet."

"Well, we need to wait for that heel print analysis and the autopsy report."

Bert nodded. "Until then, we can start by talking with these two on the list."

Both of them soon departed from the station.

Police Chief Tonew overheard the conversation between the two of them, as he walked by. He watched as the two men left and sighed. He had been getting so many calls from reporters asking if they had found the killer yet, or even crank calls from attention-seeking individuals, claiming they were the ones who did it. It was a mess.

For this reason, he was grateful that Dominic was helping out.

⌂⌂⌂⌂⌂⌂⌂⌂⌂⌂⌂⌂⌂⌂⌂⌂⌂⌂

Donna Field lived in a two-story house outside of Boston; a bit smaller than Charlotte's but equally as extravagant. She lived in a private neighborhood, next to other million-dollar homes.

Since it was 10 am, she was asleep, according to her maid. Bert decided to wait inside. As he did, he sat by the foyer and stared at the interior décor around him. There were 19th century style portrait paintings on the mahogany walls.

Donna soon emerged wearing a nightgown and her dyed brown hair was rumpled. She was around sixty years old. She didn't do much Botox unlike Charlotte. She came down the stairs asking who he was.

"I'm Detective Bert Tomlin. I'm the lead officer for the murder case of Charlotte Browning. I take it she was your best friend?"

This jilted her nerves. She struggled to find the words to say "Y—yes, she was my best friend. I was devastated when I heard the news."

"I'm sorry for your loss. Tell me, when was the last time you saw her? We know that she died two days ago, sometime in the evening from 10-12 am."

Donna walked closer to him and asked him to follow her to the kitchen and be seated in one of the mini bar stools. She offered him coffee, but he refused, politely. As she made herself a cup, she asked him to repeat his question.

"When did you see Charlotte last, Mrs. Field?"

"Please, call me Donna. My husband died years ago. I refused to be labeled as a Mrs. again." She leaned against the kitchen counter.

"Alright then, Donna. Now could you answer my question?"

She nodded. "I saw her the day before she died. We were having a get together at her place in the evening. It was for a few hours."

"Did she seem like she was in trouble, or do you know if someone was after her?"

"No, not at all. She was loved by all. She was the life of the party. Oh, but she did mention something about her husband, William wanting to visit her."

"Right, as he lives in Chicago. That's where he does his hotel business," Bert said, more to himself.

"Yep. But he apparently called Charlotte a few days before the get together and said he wanted to visit her the next day."

"Why?"

At this time, the coffee was done. Donna poured herself a cup of the hot steaming brown liquid in a cup and inhaled its flavor. She looked up at Bert and said:

"Charlotte told me, that it had something to do with an agreement of her jewels. I heard on the news that they are all gone now! How dreadful!" She sipped on her coffee and sat next to him.

"Yeah. They're gone. Someone took them from her safe."

Donna shook her head. "That's horrible…"

Bert now got down to the important questions about Charlotte and William's relationship after their divorce.

"About William visiting...did he always visit her, since their divorce? And how long have you two been friends? Sorry I forgot to ask."

"Charlotte and I? Since the 90's. We met at a gala party when my husband was still alive and was the CEO of a jewelry company."

"A jewelry company? What's it called?"

"K&I. You might have heard of it?"

"No, but go on."

"As I said, we met at a gala. Charlotte was divorced by then and was already wealthy. We became quick friends after that. She became like a sister to me. And to answer your other question: they didn't always visit each other, it was just to talk about money, that's all. But William didn't have any grudge against her."

Bert took this in. "So what time was your gathering, the day before she died?"

"Like 5:00 pm. Lasted for a few hours."

"So, you got nothing on her except the fact that she mentioned an agreement she made with William. Can you give me more details on it?"

"Sorry, I don't know." Her tone was curt and brief. It sounded as if she were hiding something. Bert studied her face. Perhaps she was lying?

"Are you sure? Anything you can remember on what she said about the agreement, maybe she owed him money, or didn't give him his ten percent...anything?" He tried to probe her into saying more. But she had nothing to say.

He then asked her where she was from 10-12 pm the night that Charlotte was murdered.

"I was at a poker game. My sister lives close by and invited me for a poker game with her friends at her place. It lasted for a while, from 9 pm until 1 am. You know I am not as old as I look. I still got some young blood in me to stay up late. Anyways, I remember that evening exactly, because I was so upset as I lost 300 dollars in one round."

Bert nodded. He believed her when she said this, but he still wanted to get more information on what agreement William and Charlotte had made regarding her jewels.

◊◊◊◊◊◊◊◊◊◊◊◊◊◊◊◊◊

Meanwhile, Dominic had gone to the residence of Gracie Anderson, Charlotte's cook. Gracie lived in a two-room apartment with her five-year-old son. She was a small tired-looking, middle aged woman, originally from Sweden. She had a sweet personality, according to her past employers.

When questioned by Dominic, she was able to tell him just enough. She didn't pay attention to the fact he wasn't an active detective; she just wanted to know who could have killed Charlotte, as Charlotte was very kind to her. She willingly said that she worked almost every day at the mansion; she arrived at 8 am and left at 6 pm to make breakfast, lunch, and dinner for Charlotte. The only day she didn't work was on Sundays.

The day Charlotte died was a Monday, so Gracie was very much at work. She claimed that she left at 6 pm like always and never came back to the mansion. When she got back home from Charlotte's, her son's babysitter told her that her son had fallen sick. Gracie and the babysitter had rushed him to the hospital where he was treated for food poisoning and a mild case of strep, for the rest of the night.

Dominic called the hospital and got confirmation from

them, that Gracie, her son, and the babysitter were indeed there from 6:30 to around midnight.

All in all, Gracie's story checked. She was in the clear.

CHAPTER 9

The clean office reeked of cleaner spray and anti-disinfectant wipes. Bert's office had just been cleaned a few minutes ago by the department's cleaning staff. His office door was wide open as an effort to let out the strong smell of chemicals. Bert sat on his swivel chair, waiting for Dominic to arrive.

As soon as Dominic walked through the door, he pressed his hands to his nose.

"Wow, that is strong. Can we talk outside?"

Bert followed Dominic out the door. They stood a few feet away from his office.

Bert gave an update on his interaction with Donna Field. He concluded that since she was one of the last few people to see Charlotte alive, she was a person of interest.

"I also got the feeling that she was lying in regard to not knowing much about an agreement between Charlotte and William, relating to her jewels. She brought it up in the first place."

Dominic let out a pensive 'hmm'. "Donna definitely a person of interest in that case," he said. "I also checked in with Gracie Anderson, the cook, and her story checks. So, we don't need to worry about her."

All of a sudden, the phone from Bert's office desk rang loudly. He picked up. It was from the medical examiner's office.

The autopsy reports were in.

⌂⌂⌂⌂⌂⌂⌂⌂⌂⌂⌂⌂⌂⌂⌂⌂⌂

The medical examiner's building was a giant three-story building, with dingey autopsy rooms on each floor. Each room contained the strong stench of death. Dominic and Bert, were led into one of the autopsy rooms on the second floor and were forced to cover their mouths with a cloth provided by the ME.

The ME, Dr. John Mieg, was an elderly man who wore glasses and a white oversized coat. He gave Bert a detailed hard copy autopsy report of Charlotte's death. He opened her body from one of the drawers and explained that Charlotte had died from internal bleeding due a blow to the head by a blunt object, from something like a small statue. She was beaten by hand afterwards, but it was the blow to the head that killed her.

"It appears the person came from behind and struck her. That explains the blood trailing out from the back of her head, on one side. This means she didn't see the person who killed her."

Both men gave each other queasy looks. *What a way to go*, they both thought.

"What about the blood on her lips?" Bert asked.

"That was caused by her falling face-first."

"Wait, but how did she end up in her bedroom, lying face up, then?" He was referring to how he first saw her when he got to her bedroom. Everything else had been spotless. Like someone had cleaned up all her blood and disposed of the evidence. Talking about evidence, they still hadn't found the object that was used to knock her out.

"Someone must have done that," the ME said, with utmost confidence.

"Because unless she rose from the dead, there is no way she could have ended up in the bedroom by herself when it's clear that she died on impact from the blow to her head."

Someone had had time to kill her, dispose of the object, steal her jewels, and on top of that, place her on top of the bed face up? Dominic thought. This had to be a two-person job. Or more than one person at least. Just like how he had his doubts when Greta Owen claimed to kill the Trent couple all on her own, he had his doubts now.

They both thanked Dr. Mieg and left the building. Dominic asked Bert for the autopsy report so he could read it in detail. Bert handed it over. After looking through it, Dominic relayed his theory.

"You think this was a two-person job?" Bert asked.

"Yep. Or even a three-person job. We know this wasn't done by one person. That would be too much work."

"Who do you think it is?"

"I think it's Donna Field or Felicia. *Or* both. I don't trust either of them, no offense," Dominic said, glancing at Bert.

"Hmm…" Bert considered this hypothesis, not quite agreeing just yet. He needed proof to convince him.

As the two were about to get in their cars, Bert got a notification from Chief Tonew, saying that Mr. Candance and his forensic team had come up with an analysis for the heel print.

○○○○○○○○○○○○○○○○○

That evening, around 7 pm, Chief Tonew handed Bert the analysis report from Mr. Candance inside his office. Dominic was also in the room. He also noticed the fact that the Chief looked a lot more fatigued than usual. *Must be this case,* he figured. He never bothered to enquire about it, though.

Bert, on the other hand, mulled over Mr. Candance's report.

"They confirmed it's a woman's heel print," the Chief said, aloud.

"What type of shoe is heel print be of? Flats? High heels?" Bert asked.

"Long high heeled boots. They said that the indentation is equivalent to *only* that of an indentation that high heeled boots make. Specifically, *wedge-heeled boots*. They also said that the mark was fresh, and could have only been made the night of Charlotte's death, not any time before or after."

Bert looked at the report. It did say that the heel print could only have been made from 10 pm-11 pm, based on technical terms that he didn't understand. But most importantly, the time frame was determined by the indentation mark that the heel print made to the ground.

"Felicia Browning-Mott wore heeled boots when she came to her mother's mansion the first time I saw her," Dominic interjected, pulling him out of his thoughts.

"Excuse me?" Chief Tonew asked, surprised by this.

"Charlotte's daughter wore high-heeled boots the first time I saw her," Dominic explained. "She was standing at the front of the mansion, talking with Bert. I'd like to know if her boots match the imprint."

The Chief didn't take kindly to Dominic's insinuations without proof. "Well, you can't ask for her boots without a warrant. Besides, you have to figure out who all could be probable suspects before jumping to conclusions."

"That's right." Bert seemed grateful for the Chief's mild reprimand towards Dominic. "Now who else wears boots? Lots of people wear boots in the winter. Maybe it was Charlotte's heel print from the many times she walked around her house,"

"How about Donna? She was at Charlotte's house the day before. Charlotte had hosted a get-together that evening," Dominic said.

Bert thought about this. "Well, it could be the heel print of any of Charlotte's friends. What was the size of the heel print, by the way?"

"Size 7. Woman's," Chief Tonew said. "It's in the report."

Bert quickly scanned the spot in Mr. Candance's report, where the size of the heel print was mentioned. "What size did Charlotte wear?" he then asked.

"Size 9," Dominic said. When Bert looked up in surprise and asked how he knew that, Dominic explained that it was in the autopsy report given by the ME, which Bert must have not seen. "So obviously *this* heel print doesn't match with Charlotte's size. Who else wears a size 7? We have either Donna or Felicia."

"But Felicia was nowhere in this area, or in this state the time of the murder! She was in LA, remember?" Bert spoke louder than necessary.

"There's no need to defend your girlfriend. If she's guilty then she's guilty. But it could be possible she made a last-minute trip here," Chief Tonew said, his tone firm as could be.

"What would the motive be?" Bert turned to Dominic for guidance.

"That's for you to figure out, right? I'm just assisting."

"Gee, thanks. That's helpful," Bert's voice seared with bitterness. "But I still think that Felicia has nothing to do with it."

There was a brief pause.

Dominic then thought of something. If Bert liked Felicia so much that he was convinced she had nothing to do with Charlotte Browning's murder, this could be an opportunity to get some dirt from her in order to *prove* her innocence.

"Why don't you talk with Felicia and *subtly* ask her what her shoe size is?" he offered. "If her size doesn't match the size of the heel print, we'll know she's innocent. I'll question Donna about her shoe size as well."

"Sure. I'd be more than happy to do that." Bert said, as he seemed more than eager to take on the task. "I also have to get information from William regarding his agreement with Charlotte on her jewels."

"Good. In the meantime—" Dominic suddenly looked down at his phone. He had just gotten a text from Berenice apologizing for her anger that last night in Costa Rica, and if he would still be down to call her back? "—I got a call to make. See you later."

He left the station in a hurry, brushing past other officers.

CHAPTER 10

After Dominic left, Bert took this time to check his own phone. He was surprised to see text from someone saying it was Felicia.

How did she get my number? He hadn't given it to her... Maybe she asked around and obtained it from an officer or fellow detective. He didn't bother to question this any further as a feeling of giddiness had built up inside him from just seeing her name. She had asked if he would like to meet up for dinner. She added, **I'm at a place called Island Creek Oyster Bar. Meet me there...if you'd like**.

Island Creek Oyster Bar...he'd never heard of that place before. Nevertheless, per Dominic's words, he wanted to take advantage of the fact she wanted to meet with him. But he couldn't help but wonder what she could possibly want. Did she want to meet up because she was interested in him? Or did she want to discuss the case? If it were both those cases, then it was a big plus for him.

He texted back saying he'd love to meet her. He made sure to look presentable, even in his work attire—his coat and tie. He chewed on a quick stick of gum and combed his hair with his hands. He was still handsome, but it still didn't hurt to put in the extra effort for a beautiful woman.

When Bert arrived, he found that the Island Creek Oyster Bar was not a bar by typical standards. It was more of a restaurant. The "bar" area was only at the front, underneath a huge neon sign that read the name of the place. Behind the bar area, wooden tables and chairs were neatly arranged. As he was in the midst of observing the place, his eyes made their way to Felicia occupying one of the two-seater tables.

He stared at her as he took in her appearance. She sported a smoky-eye look with red lipstick to complement. Her brown hair was let loose, in curls. She wore a red dress with a fur coat on top. She looked like a glamorous 1950's movie star. She looked up and stared at him up and down. Then she waved at him in an excited, yet proper manner. He waved back as he made his way over and sat in the empty seat, facing her.

"Hey, glad you could make it," she said, smiling.

"Yeah, me too." Bert grinned sheepishly.

Felicia was all business. She straightened in her seat as she spoke. "I wanted to meet with you, because I wanted to talk to you about the conversation I had with my father, at the restaurant we were at yesterday."

"Uh-huh…" Bert didn't know where she was going with this.

"He told me that he talked with mother right before she died. Mother wanted to give him some of her jewels."

At this, Bert's face turned serious.

Really?" he asked. It seemed strange, coming from a woman who wanted 90% of her business for herself.

At that moment, a waiter, a short, stout middle-aged man, came to their table and asked what they wanted to drink.

"Water's fine. I'm on duty," he said, more as a reminder to himself.

"I'll get a glass of house wine, white," Felicia said. The waiter nodded and walked away.

"Why did she want to give some of her jewels to William? And when did they talk about this?"

"Like a week before she died. She said that she wanted him to have something of hers in case something happened to her."

"So, it's like she predicted her death almost. 10% would go to William regardless—the jewels and her mansion. Charlotte's friend, Donna also told me that Charlotte mentioned to her an agreement she made with William."

"Yeah, my father said that my mother wanted to give him some of her jewels. That was what the agreement was on. But he refused to have them. Maybe it was because deep down he truly loved her, even after the divorce, and could care less about inheriting her valuables. Anyways, she insisted he have some of them. So he had to relent. He still has them with him as he had taken them back to Chicago."

Bert couldn't help but wonder, why William would refuse to take Charlotte's jewels in the first place? Was that all that was discussed between them? What about the fact that he would get her mansion and jewels, in the event that she dies?

"Did William tell you anything else, besides the fact Charlotte gave some of her jewels to him? Something about him wanting *all* of her jewels?" Bert's mind was everywhere now. He wanted to know the details of their agreement, hoping it would give him new insight or a breakthrough…

"He didn't say. That's all he told me." Felicia was unsure. Someone was lying. Either William was concealing information or Felicia was.

The waiter returned asking them what they wanted to eat. They both realized they hadn't even touched the menu. "Give us a few seconds, will you?" Bert said to him.

When he left, Bert looking through the menu options, thoroughly. He happened to look down at his feet. Then he looked at Felicia's shoes and noticed she was wearing red heels. Then he remembered. The heel print! He should ask about her shoe size to see if her shoe size matched the heel print found at Charlotte's house.

"I love your shoes; they look beautiful on you," he said out of the blue.

Felicia looked down and waved her feet forward. "Oh. Thank you. They are Dior. Got them for free for doing a YouTube video on their products."

"They look like they fit nicely…" Bert started, trying not to sound weird, or overtly obvious.

"Thanks…?" Her tone of voice instantly rose, in doubt.

He then cleared his throat and looked at his menu again. He decided to get the clam chowder soup. Felicia said she'd get the same.

Bert went back to what he was asking her originally. The agreement. The shoes would have to be addressed later.

"So, do you think that Charlotte might have made a similar agreement with her friends? Wanting to give her jewels to them too?"

"No. She was greedy as hell. She loved her jewels. I was surprised she would give some to father."

"She didn't give any of them to you? Or offer to do so?"

"Nope."

"Why? Were you two not close?"

"Not really. I wanted to break free from her legacy and name which is why I barely saw her. Only like once a year, I'd see her."

Bert leaned his head on his right hand, as they rested on top of the table.

"Explain your last name to me. Who is Mott? Your ex-husband?"

Felicia's face suddenly turned glum. "Uh, no…he's my ex-boyfriend. But we broke up a week ago. We had been together for five years. I even legally attached his name to the end of mine because I thought we were serious enough that he would propose. But he didn't."

"Is he in LA now? What does he do?"

"He's a content creator. And yes, he's in LA."

Bert cringed. *Content creator?* He thought about how job titles popular within youth culture these days had such obscure names. Content creator, influencer, Instagram model, you name it. As a cop in his thirties now, he couldn't relate. He really was starting to feel like his friend, Dominic. Older and out of touch with reality.

With that, he said, "I'm guessing you mean YouTuber, right? What's his name?"

She eyed him suspiciously. "Why are you asking? Is he a suspect?"

He didn't answer her question directly. "I'm just curious. Trying to cover all my bases."

"Well since you want to know, his name is Alfred Mott."

"Is he rich?"

Felicia hit the table with slight force. "Why are you asking all these questions about him? I don't want to talk about him. He's a disgraceful loser who doesn't know about commitment."

Bert leaned back defensively. "I'm sorry that I offended you, I just wanted to know—"

"Well, he's not rich-rich," she cut him off. "He's making over minimum wage, if that's your definition of rich. YouTubers like us don't get paid a lot unless we have like 10 million subscribers. He has like 2 million."

Bert didn't say anything to this. Regardless of how many subscribers Alfred Mott had, he didn't want her to become suspicious of all his questions. Besides, he needed to know her shoe size.

"Okay, you know what? Let's talk about something else. Like…your dress. It makes you look even more beautiful."

Her facial expression changed from a frown to a dazzling smile. "Thank you. But you already complimented me earlier… too many compliments get to me. I can only assume it's because you want something from me. Is there something else you wanted to ask me?"

"Yes…" Bert turned red. "You know me too well. I might as well ask it. What's your shoe size?"

She stared at him in surprise. "What? Why?"

"I'm looking for a gift for my niece. It's her birthday in a week," he hesitated.

She looked at him with surprise. "Oh? And how old is she turning?"

"18." Another lie.

"Well, the ones I'm wearing, are a 7. But they're $1,000. Not sure if you want to gift her something that expensive. I have some extra pairs of shoes if you want to take one for her."

Bert froze. *7? The same size as the heel print found outside Charlotte's mansion!* He did his best to hide his shock.

"Well, my niece is a size 8. So, I don't think your shoes would work for her. But thank you for offering. I'll probably just gift her something else."

To his surprise, she seemed satisfied with this.

The food had now arrived. It smelled delicious. They ate, content. As they ate, Bert talked about himself more, about how he had become a detective. He even interjected a few anecdotes about working with Dominic Rivers and how tough he found it at first. He then asked Felicia about her passions and what made her want to become a YouTuber.

"Well, you know, you have to have a pleasing personality, not just a nice face. And I really like wearing different clothes and showing them off to the world, because fashion is my number one interest. Plus, as a YouTuber, you get paid," she said, matter-of-factly. She then smiled. "So...those are the reasons why I wanted to become one in the first place."

"Well, you definitely have a pleasing personality, that's for sure. And you look stunning as always," he said, reaching over and kissing her hand. She blushed.

At the end of their dinner, Bert paid for their meals. The night was a success. The food was hearty and he had obtained everything he wanted from Felicia.

He offered to drop her back at her hotel, which she agreed to. As he drove her back, he couldn't stop thinking about the fact that *her* shoe size matched the size of the heel print. But there are so many women who have a size 7 shoe size. It could be anyone. Still...

When they reached the entrance of her hotel, he parked curbside. He got out of the car, leaned against it, and watched her walk inside. She took a few steps. Then she paused and turned around.

"Are you just going to stand there?" she asked in surprise, seeing that he was not following her inside.

Bert gulped as he stood still as a statue. "Well, yeah..."

"Sure about that? Sure, you don't wanna... you know, come up?" she asked in a sly manner, as she walked towards the front door.

Bert stood there. He didn't follow her. No matter how tempted he was, he had to remain professional. He was a detective, first.

She turned back and noticed he wasn't following her. She understood. He was a gentleman after all.

She walked back towards him, her face within inches of his. In a quiet voice she said to him, "This was the best date I've had." She pulled him closer as she kissed him on the lips, oblivious of everyone around her. She pulled away and went inside.

A *date*, huh? He now knew that his feelings were not one-sided. Bert stared at her with dreamy looking eyes as he watched her reach the elevator. He was in a daze… love struck, as they call it.

With a wide grin plastered on his face like a giddy school boy, he got inside his car.

CHAPTER 11

The following day, Dominic joined Bert for breakfast, at the Pavement Coffee House, their now usual spot for grabbing a quick meal or unwinding after work. They didn't talk about the Browning case, but instead spoke about Dominic's call to Berenice.

"So, did you two patch up?" Bert asked, sipping on his coffee.

"Sort of. She wanted to apologize for being mad at me. She said she didn't mean any of it and that she couldn't stop thinking about me."

"And...?" Bert could only assume there was more.

"She's coming to Massachusetts. She's arriving this afternoon. She wants me to pick her up."

"Wow. You must be more than excited. When do I get to meet her?"

"Soon..." Dominic said, with a smile.

Bert ordered a breakfast burrito and Dominic got a sandwich.

"So," Dominic started. "What did you do after I left the station yesterday?" he asked.

"Felicia texted me right after you left. I then had dinner with her." The manner in which he said this was very nonchalant, but still did nothing to hide his flushed cheeks.

"Really? That's taking it a step forward. What'd you do afterwards?"

Bert was bashful. "Nothing...I just dropped her back to her hotel."

"Really?" Dominic said, leaning in. "That sounds hard to believe coming from you, Mr. Casanova."

Bert chuckled. "I found out something, though. Her shoe size is also a 7."

Dominic raised his brows. "Wow. That's some news alright. What else did you find out?"

"Felicia told me that Charlotte gave William some of her jewels a week before she died. It's as if she predicted her death somehow."

Dominic was surprised. "But that doesn't sound like Charlotte."

"I know. A greedy millionaire who intended to keep 90% of the business to herself? Who would think that she'd give some of her jewels to her ex-husband? She didn't even think of giving some jewels to her own daughter!"

"That says something. Where are the jewels that she gave William?" Dominic asked.

"With him in Chicago."

"And the rest of them are gone..."

Dominic was quiet for a few seconds.

Bert noticed his pensive mood and gave him a confused look. "What are you thinking now?"

"Nothing. I just want more information on the motive behind Charlotte giving some of her jewels to William. I know you said you'd talk with William about it, but now I want to be there when you question him."

Bert nodded. "Sounds good. Now, what about Donna? We

know from Felicia that during the last meeting Charlotte had with William, she gave him some of her jewels. But what if they discussed other things as well? Donna, of all people, was aware of this meeting. It could be a possibility that Donna may be hiding something. After all, Charlotte could have told her something, afterwards."

The former detective agreed with Bert's hunches.

Bert went on, "And lastly, what about her shoe size? You said you'd talk with her right, Dominic?"

Dominic nodded. "How about we both go to Donna's house, then we'll talk to William? I do think Donna might give us necessary information if we act cool, and loosen up around her."

Bert smiled. He was grateful for Dominic's assistance. There were so many loopholes and people involved in this high profile case that it took over his mind.

But if there was one thing that preoccupied his mind the most, it would be his date with Felicia from the night before…

◊◊◊◊◊◊◊◊◊◊◊◊◊◊◊◊◊

Cars were parked outside Donna Field's house. Decorative balloons of different colors adorned the front door. Men and women, young and old, were chatting, standing around the perimeter of the house. They were formally dressed in suits, and dresses. Light jazz music played aloud. The saxophone music and the elevator tunes made for a very serene, cozy aura. It seemed like some sort of party was happening inside.

Dominic asked a man standing out front what was happening and where he could find Donna. The man told him this was a gathering to honor Charlotte's memory and that Donna was in the kitchen.

Dominic and Bert pushed past people where he finally met Donna. To his surprise, she was not crying or emotional. Instead, she was laughing with some women standing beside her. She even dressed a bit festive, as she had on a flowy white floral dress.

"Hey, I know you!" she exclaimed, once she saw Bert. She most likely recognized him from his last visit to her house. She then focused her gaze on Dominic. "And who's this? Is this a new date you got for me, honey?"

Her friends giggled at this, which the Dominic considered tactless. This was not the occasion to be making jokes, considered her best friend just died.

"No, he's not. Actually, we came here to ask you some questions about Charlotte." Bert's voice was serious.

Donna's face fell. "Like what? I'm busy."

"I can tell," he said bluntly, as he looked around.

Dominic extended his hand. "I'm Dominic Rivers. I am Detective Tomlin's friend. Former detective." He showed his badge to Donna and her wide-eyed friends. He still carried it with him, just in case. At this, her friends immediately left the kitchen.

Donna was left, standing alone.

Finally, with a nervous grin, she asked, "So...what do you want to know?"

CHAPTER 12

The three of them went upstairs to her bedroom where it was much quieter. The bedroom was lavish and spacious. Her dressers were a dark cherry color. Her queen-sized bed had silk sheets and a maroon comforter. Gold toss pillows were spread on top. Next to her bed was a dressing table with two small chairs.

Dominic and Bert sat down in each chair, while Donna remained standing by the door.

"I take it you are hosting a gathering to honor Charlotte's memory?" Dominic asked.

"Yeah, it's sort of a memorial service for Charlotte. As her friends, we wanted to come together and celebrate her life."

I can see all the celebrating of her life going on, Bert thought, as he remembered the women downstairs laughing with Donna.

"As much as we would love to stay longer to offer our condolences, we came here to ask some questions. Bert, go ahead," Dominic said, motioning with his hands.

Bert cleared his throat. "We first want to tell you what a lovely room you have. You must have lots of clothes in here."

"Oh yes. They are all in my dresser!" she chirped as she walked over to it. Inside, her clothes were neatly stacked in multiple piles. Next to the dresser was a pink shoe shelf with at least three rows of shoes, also neatly arranged.

"You must really value your shoes to put them on display like that in such an orderly manner," Bert observed.

"They are my prized possessions," she said in a show-off manner, purposely keeping the dresser open so that they could stare at the shoes for a longer time.

"Excuse me, did you say *prized possessions*?" Dominic asked, taking note of her words.

"Why yes. For example, I would never give them to anyone, I would never step out in the rain with them, unless I wear a plastic covering over them, etc. Call me silly, but these babies are my life."

"So, you'd never walk around in, say, mud, with of these shoes?" Dominic asked. He wanted to make sure of her words.

"No way! Are you kidding? I would never. I only wear these for special occasions. And the casual ones, like the ones I'm wearing." She showed off her tennis shoes by lifting her feet slightly. "I make sure to wash them before they go on the shelf."

"Your shoes don't look that big, what's your shoe size? It must be a hassle trying to fit everything in a dresser, along with your clothes. And I mean with the nice shoes you have…"

"I'm a very lady-like woman's 6. Any size more than that… it's almost like you aren't a woman anymore," she scoffed, as if her mindset was something that everyone should agree with. She bent down and picked up one of her shoes—a white, 2-inch platform heeled shoe, and turned it around. The size at the back read 6. "See?" She put the shoe back and closed the dresser door.

The two men gave each other a look. *Her shoe size* didn't *match the size of the print found at Charlotte's.*

"When you visited Charlotte, would you usually walk around outside of her house, in her backyard, for example? Specifically, the day before she died when you were at her house, did you walk around outside?" Dominic asked. He couldn't be too careful, even if her shoe size didn't match the heel print. His question caused Donna to put her hands up, indicating she had a lot to say.

"Now look, I'd never walk outside her house. Even on the day before she died. Not with the fancy shoes I had on. I wore the white shoes I just showed you. We were all inside playing cards. Gambling... I should say. In the rare case of rain, I made sure to park my car right next to the entrance, so that I can get in and out quickly. But Charlotte never usually invited me when it was raining, due to my habit of making sure my shoes were clean. They're my next *prized possession*, after my husband. But tell me, why are you asking all these questions? Did you find something?"

Bert stood up and walked closer to her. "Well, we are trying to close all loops. Just in case. We can't disclose much yet, as everything's ongoing."

"Will you let me know if you do find something?"

"That's going to be hard, but you'll know everything once this case is solved," Bert said, as he gave her a little wink.

"Thank you very much Donna, I appreciate it," replied Dominic, as he followed Bert out the door.

"Let me know if you need any more help, I'm happy to assist!" she called out.

In the car, Bert voiced aloud that he didn't consider Donna a serious suspect anymore, given that her shoe size was 6, so it didn't match the heel print, and she was conscientious about her shoes being clean at all times. She was also at a poker game with her sister the time of the murder.

"What's her sister's name?" Dominic asked.

"I don't know. I guess I'll ask—"

By the time Bert could finish his sentence, Dominic was out of the car, with Bert following suite. That's when he remembered—right, they forgot to ask Donna about her sister, and about William and Charlotte's meeting. Good thing Dominic remembered.

Donna had come down to the living room, making her rounds to everyone. That's when she saw Dominic walk up to her.

"You again? I didn't know you liked me so much," she said, with cynicism in her voice.

"I have a question to ask you. What's your sister's name?" he asked, bluntly.

"Mina," she replied instantly, taken aback.

"Mina what?"

"Mina Field."

"How old is she?" By then Bert walked over to them. He saw her stunned expression.

"She's 57. Why?"

"We want to get her information, so she can confirm you were playing poker with her the night of Charlotte's death."

"She's right here, if you want to speak with her."

Donna then left their side briefly, to find her sister.

Seconds later, Donna appeared again, this time with another woman at her side. "This is Mina," Donna announced.

Mina looked like a carbon copy of Donna, even though the two were not twins. She had the same dyed brown hair and the same outfit too. The only difference is that she had bright yellow acrylic nails, noticeable by anyone standing a foot away, whereas Donna didn't have any nail polish on. And Donna looked younger.

Bert separately led Donna to a different part of the house, and asked her about Charlotte and William's meeting, while Dominic questioned Mina about the poker game.

"Yes. Donna was playing poker with my friends and I. It lasted till around 1 am," Mina said, staring at her hands.

"And did any of you leave your house during this time?"

"No. Around 9, I left the game to go to the front door, to grab our Chinese takeout food."

"And that was it?"

"Yep."

"I see. What were the names of your friends?"

Mina gave a list of names to him, which he wrote down.

"Alright. Thank you very much," Bert cast her his trademark smile and bid her goodbye.

She watched him leave, an evil look plastered on her face.

◊ ◊ ◊ ◊ ◊ ◊ ◊ ◊ ◊ ◊ ◊ ◊ ◊ ◊ ◊ ◊ ◊

Meanwhile Donna, in fear of seeing her sister being questioned, revealed what she knew:

"I lied earlier when I said I didn't know anything else. Charlotte did tell me more. She said told me that she informed William, a week ago, that she drafted a new "will" of sorts. Originally, it had been that William would obtain her mansion and her jewels after her death. Now in her newly drafted will, she'd give him *only* ten percent of her jewels and not her mansion. As for her mansion, it would go to an auction. Why she did this, I don't know. Perhaps it was due to greed. She also said that she would give him a week to make up his mind. She even gave him some jewelry as a peace offering, to tempt him. And if he didn't agree to her deal, she would take back the jewels she originally offered him. So he had to take them. But now she's dead. And the rest of the jewels are gone. Who must have done this? Put the pieces together."

So, William was not getting Charlotte's mansion after all. This proves as a strong motive for him to kill her, Bert figured.

"Thanks Donna, you're a doll," he said, shaking her hands.

"Anytime…" Donna gritted her teeth.

CHAPTER 13

It was now around four o'clock.

On their way back from Donna's house, Dominic told Bert that Mina Field had confirmed they all played poker the night of Charlotte's death and that no one had left the house at any time. Bert also revealed that Charlotte's actual conversation with William was regarding her newly drafted will and the fact that she gave him some of her jewels to tempt him into agreeing with will's terms.

Dominic then said, "William is definitely our big suspect here. He had the motive and means to get rid of Charlotte because everything, except ten percent of the jewels, would not be going to him. This leads me to my next question: who made the heel print, then?"

"Maybe an accomplice?"

"Someone like Felicia, perhaps? As I said earlier? My bet's still on her." Dominic was adamant.

Bert didn't want to come to terms with the fact that Felicia was still a suspect. Instead, he diplomatically said, "Let's talk with William first."

◊◊◊◊◊◊◊◊◊◊◊◊◊◊◊◊◊

William Browning was staying at the Hyatt like his daughter Felicia, but was on a different floor. He was on the fourth floor; she was on the second. He was still in Massachusetts, because he refused to leave the state until he found out who murdered Charlotte.

He was seated on the queen-sized bed that faced the door. He pondered about what he was going to do next, having finished a late lunch consisting of egg rolls and noodles. That's when he heard a knock on his door. He jumped. *Who could it be?* he thought.

He opened the door, his heart raced as if he was expecting someone to attack him.

To his relief, it was only Felicia. She looked worried.

"What is it?" he asked, as she rushed inside and closed the door behind her.

"I just got a call from someone just now! I came here as fast as I could! Some person asked me if I had *"her jewels"*. I said I didn't know what they were talking about!"

"Who? Who called you?"

"I don't know…it was an unfamiliar voice."

"Man or woman?"

"A woman. I don't know how she got my number!" Felicia pressed her hands against her forehead and rubbed her temples, as if she had a bad headache. She paced near the door, anxiously.

In a calm manner, William led Felicia to sit on the bed so she could compose herself. He then stood by the door, just in case.

"Who do you think it was?" he asked, once he saw she had calmed down.

"One of mother's friends? A crank caller? I don't know!"

"Why would they ask for the jewels? How do you know it was your mother's they were talking about?"

"Because she later added, "Do not tell William about my call to you, or else you'll be sorry.""

"So, this person must know I have the jewels that Charlotte gave me. But if they are trying to frame you or me, there's nothing to expose. I'm getting ten percent of all her jewels, after all. Once they are found, that is."

"Well at least be happy you're getting her jewels. I've got nothing! Nothing from her! That doesn't mean I have her jewels or have killed her or—"

"Whoa, Felicia, calm down! You didn't kill her, you didn't do anything. This woman wants to redirect the police's attention towards you, so you can doubt yourself and land in trouble by saying the wrong things. All this instead of having them find the real killer."

"But what if *this* woman is the killer?" Felicia insisted.

"I don't know…I have no clue as to who she could be—"

He was suddenly interrupted by loud knocking at the door. At this, Felicia jumped in fright. Both of them were afraid to say a word.

A few seconds later, there were a couple more knocks on the door. Felicia looked up in fear. William bravely made his way to the door and opened it slightly.

To his relief, it was Dominic Rivers and Bert Tomlin.

"Oh, you two. I got scared for a moment."

"Sorry about that. I tend to knock really loud sometimes," Dominic said, apologetically.

"What are you here for?" William asked suspiciously.

"We wanted to ask you some questions. Are you alone?"

"No, my daughter is here with me."

Bert's heart skipped a beat, hearing this.

William opened the door wide and let the men in. "Come in. You actually came at the right time. My daughter just got a phone call that is related to the case. Felicia, care to explain?"

Felicia looked at Dominic and stopped her gaze at Bert. "I received a call from a woman asking me 'Do I have her jewels?'. Meaning my mother's jewels, I gathered. The reason I know is because she told me not to tell my father about this call, or else I'd be sorry. But I told my father, anyways. I think that this person knows about the jewels and maybe the new clause that mother enacted. The point is, we think that this woman may be the killer because of her questions on the jewels."

Bert nodded. "We know about the new clause. We know that Charlotte gave William a small peace offering (meaning some of her jewels) if he agreed to her new clause in her will. So, William, mind telling us if you truly agreed to this new clause or not. Or if you just took the jewels she gave you, but secretly harbored resentment towards her." The way he said this last line rather accusatory.

Felicia pursed her brows and gave the detective a look. "What makes you think my father has anything to do with my mother's death? And what does he have to do with the person who made the phone call?"

"I don't know if he has anything to do with the phone call, but in terms of the new clause in Charlotte's will, there's motive. William not getting the house after all, is motive for wanting her out of the picture—"

"Now wait a minute," William cut in. "Sure, at first I didn't agree to her stupid new clause. It would have been nice to have acquired her mansion. But in the end, I actually agreed to her terms because of the fact that I'm rich on my own. I have my hotel business..." He paused. Then he glared at Bert. "I also don't need to resort to stealing or murder to get her jewels."

"Then where are the remaining jewels she had? The ones that are missing?" Bert asked. He then turned his gaze toward Felicia, but saw that she was avoiding eye contact with him.

Felicia, in the meantime, couldn't sit down any longer. She stood up and paced around. She couldn't stand the fact that Bert had been outrightly accusing her father this whole time.

"The killer must be having it! Not my father!" she suddenly cried out in an agitated manner. "The woman who called me must be having it! She wants the jewels that Father has in Chicago!"

Dominic put his hands up, in an attempt to interrupt her outburst, "Okay, why don't we all calm down? We can trace the call for you right now, as this may determine if that woman is in fact guilty, instead of William."

"Fine." She sat back down on the bed.

Since the number was stored in Felicia's phone, it was easy to track it down. Bert first tried calling the number from the hotel phone. When he didn't hear anyone pick up, he then called in his co-worker to get a trace on the number. After a few more excruciating moments of waiting for an answer, they finally got one. The call was made from a phone at a Hyatt Regency hotel.

But not just any Hyatt…

It came from the Hyatt that Felicia and William were staying at!

CHAPTER 14

Someone had made that call to Felicia from the very hotel they were at, right now?! At this newfound information, Felicia and William raised their brows in shock.

"This woman must have followed me, and made the call!" Felicia exclaimed. "That can be the only explanation!"

Bert didn't have a definite answer as to who it could have been. He then whispered into Dominic's ears, "And to think we thought culprit was William. Turns out we were wrong." He had assumed all this time that William was the one responsible, but given the news of this mystery woman who had called from the very same hotel they all were at, made things more suspicious. The question was, who was this woman who was interested in Charlotte's jewels?

"But why would this woman call Felicia?" Dominic whispered back, interrupting his thoughts. "Shouldn't she know that William has some of the jewels and should therefore question him about it?"

It was a plausible question. If this woman knew that William had some of Charlotte's jewels, why not ask him about the rest of them? It just didn't make sense why this woman would call Felicia instead.

"Well, maybe the killer wanted to throw us off. That's what I was telling Felicia before you guys came in," William said, overhearing Dominic's question.

The two men looked up. "Throw us off, how?" Bert asked, confused.

Before William could answer, the hotel phone rang, causing everyone to jump. Dominic motioned for him to pick up the receiver, slowly.

"Hello?" William asked.

"Hi, I'm Dan, the concierge from the lobby. I want to let you know that room service will be a little delayed today, due to staff shortage."

"Oh, okay, thanks for letting me know." William hung up, with a sigh of relief.

"Who was it?" Felicia asked, concerned.

"The concierge, calling about room service delays for today."

"Oh." She let out a sigh of relief.

An idea suddenly sparked in Dominic's mind, from the concierge's call. He announced that he and Bert would ask one of the concierges at the front desk if they'd seen anyone make a call from the hotel's payphone. After they left, Felicia couldn't help but be apprehensive. Thoughts dwelled in her mind. Could this woman really try to pin the theft and the murder of her mother on her? Who was she in the first place? She relayed her concern to William.

"I don't know, I really don't...," he said, looking at the door.

The two men made their way downstairs to the lobby. There were crowds of people either walking in and out of the hotel, or making a reservation. Dominic noticed a payphone next to the elevator. He kept this in mind as they approached one available concierge, a young blond man in his late twenties whose name tag read James.

After explaining the whole case and asking if he saw anyone suspicious in the lobby, James said that he hadn't seen anyone using the lobby's payphone, due to dealing with customer service tasks.

"Do you have another payphone in this hotel? One that's open for the public to use?" Bert asked.

"Yes, we do have another payphone. It's in a room on the third floor. But it's not for public use. It's only for the cleaning staff."

Dominic's eyes widened at this. *This meant that the woman who called Felicia must have somehow entered that room on the third floor to use the payphone there, given that no one had used the lobby's payphone.*

"Where exactly on the third floor is this payphone?" he asked.

"It's in the staff loading room, you know, where they store pillows and sheets? It's near the exit sign. Here, I'll show you."

James took them to the third floor and led them to the staff loading room filled with pillows, towels and bins of laundry.

There was a regular phone attached to the wall, next to the bins. One had to pay fifty cents after they used the phone. On the ground, directly below the phone, was a clear plastic jug filled with coins. The lid of the jug read, PAY 50 CENTS OR YOU CAN'T USE THE PHONE.

James then pointed to the ceiling. There was a black security camera, staring down at them. "See? There's a camera up there. If you don't pay, you will get caught eventually."

"Can we view your security footage? Maybe we can get a sense as to who used this phone in the last hour," Dominic asked.

James obliged.

The three of them entered the back room where a rotund security officer sat facing three TV screens. As Dominic and Bert stood by the door, James talked with the security officer who motioned for them to come forward.

Once the tape from the past hour was pulled up, everyone watched as a woman wearing a white shawl that covered most of her face, walked up to the phone and used it briefly. The time stamp of the video read *3:55 pm,* which was right before Dominic and Bert had entered William's room. No one else was seen using the payphone after her. The person who had used it before the woman at 3:55 pm was another woman, who had used it at 1:50 pm. This woman was in the clear, as it would have been too long of a time gap for Felicia to have just reported the call to William.

"Get a close up of the woman at 3:55 pm, will you?" Dominic asked the security officer. "I would like a screen shot printed, so we can identify her."

"Sure...anything to help a murder investigation," he said in a disgruntled tone, as one would have if they were to sit in the same spot for a long time.

While the guard made the screen shot, Dominic then had to figure out *who* the woman in question called. If it was Felicia she called, then they had hit a jackpot.

"Is there a way for the hotel to figure what number the woman called?" he asked, looking back at James.

"I'm sorry, but the hotel doesn't allow anyone to do that. It's a matter of privacy," the young man said.

"Really? Even in a murder investigation?" Bert asked, raising his eyebrows.

James shrugged, unfazed. "Yep. Sorry. Hotel policy."

"But what if someone was confessing a murder on the other end of that phone line?"

"That's never happened before. Even if it has, we make sure to value our customer's safety and the reputation of the hotel, by not disclosing details like that to the public."

"That's absurd. You guys should update your policy on that," Dominic reprimanded, taken aback by the hotel's lack of accommodation.

To this, James didn't say anything. He probably didn't want to get into more trouble by arguing. Dominic turned to the security guard and said in a hasty manner, "Please get me that screen shot ASAP."

Dominic and Bert went back to William's room where they showed the screenshot of the woman who was in the hotel's cleaning staff loading room at the same time that Felicia received that call. Dominic added that the hotel would not disclose who the woman in the picture made a call to, due to their privacy policy.

The four of them stared at the photo in anticipation and silence. Now that they looked closer, they could see her hands were in view, reaching out for the phone.

"Does she look like anyone you know?" Bert asked Felicia.

"No, I don't think so, I mean her face is covered up—"

Dominic cut her off. "Hold on a second. Look at the woman's hands. Notice anything about them?

Everyone leaned in closer to examine the picture again.

"Uh...it looks like she has yellow nail polish on?" Felicia

asked.

"Exactly. Guess who else I noticed with yellow nails?"

"Who?" William asked, looking up in alarm.

"Mina Field. Donna Field's sister.

CHAPTER 15

Everyone looked at one another in utter disbelief.

William turned to Dominic. "What are you saying, Mr. Rivers? That Mina is responsible for this? Because of her nails?"

"Well, I can't be certain that she was the one who made the call. Or is the killer. But she is a likely suspect at this point."

"What do we do now?" Felicia asked. "I'll have to block this number so she doesn't bother me again."

"No. You will keep the number. Better to keep it just in case something happens. This is proof. Screenshot your "latest calls" screen, Felicia," Bert ordered.

Felicia obliged. She smiled at him. After she finished, she put her head on his shoulder. William noticed this, but didn't care. He was too engaged in his thoughts of finding the identity of the caller as well as the killer. If Mina really was the caller, what was her motive?

Dominic then brought up the fact that they still had to figure out where the object that was used to kill Charlotte was. "Maybe knowing this would help with our hunches. I also want to let you guys know that the autopsy report came through. She was most likely struck on the head with an object, most likely a statue, which has not been found yet. Sorry if we didn't inform you of this earlier, but we have been very busy going around interviewing people."

"We understand," Felicia said. "The news has also informed us a great deal. A murder investigation is tough and isn't easy to deal with sometimes." Emotions choked her voice.

Hearing about the supposed manner of her mother's death wasn't something she wished on her worst enemies. The reality of it all hit her like a brick as even if she wasn't that close to her mother, her mother didn't deserve to die the way she did.

William shook his head in pain and hurt. Hearing the manner in which she died was too gruesome for him. It was hard to hear something brutal that happened to someone he had once loved dearly.

"What if Mina has the object in her house?" Felicia asked.

"That's what I think, right?" Dominic asked Bert, who nodded. "We also found a heel print at Charlotte's that is a size 7. The same shoe size as you actually, Felicia." He gave her an expectant look, as if he were waiting to see her reaction.

Felicia stiffened. Her face reflected her surprise as she then remembered the conversation she and Bert had at dinner about her shoe size. She moved away from him.

"What is that supposed to mean? Was I considered a suspect, all this time?"

"You were," Dominic said. "After you told your shoe size to Bert, we couldn't help but assume you could be responsible—"

"Stop, okay?" Felicia put her hands up at him as she turned her gaze towards Bert. "So that's why you were asking me about my shoe size and buttering me up with compliments that day, huh? I should have known. You know, I actually liked you. Little did I know…"

She got up and slammed the door of William's hotel room.

"Felicia! Wait!" Bert ran out to follow her.

Dominic didn't know what to say to this drama. All he knew was that he hated being cut off mid-sentence. He gave William a disconcerting look.

"Lovers' quarrel. I know what that's like. She really likes him, that guy," William said, aware of his daughter's affection for the young and handsome detective.

"I know...it's helping and also it's not. Now about the object that was used to kill Charlotte. We haven't found it yet. I can't help but wonder if the object is in Mina's house. I don't think Bert has a search warrant for her house yet, but I can't help but be curious as to where she lives. We don't know anything about her, after all."

William sighed. "If there's something I want, it's justice. Whatever it takes to get to the end of this, I'm all for it."

Dominic cracked a smile. "Thanks. I'm glad you understand."

When Bert and Felicia returned, they seemed on better terms. Dominic relayed what he just told William on wanting to see Mina's house and find out if the murder object is in her possession.

"Okay, it's settled then. Mina is our lead for now. Let's leave before things get worse," Bert said, the first to walk out of the room.

CHAPTER 16

LATER THAT EVENING...

"You made it. I thought you were going to be late," Dominic Rivers said as he saw Bert walk up to his table.

Dominic had made dinner plans at the Island Creek Oyster Bar, keeping up his promise that he would introduce his girlfriend to Bert, one of these days. He and Berenice Daniels were seated at a table next to the kitchen, when Bert took a seat across from the two of them.

"Sorry about that... I was a bit tied up," he said, as he composed himself.

"With Felicia?" Dominic joked, raising his brows.

"No...Traffic was just bad."

"Oh." Dominic looked away dismissively, then turned to Berenice. "Anyways, this is my girlfriend, Berenice Daniels. The woman I have been telling you about. And Berenice, this is Bert Tomlin, my former partner in the Homicide/Missing Persons unit."

Bert shook hands with her. Her handshake was firm and her eye contact with him was powerful.

"Nice to meet you. I've heard a lot about you," Berenice said, in a husky voice. "I'm glad I'm here in Massachusetts. I was debating whether or not to come, but after talking with Dominic on the phone, I decided I wanted to see him again." She looked at Dominic with a smile so dazzling that Bert was convinced she was in love with the guy. She had on a red dress, with a touch of makeup and her beach blonde hair was tied up in a bun.

She was a natural beauty, Bert thought.

He could definitely see her appeal to Dominic. He was content that his friend had finally found someone. After being questioned about it all the time, he knew Dominic couldn't wait to break the news that he was no longer single.

"And I couldn't say no to that," Dominic said, regarding Berenice's words.

Bert laughed upon seeing his friend so love-struck. He then turned to Berenice. "Your family is in Pennsylvania, right? So how long do you plan on staying here?"

She nodded. "Yep, they are. I don't plan on going back any time soon. I may stay here for a while." She took Dominic's hands and placed her hands in his.

Bert happened to see this and for some reason felt like an awkward third-wheel.

"I agree, you never know who you'll meet," he said. His thoughts wandered over to Felicia. To that kiss he shared with her. That magical spark he felt at the moment. He ached to see her again, despite her brief anger towards him on suspecting her. Person of interest or not, she occupied his mind all the time.

Dominic seemed to read his thoughts, and inquired about Felicia.

"Did you hear from her, after what happened today? I know that you and her are on a rough patch now, with that argument from earlier."

"Haven't heard from her, but I think she'll understand eventually that everyone, including her, is person of interest."

Dominic then called the waiter, and told him they were ready to order.

Bert didn't even bother to look at the menu that lay in front of him all this time, as he was too busy thinking about Felicia.

Dominic ordered a clam chowder and Berenice requested a sandwich special—grilled cheese sandwich with spinach, feta cheese, and tomatoes. Bert couldn't decide at first. Then, he finally chose the same item as Berenice.

Berenice raised her water glass. "Anyone want to toast to Dominic being a good detective?"

"Here, here," both men agreed.

Berenice put her glass down, and said in a serious tone, "Just so you know, I am aware of everything going on with Dominic investigating the case of Charlotte Browning's death. I was mad at first, but now I see that it's important to be passionate about something. I've apologized many times to Dominic for my little outburst, his last night in Costa Rica."

Dominic knew exactly what she was talking about. He placed his hands on hers, a comforting gesture.

The rest of the evening was well spent chatting and getting to know more about their relationship.

Bert called for their waiter again and ordered three glasses of house wine.

"Drinks are on me," he said, cheerily.

CHAPTER 17

It was the next day morning. The sun was not yet up. As Dominic lay in his bed, with Berenice sound asleep next to him, he thought about what Chief Tonew had told him. That he was happy to see him after a long time.

Happy. That word meant so many things.

He felt that being in Costa Rica for a year, and finding love, put reality out of perspective. How were the people in his life really doing? How was Chief Tonew really doing? Given what was going on with his wife's health, Dominic wished he could have been more involved and less distant. When he now wanted to be in the loop of people's lives, they all seemed to have drifted farther and farther away, with new things happening in their lives, good or bad.

Dominic thought back to his detective days. He missed that life. He missed interacting with his coworkers, being on the go, teasing Bert Tomlin and other newer detectives.

He smiled.

At least one good thing came out of retirement. His eyes fell on Berenice who was still sound asleep, like a peaceful dove.

With these thoughts in mind, he closed his eyes and fell back into a deep slumber.

△△△△△△△△△△△△△△△△

Chief Tonew didn't show up to work that day. He was in the hospital to see his wife. Her health had been deteriorating ever since the time she broke her arm and had to be in the hospital to get it treated. He was at the hospital the whole day, caring for her.

When Dominic heard about this, he understood that it was important to put loved ones first, before work. He was saddened to hear that the one person who welcomed him into the Boston Police department, was facing such hardships now.

At this point, he made a decision. He would no longer shut people out, especially people who cared for him. Like Berenice. When she called him saying she was coming to Massachusetts, he was skeptical at first. He didn't know what to make about her wanting to see him after their argument. He realized he should have given love a chance and not let 'work' dictate his life.

But it had all worked out at the end. With Berenice coming here, he was no longer alone. He decided that he would try to make his relationship with Berenice work. There would be no turning back.

⌂⌂⌂⌂⌂⌂⌂⌂⌂⌂⌂⌂⌂⌂⌂⌂⌂

That afternoon, Dominic and Bert were back at Charlotte's house to search for anything else that was missing. Most importantly, could the murder weapon be at her house still? The forensic team had searched through everything on the first day, but like the heel print, something could have been overlooked.

After talking with Bert about Chief Tonew's situation, it was hard to concentrate fully on the case now.

"You got to pull yourself together, Dominic," Bert said. "I'm surprised that you didn't know about it sooner. But I wouldn't think too much about it. Did you know he has been talking about retiring soon? Don't know when, but he had been talking about it."

At this, Dominic kept a morose face. "Yeah, I do know. He told me. *I* feel bad for retiring now. I feel like so much has happened in other people's lives that I didn't know about."

"Cheer up, man. I guess what happens is for the better. I do feel for Tonew though. He's been such a huge help to both of us. He doesn't deserve any of this."

Dominic agreed with a simple nod. Then he cleared his throat. "Okay, enough of the emotional talk. Let's get going with the case."

As they entered the mansion, Bert said he'd look around the first floor while Dominic would search the other floors. Dominic had finished looking through most rooms before he remembered that he hadn't looked in Charlotte's study room. When he entered, he saw a giant sword that hung on the wall, behind the study desk.

Obviously, Charlotte's murder must have been an on-the-spot type of murder, rather than pre-meditated, because the mansion contained many dangerous objects that could easily be used as a murder weapon—such as the sword on the wall, the guns in the gun cabinet that were propped up against the wall in her guest bedroom, and many more.

So why would the killer grab something insignificant... something hard to find?

Dominic figured maybe that was the point. To either create a confusing murder for the police to solve, or perhaps it was just a rage killing. He looked around her gold-plated study desk that contained three drawers underneath. He opened one of the drawers. Inside, was a receipt. He pulled this out carefully. The receipt was for a purchase of two gothic statues Charlotte had bought at a furniture store four months ago. Attached was a picture of the two statues.

Dominic looked up and said in a louder voice, "Hey Bert, come here! Did the forensic team find two gothic looking statues in this house? Something that matches the description on this receipt?"

Bert came rushing in. "What was that?" he asked.

"Charlotte bought these two statues," Dominic pointed to the receipts. "Do you know if the forensic team found both of them? The description on the receipt reads that it is "a gothic iron statue with a rounded head and gold bottoms." The picture reflects this description quite well, don't you think?" Dominic handed him the receipts and photos.

Bert wasn't sure if the team had found two statues, but said he'd check. He pulled out Charlotte's autopsy report from his pocket.

"According to the autopsy report, she was hit with something like a statue, or small object to her right side. I could see this statue matching the mark that it made to her head...Let me call Mr. Candance. He would know if he or his team found anything."

He called up the forensics expert, Mr. Candance. Mr. Candance said that according to his inventory report, everything was accounted for except for one statue. One statue of the set had been found in the guest room, but there was no fingerprints or blood on it. He said that one of his men brought the missing statue to his attention later on, and he forgot to let Bert know about it. As for the second statue, no one had reported seeing it.

Upon hearing this, Bert slammed his hands on Charlotte's

desk with a loud thud. "Why didn't you tell me about this before?! Especially if the missing statue could possibly be the murder weapon?"

"I'm so sorry about that," Mr. Candance said, on the other end. "There have been a lot of people on our team calling in sick, so people have been filling for each other. I apologize for not letting you know. It's not that I withheld this from you, it's just that it slipped my mind."

Bert shook his head. "Slipped your mind? This would have been good to know beforehand. But anyways, thanks for letting me know."

"Anytime. And I'm sorry once again," Mr. Candace said casually.

After Bert hung up, he explained everything to Dominic.

"So, they found one statue in the guest room. Where's the other one?" Dominic asked.

"At Mina's house, perhaps?"

"I'm guessing that too."

Suddenly Dominic lowered his voice to a whisper as if he were afraid someone would eavesdrop, even though they were the only two there. "I feel like doing something illegal. Just to satisfy my curiosity."

Dominic Rivers wanting to do something illegal? That was unheard of

"What?" Bert asked, an unnerving feeling crept inside him.

"I want to sneak into Mina's house to see if the missing statue is in her house."

The way he said this made Bert believe he was serious.

"I don't think that's a good idea. Not without a warrant."

"I was just kidding." Dominic winked, elbowing his friend's shoulders.

But Bert perked up at his words. "But your idea isn't completely bad. What if we *spied* on Mina, instead? Maybe lounge out by her house to see what she's doing?"

"Why? What would she be doing?"

"I don't know. I just thought it would be a good idea to see. No harm in doing so. Plus, I can get a warrant to enter her house if the need arises, which I think at this point, there's more than enough evidence to be able to get one."

"I think that's a good idea," Dominic said. "As long as she doesn't see us, it could work. And yeah, get that warrant, as soon as you can." He then stopped. "Oh, and call Felicia and William. I want them to be in the loop about this."

"On it!" Bert exclaimed and immediately pulled out his phone.

CHAPTER 18

Mina lived in a rural area just outside of Boston. Her house was at the edge of a cul-de-sac. It was a little smaller than Donna's. Other houses stood next to hers in a row, just like the houses in Wisteria Lane from the show *Desperate Housewives.* Tonight, Mina's house was dark—there was no light coming from it. It was also 9:00 pm, so it was likely she was asleep.

Bert had gotten a search warrant approved by this time. Before entering her house, he first wanted to observe from outside. Bert, Dominic, William, and Felicia were gathered outside Mina's house in Bert's squad car. Felicia sat in the passenger seat, while Dominic and William sat in the back. The car looked inconspicuous enough, so no one would know what they were doing. Bert turned off his headlights and parked on the curb, a little away from her house.

All of a sudden, the lights of one of Mina's rooms turned on. Then they noticed what they assumed to be Mina, staring straight out the window, in an eerie way. It was as if she knew someone was watching her, but she wasn't sure who it was. She wore a blue robe and her hair was put up in a bun. She stared out some more, then turned away. The lights flickered off.

"What was that?" Dominic asked, a feeling of terror crawled up his spine. He was unnerved at the sight of Mina staring out the window like that.

No one answered him, as they also had the same feeling of fear as he did. They all continued to watch the house, but they didn't see anything suspicious just yet.

"Why are we here again?" William asked. "I don't see anything."

"Hold on, maybe we will see something," Bert reassured him.

As if at the right moment, the front door of Mina's house opened. She stepped out, looking left and right.

Felicia watched Mina with her observant eyes. "What's she doing?"

"I have no clue," Bert whispered.

They watched as Mina took a shovel that was propped against the side of her house and went to the backyard. After twenty minutes, she returned with the shovel and placed it against the side and went back inside. Then she came out again, this time with something sticking out from her robe pocket; her hands clutched tightly at it, to make sure whatever was inside wouldn't fall out.

"What's that in her pocket?" Dominic asked.

"I don't know," said William, as he watched Mina just as closely.

All of a sudden, Mina disappeared out back, holding on to her pocket as if her life depended on it.

CHAPTER 19

Everything happened so fast. One moment they were watching Mina carrying an item that jutted out of her robe, the next, Mina was running towards their car with the shovel in her hands. The frightening way in which she ran was as if she were a killer in a horror movie, chasing her victim.

"Who are you?!" she yelled as she banged the shovel on the hood of the car. Felicia screamed. Bert steered the wheel and reversed the car back several feet from Mina. He hit the brakes and held his breath.

"Who are you?" she called out again.

Bert got out of the car, with his hands up. "Hey, hey, hey! It's me!" he shouted. "I'm Detective Tomlin." He then pointed to Dominic. "Remember, you talked with my friend, Dominic today?"

Dominic got out of the car and motioned to himself. Mina paused as her eyes darted back and forth between the two men.

"Oh. I thought you were some creepy guys watching my house, or something."

"If that were the case, running up to their car and banging on the hood of their car is not a way to make them leave. That's only going to get you arrested," Bert advised, narrowing his brows. "But I'll let it slide, if you agree not to do that again."

She softened her demeanor. "I'm sorry. I was just scared."

Bert nodded. Then he pointed to the shovel in her hands. "Mind telling us what you were burying with the shovel?"

She froze. Then in an icy tone, she said, "None of your damn concern. It's my house, I can do whatever I want."

Bert wouldn't settle for it. "Do you want to talk more inside? We *all* a little cold out here."

"What? Why? And who's *we all*?" she asked, peering through the windshield of his car.

"Including Dominic and myself, we have Felicia Browning-Mott and William Browning." Bert pointed them out. "There are some things we wanted to ask you. Since you're already here, why not ask about them now?

Her eyes widened upon seeing Felicia and William's distraught faces.

"Sorry. I can't. I'm tired and it's late. You all better leave." she said, as she started towards her house slowly.

"Tired? You weren't too tired to dig just now, surely you can't be tired to invite some people over. Especially people you know?" Dominic asked.

She stopped in her steps. "I guess?" she said, her words appeared more as a question.

She went inside.

Once they were in her living room seated comfortably on her white four-seater couch, Bert resumed his questioning. "Mind telling us what you were burying out back?" he asked.

"Nothing important. Just an old item."

"A statue?" Dominic asked out of the blue.

She froze. "Well, uh, not exactly but—"

Felicia and William looked at her disapprovingly. Since Mina was not answering the question, Felicia countered. "Did you happen to call me today? Around 4:00? From the Hyatt Regency Hotel? The same one I stay at?" she asked.

"No! I'd never!" Mina answered almost immediately. The tone of her voice went up a few decibels.

"You didn't threaten me on the phone today? From the Hyatt's hotel's staff loading room?"

Mina's eye's widened at this. "No! I was here at home the whole day!"

"Got proof?" William asked.

"No! I, uh, uh..." She stuttered as she spoke. As they waited for her answer, suddenly, they heard the sound of Mina's bedroom door crack open. Someone was making their way to the living room. Everyone paused. The room was now eerily devoid of any sound.

They had assumed Mina was alone in the house. Then who else was here?

CHAPTER 20

A tall man walked to the living room, slowly. "Who's there, Mina?" he asked groggily.

Everyone turned their heads. To Felicia's horror, the man was none other than Alfred Mott, her ex-boyfriend. What the hell was he doing here?

"Alfred?!" she asked, as she got up immediately and walked towards him. "I thought you were in LA."

Alfred Mott, an average looking man of thirty-eight years, had brown hair, green eyes and a smirk of a smile that made him look cocky. He wore a blood red robe and bathroom slippers. His hair was a mess, all tousled up, like someone had given him a head massage. His appearance was as if he had just woken up from a nap. He seemed oblivious to everything that had been discussed so far.

He first started dating Felicia five years ago, after meeting at a YouTubers Meet-Up convention. Recently, he had broken up with her as he realized he didn't love her anymore and 'wanted to see other people'. So one could imagine his shock to see Felicia here of all places. His eyes had widened and the lines on his forehead had creased even more.

"What are you doing *here?*" he asked.

"I came here because my mother's dead and I wanted to find her killer. What are you doing here with *her?*" She pointed at Mina. "She's old enough to be your grandmother!"

Mina looked offended. "Excuse me?" she asked.

"I can't believe you dumped me...for *her*?" Felicia continued.

"No! I just met her recently! After the news of your mother's death broke, I figured you must be in Massachusetts now, and I wanted to see you. When I came here, I happened to bump into Mina at a local diner. We started talking and she told me that she was the sister of your mother's best friend."

Felicia shook her head. She knew it was all bull.

"Liar! You were here before my mother's death! In fact, you both must have killed her!" Felicia pointed her fingers at both Alfred and Mina.

Seconds later, there was a loud *smack*. Alfred clutched his cheeks in pain.

"You did not just do that!" Alfred spat at her.

Bert drew Felicia back and asked her to sit down in a collected manner. He put his arms around her shoulders as a way to calm her down. She shook him off as she continued to stand right in Alfred's face.

Upon seeing this, as if a cloud of jealousy overcame Alfred he added, "By the way, this bozo your new boyfriend?"

"None of your business. We aren't dating. Remember?"

"Watch who you call bozo, I'm an officer of the law," Bert said showing his badge.

Alfred ignored him as he resumed his conversation with Felicia. "You're right. So why should it matter to you who *I'm* with?"

"It doesn't. Not anymore...but *her*? Really? This is who you meant when you said you wanted to see other people?" Felicia repeated, pointing at Mina again.

Dominic rolled his eyes. "Okay you both, let's drop the Jerry Springer act, okay?" He put his hands in between Felicia and Alfred to prevent them from coming any closer to each other. "We don't have time to listen to your personal quarrels. We came here for a reason. We were in the process of finding out if Mina made the phone call to Felicia today."

"And who are you?" Alfred asked sharply as he gave Dominic a look of annoyance.

"Name's Dominic Rivers, former detective. And in case you're wondering, the man with your ex-girlfriend is Detective Bert Tomlin."

"Wait, what phone call?" Mina suddenly asked, as if she just understood Dominic's earlier words.

To this, Bert glared at her.

"You know exactly what he's asking about. Better speak the truth now or you'll be spending the night, or as long as it takes, downtown."

This got her to be silent. Mina sat down on a bar stool that stood in front of the couches, and put her head down. Everyone looked at her in anticipation.

"Fine. I will admit. I made the call. But I didn't kill Charlotte."

"Why did you make the call?" Dominic asked.

"I wanted to know where the rest of the jewels went. Donna told me all about Charlotte's new clause in her will beforehand."

"When did Donna tell you this?"

"The day before Charlotte died."

"So were you also at Charlotte's get together?"

"I wasn't. But Donna told me about it right after she got back. This made me wonder where the rest of the jewels were. I definitely couldn't ask Charlotte about them directly."

"Why would you call Felicia asking about them after Charlotte's death?"

To this, Mina didn't answer.

△△△△△△△△△△△△△△△△△

Many thoughts flowed through Mina Field's mind at the moment.

How can I possibly reveal the reason why I called Felicia specifically, without making myself look guilty? she thought.

The reason why she had made that call was so that the police would suspect Felicia and later take the fall for Charlotte's death.

But at the moment, Mina knew the detectives didn't suspect Felicia anymore because instead of arresting her, they were at Mina's house, asking all sorts of questions.

Mina decided she dared not say anything that would draw suspicion onto her.

And if by any chance Alfred opened his mouth, that will the moment when she'd reveal everything...

△△△△△△△△△△△△△△△△

While everyone waited for an answer, they hadn't realized that Alfred had disappeared from sight.

"Where's Alfred?" Felicia asked, looking around the rom.

Everyone looked up.

Alfred Mott was nowhere in sight.

Mina started frantically calling out his name.

"Oh my god, he probably knows something and has run away!" Felicia cried out.

"Wait here then. William, you too, stay with the ladies, Bert and I will search around," Dominic instructed.

CHAPTER 21

Alfred Mott hadn't planned on getting caught. It was already a mistake to come to Massachusetts, to see Felicia. He really did want to see her, but after meeting Mina at a diner a few days before Charlotte's death, he thought he could get his hands on something that would help him. He was in debt after all. What better way than to butter up someone with a connection to the richest woman in Mass state?

He remained hidden. his heart racing like never before.

⌂⌂⌂⌂⌂⌂⌂⌂⌂⌂⌂⌂⌂⌂⌂⌂⌂⌂

Bert and Dominic searched every corner of the house. Alfred was nowhere to be seen. Bert decided to search the backyard while he told Dominic to circle out front. When he reached the backyard, he got chills. He was able to see from the moonlight that lit his surroundings. What he saw was nothing but grass and mud. Not even a single plant was in sight. While looking around, he also thought of searching for the object that Mina had presumably buried here.

He then saw something sticking out of the mud. He grabbed his phone and turned on the flashlight. He shone the light on whatever was sticking out. It looked to be green or black... Just as he was about to reach for it, a figure sucker punched him. Bert fell to the ground, reeling in pain. He looked up. It was a dark figure, wearing all black. The figure struck a tough punch at him again, which caused Bert to scream in agony.

Dominic heard his friend's screams. He immediately rushed to the backyard. He was horrified to see a tall, lean figure standing over Bert, about to throw a punch. He ran to the figure and pinned their arms down.

It was then that he saw it was none other than Alfred.

"What are you doing?" he asked.

"Let me go."

"Not unless you tell me what you were doing. Why did you disappear all of a sudden?"

"I won't say—I can't tell you…"

Dominic pinned his arms down harder.

"Ow! Ow! Okay fine!"

"Tell us now. Did you have anything to do with Charlotte's death?"

"No! No!"

"Don't lie."

At this point, Bert was able to get up.

"Tell us," Dominic probed. "Or else you will be treated a lot worse in jail tonight." His cold voice permeated through the air, making the hairs on Alfred's hands stand up. The usually confident man was now terrified for his life.

"I didn't mean to! I saw her and…"

At that moment, Mina, Felicia and William made it in time to the backyard to see what was happening.

Having heard Alfred's last line, Felicia asked, "You saw who?" with her hands on her hips.

"Charlotte, you mean?" William interjected.

"Guys, please." Dominic put one hand up defensively. He

turned to Alfred, loosened his grip on him and allowed him to speak. "Who did you see?

There was no running away or lying now—Alfred was as trapped as one could be.

Alfred took a deep breath. "I just wanted her jewels."

"Whose jewels?"

"Charlotte's. After meeting Mina, I realized that since she had a connection with Charlotte through her sister, Donna, the idea of taking her jewels popped in my mind. Especially after Mina told me about Charlotte's new clause. And everything about how Charlotte was greedy and liked to keep things for herself."

Felicia shook her head. It was one thing to steal, but it was another to insult someone's mother. But she knew Alfred well. He was not the husband-material she thought he was. He was just like the other fake people in her life—they were all just after money. In the world of the rich and famous, no one was truly one's friend, unless they stuck by them during their bad times.

"So, what prompted you to steal her jewels?" Dominic asked.

Alfred paused for a moment at this. "I thought knowing Mina was perfect opportunity to get a gamble at the rest of Charlotte's jewels. I concocted a plan to steal Charlotte's jewels and eventually pin the theft on Mina."

At this, Mina's face turned white. This was the first time she knew anything about pinning any sort of theft on her.

"What did you do next?" asked Bert.

"I stole one of Mina's shoes after spending a night at her house. I used them to place a footprint outside in the mud, before running away."

Dominic took this in. So, Alfred stole Mina's shoe, trying to pin the theft on her. Then what happened for Charlotte to end up dead?

"So how did Charlotte die then?"

Dominic's harsh tone took Alfred by surprise. He looked down. Admitting to a theft was easier than admitting to a murder, obviously. Even if one was innocent, trying to prove oneself as so in front of a cop was difficult. One stutter, one hesitation, and a cop would automatically sense guilt.

"*How* did she die?" Dominic repeated after hearing no response.

"I won't say."

"Why not? You already had no problem admitting to the theft."

Alfred gulped. He didn't feel guilty for his actions, but the fact that he was getting caught was humiliating. He couldn't let this ex-detective force a confession out of him.

"I'm not going to say anything. Not unless I get a lawyer. Let me go, so I can call him—"

"You're not going anywhere, Alfred. I know what you'll do —you'll run away. People like you are so easy to decipher. So, don't test my patience now."

"Try me," Alfred flashed a corny smile as he laid a kick at Dominic's legs. Dominic fumbled to the ground.

As Alfred was about to get up, Bert immediately grabbed his arms and threw him to the ground. "You, sir, are in big trouble!" he yelled.

"Let go of me! I'll file a complaint against you! I plead the fifth! Please!" Alfred screeched, as he tugged and scratched at Bert's hands.

"That's not going to work," Bert said in a condescending manner. "You better tell the truth. Why were you running off in the first place? It has to be because you're guilty, right?" He turned to Felicia, who gave him a little nod. William and Mina stood still as statues as they watched the commotion. They didn't dare say a word until they heard the confession from Alfred...that is, if he was even going to give it.

At this point, Dominic was able to stand up.

"Did you kill Charlotte? After you stole her jewels?" he asked as he looked at Alfred still on the ground.

"Talk to my lawyer," he insisted.

To this, Bert grabbed him by the collar, harder. "Listen here you self-entitled jerk. Be lucky that we are only asking nicely. Because you are a second away from getting your last taste of freedom out in the open here. So, I'm asking you one last time —did you kill Charlotte or not? You obviously thought this through well, coming up with an elaborate plan to steal her jewels. You yourself admitted you stole Mina's shoes to pin the theft on her. Now I think it's unlikely that someone else could have killed Charlotte, hmm?"

He waited for Alfred to react to his words, but the man kept a grim face, refusing to talk.

CHAPTER 22

The scene at the moment was something out of a noir film—one suspect, one object in question, one detective, one ex-detective, and three frazzled bystanders.

Bert looked at Dominic as he wondered how to get Alfred Mott to confess. He heaved Alfred to his feet and handcuffed him.

It was then that Dominic suddenly remembered a tactic he had learned in training—*get a confession by using psychological tactics. Get into the perp's mind by saying certain words that will catch them off guard, so that they confess to the crime.*

"What we know is that you acted alone, am I right?" he asked Alfred. "You may not give me an answer now, but the proof is all there. Once we get a hold of the murder weapon, we will look for fingerprints. We will keep digging until we find an answer. So, you're not off the hook just yet."

As he went on about how the police were not going to take his silence as an answer, Mina looked around nervously. She focused her gaze on Alfred. He, in turn, looked back at her. He shook his head.

"Alfred, you better tell us, did you do it or not?" Bert asked, interrupting Alfred's momentary glance.

With dismay, Dominic watched how this line of questioning was going nowhere. His looked at Felicia, who shook her head with disgust, then at William, who put his arm around his daughter.

He then turned to Mina who seemed to be doing something with her fingers. Like she was signaling something to Alfred. He narrowed his gaze at her.

What is she doing?

Alfred saw her fingers and his eyes widened.

What is going on? Dominic thought.

Alfred suddenly spoke: "You want me to talk? Alright, I'll talk. I am innocent, that's what I have to say."

"Oh really?" said Bert, with a scoff. "Tell that to your lawyer. We're taking you downtown." He was about to lead Alfred away when Dominic stopped him.

"Wait, Bert. Remember when we talked about how this job could have been a two person or three-person job, and we quickly rebuffed that theory, given the evidence and motives we have now. But what if this really was a multiple person job?"

Felicia inched closer. "What do you mean?"

Dominic put his hands up. "What if Alfred was the one who did the murder and theft, and someone else hid the murder weapon?"

Upon hearing this, Alfred wriggled at his handcuffs, as if he were aching to escape. Mina clutched her hands to her chest. It was like she was thinking, *if Alfred had already tried to pin the theft on her by taking her shoes, what was he going to say to what the detective had said? Would Alfred spill her name? Before he does anything, she had to say something.*

"What if Alfred somehow killed Charlotte, perhaps with the object that Mina was trying to bury tonight? And then Mina hid it for him?" Dominic continued.

This caused Mina to break down. "That's a lie!" she cried.

"Is it though? Why don't you tell us what you were trying to bury out here?"

"Why are you questioning me, why don't you question Alfred? He did it!"

"Shut up you old woman, shut up!" Alfred yelled.

Felicia and William were in a daze upon what they had heard. It seemed impossible that Alfred would do such a thing!

"Did what, kill Charlotte?" asked Bert.

No one answered. Mina and Alfred kept silent. The night had become more tense by the minute.

Finally, Mina let out a loud sob. "I didn't kill her, Alfred did! But I saw the statue in my basement, a day after the news of the murder broke. I didn't know how it got there. I recognized the statue, having seen it in Charlotte's house when I went over several times. So, you can imagine my surprise when I saw the statue in my basement and saw blood on it. Now that I think about it, Alfred must have put it there without my knowledge in an attempt to frame me for the murder. I got scared and didn't tell anyone, not even my sister. I—I tried burying it tonight…I didn't want you all to think I killed Charlotte because I had murder weapon with me."

"Now that is the biggest lie I've ever heard!" Alfred raised his voice as he spoke. "Don't believe a word of what she said! She knew exactly how the statue appeared! I put it in her house for her to hide, after Charlotte died! And she knew it too!"

Mina waved her hands trying to stop him from talking. But he went on.

"You think she's innocent? No…she may not have killed Charlotte, but she sure did help with hiding the statue in her basement." He shot Mina a stare so cold and evil. "Yeah, that's right. I came to your house the next day and I asked you to hide the statue. And you agreed, if we split the jewels that I had stolen."

After Alfred finished, there was a deafening silence. He then covered his mouth in horror.

Without realizing it, he had confessed.

Mina almost lunged at him when Dominic stopped her by pulling her away.

"So...where are the jewels? The *rest* of the jewels?" Felicia asked.

Alfred let out a large sigh. Since he knew he had nowhere left to run or hide, he had to tell the truth. "Right here, in Mina's basement."

This prompted Dominic to jump into action. "Stay here," he instructed Bert. "And call for backup."

He motioned for William to follow him as the two of them went inside the house. After sifting through items inside the basement, they found a huge suitcase. Inside the suitcase was a duffle bag which contained the jewels.

"Looks like we got another cat out of the bag," Dominic announced smugly.

When backup came, Alfred and Mina were escorted into two squad cards and taken downtown. Upon finally learning the truth of her mother's death, Felicia sobbed in her father's arms, overcome with emotions.

Leaving the two of them to grieve in peace, Dominic looked up at the night sky, feeling a sense of pride upon getting to the bottom of this high-profile case.

CHAPTER 23

Inside the interrogation room, Alfred confessed to how he killed Charlotte:

"I snuck into her house through the front door. Then I went to her guest room which was where the safe was. I did my research beforehand, so I knew the layout of her house well. When I had gotten to her safe, I realized it had a complex lock system. I still managed to get the jewels out of there, though." (Alfred had fixed safes when he was in college as a part-time job. He had mastered the skill so well that even now, he had the knack in opening complicated safes.)

"After I stole the jewels, I tried to escape. I saw Charlotte coming down the stairs. In fear of getting caught, I went back to the guest room, grabbed a random object and hit her with the statue. Once I saw she wasn't moving, I carried her body to her bed."

His story was validated by the fact that his and Mina's finger prints were found on the duffle bag which carried the jewels. Alfred's prints were also found on one of Mina's shoe (a red wedge heel, size 7)—the shoe that was used for the heel print. And finally, his fingerprints were all over the second gothic statue that Mina had buried, which was the same statue used to kill Charlotte.

Mina, in the meantime, revealed why she made the phone call to Felicia and confirmed what Alfred had revealed earlier about agreeing to hide the statue if she got half of the jewels that he stole.

In the end, both of them got huge sentences—Mina got a hefty sentence for conspiracy and cover up and Alfred got a life-in-prison sentence.

⌂ ⌂ ⌂ ⌂ ⌂ ⌂ ⌂ ⌂ ⌂ ⌂ ⌂ ⌂ ⌂ ⌂ ⌂ ⌂ ⌂ ⌂

When Donna heard the news of Alfred's arrest, she was shocked. But she was glad that justice had been served for her best friend. She also cut off all ties with her sister and refused to visit her in jail.

Felicia, on the other hand, returned to LA, packed all her things and moved back to Massachusetts to live with Bert. She was now an advertising consultant. Even though she had moved on with her life, she couldn't help but think about Alfred and how she wished she had never known him. Then again, if this case hadn't happened, she never would have met Bert Tomlin.

Talking about him, Bert was still a detective, involved in investigating more grisly cases, and was content with Felicia by his side.

William remained in Chicago where he continued to run his hotel business.

As for Dominic Rivers...well, everyone deserves a happy ending, don't they?

CHAPTER 24

Two years later, *July*

Palm Beach, Florida

Sounds of the wedding march rang happily in everyone's ears as the priest pronounced the couple as husband and wife. Dominic Rivers and now Berenice Rivers, walked down the aisle as a newlywed couple. Met by hundreds of cheers and claps, they danced to the recession song which was Crazy in Love by Beyoncé featuring Jay Z.

Berenice was glowing in her gorgeous $1,000 mermaid style dress, customized with embellished diamonds and a five-foot veil train. Dominic wore a black tuxedo, which showcased his tan (having been in Florida for a while). His hair was professionally styled and gelled to perfection.

The wedding ceremony took place on a large grassy area, outside of the Hilton Hotel. The decorated canopy where they exchanged their vows, overlooked the beach. The view of the stretch of sand and the waves pattering on the shore was a sight for sore eyes. The Florida sun that glistened in the vibrant summer afternoon added to the romantic and celebratory mood.

Guests who were invited included Dominic's brother Mario Rivers, Felicia Browning (she had legally dropped the surname Mott at this point), William Browning, Donna Field, and of course, Bert Tomlin. Steve Boden and Taylor Boden were also in attendance as they were happy to support the detective who had helped give them closure regarding their son, Eric.

Everyone sat at round tables, underneath a silk canopy as they ate the delicious food. Berenice's family made sure to cater from a five-star restaurant so the food and drinks were of high-quality. Assortments of cheese slices and caviar and servings of quinoa, rice, vegetable rice, and steak, clams, and wine were neatly placed on the "Food and Drinks" table.

"Can't believe it. Who'd have thought you'd settle down?" Bert asked, putting a spoonful of rice into his mouth. He didn't want to admit it, but he had gotten emotional after seeing Dominic and Berenice walk down the aisle. There was something so surreal and special about a wedding as it was a once in a lifetime event.

"Yep. I may be a tough cop, but I realized I can make a committed life partner too. I learned that the hard way," Dominic said.

"Amen," Berenice agreed, planting a kiss on his cheek.

"Congrats to you both. I wish you two the best of luck," said Bert.

Berenice then motioned at Felicia and Bert. "When will you two marry? Do I sense wedding bells anytime soon?" she teased.

Felicia gently elbowed Bert. "Not sure, but I'm waiting..." Bert, in turn, stared back at her as if she were the only woman in the world. "You know you're the only one for me and that I intend to marry you."

At this, Berenice put her hands to her cheeks. "Aww... how cute," she gushed.

There was a silence between them all. It was then that Bert suddenly remembered something important. "I'm taking a little break until my next assignment," he announced.

"How long a break?" Dominic asked, taken aback.

"Like 2 months."

"Wow, is Chief Tonew being generous?"

"Chief Tonew retired actually." Seeing Dominic's shocked face, he continued, "He said it was a family emergency and he left the U.S, hastily. I thought he would have let you know first, of all people. I'm quite surprised you didn't know."

Dominic pursed his brows. "No, no he didn't tell me anything. I wasn't aware of his retirement. I'm guessing it had to do with his wife's health? I knew about that, but—"

Bert cut him off. "His retirement aside, I tried calling and texting you, but you wouldn't respond. Thank god I received your wedding invitation through UPS mail, or else I wouldn't have even known you were getting married."

"Well, I was in Norway in the mountains this whole year. Wi-fi was bad there. Berenice and I have discussed traveling around the world full time. Hopefully after our honeymoon, we can begin doing so."

That must have been the reason Dominic hadn't contacted him in so long, Bert thought. Regardless, he was happy for Dominic's new life plan. Not something he expected the tough and stern officer to do after retiring, but life experiences did change people. Marriage, especially.

"When did the Chief retire, though?" Dominic asked, his thoughts were back on his former boss.

"Six months ago. He gave his regards to you before he retired. He hadn't forgotten about you, you know."

"Where does he live now?"

"Poland, where his wife's relatives are."

Emotions overcame Dominic when he realized he'd never see Oscar Tonew in person again, not for a while, that is. He knew that the Chief's retirement did have to do with his wife's health. That explained why he wasn't able to attend Dominic's wedding.

It would have been nice if he was here, Dominic thought. He wasn't offended that the Chief didn't tell him about his retirement. Dominic remembered the last time he heard from him was a year ago, when they had a quick dinner. After that, there was no formal contact between the two of them. He knew that the Chief had a lot on his plate to deal with, even back then. It now reassured him to know that Chief Tonew's wife was in good hands, knowing she had a loving husband by her side. He wished his former boss the best in life. Just as he, himself, was starting a new journey in life, he figured Chief Tonew was doing the same...

△△△△△△△△△△△△△△△△△△

After Dominic got married, he still kept in touch with his friend, Bert Tomlin. Their friendship never seemed to fade as the months went on.

With no looking back, the two of them went on to live fulfilling lives without any regrets.

THE END

AUTHOR'S NOTE

This is my first attempt at a full-length mystery book. I started this book in August 2020, and since then, this book has grown immensely. This book was inspired after I watched the Apple TV crime drama show, *Defending Jacob*, which is about a boy who is accused of murder.

After watching it, and given my love for mystery/thrillers, I got an idea of writing a book in that genre, specifically a cozy mystery about two detectives who solve different cases. My second story "He Saw it Coming", as well as the overall mood of this book were definitely inspired by the show.

I would also like to point out that this book is set in real-life Boston, Massachusetts, with a mix of real and made-up locations. Real locations mentioned are Salisbury, the Boston Public Library and the Boston Police Station, Island Creek Oyster Bar, The Pavement Coffee House, the Marliave and the Hyatt Regency. Shout out to Google Maps being a helpful aid for location logistics and helping me with deciding the various cafes and restaurants in this book. Everything else, from the characters and names to the locations not mentioned above, are fictional.

I couldn't have written this book without additional research into certain technical terms as well.

Sources are below:

[1] *https://www.newburyportnews.com/*

[2] "Test Instructions". *testingcolorvision.com*, Wagoner Color Vision Testing, LLC. 2018. https://www.testingcolorvision.com/test-instructions-conditions.php

ACKNOWLEDGEMENTS

It wouldn't have been possible to complete this book without the following acknowledgements:

I would like to thank my editor Alyssa Matesic, for giving helpful and critical editorial and developmental feedback for my first two drafts of the book. I've definitely learned a lot more about the art of effective storytelling and plot/character development from her comments.

I would also like to thank my copyeditor and proofreader Jessica Powers for giving my manuscript a grammatical polish during its final stage.

I would like to thank my family and friends for being supportive of me in my journey as an author! This goes to you!

Lastly, to fellow readers, I hope you enjoy reading this book, as much as I enjoyed writing it!

~Deepika Viswanath

ABOUT THE AUTHOR

Deepika Viswanath (pronounced dee-pee-ka) is an author and writer from the Bay Area, California. This is her first book. She also submits short stories and blog posts to various writing sites. Aside from writing, she creates and sells self-care journals and productivity planners.

Website: www.deepikaviswanath.com

Twitter: @itsdeepikav and @deepikaviswan

Instagram: @itsdeepikav

Made in United States
Troutdale, OR
10/04/2023